CALL YOU HOME

BOOKS BY JAN THOMPSON

Protector Sweethearts (6 Books)
JanThompson.com/protector

Defender Sweethearts (6 Books)
JanThompson.com/defender

Binary Hackers (4 Books)
JanThompson.com/binary

Seaside Chapel (7 Books)
JanThompson.com/seaside

Savannah Sweethearts (12 Books)
JanThompson.com/savannah

Vacation Sweethearts (8 Books)
JanThompson.com/vacation

Midtown Christmas (4 Books)
JanThompson.com/christmas

CALL YOU HOME

SAVANNAH SWEETHEARTS
BOOK ELEVEN

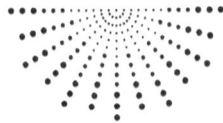

JAN THOMPSON

GEORGIA
PRESS

CALL YOU HOME (SAVANNAH
SWEETHEARTS BOOK 10)

Author Website: JanThompson.com
Book News: JanThompson.com/newsletter

Published by Georgia Press LLC

eBook Cover Design: Georgia Press LLC
Paperback Cover Design: Georgia Press & Deranged Doctor Design

eBook ISBN 978-1-944188-47-4
Paperback ISBN 978-1-944188-48-1

To my Lord and Savior, Jesus Christ, who died on the cross to save me from my sins and rose again from the grave to give me eternal life in heaven.

For God so loved the world that He gave His only begotten Son, that whoever believes in Him should not perish but have everlasting life.
—John 3:16

READ A FREE EBOOK!

TIME FOR ME (A VACATION SWEETHEARTS PREQUEL)

When art gallery archivist Sheryl Breckenridge tries to get world-famous sculptor Winton Pace to display his artwork at Simon's Gallery, she doesn't expect him to fall in love with her. Will she reciprocate in this friends-to-more romance?

Read *Time for Me* (A Vacation Sweethearts Prequel) for FREE at the link below. This story starts thirteen months before *Smile for Me* (Vacation Sweethearts Book 1).

Download the FREE prequel here:
JanThompson.com/time-free

Sign up for Jan Thompson's mailing list to keep up

with her book news. She writes Christian beach romance, romantic suspense, and suspense thrillers.

Subscribe to Jan's book news:
JanThompson.com/newsletter

ABOUT CALL YOU HOME

SAVANNAH SWEETHEARTS BOOK 11

She speaks fluent sign language. But she can't interpret his mixed signals.

To save a landmark family restaurant in Savannah, two chefs must put aside their twenty-year-old feud and cook together. Can they at least try to be kind toward each other without digging up old hurts?

I can't wait for you to read Piper's story. Fans of my Savannah Sweethearts Christian beach romance series might recall that Piper is Deaf. Here comes Chef Isaac, her nemesis, who does not speak American Sign Language. How are they going to resolve their old feud if they can't understand each other?

PIPER'S PICKLES...

Right before a long and busy Thanksgiving week-end, chef and restaurateur Piper Peyton is confronted with a series of impossible problems.

Piper can handle one disaster at a time in her restaurant, but not two unexpected catastrophes in the same day that threaten to shut down Piper's Place for good and possibly end her career as a restaurateur.

Sometimes bad things happen.

But hopefully not all at once, right?

Yet, no matter what, she has to keep Piper's Place open for business. Her customers expect it. This is their favorite twenty-four-seven restaurant where Riverside Chapel members frequent after church on Sundays and throughout the week. This is where people, young and old, gather to talk about life, solve their problems, meet new friends, and critique her new test dishes.

Oh, this place absolutely needs to stay open.

What to do, Lord? What to do?

ISAAC'S INGREDIENTS...

How long can a person bear a grudge? For cruise ship chef de cuisine Isaac Untermeyer, he can hold it for twenty years and then some.

How can he forget that high school sophomore with the topknot bun on her head and a big smile on her face, who robbed him of the high school cooking competition trophy, and ran off with the prize of full tuition paid to any college of her choice? Not that Isaac needed the money. It was a matter of pride.

Even if he tries to get over how he lost the championship to a supposedly better cook, his family won't let him forget it. As soon as he arrives in Savannah for his holiday break in between jobs, his mother takes him to none other than Piper's Place.

However, something is wrong in their kitchen that night when meals don't arrive and the customers start to leave without eating.

The chef in Isaac senses a crisis.

He wants to help his nemesis, but his pride says *don't bother*.

Yet, somehow Isaac finds himself responding to the call for help and going to her rescue...

And he doesn't know why.

Call You Home is the last novel in *USA Today* bestselling author Jan Thompson's Savannah Sweethearts series of clean and wholesome contemporary Christian beach romances celebrating faith, hope, and love in Jesus Christ. The series is set in the historic southern coastal city of Savannah, Georgia, and on the nearby idyllic beach town of Tybee Island by the Atlantic Ocean. If you enjoy *Call You Home*, you might also enjoy the other books in the series.

Call You Home (Savannah Sweethearts Book 11)
JanThompson.com/call

Savannah Sweethearts
JanThompson.com/savannah

For book news, subscribe to Jan's mailing list
JanThompson.com/newsletter

CALL YOU HOME

PROLOGUE

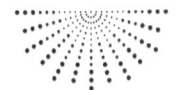

*P*iper Peyton's hands shook as she continued the online chat with her bank. She couldn't type any faster, but there was no other way to talk to the bank at five o'clock on the night before Thanksgiving.

Her local branch was already closed for the day. Regardless, her favorite banker, who understood rudimentary American Sign Language, had the whole week off. This customer support person she was chatting with wasn't even in Savannah.

Piper drew a deep breath, prayed for calm, and slowed down her typing, mulling over the day's double catastrophes as she attempted to answer questions.

Yes, my financial manager took everything.

Yes, he's the only other person with access to my account.

No, I don't know where he went or when he left. He's not answering his phone.

Yes, I just found out. I told you my butcher told me that he couldn't get paid.

Piper glanced at the clock on her laptop.

Even though Piper's Place opened for business around the clock, dinner wasn't served until five. She had to get back to the kitchen as soon as possible.

Never in twelve years had she expected to cook around the clock. That had been why she hired three chefs to help her. Each of them would work eight-hour shifts with two days off per week. As the executive chef, Piper oversaw the entire restaurant, planned new seasonal menus, and filled in whenever a chef was out. If she wasn't in her office, she was in the kitchen, working full shifts.

For the last three months, Piper and her sous chefs had taken turns to fill in for Chef Lillian, at home on a five-month maternity leave. Piper didn't mind, as she loved to cook. It was quieter at night, and she liked to look out of the third floor window at the night landscape: the moon in the sky and the river beyond the riverfront.

At the moment, Piper wasn't enjoying anything.

At eight o'clock in the morning, Piper was about to go home to sleep for several hours before returning to her office after noon, when the lunch shift sous chef, Forsythia McDevitt, informed her that the dinner chef, Torkel Le Tissier, had eloped with the lunch chef, Seraphina Moulton, and they had left the country.

That meant Piper had no main chefs from eight to midnight, for a total of sixteen hours. Maybe they could still survive Thanksgiving Eve, with two sous chefs, one for each shift, plus a bevy of rotating prep cooks and line cooks.

However, Forsythia was in some sort of emotional breakdown because Torkel was gone. Unable to function, Forsythia spent the entire morning crying in the hallway, refusing to go home and refusing to help Piper in the kitchen. Normally, it meant that Piper could fire her, but she felt sorry for Forsythia.

By four o'clock, Piper was exhausted. The lunch shift was over, and now she had to cover the dinner shift—unless her other sous chef, Lennon Bao, could handle it. Forsythia was still hanging around, embarrassed that she had been dysfunctional. She offered to help Bao with the dinner shift.

That was when the other shoe dropped.

Around four in the afternoon, the butcher

texted Piper, saying his payment had been declined. Leaving the kitchen to Bao and Forsythia, Piper rushed to her office at the back of the kitchen to log into her bank account on her laptop to see what was going on.

That was when she discovered her checking account had been zeroed out. So had her business savings account.

Money for her rainy days was gone.

The only person who had access to her accounting system and bank was her bookkeeper, financial manager, and cousin, Regis.

Piper couldn't believe he would do this to her. Flesh and blood!

She texted her investment broker to see if everything was okay over there. She was relieved to find out that her stocks and mutual funds had not been touched.

However, three hundred thousand dollars are missing.

My operating fund and savings.

Salaries for my employees. Christmas bonuses. Grocery money.

By the time the bank customer service continued typing, Piper had developed a headache, even before she was told what she had suspected.Her once-trusted cousin Regis Peyton had transferred the funds to another account, to which Piper had no access.

What should I do?

Piper prayed again. She might have been saved for only about ten years, but she had learned how to pray in church.

She read what appeared on her chat screen, mulling over what her bank was doing. They had canceled her debit and credit cards, and contacted their fraud liaison. They wanted her to report the theft to the local police.

My cousin is a criminal.

She continued reading. They had safeguarded her account, but it was up to her if she wanted to close the account and reopen a new one. Piper wondered if she should go to another bank, but then decided that would make her look paranoid.

I'm not afraid of my cousin.

However, not only did Regis have access to her bank account, he also had access to all her business dealings—from the butcher to the florist, from the fishmonger to the restaurant equipment supplier. Did she have to contact all of them to make sure Regis had not messed with them as well? Would that cast a bad light on her as a businesswoman? Would her integrity and business dealings be called into question?

Piper realized that perhaps the best thing for her would be to close that offending bank account, open a new account, and basically start over?

Piper nodded, then realized she could not be seen on the chat. She typed an affirmative reply.

A light lit up on her office door. That meant someone was knocking on the other side. She ignored it while she finished her conversation with customer support.

Yes, the next day was Thanksgiving, and the bank would be closed. She'd have to go on Black Friday, the busiest day of the year to be out and about, to open a new business account—if she could transfer some money from her investment funds into her new checking account.

Yeah, so that I can pay my employees next week.

She wondered if her fund manager was available. She texted him.

I need to sell some stocks right now. Emergency. Please and thank you.

Even though it was Thanksgiving in the USA, it was still a working day in the other parts of the world. Maybe Jefferson could sell some of her Asian stocks since it would be daytime Friday in Hong Kong and Japan.

All her operating fund and company savings gone, Piper had a hard time focusing on the other problem: she had no other chef besides herself working for the rest of the holiday weekend.

The door light flashed again.

Reluctantly, Piper got up and walked to the door.

As soon she opened it, Nelson Guilmard, her restaurant manager, nearly barged in. He looked very worried. He spoke and signed frantically. "The customers who made reservations are here."

Even though Piper was profoundly deaf, she had insisted that Nelson spoke as he signed. That way, she could perfect her ability to read lips.

"Forsythia is a wreck. Bao is doing his best. He wants her out of the kitchen."

Piper nodded as Nelson finished, wiping off sweat from his forehead as a gesture of defeat.

They were both stressed. Customers were waiting.

Piper felt drained all of a sudden. Sapped of energy.

She hadn't slept since midnight last night.

She glanced at the clock on her office wall. In seven hours, it would be her shift again. She wasn't sure if she could make it until midnight, let alone through the night until eight in the morning.

The restaurant would be full again the next day. More and more, people were eating out for Thanksgiving these days. Sometimes they ordered out, but either way, this was one of the busiest times of the year for Piper's Place.

Piper's Place closed only once a year: Christmas. The restaurant was open all week long, including Sundays at noon.

It used to be closed on Sundays when Grandma ran this place, but not when Piper took over. Even after she became a Christian some ten years ago, she kept the doors open on Sundays for churchgoers to have their after-church lunches.

Piper held back tears.

"I tried to send Forsythia home. She won't leave. Maybe if you asked her, she might," Nelson said as he signed the equivalent in ASL.

"Is she still crying?" Piper shook her head.

The only person who could keep Sous Chef Forsythia calm in the kitchen was Chef Torkel.

Piper wondered why she hadn't known about this side of Torkel. When she had hired him to be her chef of cuisine, he was the perfect man—uh, chef—for Piper's Place.

Everyone swooned over him then, but not Forsythia, who kept her distance. No one knew she had any interest in Torkel until today. If the two had been an item once upon a time, it was all behind Piper's back.

Nelson tilted his head. "Now Forsythia has

locked herself in the pantry. Bao offered to buy her dinner if she would get out of his pantry."

Piper frowned. "If she keeps on like this, I'll have to fire her."

Nelson plopped on the couch. "So we lost our lunch and dinner chefs, and our night chef is on maternity leave. We still have two sous chefs, who may or may not be able to step up to fill the empty positions."

"Forsythia is in a bad shape. I don't want any accidents in the kitchen. I'll take care of it." Piper sighed. "I also need you to come with me to the police station to help me report this crime, but first we need to put food on the table."

Nelson nodded.

Piper wondered if that was okay to wait a few more hours before she reported the crime. She knew she couldn't call the police right now because she couldn't hear them talk to her on the phone, and they wouldn't be able to see her sign.

Meanwhile, her restaurant was going under.

Piper's Place, a landmark in Savannah that her grandmother had named after her, was housed in a late eighteenth-century store with underground tunnels and uneven old floors. Most of the front of the building had been rebuilt in the nineteenth-century. It cost a fortune to maintain this historic building and keep it looking like the storehouse it had been so long ago.

It was a piece of history.

And now it could be history.

"I have a suggestion," Nelson signed.

"What?" At this stage, Piper was open to anything.

"I talked to a friend of mine, and her son is a chef. He happens to be home for Thanksgiving and Christmas—and get this, not working."

Piper waited.

"His mom said he just sleeps all day and watches TV when he gets up."

"I don't want a lazy bum to work in my kitchen."

"He's on vacation."

"What does he do when he's not?" Piper signed.

"He's been chef de cuisine on a cruise ship for the last five years." Before Piper could reply, Nelson continued to sign. "Maybe he could help us out for a couple of weeks while we interview new chefs."

"He sounds like he could be expensive." Piper had some stock left, but not a lot. In the last few years, she had to cash it out and spend most of it on medical bills, when Mom's health insurance didn't cover her colon cancer treatment. Compared to how much she had to dig into her savings for the cancer treatment, her mother's funeral expense paled in comparison.

If the medical expenses hadn't been that high, Piper could have made more progress toward paying off the mortgage on the commercial building that housed Piper's Place. The historic building came with special preservation rules to which she had to adhere. The cost of maintaining the historic structure was another reason she had not paid off the mortgage on the building.

At her deathbed, Grandma had said she wished that the back wall of the old building hadn't collapsed twenty years prior. It had been costly to restore the wall because her commercial property insurance was bad. It would never collapse again, she had promised, since it was newer than the other three walls.

Piper hadn't banked on her grandmother's word. After she took over the restaurant, she bought a better commercial property insurance.

Mortgages, insurance, salaries, utilities...

Some of these recurring payments would be due come the first week of December.

In nine days.

"In an emergency, we don't have a choice," Nelson spoke and signed. "Besides, he's having dinner in town."

"How much are you thinking of paying him?"

"Two or three times the usual rate per hour. He could possibly work tonight all the way through the next two weeks, but he would want Sundays off."

"You've talked to him?" Piper frowned.

"No. I talked to his mother, and she wants him to go to church with her this Sunday. I know he won't be able to work that day." Nelson smiled nervously.

"Oh, I see."

"He is available. Who else can we call on short notice?" Nelson persisted.

Piper was thinking about her situation beyond this week. She had to pay her employees—all of them.

How fast can I sell my house?

Her Tybee Island beach house was probably worth something. She still had five years of mortgage left on the house, so she wasn't sure how much she could get out of it.

Piper made a note to herself to call her real estate agent friend from church. Sabine Wei would know how much her house was worth. Would that be enough to save her restaurant?

"Let me think about it for a little bit, okay?" Piper signed. "I need time to breathe."

"And pray," Nelson reminded her.

And pray.

Piper nodded.

She logged out of her laptop, threw on her cotton denim chef coat from her closet, and drew a deep breath as she shut the office door behind her.

At the end of the kitchen, she tied up her hair into a topknot bun, washed her hands in an open sink, and entered the war zone.

What to do, Lord? What to do?

CHAPTER ONE

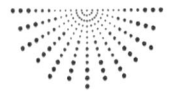

"*I* can't believe you two have been married for over a year, Mom." Isaac Untermeyer tried not to look bewildered as he walked with his mom and Jerome Pendegrast down River Street.

"Don't ask us when we're going to have more kids," Jerome said.

"Is he serious?" Isaac asked Mom.

"He's always serious." Mom was still holding Jerome's hand. They looked like they were madly in love.

Strike madly. *I have no idea what that means.*

The sun was setting, and the sidewalk was still crowded. Nothing had changed in Savannah while Isaac had been gone.

A year ago, he had come home for one day for his sister's wedding, but he didn't have time to hang out in his hometown. He flew back to work on the other side of the world as soon as Amy and Cyrus had left for their own honeymoon.

Shortly after that, Mom and Jerome married—without as much as an email to let Isaac know.

Mom could be like that sometimes. Soon, she had regretted it, and tried to make amends, but there was nothing left to be done. Married was married.

One year later, Isaac had quit his job as chef de cuisine onboard the luxury cruise liner. He had to do it. They decided not to give him a pay raise, but that wasn't it, really.

Isaac had always wanted to run his own restaurant. He was tired of working for someone else, taking orders from the corporate office, cooking for five thousand people.

He wanted a smaller establishment, maybe a corner cafe somewhere. He'd cook breakfast, lunch, and dinner, of course, but then he could lock up and go home for the night. He wouldn't have to live onboard a cruise ship all year long, surrounded by water, bouncing from port to port.

It gets old after a while.

He wanted to plant a vegetable and herb

garden in his backyard, harvest them for his kitchen, and create new dishes whenever he wanted.

Yeah. I want to be my own boss so badly.

He would even entertain the idea of a food truck if he couldn't save up enough to open a restaurant.

Which was why he quit his job and came home to Savannah.

And so began the next chapter of his life. It was an unknown chapter, but Isaac prayed it would bring him closer to his dream job.

Through various channels and connections, Isaac found out that there was to be a cooking competition in the Bahamas in January, where the prize was fifty thousand dollars. That would definitely bring him closer to his own brand new food truck, though it would still be a long way off to buying a building somewhere and opening a new restaurant.

He hadn't decided which he'd do yet, but Nassau was a step forward either way.

He had six or seven weeks left to come up with some sort of seafood menu that would blow away the judges. He had been thinking about his new beginning for weeks.

A cargo ship horn pulled Isaac's attention

toward the Savannah River, where a riverboat chugged downstream the other way.

"That one of your riverboats?" Isaac asked his stepfather.

Jerome nodded. "That's my *Carleigh*. I don't have any opening there, but if you want me to keep you in mind for a position, I could."

Isaac was stunned.

He didn't know whether to feel insulted or make a decision to ignore his stepfather.

"You might have misunderstood my question," Isaac said. "I'm not looking for a job. I guess Mom told you I quit my job, but I just need a short break. I'll put feelers out later. I have savings, so I'm not going to starve between now and Christmas. I'm preparing for that cooking competition, remember?"

The crowd hampered their progress, and it was closing in on seven o'clock. Isaac felt hungry, but he didn't say anything.

As soon as his cruise ship docked in Sydney four nights ago, he had flown out and returned here. He had been suffering jet lag ever since. The time change between Australia and America was night and day.

For three days, Isaac wandered around Mom's house at night, and slept in all day. Today was better. He only slept through lunch, waking up sometime in the middle of the afternoon. Still, this would be his first real meal of the day, not counting the coffee he'd had, whenever that was.

"Here we are!" Mom declared.

Isaac looked up, and suddenly his muscles stiffened from his shoulders all the way down to his calves.

Not here.

He glanced at Mom, who seemed to know what he was thinking.

She smiled, leaning against Jerome. "This is where we sort of hit it off."

Jerome kissed her forehead. "In our Super Senior luncheons."

"What?" Isaac barely muttered.

"Super Seniors from church," Mom explained. "You wouldn't know. You're underaged. You have to be at least sixty to join our club. We do more than weekly lunches, but we eat here most of the time."

Do I care?

Isaac cleared his throat. "I can't go in there."

"They have really good food," Jerome said.

"I'm sure many area restaurants have good food." Isaac could hear his heart beating hard now. Or was he imagining the noise?

"What's wrong with Piper's Place?" Mom

tugged at Isaac's arm, leading him to the slaughterhouse.

Isaac's feet were cemented to the pavement.

"Come on, dear."

Isaac didn't move.

Jerome frowned. "We have a reservation for seven. If we show up even five minutes late, they will give the table to someone else. It's that busy."

"Ah..."

"Isaac Untermeyer!" Mom gritted her teeth.

Isaac wasn't going to budge. Did Mom think that she could use that on him twenty years later? He wasn't seventeen anymore.

"I'll eat somewhere else."

"What's going on?" Jerome asked Mom.

"Hang-ups," Mom said.

"She got away with it. The judges favored her." Isaac clammed up.

"What is he talking about?" Jerome asked.

Mom didn't laugh. "Piper Peyton won the cooking competition fair and square. Your dishes didn't taste as good as hers, so you lost."

"Piper? When was Piper in a cooking competition?" Jerome glanced at his watch.

"Twenty years ago. Savannah High," Mom explained.

"High school? When they were kids?" Jerome

laughed so hard he began to cough. "Are you *kidding* me?"

"Very *punny*, honey." Mom elbowed Jerome.

They both laughed until tears came out of their eyes.

Isaac stood there in disbelief.

He shook his head.

And they laughed some more.

Two grown adults in their seventies, laughing at his misery.

Jerome wiped his eyes. "Look, Son. Let me challenge you to be man enough to step into Piper's restaurant and order from her menu."

Man enough?

"What did you say?" Isaac couldn't believe his ears. Did his stepfather challenge him?

"You heard what I said," Jerome replied. "Now let's see if you're going to come to dinner with us or walk away with your tail between your legs."

Tail?

"What did you say?" Isaac wasn't sure how to respond.

Jerome checked his watch. "Rhoda, why don't you go in there and save our table? Isaac and I are going to have a little talk to clear our thinking."

Mom nodded. "Don't take too long. I'm famished."

"So am I." Jerome put his large arm across

Isaac's shoulders, as they stood outside the windows of Piper's Place.

Isaac didn't like the man strong-arming him, but Jerome was at least six-five to his five-eleven, and yep, the seventy-something man had the physical advantage. He must lift weights or something, because Isaac couldn't even move his neck.

Isaac cleared his throat. "I don't know if you meant to be buddy-buddy, but my shoulder muscles sort of hurt."

"Oh." Jerome's arm sprang off.

"Thank you." Isaac made a show of rubbing his muscles.

As he did that, hoping to buy time, his eyes wandered back to the old glass window. The restaurant was crowded and noisy, almost sounding like a tavern, and the music was...

Christian?

He heard Christian hymns.

Isaac tried to recall his last interactions with Piper back in high school. He did not remember her going to church at all. So why would she play Christian hymns in her restaurant?

Was Piper a Christian?

Or maybe her business partners were.

Yeah, that has got to be it.

If Piper were a Christian in high school, she

wouldn't have used his family recipe to win the cooking contest against him.

Suddenly it hit Isaac.

What about me? I'm a Christian. And here I am angry with her for twenty years.

What does the Bible say about anger?

Festering anger?

The front door opened and more customers entered Piper's Place. Before the door slowly closed, Isaac was able to see the hostess station. Standing behind the two people there was a rather tall woman, facing away from the front door. She was talking to a couple of the servers.

Isaac recognized her at once.

That twisted topknot bun on top of her head gave her away. It had been so many years, and yet her hair was still tied up. Back in high school, she would sometimes tie her hair in a chignon at the back of her head, but most of the time, it was usually a variation of a bun on top of her head.

If only she would let her hair down, even once...

She turned around, walked down a short hallway, and disappeared through a bright green traffic door.

Green had always been her favorite color, Isaac remembered.

The color of herbs and vegetables.

Isaac wondered if she still maintained her grandmother's herb garden.

Surely she did.

To keep up, Isaac also kept his own herb garden on the top deck of every cruise ship he worked in. One of these days, he wanted a cooking rematch against his nemesis.

And I'm going to win.

CHAPTER TWO

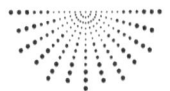

Isaac couldn't believe he fell for Jerome's persuasive words, but five minutes later, he found himself entering Piper's Place and following Jerome and a hostess to their table on the third floor, where Mom waited by a gorgeous view of the Savannah River and the night sky.

Mom seemed happy that Isaac had changed his mind. She literally clapped her hands in glee, as though she were a little girl getting everything she wanted.

Well, Mom always got what she wanted.

Even when Dad had been alive, he made sure Mom was happily spoiled.

After Dad passed away so many years ago, Mom kept the family business going for years alone, keeping his memories alive all by herself.

Isaac felt bad that once he left for college, he hadn't come home often, but then none of his siblings had either, not until Amy got married the year before. It was a miracle that their youngest brother, Garrett, made it to the wedding. Most of the time, no one could contact him.

Still, Isaac was the oldest son in the family, and wasn't it his role to show some sort of example to the younger ones?

Granted, he had been fostered and adopted when he was four years old, but Mom and Dad had treated him as their own.

They will always be my parents.

And that was why he swallowed his pride tonight.

Only a few minutes prior, in as few words as possible, Jerome had reminded Isaac of all the things that poor Mom suffered through all those years alone, at the begging mercy of her church. Her wish at every Christmas was to see her three children come home to visit her, to be a family with her again before it was too late.

Amy had come home last year.

Isaac was here now.

Jerome said that if Isaac could get along with Mom—and survive Thanksgiving and Christmas with her—then perhaps his brother Garrett would come home too.

Isaac didn't need Jerome to remind him that Mom missed Garrett most of all.

Garrett was the only biological son that Mom and Dad had together. He was a piece of Dad that Mom had missed all these years, although she had treated all three of them equally.

Yes, equally harshly.

There she was, sitting across the restaurant table from Isaac, seemingly happy as could be that Isaac had not decided to eat elsewhere tonight.

Time had aged her. Her once reddish hair was now completely white. Lines scored her face, all the way to her forehead and hairline.

Isaac wondered how much time they had with her.

He wondered if he should give Garrett a call and talk to him—as Jerome had done with Isaac ten minutes ago.

Maybe Garrett would be open to reason.

Come home, bro. Time is always running out.

Then again, the Special Forces often sent Garrett to places where no family member could contact him at all.

Truly, the best thing Isaac could do was to ask God to tell Garrett to come home to Savannah.

"I like all their seafood dishes," Mom said, obviously oblivious to Isaac's thoughts. "There's no bad food at Piper's."

"That's why it's all so expensive." Jerome chuckled, thumbing his menu. "Do you like seafood, Isaac?"

"We cook it all the time on the cruise ships, so I've got a hankering for some fried chicken right now." Even as he said it, Isaac's eyes were scanning the seafood dishes. Maybe he could get some ideas for his menu—

No. I'll make my own ideas.

There was no way he was going to give Piper any credit if he won the cooking competition coming up.

"Get the buttermilk fried chicken." Mom pointed to an item on her menu. "It's Piper's own personal recipe."

Piper again.

Can everyone not remind me I'm in her restaurant?

Against my will, to boot!

Isaac took a deep breath and looked out of the window. The twinkling of stars in the sky made for a pretty night this Thanksgiving eve.

Yet, Isaac didn't feel thankful at all.

He had been griping and complaining, hadn't he?

He had quit a rather good job on the cruise ship. Was it a mistake?

He was now sitting in the restaurant owned by the person who had haunted him for twenty years.

The server appeared, flustered, sweating.

What on earth?

"I'm sorry," she said. "We're running behind a little bit. What can I get you for an appetizer? Anything to drink?"

Running behind?

It was all Isaac heard. He looked around the restaurant and noticed something bad that could take down the entire establishment.

Most of the tables didn't have food.

Servers filled drinks, brought more bread for some.

But no one appeared from the service elevator door with trays of dishes. No one came up the stairs. And customers were leaving.

"Is something the matter?" Isaac asked. "I don't mean to pry."

Jerome cleared his throat. "It's Thanksgiving. The place is always crowded this time of year."

So? Surely a busy restaurant had prepared itself for the holiday crowd.

Isaac waited for the server to say something.

"I can take your drink and appetizer order." She smiled.

She did not answer his question about what

was going on in the restaurant with all these people waiting for food.

"Curiosity killed the cat," Mom said.

Curious? Is that a challenge?

Isaac had been challenged twice tonight.

Jerome had implied that he should not run away like a cowardly dog.

Now Mom said the curious cat could die.

"Why am I hearing all these metaphors about cats and dogs?" Isaac turned his attention to the menu.

He salivated at the names of all the dishes he wanted to try.

Only because I haven't eaten all day.

"Are we having turkey at Amy's tomorrow?" Isaac asked.

"Yes," Mom said. "So don't order turkey tonight."

Yep, Mom is back. Always telling the kids what to do.

"I'm not a kid anymore, Mom. If I want turkey for two nights in a row—"

"More than two nights. You'll be eating leftovers all weekend."

"Oh, good point."

If Mom could explain herself, it might help Isaac and his siblings think less unkindly of her.

Then again, didn't the Bible say to turn the

other cheek and to return good for evil? Not that Mom was *evil*, but sometimes what she said could have been more thoughtful.

Just as Isaac was about to change his mind from chicken to red snapper, he saw several more parties of people get up from their tables and leave. "Uh-oh."

"*Uh-oh* is right," Mom said. She turned to the server. "Tell me, Rosalinda dear, Is Nelson downstairs?"

"Yes, ma'am." The server knew whom Mom was talking about.

The name was familiar to Isaac.

Too familiar.

Nelson? Do I know a Nelson?

Mom continued to speak to the server. "Please tell him that Rhoda Pendegrast and her party are here. He knew we're coming tonight."

"Yes, ma'am."

After the server left with their drinks and appetizer orders, Isaac waited for Mom to explain.

When she did not offer any information, Isaac asked. "What was that about?"

Mom turned to Jerome. "Isaac's always been the curious one among my kids."

Then it dawned on Isaac.

Nelson Guilmard.

"Nelson, my classmate from Savannah High?"

"The one and the same," Mom said.

"Why did you have to tell him we're here?" Puzzling.

In high school, Nelson Guilmard's younger brother had dated Piper Peyton, the girl who had robbed the cooking trophy from Isaac.

No, Isaac didn't need the full scholarship to college, but he wanted the trophy as a claim to fame in their Cumin Cooking Club.

"Mom, you kept in touch with Nelson all these years."

"Well, hard not to when he works here."

"He and Piper...?" Isaac almost felt embarrassed asking.

"No. Nelson's married to some sweet girl, and they're expecting their third child. I'm still in touch with his parents. They live on St. Croix now." Mom turned to Jerome. "Warm and sunny all year round. Maybe it's a place we could move to?"

"Or visit." Jerome pecked Mom on her puckered lips.

Isaac tried to get the two lovebirds to his topic of conversation. "Nelson. We were talking about Nelson."

"What about him?" Mom asked.

"He's working here."

Mom nodded.

"Is there anyone in my high school cooking club who is not working for Piper today?" Isaac snapped.

"Nelson's brother Marlon isn't. He got that basketball scholarship to Ohio State, and he was out of here."

"I remember. What's he doing now?" Isaac expected Mom to know.

"He graduated with some sports degree and teaches high school basketball now."

"Where?"

"He married and moved with his wife to Oklahoma, where she's from."

So Marlon and Piper had broken up.

Well, what did he expect? Those two had only been high school sweethearts.

Marlon hadn't really been as interested in cooking as he was in Piper. They were the same age, and Piper only joined the cooking club because of Marlon.

Still, they had a wonderful time, didn't they? All six members!

Isaac recalled their exclusive Cumin Cooking Club, how Dad funded their "research dinners" at five-star restaurants.

Isaac remembered boasting about how he was going to Paris, France, to learn how to cook from the master chefs of Europe, et cetera, et cetera.

But losing that trophy to someone three years his junior, though...

That stung.

Especially since Isaac had been the one who taught Piper Peyton everything she knew about cooking. Her mother was sickly all the time and didn't cook. It was up to Peyton to feed herself.

And Isaac had a soft spot for—

Yeah, it stung.

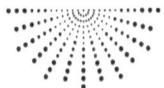

CHAPTER THREE

"As your restaurant manager, I want to be sure that we're in agreement," Nelson signed quickly.

"What agreement?" Piper wiped her hands on a kitchen towel, which she then flung over her shoulder. She was at the grill station. Her shoulder muscles were hurting something fierce, but she pressed on.

"You said I could call in an emergency chef."

Piper nodded.

"He has arrived." Nelson looked excited.

"To work?"

"He's eating dinner with his mother upstairs. Shall I go get him?"

"Oh. You said that he was eating in town."

"We are the best restaurant in town," Nelson signed.

Piper felt sweat dripping down her forehead. She had been working for twenty hours straight, and hadn't gone to the police station to file a report. She had almost left the kitchen to Bao, but he was reluctant to take over as the main chef. He only wanted to assist as the sous chef—and he did not want Forsythia anywhere near him.

It was almost eight at night, and they were in the weeds, failing miserably to fill all the food orders. Nelson had already told her that a third of the customers had left.

Her skeletal crew was upset about the two eloping chefs. Piper herself hadn't seen it coming.

The stress of the last four hours had taken a toll on her. She wanted to sit down, but there was no time.

She leaned against the steel counter behind her, one hand still holding a spatula, and both of her eyes on the two frying pans on the stove—one with soup and one with sauce.

Around her, the kitchen was busy, busy, busy.

Thank God that Forsythia had stopped crying, not that it helped too much. At least she wasn't pouring tears into the dishes she was helping Piper cook tonight. Piper had sent Forsythia to the chef garde manger. The poor girl was fussing at having been "demoted" to preparing cold cuts and salads.

Chill, girl.

Piper prayed that Bao would step up. He had so much potential to be the main chef, but he'd rather remain a sous chef. Even the notion of getting more pay didn't make him budge from his mental barrier.

They'd have to deal with that later. First, they had to survive tonight. Everyone outside was waiting for their meals.

Piper walked toward where Bao was standing and turned down his burner, as he continued stirring the buttery, nutty sauce.

"Did I make a mistake with Torkel and Seraphina?" Piper signed to Bao.

Surprised that Piper asked for his opinion, Bao nearly dropped his wooden spoon. "I don't know, ma'am. All I know is that we lost two chefs and I feel overwhelmed."

"Don't be overwhelmed. If you are, imagine yourself in my position."

"You must be under tremendous pressure."

"I am, but God is greater still."

"So this is when your God comes in to rescue you."

"He's always with me, through good times and bad. But yes, right now, I need Him the most." Piper spotted Nelson walking toward them.

Nelson should have gone home at five o'clock. The night manager had probably arrived by now, dealing with the front of the house.

"We'll debrief ourselves later," Nelson signed. "Right now, we need the mercy of God. It's possible that the mercy includes an emergency chef. Have you decided?"

"Bao and I are doing fine now," she signed to Nelson.

"We have a night shift to fill. You've been here since midnight. We haven't gone to the you-know-where. If you're going to cook all evening and all night—after cooking last night and all morning—I think you're going to collapse."

Night shift. That was coming very soon. "I know what you're saying, but we don't even know this guy you want to hire."

"Just for two weeks to tide us over. I'll send out emails even today for chefs who might be interested for the long term. I am guessing you will want to hire two chefs to replace Torkel and Seraphina."

Piper didn't have time to argue with Nelson right now. "I do trust you."

Yes, Nelson had been a loyal friend to her for many years. When Piper took over the restaurant from her grandmother twelve years ago, she called Nelson—who was then working as a restaurant manager somewhere in Charleston.

Nelson had been here at Piper's Place ever since.

A loud clatter and clanging startled Piper. She spun around to find Forsythia on the floor, batter all over her head and her black chef coat, and a stainless steel mixing bowl upside down on the floor near her.

Forsythia burst into tears.

"Clean up, please," Piper signed.

Bao rushed to Forsythia to get her up from the messy floor.

Forsythia reached for her ankle and moaned.

Oh no.

Piper waved for a mop. She and Nelson started cleaning up the mess, as Forsythia hobbled.

"I think I twisted my ankle," Forsythia mumbled.

"Take her to my office," Piper signed to Bao. She turned to Nelson. "Call your emergency chef."

CHAPTER FOUR

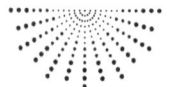

*I*t was pushing eight o'clock and dinner still hadn't been served.

Something must be terribly wrong in the Piper's Place kitchen downstairs. It was all Isaac could think of, while he tried to keep up with Mom and Jerome.

They were planning a vacation or something in Key Largo or somewhere.

Isaac sipped water. If he drank more, he wouldn't be able to eat dinner tonight.

If dinner came at all.

Mom reached across the table and patted the back of Isaac's hand. "I want you to handle our anniversary dinner next year. I want it to look somewhat like a wedding reception—because we didn't have one."

"Of course. It'll be better than Amy's wedding reception."

Mom frowned. "Watch that pride, dear."

"Amy's reception wasn't bad," Jerome said. "Piper gave Amy a discount because of your mom."

"A discount. That explains it."

"Stop, Isaac. You have logs in your own eyes too," Mom said.

Isaac felt chastised. He remembered clearly last July—it was hot in Savannah—when he had attended his sister's wedding.

He had sneaked into the kitchen of that small private home where the wedding and reception were held. Piper wasn't there, but her chef de cuisine and several of his assistants were.

Isaac tried to recall his name, but he couldn't remember.

The finger food was all right. Isaac had to give him that.

But as always, Isaac considered himself a cut above Piper and anyone who worked for her.

Mom wiped her eyes. "I wish Felix had been there to walk Amy down the aisle. He would have loved to do that."

Oh. Isaac blinked. "I'm sorry, Mom. I shouldn't have brought up the past."

"I mentioned it first." Mom sniffled.

"But it's true. Dad would have loved to be there

for his only daughter," Isaac said, not looking at Jerome.

"I bet he would." Jerome's voice was even. "When I walked my daughters down the aisle at their weddings, I wished that my wife could have been there."

Isaac looked up. He knew that Jerome was widowed, but he wondered how they could talk about their past like that.

"Were you thinking about how we could be talking about our deceased spouses?" Jerome asked.

Isaac nodded. "Isn't it painful?"

"My wife died years ago. And so did your dad," Jerome said. "It was all a long time ago. We don't forget our history, but we also don't let our painful past prevent us from moving on, Son."

Painful past?

What is he saying?

"Jerome is positive that way," Mom said. "That's why I love him."

Love? Isaac wondered how Mom could love anyone else but Dad.

"I loved your dad dearly, but he is not here anymore." Mom patted Isaac's hand again. "Jerome also loved his wife, but it's over now."

"Death is the end of a marriage," Jerome said.

Isaac leaned back. "That sounds morbid. I thought a marriage is forever."

"Nope." Jerome sat up. "Only until death. You remember the vows, right?"

"No, I don't. Never been married."

"Figure of speech, Son." Jerome laughed. "Go read your Bible. There's no marriage in heaven."

"What about all those sayings about marriages being made in heaven?"

"Sayings. They're just sayings." Jerome whipped out his phone. He found something and started to read. "Listen to what Mark 12:25 said."

For when they rise from the dead, they neither marry nor are given in marriage, but are like angels in heaven.

He scrolled. "Says the same thing in Matthew 22:30."

For in the resurrection they neither marry nor are given in marriage, but are like angels of God in heaven.

"So marriage is only on earth." Mom looked at Isaac quite intently.

Uh-oh. Isaac almost knew where she was going.

"How about you, dear?" Mom's voice was sweet —too sweet.

Jerome rubbed his chin. "You know that Piper is still single—"

"Jerome!" Mom swatted his arm. "Leave Isaac alone. He probably won't ever marry."

Why did Mom say that?

Isaac was afraid to ask.

But Jerome asked for him. "Why is that?"

"Because"—Mom rolled her eyes—"he is too full of himself!"

Isaac's jaw dropped. "I am not."

"You are too." Mom pointed a finger at him. "Amy would agree with me."

"Don't drag Amy into this."

"Then why are you still single?"

"Because I've been busy working and saving up to open my own restaurant. Life is not all about kisses and hugs, you know."

Well, unfortunately, Isaac had quit his job in a huff. He didn't feel like going back on another cruise ship any time soon.

Around them, more people left.

Then the service elevator door opened, and someone came running out of it.

A balding man with a familiar reddened face.

And batter all over his vest and pants.

He made a beeline toward their table. "Isaac Untermeyer, you're hired!"

CHAPTER FIVE

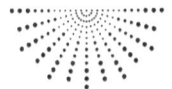

"*B*ut I didn't apply for a job," Isaac said as Nelson ushered him into the elevator.

Nelson Guilmard wiped sweat off his forehead. The more he did so, the more he smeared batter all over his head.

Isaac didn't have the heart to tell him—

Well, okay. "Nelson, my friend, your hanky is covered with batter, which you then rubbed all over your face—and what happened to your hair?"

"Started losing it since the day I got married." Nelson put away his handkerchief.

"Who uses handkerchiefs anymore?" Isaac asked.

"Tell that to my wife. She irons them. Can you believe it?"

"Your wife irons?"

"Does anyone these days?" Nelson sighed. "She also dresses in vintage clothing only. Always the twenties. Laces and frills and whatnot. I have to draw the line somewhere, and that's where I drew the line. I'll wear a vest, but that's it."

Suddenly his jaw dropped. His eyes were on his own chest. "Yikes. She's going to kill me for ruining this silk vest."

The elevator door opened to a battlefield so loud that Isaac had to cup his ears.

"This way!" Nelson yelled.

Isaac followed him to a room—office—at the back of the kitchen. Inside was a woman on a couch —also drenched in batter.

She was crying.

"Isaac, meet Sous Chef Forsythia. Forsythia, meet Chef Isaac."

Forsythia bawled.

"You need to have that ankle looked at." Nelson glanced at his watch. "I'll have someone take you to the ER or the closest clinic."

Nelson opened a closet and selected a chef's coat. "Does it fit you?"

"Wait a sec." Isaac put up his palm. "Like I said, I didn't apply for the job. Any job."

"Your mom said you're jobless at the moment."

"I've got a cooking competition coming up in January."

"She said you quit your chef de cuisine job on that cruise ship. They don't pay enough or something."

"Mom talks too much."

"She also said you don't have enough money to open your own restaurant." Nelson rummaged through a file cabinet, obviously looking for something. "Ah, here it is."

"Mom needs to shut—"

"How about we pay you twice the rate per hour you got on that cruise ship?" Nelson shoved the stack of paper in front of him. "It's only for two weeks, with Sundays off, but you can extend any time you want."

What?

"Whatever you were paid last month per hour, we'll double it. It will help you save up for that dream restaurant of yours."

"I heard you." Isaac found himself calculating.

So in two weeks, he'd earn what he would have in a month.

"How many hours a week?" Isaac asked, against his better judgment.

"Actually, the working conditions are great here. We have three rotating chefs, including Piper herself. She lost two of her chefs today, but when they were here, each chef only worked for eight hours a day, even though Piper herself stays most of the time. She works like fourteen to seventeen hours a day."

"Did your two chefs get fired or did they quit?" Isaac asked.

"They eloped with each other."

"Seriously?" Isaac chuckled, though it was no laughing matter.

Piper had lost her chefs. Even if he were running his own restaurant, Isaac couldn't possibly work twenty-four hours straight without sleep.

"What about the others? Doesn't she have sous chefs?"

"We have various types of assistant cooks. We have two sous chefs—including Forsythia with the bad ankle." Nelson pointed to Forsythia on the couch. "She assisted Chef Moulton, and Bao assisted Chef Torkel."

At the name, the woman on the couch began to cry.

"This restaurant is doomed," she moaned. "We're all going to lose our jobs."

Isaac recalled how customers had left the restaurant without getting their food.

The woman blew her nose. "I thought Torkel loved me."

Nelson tried to shove the chef's coat into Isaac's

hand. "Right now we only have one main chef, and she hasn't slept since last night. So you and she will tag team—"

"She who?"

"Piper—"

"Oh, no." Isaac stepped back. "We don't get along."

Nelson gave him the eye. "Twenty years ago, you did not get along, but today is not twenty years ago. You're both in your thirties now. She approved this, anyway."

"She approved me?"

"Well..."

Isaac shook his head. "She didn't know it's me you're hiring."

"It doesn't matter," Nelson said. "It's divine providence. God sent you here to help us."

"Are you sure you want to bring God into your little scheme?"

"It's not a scheme. We're desperate. You might be an answer to our prayers."

"I might not be."

"Just about everyone is freaking out in the kitchen."

"Yeah, if you don't have a chef in the kitchen, the crew is headless."

"Exactly."

Isaac studied Nelson. There was something else he wasn't saying. "What is it?"

Nelson's eyes twitched.

"Out with it, Nelson. Your eyes are giving it away."

Nelson slumped into an armchair. "I can't say anything, but it's worse than losing the two chefs."

What could be worse?

Is the restaurant in deep debt?

Nelson glanced at the woman on the couch.

Ah. He can't say much more with Forsythia in the room.

"I'll let Piper explain everything," Nelson said.

Isaac moved toward the door. "I came for dinner, against my will, with my mom and Jerome. That's all I'm here for."

"Your mom said..." Nelson's entire face turned red again. "She said you can cook anything at a moment's notice."

"That, I can." *It's the truth.*

"Like I said, Piper needs you. She has been filling for Chef Lillian—away on maternity leave— at night. So she hasn't left the kitchen since midnight last night. She's exhausted."

Poor thing.

"We're in the weeds. I've closed off sections, and we're turning people away. We're losing money, and on top of it, our sous chef right there fell and sprained her ankle or something."

"So you're shorthanded."

"As we speak. I fear Piper's going to pass out or have an accident in the kitchen—she has been cooking for almost twenty hours." Nelson drew a deep breath.

Isaac wasn't sure if he wanted to have anything to do with Piper, but she needed help.

And oddly enough, Isaac was wide awake due to his jet lag. It was daytime on the other side of the world, and he could certainly cook all night, given the recipes and with some help from the others.

But...

Here we go again.

She needs me to help her once again. To what end?

Twenty years ago, Piper needed Isaac to teach her everything he knew about cooking, only for him to see her beat him at the cooking contest.

Now she needed him again.

And she owns her own restaurant, while I don't.

"I mentioned the hourly rate," Nelson whimpered. "Would you rather I triple it?"

"It's not about the money."

It was a matter of principle—or maybe bitterness that had simmered for twenty years?

Isaac wasn't sure what he wanted Piper to do. Apologize? Give up the trophy?

Whatever it was, he didn't want to have anything to do with Piper.

"I'm sorry, but I can't help her." Isaac walked out of the office.

Nelson tried to stop him, but Isaac wouldn't hear of it. Someone called Nelson's name, and Isaac took the opportunity to keep walking. He turned down the first hallway he saw. It was a long one.

Weird, these old buildings.

He had no idea where to go.

He remembered Nelson leading him from an elevator to the office somewhere, but he didn't remember if they went through this hallway in particular.

Okay, maybe if he went back the other way...

Which way was that?

All he needed to do was find the service elevator and go back upstairs where he had come from.

After dinner—if dinner would be served at all— he would go home.

Mom had set him up. Isaac was sure that she had found out about the crisis somehow, and made arrangements for them to eat at Piper's Place tonight.

Not only that, she had gotten in touch with

Nelson, who turned out to be the restaurant manager doing the hiring.

Whether Mom had manipulated the circumstances, Isaac couldn't tell at this time.

All he knew was that as of this afternoon, Piper's Place didn't have a chef de cuisine, and they had been flying headless for the four busy hours—with Piper doing everything.

He turned around and walked down the other end of the hallway.

Several servers walked past Isaac, and he knew he was in the right hallway. He followed them.

Out of the corner of his eye, he saw a woman in a chef's coat exit an elevator door. Her hands were on her face—or forehead. He couldn't see from the back view.

But he recognized the familiar hairstyle.

And then he heard her sobbing quietly.

No, no. Don't do that.

Please don't.

Isaac's mind transported him back to Piper Peyton's first year at Savannah High School. She had attended another school somewhere in Tennessee for her freshman year, but she moved with her mother to Savannah that summer, before her sophomore year, to care for her grandmother, the original owner of Piper's Place.

In the middle of the fall semester, Isaac had

been playing basketball with the Guilmard boys, when he found the awkward sophomore crying outside a nearby building. Since Piper could not hear herself, she had no idea how loud her sobs were.

It had gotten to him then.

And it got to him now.

Bracing himself, Isaac tapped her left shoulder —not her right, because she had a high school volleyball injury there.

She spun around.

And shrieked.

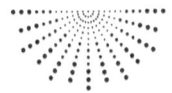

CHAPTER SIX

"*N*elson! What have you done?" Piper signed furiously, as she stepped into Nelson's personal space in her office.

He backed toward a couple of armchairs, next to the couch—where one of the dishwashers was helping Forsythia to her feet.

Piper glanced over to find them staring at her.

At least Forsythia had stopped crying.

"Take her to urgent care now," Piper signed to the dishwasher.

He nodded, and they hurried out of there, as quickly as Forsythia could hobble.

Piper turned her attention back to her restaurant manager and old friend Nelson.

She could tell by the uncomfortable look on

Nelson's face that he knew he had done something he shouldn't have done.

Not that it was *wrong* wrong, but never in a million years would she have expected this from him, her most loyal and trusted employee—more trustworthy than her no-good cousin.

"You agreed to hiring an emergency chef," Nelson signed back.

"Not him!" Piper turned around and jabbed Isaac on his chest.

Taut muscles there.

She almost blinked.

Isaac Untermeyer didn't move from where he stood, a few feet behind Piper and Nelson having a row.

Truth be told, Isaac probably didn't understand sign language.

Just as well, as Piper was about to take it out on Nelson.

Poor Nelson.

She couldn't fire him. Nope. His wife was expecting their third child any day now. The entire family depended on his salary to pay for the delivery and health insurance. His wife quit her job as a preschool teacher back in the summer to be a stay-at-home mom.

Must be tough to have two kids under four, and now one more.

So I can't fire Nelson.

"You didn't ask who it is," Nelson signed back. "You gave me permission, just like that."

"You knew you should've told me whom you already had in mind. You know I would've said no."

"It was all very sudden. I knew you two have a history, but..." Nelson's shoulders sagged. "When all this happened this afternoon, I remembered that Mrs. U—I mean Mrs. P—had reserved a table tonight. She told me Chef Untermeyer is in town."

Chef Untermeyer.

Isaac cleared his throat. "Just call me Isaac. No need to be formal."

Piper didn't know that Isaac had been speaking until the last word. She caught *formal*. "What did he say?"

Nelson interpreted.

Piper hated being manipulated, but maybe Nelson wasn't trying to. Maybe Nelson just wanted Piper's Place to keep its doors open so that he could have a job.

So that they could all keep their jobs.

If only through Christmas. She wasn't sure if she could keep the restaurant doors open past the first of the year if she didn't recover her stolen money or sell her house or find another source of funding.

Truly, Nelson pulling a fast one and hiring Isaac Untermeyer was the least of her problems.

Or is he a potential problem?

"I wouldn't have brought him in if not for the other matter," Nelson signed and spoke. "You and I need to go to the police station, but we can't leave the kitchen without a chef."

Isaac lifted a finger. "Hold on a sec. Police? What's going on?"

Piper felt woozy. She leaned against her table. "I've failed Grandma."

Thankfully, Nelson did not interpret that to Isaac.

"Maybe if you told Isaac about it, he might agree to help us for two weeks."

Piper looked at Isaac and then back at Nelson. "He doesn't want to work here."

"And you don't want to hire him," Nelson signed back. "But he might be just what we need right now. I promise to stand between you and him to prevent you two from killing each other."

Piper blinked.

"Shall we tell him about the other problem?" Nelson asked.

Slowly, Piper nodded. Then she turned away so that she didn't have to see Isaac's face. She assumed that Nelson was telling Isaac about her missing money.

A gentle tap on her shoulder made turn back. Nelson wiped sweat and batter from his face.

Standing closer now, Isaac's face was one of...

Pity.

"I don't need his pity," Piper signed to Nelson.

"He said that you need to report to the police as soon as possible, and he can at least cover for you tonight," Nelson signed. "I told him he could work until midnight, when the shift ends. Let's just get through tonight."

"Bao and I were going to tag team this evening," Piper signed.

"You still don't have a night chef," Nelson replied. "And no sous chef to help you between midnight and eight."

"I have line cooks. Besides, in the night, most people order soup and sandwiches." Piper stepped away from Isaac. She felt nervous around him, like it was high school all over again. The memories flooded her mind...and heart.

"You're going to cook for twenty-four hours?" Nelson asked. "Let Isaac cook this evening. You get some sleep. Get up at midnight and the kitchen is all yours."

"Who died and made you the kitchen manager?"

"If you carry on like this, you will drop dead, and then I'd have to run this place." Nelson tried not to laugh. "Once we all get some sleep, we can think much more clearly, and regroup to find a more permanent chef."

Piper thought of her other chef Lillian. She was still on maternity leave, but if she could return one month sooner, she could have Torkel's job. If Piper added a Christmas bonus or offer to pay for full child care, Lillian might take it.

But my bank account is empty.

Why did you do this to your own flesh and blood, Regis?

Was it because their grandmother had cut Regis out of her will some twelve years prior? Grandma had explained in her letter to the family, read after the funeral, that she had supported Regis and her parents way more than she had any money left. So everything she had left would go to Piper only so she could keep the family restaurant going.

Piper recalled that at first Regis seemed disappointed when the will was read, but he had a good job, and some inheritance money from his mother's side.

However, a few years later, Regis lost his job and decided to start his own accounting firm to work on people's taxes. And he would be happy to manage her finances to free her up to do what she did best: cook and operate the restaurant.

She should have said no.

However, Piper wanted to give Regis more business. He was her only cousin in town. She wanted the family relationship. Also, she felt sorry that their grandmother had cut him out of her will. It meant that Regis did not get a share of the restaurant nor the Peyton house. So when Regis needed a job, Piper gave him one.

Well, Regis turned out to be not much of a family.

Now he had not only jeopardized Piper's restaurant, he had also caused her to lose Grandma's house.

Is this payback, Regis? After twelve long years?

Piper wondered if the police could force Regis to return her money—or what was left of it. She needed it all back, of course. She had been operating the lucrative restaurant for ten years. She wasn't about to take out a loan now—although she could do that against her house.

Ah, better sell the house.

She closed her eyes.

So many problems.

But first, we have to get through tonight.

She checked her watch. This shift would end in about four hours.

Piper studied Isaac, standing there, looking lost in a world of sign language. He seemed to be waiting for someone to talk to him.

One evening. Four hours.

What could possibly happen in one evening?

Piper was thinking about the option, when Nelson's face contorted.

He must have heard something she could not.

Nelson signed quickly. "Fire in the kitchen!"

Horrified, Piper spun around, expecting to push Isaac out of the way—

But he was not there.

She rushed out of the office, Nelson right behind her.

There, by one of the grills, Isaac was putting out a grease fire.

Piper signed as she walked toward him. "What happened?"

Nelson's mouth opened and closed. The other people's mouths opened and closed.

Piper could not hear a thing.

She kept signing. "Someone tell me what happened."

Nelson finally did. "Something caught fire."

Piper rolled her eyes. "I can see that something caught fire. Who did this?"

No one owned up.

Piper watched Isaac scrape a charred pizza off the grill. It must've been a special order. Sometimes guests asked for something from their old menu from decades ago, back in the days when her grand-mother ran the place.

Now Piper was going to lose it all—the entire family farm, so to speak.

Because she trusted a cousin, who turned out to be a crook.

Piper held her tears.

She felt teary these days for some reason. Maybe it was the stress of work. The stress of life. Something.

I'm so tired.

Isaac said something. Piper tried to read his lips.

They were nice-looking lips. He had used lip balm or something, so they weren't chapped—

Wait. What did he say?

"Please repeat," Piper signed. "Clearly."

Nelson interpreted for her. "He said it's fine now. Let's cook."

Piper nodded slowly.

Nelson handed Isaac a chef's coat.

Isaac put it on. "Give me some instructions, and then don't you have to head over to the police station?"

"What?" Piper signed.

Nelson told her what he said.

"I better stay," Piper said.

"You don't trust me?" Isaac asked, motioning for Nelson to interpret for him.

"Never," Piper signed back.

Nelson looked almost reluctant to tell Isaac what she said.

"Your customers are waiting." Isaac pointed to the full order wheels behind Piper. "Go to the police ASAP and return. I need you here tonight."

Nelson's ears reddened as he interpreted what Isaac said to Piper.

Piper sighed. "Of course he needs me here. This is my kitchen. Tell him."

As Nelson interpreted, Piper felt her heart soften. It had been a disastrous day, but God had sent help.

In the middle of her chaos, God sent calm.

Somehow, Isaac's presence quietened her heart. She had heard bits and pieces of what he had been doing the last twenty years, whatever the Super Seniors cared to tell her. They seemed to be talking about their sons and grandsons every time they had the chance.

Was it because Piper was still single at thirty-five years old?

That was by choice, didn't they know?

Still, all that trivial information they had given her about the Untermeyers piled up over the years. Piper knew quite a lot about what Isaac had been up to. He had traveled across the world in search of new spices and dishes to create for some future restaurant he was going to own.

Piper felt sorry for him. First, she beat him at the high school cooking competition by only two points—which he probably didn't know. Then, she owned her own restaurant sooner than he could start his own—although it was because Grandmother passed away too soon.

Now, he would be working as her employee—even if it was only for several days until this weekend was over. Surely he wouldn't stay longer than that.

She was willing to pay whatever he asked, although Nelson had hinted that they had agreed on something she could afford.

His words were probably benign.

I need you here tonight.

Sure. He needed her to give him directions on how Piper's Place worked, although this was a strange weekend before it even began. In one day, two Goliaths emerged in the form of runaway chefs and runaway money, two problems bigger and more severe than anything Piper had ever faced.

And I need a champion.

An emergency chef.

CHAPTER SEVEN

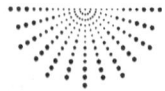

*a*round midnight, the crowd tapered off, but Piper hadn't emerged from her office. When she didn't return to the kitchen half an hour later, Isaac felt like he should check on her, but he didn't want to be a busybody.

Officially, his shift had been over at midnight, but if Piper didn't take his place, there was no other chef to whom he could hand over the spatula.

It had been a very hectic four hours, but Piper had shown him some of the signature dishes, before she and Nelson went to the police station. They had returned by eleven o'clock, and Piper helped out in the kitchen again before disappearing into her office.

Isaac wondered where she got her energy, as she had stayed up for hours the night before and then stayed at work the entire day, with the exception of her trip to the police station.

Piper's Place had fed hundreds of people between the hours of eight and midnight. People from all over the country and world had poured into Savannah for the long Thanksgiving weekend. Many were looking for places to eat dinner.

Isaac knew that this location on River Street was practically everything. The godsend spot right in the middle of a touristy downtown Savannah meant that tourists didn't need a map to find Piper's Place. They could just walk by and there it was, across from the riverfront.

Even Nelson had stayed back past his bedtime to keep the calm at the front of the house, while Piper and Isaac kept the kitchen going. Apparently, none of the servers knew that Piper's cousin had stolen her operating fund.

It was past 12:30 a.m. Isaac wondered whether he should find Nelson to get a ride home to Mom's house, or whether he should stay here and keep cooking until Nelson came to get him and Piper showed up.

Isaac didn't want to admit that he had rather enjoyed this fast-paced kitchen this evening. It was different from the cruise ships he had worked on because he didn't have to worry about these chefs and cooks getting motion sickness, or running out of ingredients while they were far from shore.

This restaurant also had a smaller staff than his kitchen brigade on cruise ships. He was able to get to know each and every one of them. He had no idea how Piper managed to put together a group of people who worked so well together.

Too well, considering that her two head chefs had eloped with each other and left her establishment in a hurry.

However, it was nice to be able to go home to a bed that wasn't in a small, tiny cabin, with a small, tiny bathroom. Everything was small on a cruise ship, even on luxury liners. Sure, if he was a paying customer in one of those expensive balcony staterooms, it would be different. However, as an employee, his living quarters in the cabins were not as luxurious.

Yeah. I made the right decision to ditch cruise ships.

Isaac recalled that Nelson had initially offered him a two-week job. At this special rate, it was a lot of pay. It sounded like he would work only eight hours, but Piper would do the rest, with help from her other cooks.

They could probably find a permanent chef in two weeks.

But overnight? Not likely, unless they had

another chef in mind. According to Nelson, they would ask Chef Lillian if she could come back a month before the end of her maternity leave. That could be next week or the week after.

Until then, Piper had to do a lot.

Even if Isaac felt heartless, he couldn't imagine anyone working non-stop around the clock. Perhaps Piper was strong, but Isaac distinctively remembered her crying all by herself in the hallway, when she thought nobody was looking.

It was the same Piper who had cried behind the sports building back in high school.

Don't let her fragility fool you again!

Still, Isaac wondered if it wasn't real.

To think he had borne a grudge for twenty years.

At the back of his mind, Isaac knew it wasn't pleasing to God.

Now that Piper had become a Christian, it was even more displeasing to God for believers to be enemies of one another.

What did the Bible say about that? That was the one question Dad had said to ask. Dad had been gone for decades now, but Isaac still remembered some of his last words.

Never go forth before you check with God.

And yet, for twenty years, Isaac had gone forth, hating Piper for winning that cooking competition.

Hate? Well, I don't think I hate her. I hated the results, though.

For twenty years, he could not bring himself to congratulate Piper on her win. Everyone said she had won it fair and square, but both Piper and Isaac knew she had used *his* recipe.

Which I gave to her myself.

Isaac sighed.

He checked off his tasks on his handy dandy iPhone app. He glanced over at the mostly empty order wheels hanging over the counters by the door.

Why doesn't Piper go paperless?

It might make the kitchen more efficient.

Ah, but it wasn't his place to suggest this or correct that. He was here to work for a short while and then he'd leave. When he ran his own show, he could do what he felt was best.

Perhaps that was what Piper was also doing: her best.

The traffic door swung open as orders started all over again.

"Does this place ever sleep?" Isaac asked Lennon Bao, who was inventorying his pantry.

"On Christmas Day. Otherwise we're open twenty-four-seven, as you can see."

And therein was the problem.

Isaac wasn't sure if he could work ten or twelve

hours straight. But there was nobody else to replace him and Piper.

"Piper needs to get some sleep," Isaac said to no one.

"She takes power naps in her office," Bao replied from inside his pantry.

So that's what that couch in her office is for. "Does she ever go home?"

Bao put ingredients on a counter. "Yeah, but for the last three months, with Chef Lillian on maternity leave, Piper has been covering for her at night."

"You don't call her Chef Piper or Chef Peyton?" Isaac asked.

"She doesn't want to be called chef, though she's one of the best chefs I know."

Isaac cleared his throat. *I don't know about that.*

"You sure you can't work through the weekend, at least?" Bao asked. "I know it's sudden, but I can help you with the dishes. With all her chefs gone, Piper is on her own. She's not going to get any sleep through Sunday night, I can tell you that."

Where was Piper going to find a ready chef on Thanksgiving Day? She couldn't interview anyone in the middle of the night.

"I wonder sometimes if she shouldn't have hired so many chefs," Bao said. "But the boss is stubborn, and she only lets them work eight hours a day so that that each chef has a life after work. Some good it did. Lillian had more kids, takes more maternity leaves. And the other two chefs had too much time on their hands."

"I don't need to know all that," Isaac said. "I'm only here until midnight."

Bao nodded. "I think I spoke too much."

"Forget it. We all speak too much."

Mom, too.

Isaac made a mental note to have a chat with Mom about putting him in this awkward position.

Ironically, Isaac had enjoyed the last three hours he had been in the kitchen. Most of the dishes were basic, so basic that it didn't take long for Bao to bring him up to speed.

Sure, the meat and vegetables were fresh, and the spices were all there. If the mixes were not ready, Bao did it for him.

Isaac made a mental note to suggest to Piper that Bao had potential to be head chef. "Why are you still a sous chef?"

"Because I want to."

"Less pay."

"However, less pressure and less stress."

"A tradeoff."

"I like Piper's Place. It's controlled chaos, and it's family."

In a way, that had always been true, even when

Isaac worked here in high school, bussing tables, back when Piper's grandmother had been alive, and before he and Piper had become foes.

Piper might not feel the animosity as much as Isaac did. Otherwise, why would she hire him or agree to hire him in the first place?

At the back of his mind, Isaac knew that at some point, they'd have to clear up their feud, especially now that Nelson had let it slip that Piper accepted Jesus Christ as her personal Lord and Savior some ten years ago one Sunday when she visited Riverside Chapel.

That is to say, pour on the Christian forgiveness.

Yet, Isaac didn't feel forgiving. Piper had bruised his pride, and he wanted justice.

For twenty years, he had carried this bruise around with him everywhere he went. Every time he stepped into a kitchen, he felt the heaviness of having lost a competition he should have won.

He had heard many sermons and read many passages of the Bible saying that it was not a good thing for him to hold a grudge.

Yeah.

He reached up to pick an order from the order wheel. The orders were arranged in chronological order.

Now Isaac felt like a line cook. Except he had

to make some breakfast. The items sounded like specialty dishes.

Isaac walked toward Bao. "What is this?"

"Ah, that's just eggs Benedict with a twist," Bao said.

"At one in the morning?"

"Yeah, we serve whatever is on the menu. If the customer orders breakfast at midnight, they get breakfast at midnight."

"Okay."

"I can handle it. You can watch and learn."

Isaac laughed. "I'm teachable."

It was a quick dish, and Isaac was back to the order wheel for the next order.

Isaac was getting another pan from the rack, when he saw Nelson opening Piper's office door. Through it, Isaac spotted Piper's topknot bun at one end of the couch. The alarm clock was ringing and flashing all sorts of lights. Nelson shook Piper's shoulder.

She must be dead tired.

She had to get up and work through Sunday.

Suddenly, Isaac felt like a villain, as though he were punishing Piper for something.

It wasn't his place to help her, but didn't Nelson say something about God answering their prayers?

They had prayed for God to help them in their disastrous situation.

And I showed up.

Isaac wasn't sure if he was truly God's answer to Nelson's prayers. Would God use a bitter man to answer prayers?

Bitter?

Yes, Isaac was bitter. He had been bitter for twenty years.

However, seeing Piper this evening made Isaac realize that they were not bickering teenagers anymore. They were so far removed in time and space from those high school years that the memories of old were fading more and more with each passing year.

For the last twenty years, Isaac and Piper hadn't caused trouble for each other.

Piper had been busy running a successful family restaurant in Savannah, while Isaac was working overseas.

Piper had been keeping the historic building alive. Isaac saving up to open his own future restaurant.

For all intents and purposes, they lived in separate spheres, and their paths hadn't crossed.

Maybe I owe her an apology.

So. What did the Bible say about it?

Just like that, a verse popped into his head. No

doubt, all those years of memorizing verses in Sunday School, summer camp, and Bible studies had helped. He couldn't have recalled what he hadn't learned.

> *Do not withhold good from those to whom it is due,*
>> *When it is in the power of your hand to do so.*

"Proverbs 3:27," Isaac muttered as he put down the frying pan on the counter.

As he walked to Piper's office, Isaac prayed that he would not regret the decision he was about to make.

Nelson was still standing by the couch.

"Let her sleep," Isaac whispered.

CHAPTER EIGHT

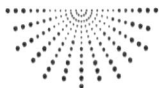

*A*t seven o'clock in the morning, Isaac had worked a total of eleven hours straight, and he was finally exhausted.

His jet lag had made him a night owl this week, but now it was around eight in the evening in Sydney, Australia, where his cruise ship last docked, before it sailed again for a fifteen-day tour of coastal Australia and New Zealand without him.

Isaac missed the summer months in the Southern Hemisphere, although winter in southeastern USA would be mild. No snow here, unlike Japan, where he had thought of going. His sister, Amy, had photographed weddings in Japan many times, and had business associates there who would hire Isaac as chef in their restaurant in Osaka.

However, Isaac still dreamed of owning his own restaurant someday. He had been saving up most of his income the last ten years so that he could open a restaurant without having to borrow money, but it was still an arduous, uphill climb to business ownership.

Taking two months off from work was perhaps counter-intuitive, but the cooking competition in Nassau in January held promise for him. If he won first place, he'd take home fifty thousand dollars. It would be about half of what he earned in one year as chef de cuisine.

He wasn't an award-winning chef or anything, but he knew he could cook.

And he proved that again all night at Piper's Place, completing orders, and getting little notes from customers complimenting him. Word somehow had gotten out—through the servers and maybe even Nelson—that they had a special guest chef for the weekend.

The whole weekend!

What on earth am I doing?

Isaac was reaching for another order when he spotted Piper coming his way, wearing a clean chef's coat. Her face looked washed, but she still looked sleepy.

He wanted to suggest that she go home for the rest of the day, but it would be presumptuous for him to take over, when he was still learning about all the dishes from the pantry chef.

"Did you get any sleep?" Isaac spoke slowly when Piper approached him. He found out from Bao that Piper could read lips—but only if you spoke clearly while facing her.

She signed back.

She could read lips, but I can't understand ASL.

Isaac stared at her.

Her perfect topknot bun was still on top of her head. She didn't wear any earrings. Isaac remembered her saying, back in high school, that she had been too afraid of getting her ears pierced.

Somehow he liked it that way.

Piper waved to a line cook nearby to interpret for her.

"She says you can go home, since you over-worked by six hours," he said.

"Me?" Isaac pointed to himself.

Piper must have read his lips because she nodded.

Isaac reminded himself to be careful what he said around here, in case Piper misunderstood his intentions when she read his lips.

She signed again.

"She said she'll send you a check in the mail to your Mom's house."

Isaac didn't move. "Ask her who is cooking today."

"She said that even though she lost two main chefs, their sous chefs hadn't left, and she has asked everyone who could fill in to do so." He paused to let Piper sign more before she continued interpreting. "So you can go."

"Ask her if I can help. Nelson offered me two weeks of work. I can help today as well."

Piper frowned.

Isaac was certain Piper had no choice. She had to make a decision. Once upon a time, she had three main chefs, plus herself as the executive chef. The only kitchen staff remaining were sous chefs, pantry chefs, and prep and line cooks. Piper didn't have any pastry chefs because she had outsourced that department to a local bakery.

Isaac looked at Piper squarely in the eye and spoke slowly. "Your sous chef, Forsythia, is out with a bad ankle. You have one other sous chef left, the talented Bao. Your prep and line cooks are stretched thin. You yourself are overworked. Am I right?"

Piper drew a deep breath. She signed for the interpreter. "I don't need your help."

"Nelson can vouch for me." Isaac waited.

And waited.

Finally Piper signed again.

"She said if you want to work today, you can come in at four o'clock for the dinner shift."

"Fair enough," Isaac said. "I'll see you at four."

CHAPTER NINE

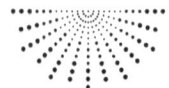

*L*eaving Piper and Bao to handle brunch and lunch, Isaac called Uber to get a ride home to Mom's house. He took a hot shower, climbed into bed, and prayed for Piper.

He closed his eyes—

And heard his phone rang.

It was his sister.

"Up early?" Isaac said into the phone.

"It's three o'clock." Amy laughed. "In the afternoon!"

"What? What?" Isaac sprung up from his bed.

His phone clock agreed with Amy.

"I slept for seven hours!" Isaac scrambled to his feet.

He wandered to the bathroom, passing by his

open suitcase on the hardwood floor. "So whassup, little sister? Why are you calling?"

"Well, I heard," Amy said.

"About what?" He turned on the speakerphone and splashed water on his face.

"You and Piper."

"There's no *me and Piper*. Extra pay is what I get. It will help me buy better ingredients for my cooking competition in January."

"That's all?" Amy asked.

"That's all. Tell Mom that."

Amy laughed at the other end of the phone. "I will when she comes over for Thanksgiving dinner tonight. What time are you coming over? We eat at six."

"Oh, no. I'm sorry." Isaac let out a loud moan. "My shift starts at four. I wasn't planning on it, to be honest, but Piper needs help. Did you know that Nelson works here now?"

"Nelson Guilmard. Yeah. Cyrus and I see him when we eat at Piper's."

"I didn't think you knew him from high school since you were so much younger than we are. He and I graduated the same year."

"Well, his wife takes the kids to some of our church activities, so I have met her."

"They don't attend Riverside?"

"No, but Piper does. She works a lot, so I don't see her much besides Sunday mornings."

"Well, I came home Monday."

"Whatever you do, don't kill each other at work." Amy laughed. "Or at church."

"What do you mean?"

"You've hated her since your senior year in high school. Are you saying things have improved now to the point that you could work for her without animosity?"

"I don't know if I *hated* her. Hate is such a strong word."

"Wow. For years we couldn't even mention Piper in front of you, remember? Every time we talked, her name was taboo. We couldn't even tell you that Piper was catering my wedding last year."

"Good thing I didn't run into her at the reception."

"She sent one of her chefs instead of taking care of it herself. When Mom told her you were going to surprise me at the wedding, she didn't show up at my wedding, even though I had invited her. Bet you didn't know that."

"No, I didn't."

"Now I found out from Mom that you worked at her restaurant last night."

"So you called me to make sure I'm okay," Isaac said.

"You know me so well, big brother. And we have always been honest with each other about everything."

Isaac knew it was coming. Last year, when Amy had problems with Cyrus, she had called him.

Somehow the two siblings instinctively knew the other needed encouragement.

"Amy, I appreciate your calling me. It's just a job and I'll be done in two weeks."

Slowly, Amy spoke again. "You've always had a soft spot for Piper."

I don't want to think about it. "Maybe we can talk later? I need to brush my teeth now. You know I can't ever talk with toothpaste in my mouth because I inevitably swallow it and then throw up."

"I'm sorry. I'll let you go, but I want to remind you of a verse."

"One of the guilt verses?" Isaac raised his eyebrows.

"I don't know, but I see it as an encouragement. Do you remember what Dad said to me before he died?"

"You told me, maybe, but I forget."

"It's Ephesians 4:31-32."

Let all bitterness, wrath, anger, clamor, and evil speaking be put away from you, with all malice. And be kind to one another, tenderhearted, forgiving one another, even as God in Christ forgave you.

"Dad said I need to be kind to Mom because she's had a hard life," Amy added.

"She sure has," Isaac agreed.

"I'm saying to you now that you need to be kind to Piper."

"Because she's had a hard life?" Isaac asked.

"Because both of you have had hard lives."

"I can't imagine hers being harder than mine," Isaac said. "But we never know."

"Right. I am praying for you and Piper."

"Thanks, little sister." Isaac tried to change the subject away from himself. "By the way, if you know of any really good chefs who need a new opportunity, maybe send them this way to fill out an application? I don't plan on staying beyond Monday, but it would be bad if this landmark restaurant shuts down."

"Sure. I'll ask Cyrus if he knows anyone. I'm sure Piper will be interviewing soon, if she hasn't been thinking about it already."

"Thanks. That will be so helpful. We're treading water right now..."

"We? You said *we*."

"I mean, she is, since I'm only the emergency chef."

"Emergency chef? Sounds gallant, knightly, heroic, and all that." Amy laughed.

"Haha."

Amy calmed down. "I'm sorry you probably can't make it to Thanksgiving dinner tonight. I wanted your critique on my turkey. But maybe you can stop by tomorrow for leftovers."

Isaac would rather not miss this family meal if he could help it, but at the spur of the moment this morning, he had agreed to help Piper.

"I might be able to come over for lunch tomorrow."

"Just text me."

"Sounds good. Thank you for understanding."

"Don't mention it. Maybe this is God's opportunity for you and Piper to get over your issues."

Speaking of Piper, Isaac wondered if she had any family to go home to for Thanksgiving, since her mother and grandmother had both passed away, and her father had left the family when she was a baby.

And her only cousin in town was on the run.

Maybe he could ask Piper to—

Better not.

Too much and too soon.

CHAPTER TEN

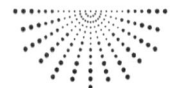

*P*iper tried not to laugh when she saw Isaac emerge from the hallway ten minutes to four o'clock wearing a faded sweatshirt and sweatpants. It wasn't that the colors or designs that were jarring together or that they looked like rags, but it was the way Isaac carried himself, as if he was lounging around at home.

He must have been self-conscious of her looking at him, because he glanced away, and quickly put on his chef's coat, covering up his sweatshirt.

Piper went back to cooking. Most of her customers were out-of-town visitors, spending Thanksgiving in Savannah. Imagine going to a resort for Thanksgiving week, only to find every restaurant closed. Well, Piper's Place was open today for those tourists.

And also locals who didn't feel like cooking today. In fact, some had already picked up their roast or smoked turkey for their Thanksgiving meals at home.

Piper wondered if she should add a delivery service, but business had been busy enough that so far, there had been no need.

She was so busy making a new batch of gravy that she didn't realize Isaac was standing next to her until she smelled the eau de toilette.

His hair was a bit damp, but combed.

He was looking at her, as if he had something to say, but didn't.

She wanted to ask him what it was like working on a cruise ship overseas, but they didn't speak the same language to make small talks like that worth the time.

Someday, Piper might go on a cruise—or a vacation, at least.

Truly, she had no idea when she had taken a vacation.

Once a workaholic, always a workaholic, I guess.

Isaac was wearing clogs today, but it didn't add much to his height. He was still three or four inches taller than she was.

"Good afternoon," he said slowly.

His lips were...

Ahem.

Piper signed the word *afternoon* to him.

Isaac lifted his hand fingers, tried to copy her.

Not bad. She nodded.

Piper waved to Bao, who had come to work groggy an hour ago. Bao was also working long hours today, but Piper was hoping that they could still impart enough information to Isaac.

With Torkel gone, Piper was leaving the dinner shift to Chef Isaac, with the able assistance of sous chef Bao. In all honesty, Piper would have promoted Bao to chef de cuisine if Torkel hadn't been there.

It wouldn't be too bad. Bao and Isaac would be assisted by two prep cooks and two line cooks, who had told Piper they would stay.

On Monday, Lillian would return to work—a month early in exchange for all paid childcare one block away. Lillian could take over dinner. They'd try to hire a new chef, and then Isaac could leave in two weeks.

Bao greeted Isaac, but Piper didn't know what they were talking about.

"Tell him that he and I are rotating two shifts between now and midnight on Monday," Piper signed.

"Midnight?" Bao asked.

"Yes. We have no choice but to close the restaurant between midnight and six until Monday. I will come in at six when the bakers deliver."

"You're going to work until four?" Bao's eyes widened.

"It's my restaurant and I can work ten hours a day if I need to. It's only until Monday though. We're going to hire a new chef, and then we'll be back on three shifts, and he can leave." Piper pointed to him.

"Do you want me to interpret that?" Bao asked.

Piper nodded.

They waited for Isaac to speak.

"Yeah, sure. One chef, she says?" Isaac then realized that he should address Piper. "Didn't you lose two chefs?"

"Yes, I'm putting myself back in rotation. I filled in for Chef Lillian at night, and I miss being in the kitchen more."

After Bao interpreted, Isaac nodded. "I know the feeling. There's nowhere else I'd rather be than in the kitchen."

Piper managed a smile.

Every now and then, Mrs. Pendegrast would let it slip that Isaac was saving up to own his own restaurant. After ten or fifteen years, how much had he saved?

It cost her a fortune to keep this place going. Maintaining the historic building and keeping it up to code were costly, but her biggest expenses were in salaries. Three main chefs and their sous chefs, a bevy of prep cooks and line cooks, servers, dishwashers, bussers, and so forth. She often did not pay herself if she had to give bonuses to her employees.

This time, it would be a sad Christmas for everyone.

Piper wasn't sure if one chef was enough to replace Torkel and Seraphina, even if she put herself back into rotation.

The other alternative was to close Piper's Place at midnight and reopen at six o'clock permanently.

Would her customers be upset?

She looked at Bao. She trusted the sous chef, but would he be able to rise to the challenge? She had reread his resume. He had worked at a prestigious New York City restaurant as a main chef for three years. Having burnt out, he came to Savannah to do something easier—with less pay.

Piper wondered if she could perhaps persuade Bao to become a chef again. She could start him at something easy, like breakfast and lunch. Lillian could take the dinner shift. The prep cooks might be enough to cover for the sous chefs whom Piper had lost following the elopement of her two top chefs.

Isaac seemed to be waiting for her to tell him more.

"I can handle lunch by myself—since our prep cooks can help me," Piper signed. "I want you to work the dinner shift until Monday when Chef Lillian returns. Bao can help you."

"Except on Sunday," Isaac reminded her.

"Yes, you're off on Sunday." Piper swiped her phone and displayed the schedule she had set up for them between today and Sunday night. She showed it to Isaac. "Tell him I'm going to email it to him."

Bao interpreted as fast as he could to keep up with Piper.

"Do you have my email?" Isaac asked.

"Yes, I do. It's in your personnel file."

She sent it off.

"Last night, I showed you some signature dishes. Now I will show you the rest," Piper signed. "They're very popular."

"I bet," Isaac mouthed. He reached for the folder on the other counter.

It was the same folder Piper had shown him the night before.

"I still think you should have made a cookbook," Isaac added.

Piper ignored him.

"After I cook a few more signature dishes, Bao will assist you as your sous chef until midnight," Piper signed. "At midnight, we close."

"Who's your sous chef at lunch?" Isaac asked.

Piper understood even before Bao interpreted what Isaac said.

"It would have been Forsythia, but she is out," Piper signed for Bao to interpret. "She has a bad sprain, and she can't put weight on her ankle. I told her not to come in until next week."

"Who will assist you?" Isaac asked.

"I'll be fine. Don't worry," Piper signed. "Tomorrow, I have a favor to ask."

"Already?" Isaac laughed.

"I need to leave by one o'clock and won't be back until maybe four." Piper waited for Bao to interpret. "Would you be able to fill in for me from one to four? When I get back, I will work in your place from from four to seven."

"Going shopping?" Isaac laughed.

If only.

She didn't have to tell him where she was really going. Heidi Wei-Flores, her pastor's wife, had offered to go with her to the bank and then back to the house to wait for Sabine, her real estate agent.

Thank God for Heidi.

Otherwise Nelson would have to miss work,

since he had done a lot of interpreting for her. On some other days, she hired interpreters. It wasn't easy to get people to work during the holidays, though.

Fortunately, the college where Heidi taught history was closed for the long weekend. Not being a shopper, Heidi would have stayed at home. She was more than happy to help Piper in a non-shopping situation.

Piper herself wasn't a shopper either, and would rather stay in her kitchen on Black Friday than battle shoppers clogging up the streets, driving everywhere to save a buck on sales.

However, it had to be done. First, the bank, and then the house.

She did not want to sell her grandmother's Tybee Island house, with the vegetable garden and greenhouse in the backyard. However, it would fetch enough money to keep her out of debt.

Piper felt her eyes sting.

She felt a hand on her shoulder.

Isaac's lips moved. "Are you okay?"

Piper took a deep breath.

"Let's get started," Piper signed. "Customers are waiting."

CHAPTER ELEVEN

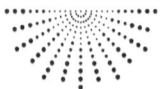

or everyone's sake, Piper closed off
the entire third floor of Piper's Place
for Thanksgiving Day, giving Isaac, Bao, and the
kitchen staff a reprieve. Fewer tables to handle
meant less pay for the restaurant, but at such a time
as this, sacrifices had to be made.

Isaac found it compassionate that Piper also
allowed everyone to take turns to go home for
Thanksgiving dinners with their own families,
which opened a door of opportunity for Isaac to
invite Piper to his sister's house. However, it wasn't
going to work out.

Amy's house was in Pooler, near the Christmastown warehouse where she worked more than the
photo studio she still maintained downtown. The
driving distance from River Street to her house

before and after dinner would take up too much time.

Isaac texted Amy, letting her know about his dilemma. He wanted to help out Piper in her kitchen, but Amy's dinner was smack dab in the middle of the evening.

And he wanted to be with Piper.

He didn't know why.

Maybe it was because he couldn't help himself. Way back when, if Piper had needed help cooking or learning a new dish, he was the first to rush to her side. It could be that he was trying to show off his culinary skills, but he also enjoyed her company.

Right now, they weren't having fun, but Isaac wanted to make sure she survived this weekend. It was hard to lose one chef suddenly, let alone two. Being shorthanded could put the restaurant under.

At the same time, this was Piper, the girl who took his prized trophy away from him.

He could never forgive her for it—

Or could he?

Amy said she didn't mind if Isaac visited her the next day instead for sandwich leftovers. In fact, she wanted to see Isaac and Piper on good terms. She repeated that it couldn't be good for him spiritually if he bore grudges the rest of his life.

In many ways, working at Piper's Place this

Thanksgiving weekend changed Isaac's perspective of his past. Perhaps he had gotten older, but twenty years away from Savannah had taken the edge off his bitterness toward Piper.

Regardless, the bitterness was still there. Maybe it was because Isaac hadn't truly apologized for being a sore loser all those years ago.

Wait a sec. Sore loser? Me?

Amy had hinted as much when she reminded Isaac of that verse in Ephesians 4 this morning.

Let all bitterness, wrath, anger, clamor, and evil speaking be put away from you, with all malice. And be kind to one another, tenderhearted, forgiving one another, even as God in Christ forgave you.

Isaac wasn't sure whether he was still angry about losing to Piper in that cooking contest, but he knew he was still a little bit bitter, even though at the same time he could not bear to see Piper in distress.

And yet, after all these years, Piper was still ahead of him in the restaurant business. Piper still won.

And be kind to one another...
Tenderhearted...

Forgiving one another...

Customers coming and going kept Isaac and Bao busy all through the evening, until Bao left for a couple of hours of family and football.

Six o'clock came and went.

Isaac found it interesting that in a twenty-four-seven restaurant such as this, customers sometimes ordered breakfast at dinner and dinner at breakfast. Sometimes he was making pancakes at four in the afternoon, covering for line cooks who were at home, and sometimes he made ice cream at three in the morning.

Eight o'clock struck, and Isaac hadn't left the kitchen.

Nelson stopped by to see how everyone was doing. Apparently he lived only a few blocks from here, and he could even walk home. He had finished Thanksgiving dinner with his wife and kids. He came to the kitchen to wish Isaac a Happy Thanksgiving and to make sure Piper wasn't there.

Isaac thought that was funny.

"Not funny, old friend," Nelson explained. "If she is here right now, hovering over you, she's not getting her sleep. She's going to regret it tomorrow morning."

"And she might be exhausted if she has to go

somewhere after lunch." Isaac remembered the time swap.

Nelson nodded. "Since her grandmother and mother died, Piper has made this restaurant her home. She practically lives here, and we have to tell her to go home," Nelson said. "In the last several years, my wife and I have invited her over every Thanksgiving. Sometimes she came, sometimes not. This year, my wife invited her again, but she turned us down, even before the two chefs ran off."

"She's worried about this place."

"Or maybe it's because I'm taking home the turkey she roasted." Nelson laughed. "I think she has eaten the same turkey all day long."

"I would be tired of it too." He flipped the hamburgers on the grill. An assistant brought him two plates, each with different types of buns. One didn't have pickles on it, and the other didn't have tomatoes. Customers could be picky.

"Well, we asked her over this time because she has no family in town. Her only relative ran off with her money. Tomorrow, she's going to put her house on the market."

Isaac froze. That was news to him. "What?"

"Oops. I shouldn't have said a thing, but your mom will find out sooner or later. She and the Super Seniors fancy themselves to be Piper's buddies."

"Was that why she swapped three hours of work with me Friday?"

Nelson glanced at his watch. "I better go."

"Have a good one, okay? Say hello to your wife for me."

"Will do. I'll see you in the morning."

Watching Nelson leave the kitchen, Isaac wondered if any one of them would have a job at the end of the year. If Piper had to sell her house, she must be seriously short of money.

How much did her cousin steal from her, anyway?

How empty was empty?

Isaac said a prayer for Piper that the police would catch her cousin soon, and perhaps return all her money or at least some of it. He wondered why he would steal her funds in the first place.

What if Piper lost her grandma's restaurant?

It would be a shame indeed.

Such a historic landmark in Savannah, with the building traceable to the early nineteenth century, when Savannah was a busy port for cotton and whatever other exports they sent overseas.

She might have to sell the building too.

It would never cross Isaac's mind to invest in someone else's restaurant, but he nearly came close to thinking that though this evening.

I must be tired.

He had been saving for years so that he could open his own restaurant. There was no way—just no way—for him to even consider buying a share of Piper's Place. Since he didn't have enough money to buy a majority share, he would always feel beholden to Piper's final decisions.

Nope.

Even if Isaac didn't have enough for a restaurant, he could always go to Plan B. Yeah, a food truck would work too. He would run it without debt, and cook whatever he wanted, whenever he wanted.

And that meant neither he nor his employees would work on Thanksgiving Day, Christmas, New Year's Day, and Easter Sunday.

Unlike Piper's Place.

Isaac caught Bao's attention. "Say, can I ask you something?"

"What, Chef?" Bao replied, carrying a mixing bowl.

"Why is Piper's Place open today?"

"I don't know, to be honest. Tradition, maybe?"

Isaac nodded.

"I also don't know why we're open on Sundays either. I mean, Piper says she's a Christian, so why not close on Sundays too?"

"Good question, Bao. Good question." *If I ran this place, we'd have holidays.*

Nine o'clock came.

Isaac cooked more hamburgers. Nobody ordered turkey this evening. He hoped that Piper hadn't cooked too much turkey. What would she do with all that extra food?

Then ten o'clock.

Isaac was alone with a skeletal crew.

Somehow Isaac didn't feel tired. Two more hours to the end of his shift at midnight, and then he'd go home and sleep.

Dinner at Amy's house would have been over by now. They were probably putting away the leftovers and clearing the table. Watching television. Playing board games. Chatting.

Taking it easy.

Relaxing.

Something he needed badly.

Isaac second guessed himself now. Should he have stopped work and gone over to Amy's for Thanksgiving? After all, Piper said he could. However, if he left, Piper would fill in for him while he was with his family.

And it would add hours to her workday.

Piper hadn't left the restaurant since Tuesday night. Isaac guessed that she had slept for maybe four hours in two days. At this rate, she must be exhausted. If she didn't get her rest, she would be heading towards a burnout. He had seen burnouts before. Some of his friends had quit and left the business when the furnace was too hot in the kitchen, searing their souls.

There was a reason God created a rest day. At least once a week, usually Sundays, Isaac didn't work. Why couldn't Piper's Place close on Sundays?

Isaac decided that when he had enough funds to open his own restaurant, it would close on Sundays so that his employees could have a day of rest to spend time with their families or sleep in—or go to church, if they were Christians.

Until then, he was at the mercy of his employers.

In this case, it was Piper.

Never in a million years would he have expected to end up working for Piper Peyton, who had snatched the championship from him.

Be kind.

Forgive.

But how do I forgive her through this disappointment, Lord?

Isaac plated the shrimp scampi. Just as he was sprinkling extra chopped parsley on top, Bao appeared out of nowhere, startling him.

"How was your Thanksgiving dinner?" he asked.

"I haven't left." Isaac put the plate on the

counter. Bao checked the order and took care of the rest.

"Your family, though?" Bao asked.

"They'll make me sandwiches tomorrow. The way my sister described her turkey, she's going to have leftovers for days. Besides, we have turkey here, so in many ways, I'm turkeyed out. I want some ham, to be honest."

"Have you eaten dinner?" Bao asked.

"Actually, no."

"Please, Chef, go eat. You have less than two hours left to your shift. The crowd has tapered off." Bao reached for Isaac's wooden spoon.

Isaac forgot what he was stirring or doing. "Yeah, I better take a break."

"So we have a little break room in the back."

"I know where it is."

"There's turkey and fixings in the fridge. There's a microwave near the sink. We usually take our plates and go elsewhere if there's not enough chairs. Since the third floor is closed off today, that's where you might eat." Bao pointed to the back of the kitchen. "Outside the break room, hang a left until you see the service elevator."

Isaac nodded. "Thanks."

CHAPTER TWELVE

*W*hen Piper accepted Jesus Christ as her Lord and Savior some ten years prior, she hadn't expected a perfect life, but at the back of her mind, she hoped that life would be easier in some tangible ways.

Didn't the Bible say in Matthew 11:28-30 that Jesus would give her rest?

> *Come to Me, all you who labor and are heavy laden, and I will give you rest. Take My yoke upon you and learn from Me, for I am gentle and lowly in heart, and you will find rest for your souls. For My yoke is easy and My burden is light.*

Sitting at the quiet booth at the corner of the third floor of her restaurant, Piper watched the night scenes outside. The streets were empty. Every now and then, container ships passed by on the Savannah River.

The faintly starry November night beamed down over Savannah, casting a dark gray shroud over the old cobblestone road and cement waterfront. Sometimes she wished Savannah could turn off all of the city lights so that she could see the stars.

In times like this, she felt alone.

Yes, God was with her. Always with her. But she felt as though no one was holding her hand on earth, to walk this difficult path with her.

Even Adam had Eve. But I have no one.

Piper tried to hold back tears. She chided herself for not being strong, for being weepy and emotional.

Well, if Isaac hadn't shown up, she wouldn't have felt this bad. His presence at her restaurant reminded her of their spat all over again. She didn't need that added to her already full plate at work.

Was it all about their spat, though? Piper knew that wasn't all there was to it. Isaac had been the high school boy whom Piper had a crush on. She thought she had gotten over it. However, that puppy love had now resurfaced, morphing into a stronger feeling she wasn't prepared to address.

Maybe I'm just tired.

It was Thanksgiving Day again—the end of it, anyhow—and she hadn't done much all day except trying to keep her business going, customers fed, employees working.

Lord Jesus, give me rest, please.

Piper felt that maybe she should talk to Heidi Wei-Flores, her friend and Sunday School teacher. As pastor's wife, Heidi ministered to women in the church, when she wasn't teaching class at the University of Coastal Georgia. Maybe if Heidi had a minute, she could give her a word from the Lord. In fact, the verse from Matthew 11 had been a reminder from Heidi a few months ago, long before these double disasters struck.

Piper would see Heidi on Friday. Heidi had agreed to interpret for her at the bank and on the meeting with Sabine, her real estate agent, though there might not be any time to add Isaac to their agenda. Piper did not want to take Heidi away from her husband on a Friday evening.

Piper's eyes wandered around the third floor of her restaurant. The silent grand piano at the corner, where this year's Christmas decorations would not be, reminded her that come Friday, she would have to tell her regular jazz pianist that she could no longer pay him.

The sofas and small circles of armchairs here and there had been her own idea to make this third floor a special place for people to hang out. It was supposed to be like a lounge on the top deck of a cruise ship, with the windows mimicking the view of the sea—in this case, the river.

She had spent a bit of money upgrading this floor a number of years ago, and her customers loved it.

Today it was closed off because of her smaller workforce this Thanksgiving day.

She wondered if she could ever open up this floor again after Christmas when her money ran out.

Why did you steal from me, Regis? This restaurant is all I have. I have no life. I spend my days and nights here. How could you?

Piper could not bring herself to say a prayer for Regis. She wanted him to be caught and jailed, and then she'd think about praying for him. What kind of trouble was Regis in that he dared to steal from his own flesh and blood?

If he had any money trouble, he should have asked for help. Perhaps they could have worked out something.

But to steal?

She blinked away sudden tears.

I'm sorry I have to sell your house and vegetable garden, Grandma.

And the kitchen you taught me to cook in.

I might even have to sell this restaurant.

Or at the least find a business partner to offset the cost.

Had there been warning signs with Regis? He had done her taxes well for the last few years. He hadn't shown her that he couldn't be trusted.

Then again, Piper had been so busy with her restaurant that she had no time for people, so she hardly knew her own cousin. In fact, she hardly knew most of the people who worked for her.

That's the honest truth.

In a way, she should have hired more deaf or hearing impaired workers, so that they could be a community. And yet, that had not been her hiring practice. At Piper's Place, she hired by merit, nothing else.

That had ironically led her to allow Isaac Untermeyer to work in her kitchen this weekend, even though he refused to work on Sunday, insisting that he needed his day of rest to go to church with his mother and sister.

I go to church too.

In fact, there were other people working for her who went to church on Sundays. Piper worked out their shifts so that they could spend time worshipping God.

I wonder if it makes sense to close on Sundays.

Don't I need a day of rest too?

Outside the window, the night was clear once again, but looks could be deceiving. It was cold tonight, though one couldn't see that.

All Piper could see there was the cloudless sky, the dark of the river, and the hotel lights across the river on Hutchinson Island. She could not see the bridge upriver because of the hotels and buildings that blocked her view.

She closed her eyes.

Didn't want to look at her wristwatch to find out how late it was now, and how exhausted she was.

What she wouldn't do for a hot bath in her bathtub at home.

Alas, she had to make do with quick showers in her office and short naps on her couch.

How long can I do this before I collapse altogether?

❧

*I*saac was humming a tune he made up as he exited the elevator to the third floor, where Piper's Place staff and servers could have a quick Thanksgiving meal. He figured nobody would be up here this late when the entire restaurant would be closed in two hours.

Isaac wondered whether he should tell Piper

what he thought about Christians working on Thanksgiving Day, and for that matter, on Sundays. Then again, it was none of his business.

One and a half more weeks, and he would be paid and gone.

He had sent a text to Jerome, asking if he could use his riverboat galley kitchen to practice for his cooking competition. He was quite confident that he would be placed. It was an international competition, and he had sailed the seven seas—

Seven Seas.

That's it!

Isaac chuckled. He couldn't believe it. He'd found a name for his future restaurant or food truck.

He would call it Seven Seas. He would google later to see if anyone else had taken it, but for now, Seven Seas sounded pretty clever.

Still humming, he looked for a table by the window.

He passed a few servers who had finished eating. It was almost ten o'clock at night, and most of the employees had eaten their dinner.

Isaac was late because he had been busy.

Most of the tables by the windows were booths. He walked up and down to find the best view.

And there she was.

This time, her hair was in a chignon at the back

of her head. She was looking out of the window. In front of her was an emptied plate on the table.

Isaac held his tray of turkey with gravy and apple pie with one hand, and tapped her shoulder with the other.

She rubbed her eyes, and turned to face him. She looked sleepy, like she needed to be held.

Isaac forgot what he was going to say.

"May I sit here?" Isaac asked.

Piper nodded.

Isaac slid into the seat across from her, and prayed before he ate.

"Want some?" Isaac pointed to the turkey. "It's good."

Piper shook her head.

Isaac needed to find a way to talk to her. They didn't speak the same language. His interaction with Piper reminded him of the first time his cruise ship docked in Kagoshima, Japan, and he decided to join a shore excursion. He could only speak to the tour guide and the checkout workers in the stores, but he could not speak to quite a number of the local Japanese people.

Because he didn't speak Japanese.

And now, with Piper, he didn't speak sign language.

What if he could sign? He wondered what conversations he would have with Piper. They could catch up on the last twenty years. He could tell her of all the cuisines he had tried to cook in all the countries he had visited the last five to ten years. He could tell her about the exotic dishes he had been afraid to try. He could...

He could apologize to her.

Isaac chewed slowly, frowning.

His phone chirped.

He retrieved it from his pocket. There was a partial text message on it from a number he didn't recognize.

Piper tapped the table, and Isaac looked up. She pointed to herself and then to her phone.

Isaac swiped her phone to read the entire message.

It's me.

"Oh." Isaac updated the contact, adding Piper's name.

His first text from Piper. Three feet away from him across the table.

PIPER

Is something wrong with the turkey?

ISAAC

Why do you ask?

PIPER

You were frowning as you ate.

ISAAC

No. I was thinking of something else.

PIPER

What?

ISAAC

Do you really want to know?

PIPER

I had a long day. Distract me.

ISAAC

OK.

He continued eating, even as Piper waited for him to explain what was in his mind. Would he lie and say it was something else? He felt that he couldn't.

They were almost alone here on the third floor. There were some other employees, but with texting, they wouldn't be privy to their conversation.

ISAAC

I must apologize for what happened twenty years ago.

Piper was staring at her phone, as Isaac waited. *This is awkward.*

Isaac kept eating. Before he knew it, he had

finished the turkey, gravy, stuffing, and all the cranberry sauce.

Still no reply from Piper.

Isaac watched her now. She drew a deep breath and finally looked up. She sighed. And still texted nothing.

"I'm sorry I got mad for losing the cooking competition to you."

There, I said it.

That was all Isaac wanted to say, and had to say. He figured that if Piper didn't respond, then it was upon her to get right with God, since he felt that he had done all he could to straighten this wrinkle in their relationship.

Our what?

There was no relationship between them other than chef and restaurateur. Technically, Isaac could list all the possible improvements Piper's Place could make, and that would also make him a consultant.

In less than two weeks, he'd be gone.

In six weeks, he'd be in sunny Nassau, cooking his way to the grand championship. He could imagine the prize money now, plus a chef de cuisine position at one of the five-star hotels in the Bahamas. All that would get him closer to owning his own restaurant. All it took was funding, funding, funding.

And God.

Of course, God.

Forgive me, Lord. I have wanted my own restaurant for so many years that it's all I ever see. Am I missing something?

Something appeared on his phone. Isaac tapped it.

PIPER

By two points.

ISAAC

What? I thought the results were sealed.

PIPER

I found out two years ago.

ISAAC

How?

PIPER

I can't tell you.

ISAAC

But two points?

PIPER

That's what I was told.

ISAAC

Margin of error.

PIPER

We tied for first place.

ISAAC

Why didn't they give both of us the prize?

PIPER

Rules. There could only be one winner. I think they gave it to me out of pity.

"Pity? Not at all," Isaac said. "You're a very good chef. That turkey was delicious. If I wasn't on the third floor, I'd go for seconds."

She didn't reply.

"Do you want half of my apple pie?" Isaac pointed to his pie.

Piper shook her head.

"No?" Isaac took a bite. "Mmmm... Did you make this?"

Piper nodded.

And smiled.

"Got a smile out of you." But inside, Isaac felt awful in every way.

Two points.

And it had caused twenty years of bitterness.

He wondered if it had affected Piper at all, when he closed the Cumin Cooking Club shortly afterwards. Then again, he recalled that Mom had mentioned Piper's ailing grandmother and family issues. Piper was probably too busy to be bothered by Isaac's woes.

"Twenty years. I can't believe I carried this grudge so long," Isaac said.

Piper didn't respond. Isaac waited. He wanted her to say something. But she didn't.

He tried to remember if Piper was this quiet in high school. He seemed to recall that Piper had been a loner. She had three friends: Nelson, Marlon, and Isaac.

The Cumin Cooking Club had been her hangout and hiding place after school.

And Isaac had destroyed it.

He wondered what else he had destroyed.

CHAPTER THIRTEEN

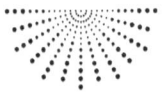

"*Y*ou wasted a lot of time." Amy swiped her key card at the door to the Christmastown warehouse just outside of Savannah.

Isaac followed his sister into the huge room. She picked up an iPad from an office along the way.

"Wow. Lots of stuff in here." He looked around. "What happened to the aisles we used to skate down?"

"Gone. And not allowed." Amy led him down an aisle. "We have new pop-up Christmas trees this year—they're selling like hotcakes—and this is not the place for kids to play in."

"You sound like Grandpa."

"It's your fault I have a scar on my knee. Remember?"

"I said I was sorry years ago," Isaac protested.

He followed Amy to a row of giant boxes.

"You sure you want to do this?" Amy asked.

Isaac nodded. "The least I can do for her. However, if you must know, I wouldn't have been able to afford it if you hadn't given me a discount."

"I gave you a fifty percent family discount. Remember that next time I need a favor, big brother."

"I owe you one, little sister."

Amy smiled some kind of mischievous smile that took Isaac back thirty years at least into their childhood.

"What?" Isaac asked. He didn't want to figure it out.

"You're getting a bit soft for Piper, I see."

"Am I? It's Christmastime. That's all." Isaac tried to keep a poker face. "When you told me this morning that she canceled her Christmas decorating order, I was like—that place won't look Christmassy without Christmastown decorations."

"How would you know? You weren't here this time of year for a while now."

"I can imagine."

"I think you're imagining an awful lot." Amy tilted her head. "Still, our decorations are the best in town, and they look great in her restaurant."

"If you have some photos from last year, maybe we could recreate what she likes."

"I can email them to you. What if she gets mad at you?"

"For surprising her with what she already approved from last year?" Even as Isaac asked the question, he wondered if he was making a mistake.

"I think she meant to DIY. Long before she outsourced to Christmastown, her employees decorated all three floors themselves."

"Well, now we're going to do it again." Isaac stopped at the three large boxes marked *Piper's Place.*

"Sign here." Amy handed her iPad over to Isaac.

He paused at the number. "Thanks again for the discount."

"I'll get someone to load up the truck for you," Amy said.

"Well, I brought Mom's truck."

"Then you won't have room for all three boxes."

"I'll just take one with me now, and then I'll try to sneak in the other two over the next couple of days."

Amy wagged a finger at him. "You're going to be in so much trouble with Piper."

"We'll see." Isaac handed the iPad back to his sister.

Amy tapped it. "I just emailed you the receipt. Now let me show you how the pop-up Christmas trees work."

"A pop-up Christmas tree. Who'd thunk?"

"It was Cyrus's idea," Amy said, her eyes far away. "The first time I saw it working properly, I was photographing in Oregon. He flew it all the way there to show it to me."

"Nice."

"Yeah, considering he had never flown before."

"Wow. It must be love."

"It was." There was a glow on Amy's face.

"And you're still in love."

Amy smiled. "It's for life. God gave us more and more love for each other. But don't be fooled. We have good days and bad days alike, especially since we're also business partners. God's love keeps us together, though."

"At least you can communicate with each other."

"What do you mean?"

"What if you don't speak the same language as the other person?" Isaac regretted asking.

She seemed to be studying his face. "Something on your mind?"

"You got that reading my face?" If Amy could read his face, Isaac wondered if Piper could have too, back at the restaurant.

"After I show you how to pop up the tree, we can step into my office, and you can tell me all about it."

CHAPTER FOURTEEN

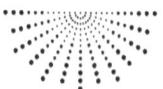

*A*fter they loaded the Christmas box onto Isaac's truck, they returned to Amy's office. Cyrus was in the warehouse somewhere, taking inventory, so the siblings were alone.

"Everybody's in some sort of hurt because of me," Isaac said quietly.

Amy knitted her eyebrows together. "Is that a philosophical thought or are you literal?"

Isaac shrugged. "I don't know, Sis."

They sat down in two office chairs. Amy didn't log into her computer. "Tell me what's going on."

"Does this session cost money?" Isaac chuckled.

"No, but I want two giant pumpkin pies for Christmas. With homemade crust. And real pumpkin. Not from the can."

"That's going to cost a lot."

"I'm eating for two, and I don't want cheap food."

Isaac nearly jumped out of his chair. "You what?"

His jaw dropped as Amy nodded.

"Just found out this morning." Amy smiled. "God is good to us."

"I know. If not for God, I wouldn't have a family." Isaac wasn't sure how much he could recall, but he vaguely remembered being shuttled from house to house, until the Untermeyers became his foster parents when he was three years old, eventually adopting him when he was four years old.

"I wouldn't have a mom and dad," Isaac added.

"And I wouldn't have a big brother." Amy patted his knee. "Now tell me about your great epiphany."

Isaac glanced at his watch. "I don't know if I have enough time. I need to be at work around eleven or so. I have to fill in for Piper."

Even though he didn't have to be there until noon, he felt that he had to show up to make sure his assistants did what they were supposed to do. Granted, they had worked there longer than Isaac had, but still.

He wanted to impress Piper.

Ah.

He cleared his throat. "I found out last night

that Piper and I could have tied in that cooking competition."

Amy didn't flinch. "Did you practice the verse we talked about? Being kind and forgiving?"

Isaac remembered the last part of that passage in Ephesians 4.

And be ye kind one to another, tenderhearted, forgiving one another, even as God for Christ's sake hath forgiven you.

"I decided I had to apologize to her," he said. "God forgave me. Why is it so hard to forgive others?"

"Human nature."

"Yeah. So anyway, I had an opportunity last night to apologize to her for being upset all those years ago that she won instead of me. That was when I found out she had done some digging around two years ago, and found out that we both were practically tied for first place."

"And you didn't feel bad about that?" Amy asked.

"What do you mean?"

"You tied at first place with a sophomore who had just learned to cook."

"Well, she is a very good cook. Have you tasted her turkey and apple pie? She cooks like her grandmother."

Amy frowned. "That spoils it all, big brother.

Now you won't eat my turkey any more. I saved some for you from the dinner you missed yesterday. Everyone wanted to know if you were hiding out in the kitchen with Piper. Mom was all—"

"Wait. What?" Isaac's jaw dropped.

"If I didn't know any better, Mom wants you reconciled with Piper."

"What does she have to do with..."

"She's in this phase, where she's trying to do all sorts of good," Amy explained.

"To make up for all those years when she had been such a difficult mom to live with?"

"Well, she wasn't difficult for you."

"No. She's the best mom I ever had." And it was the truth, if all foster moms were mothers of some sort. "I think she was always kind to me because she pitied me."

Pity.

That word. It reminded Isaac of what Piper said yesterday.

I think they gave it to me out of pity.

Isaac could not imagine anyone pitying Piper. She was stronger than people gave her credit for. She was sure of herself, certain of what she was doing, and she stood tall in the midst of her difficult situation.

If the police didn't find her cousin on the lam and return her money to her, Piper's Place might go bankrupt or something. Isaac wasn't privy to Piper's finances, but it took a whole lot of money to operate a restaurant. That much, he knew.

On top of that, Piper had lost two chefs in a day. She seemed to be taking it calmly. Yet, it must have taken a lot of strength of character for her to agree to hire Isaac for two weeks.

Isaac knew she would rather have nothing to do with him.

And yet, her objectivity impressed him. She had put the well-being of her restaurant over her own personal problems.

In retrospect, Isaac was sure now that Piper had won the cooking competition fair and square. In fact, since Piper was in a single parent home, she could certainly use the scholarship. Isaac didn't need it.

It was his pride that had been bruised.

And what does the Bible say about pride?

"So she forgave you?" Amy asked.

"She never said. In fact, she didn't say if she accepted my apology. All she said was that she found out we were two points apart."

"Now things have changed. You've grown up. It's a good thing you talked."

"Texted. We messaged each other sitting across the table." Isaac wondered if he should learn ASL or whether he was just passing through Savannah, on his way to somewhere else where he would not have to learn a new language.

"You said that Piper found out about your scores two years ago."

"Yeah?" Isaac wondered what her sister was up to.

"Did she say if she stumbled onto the information, or if she actively sought it out?"

"Why does it matter?"

"If she stumbled on the information, it tells me she wasn't pursuing it. If she sought it out, then I'd say it bothered her some that things were not friendly between the two of you."

"And why would I be in her mind?" Isaac asked, just as the answer became clear. "Ah. Mom. Mom, Jerome, and the Super Seniors eat at Piper's Place all the time."

"Watch out, big brother. Mom's up to something."

"Like what?"

Amy shrugged. "I don't know, to be honest, but she sold fifty-one percent of Christmastown to Cyrus two years ago, remember?"

"And?"

"She has money to spare. She's got to be thinking about investing in something."

"She still has the Christmas tree farm?"

"It's mine now, but she has to just give it to me because Dad willed it that way."

"I cashed out my inheritance and put it in the bank," Isaac said. "I don't know whether that was good or bad. But I'm such a long way from owning my own restaurant."

Amy seemed to be waiting for Isaac to say more, but that was all he had to say today.

He needed direction from God for his personal and professional life.

"God guided you last year when you came home, thinking Mom had gone nuts selling the majority share of Christmastown," Isaac said.

"Yes, and He did in unexpected ways. I thought that Cyrus was my enemy, but somehow he wasn't."

"I don't think Piper and I would ever be business partners, if that's what you're thinking of," Isaac said.

"I'm not thinking of that, but I wouldn't put it past Mom to think that way. If it worked for Cyrus and me, she might think it'll work for you."

"That's where she would be wrong."

"I'm just warning you."

"Piper and I could be friends, I think. But beyond that, I don't think we want to see each other in the same kitchen. We're both fiercely independent, and we'd rather have our own restaurants."

"Hmm. You know so much about her, and you've only seen her two days?"

Isaac wondered if he was mistaken. "Maybe I don't know anything."

"Maybe you don't need to come to any conclusions yet. Maybe let it play out?"

"There's so much I don't know about life." *And maybe love?* "To be honest with you, I'd rather be where I know exactly what I'm doing, and where I can see the end results, and that's in the kitchen."

"Well, good, because now you're officially late for work."

"Oh no!" Isaac tore out of the office like a whirlwind.

CHAPTER FIFTEEN

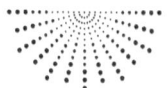

*I*saac parked his mother's truck as close as he could to the back entrance of Piper's Place. There was a chill in the air, but the sky was clear. He could leave the Christmas box in the back of the truck until later, but maybe he should ask Bao and someone else to help him carry it inside and hide it from Piper until he was ready to reveal it.

When Isaac reached the back of the restaurant, he spotted its catering van at the loading dock, with its doors opened.

Piper and another employee were putting boxes and plastic containers into the van.

Isaac reached Piper. He waited until she was looking directly at him.

"I'm sorry I'm late," Isaac said as clearly as he could.

Piper nodded.

"Do you need any help?"

Piper shook her head.

Isaac watched her close the door, wave, and drive off. The employee waited at the door, holding it open for him.

"Do you know where I can get a platform cart or something to carry a big box?" Isaac asked.

She nodded. "We have a few kinds, including utility carts."

"Thanks." Isaac closed the door behind him. "Where is Piper driving all those boxes and containers?"

"To the local homeless shelter," she said.

"Oh." Something new about Piper that Isaac didn't know.

"We take all the food we can't finish cooking and send them to Sunrise Hill twice a week."

"Really?"

"We take turns, but since Piper's going to be out and about, she's doing it today."

"Where is this homeless shelter?"

"The other side of town. Maybe you can go next week, and see what else Piper's Place does for the community."

"Maybe I will." A new respect for Piper rose in Isaac's heart.

What else does she do that I don't know about?

Lunch came and went, and Isaac said a prayer for Piper that all would go well this afternoon, whatever she was doing.

So much was going on with her.

He was starting to get curious about his old friend from high school.

~

That Isaac Untermeyer was late for work.

It bothered Piper all the way to Sunrise Hill, where she dropped off the containers of leftover Thanksgiving turkey, ham, sides, and other various food items that Piper's Place hadn't served in the last two days.

It bothered her on the drive to her bank, where she would meet Heidi Wei-Flores, her interpreter and confidant.

Isaac Untermeyer came to work late.

And all he had to say was *I'm sorry I'm late.*

His facial expression hadn't been one of remorse—

Maybe she was reading too much into it.

Isaac had always worn a can-do attitude, and

that much hadn't changed since high school. It might have masked all his pain and shame for losing the cooking competition. Like it didn't matter to him that he had come in second, even when Piper knew it had hurt him deeply.

That was why she hadn't tried to contact him all these years.

Even two years ago, when she found out that they could have tied, she didn't try to send feelers out for him. His mother, then Mrs. Untermeyer, whom Riverside Chapel members had called Mrs. U for decades—now Mrs. Pendegrast, whom the same church members now called Mrs. P—had said he was on a cruise ship on the Sea of Japan. After that, he was in Australia and New Zealand in the southern hemisphere, where it was summer in December.

Piper had no desire to contact him and bring up old hurts.

In fact, she was a bit angry at him for not showing good sportsmanship all those years ago.

Sure, they were kids in high school.

But still...

Even kids knew how to play fair in sports.

If you won, you won. If you lost, you lost. Get over it.

And then on Thursday night...

Piper was surprised that Isaac had apologized.

If he had done so twenty years ago, they would have kept the Cumin Cooking Club going. Due to Isaac's poor loser attitude, they shut down the club, and Piper lost a friend.

I don't know if I can ever forgive him for ruining my entire school year.

Somehow Piper made it to the bank parking lot early. She could sit in her car for another fifteen minutes, and be on time. She checked her text messages. Heidi was on her way, driving from her college campus.

See, Isaac? This is how to be early to a meeting.

Piper didn't know why Isaac bothered her so, and why he was renting space in her head.

She had so much to talk to him about, so much to tell him—about her new faith the last ten years, her fears of losing her restaurant, her feelings for...for...

For him.

Over the last ten years since she had been saved, Piper had wondered what it would be like to date a Christian man, and somehow her thoughts kept going back to the only Christian guy she had ever known who had shown genuine care for her.

When she had first arrived at Savannah High and didn't know anyone, Isaac had taken her under his wing. He seemed so excited about life, even though he didn't speak ASL and she couldn't hear

137

him at all. Somehow, just by looking at each other, they had a connection—

No.

If Isaac hadn't realized it already, she didn't accept his apology on Thursday night, and neither did she say she forgave him.

CHAPTER SIXTEEN

*L*ike a tempest in a teacup, Bao ran circles around Piper to keep her occupied in the kitchen downstairs, while Isaac and three other cooks—who had gotten off work the same time as Isaac—ran upstairs to the third floor and decorated the place for Christmas according to last year's photographs.

There were no customers on this floor tonight, as Piper had made an executive decision to keep all the sections here closed until she could hire one replacement for her two chefs who had left.

Isaac applauded her decision, because it would take time for Sous Chef Bao to become Main Chef Bao. From what Isaac understood, Bao didn't want the top job. Still, he was a good sport to do whatever Piper needed in the interim while Piper reorganized her kitchen staff, with Forsythia nursing a sprained ankle at home.

Meanwhile, Isaac was running on fumes after twelve hours of cooking in the kitchen.

But he wanted to do this.

For Piper.

While the other two employees decorated the window frames with lights, Isaac had taken the Christmas tree out of the box. He was reading the printed instructions now, trying to remember what Amy had told him on Friday morning.

He searched for the remote.

Before he did anything, he moved the tree into place, near the grand piano. He made sure that he left four feet on all sides, according to the instructions. He plugged it into the wall socket.

The two employees came up to him. "How does it work?"

"Well, my sister said all you have to do is push this button." Isaac hesitated, staring at the remote in his hand.

Everyone waited.

He pushed the button.

The magic Christmas tree popped open with a whooshing sound and a rattling of the attached multicolored ornaments.

"Okay, someone turn off the lights," Isaac said.

He waited until the lights were off before he pushed another button.

Lights appeared all around the tree, sparkling, glowing, chasing.

"Wow." Even Isaac was impressed at his brother-in-law's creation.

Nobody said a word.

Isaac spun around.

"Am I the only one impressed—"

His mouth shut up as he met the glare of a pair of bright and angry eyes.

He had never seen anyone look so angry and pretty at the same time. Was it possible?

Piper suddenly signed something. Her fingers and hands swiped here and there, up and down, sideways.

She seemed upset, but Isaac couldn't understand a word.

She yanked her phone out of her pocket and tapped furiously.

Isaac heard the tone on his own phone. He was afraid to look, but he had to. The message from Piper was loud and clear.

This is not your restaurant!

And she stormed off.

"Wait! Wait!" Isaac chased after her, but her strides were faster than his.

She reached the elevator and punched the button.

Isaac put his foot in the door. The door opened.

He wondered if he should even enter the elevator.

Maybe Piper needed space.

Inside the elevator, Piper fumed, folding her arms across her chest.

Isaac retracted his foot.

"We'll talk later," he said.

Piper didn't respond, but Isaac expected that she had read his lips.

He watched the elevator door close in his face, separating him from Piper.

He took the stairs, walked down the lonely hallway leading to the back parking lot, and went home.

❧

"*W*hat was he thinking?" Leaning against her office table, Piper signed to Nelson.

Nelson had a sly smile on his face. He was sitting on the couch looking over the schedule that Piper had handed to him.

"Don't tell me you're taking his side." Piper plopped down on an armchair.

She had a few more minutes left in the short break before she went back to work in the kitchen. It was almost eight o'clock in the morning. Four more hours, and she'd go home to sleep all afternoon.

Nelson would hold down the fort until she came back this evening.

"I'm not taking anybody's side," Nelson signed back.

"I was going to forgive him, but now..." Piper buried her face in her hands.

When she opened her eyes, Nelson was looking at her.

"I think we need to choose our battles," he signed. "I'm not as worried about the Christmas tree as I am about your not being able to pay your employees next week when December comes."

Piper drew a deep breath.

He's right.

"Any word from the police?" Nelson asked.

"No, but they've assigned Detective Zimmerman to the case. You remember him?"

Nelson nodded. "He helped Iris Delaney find her sister several years ago."

"They're conducting a nationwide manhunt. Apparently I wasn't the only person Regis stole from."

"I'm sorry."

"Me too." Piper stood up and stretched. "I guess you're right. What's a Christmas tree compared to losing a restaurant?"

"As long as you don't have to pay for it."

Piper shook her head. "I called Christmastown. It's paid for, but they won't say who. We can guess."

Nelson made a face. "Why did Isaac do this?"

"I don't know."

"Do you want me to ask him?"

"I don't care if you do." Piper rubbed her temples. "I care that I have to hire a full-time chef to replace two chefs. I care that I may not be able to afford that chef, but I don't see either Bao or Forsythia wanting the position. Even if they did, I'd have to find their replacements."

"Lillian comes back on Monday," Nelson reminded her. "So will Forsythia, supposedly."

"Thank God."

"I wish I could help more. If I had the money, I'd invest in Piper's Place."

Piper wondered if Nelson was serious. She decided not to ask.

Regis stole three hundred thousand dollars.

How much could Nelson invest on his salary?

"Even if you sell your house, will we stay afloat?" Nelson signed so slowly that Piper almost asked what he was worried about.

"My house is old, and I'm not sure if it's going

to sell for much. Sabine said she's going to do her best—they all say that—but even after I do sell the house and pay off the bank, what I have left is not enough to sustain us past Christmas."

"Whoa."

"I'm going to sell as many stocks as I can, and that will take us through January. After that, I don't know what's going to happen."

"That bad?"

Piper nodded. "Now you know the truth."

"Can you get a loan?"

"I don't borrow money."

"What about investors?"

"I don't know."

"Let's pray and ask God for help," Nelson suggested.

When they were done praying, Nelson asked if Piper would like him to go upstairs to inspect Isaac's Christmas decoration.

"I don't care." Piper walked out.

CHAPTER SEVENTEEN

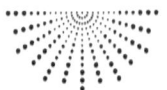

$\mathcal{I}$saac could hardly sleep all night. In the morning, he called his sister to cancel the other two Christmas boxes.

Amy and Cyrus were at home this Saturday morning. Cyrus would be leaving for work after breakfast. Amy was going to stay at home all day. They invited Isaac over for breakfast at their house in Pooler, on the other side of Savannah.

Isaac took a quick shower, and he was on his way, forgetting his jacket. He figured he'd just run inside his sister's house as soon as he arrived.

"So much on your mind that you forgot it's winter?" Amy laughed.

"You can borrow my jacket. I have a few." Cyrus kissed Amy on the way to the coffee maker. "Want cream with your coffee?"

"Just a dash." Isaac sat down at the breakfast table, where there was a spread of hot pancakes that Amy already made while Isaac was in the shower.

"Girl trouble?" Cyrus asked, helping Amy with her chair.

Isaac thought Cyrus was being extra careful. He must be excited to become a dad.

"I don't know what kind of trouble I'm in," Isaac said. "I thought that since she couldn't afford to hire y'all this year, I could help. Apparently she didn't like that kind of help."

"You can't read people's minds," Amy said.

"I overstepped my boundaries. I thought I'd surprise her. I don't know why she was upset when we decorated it the same way she had it last year."

They said grace before they ate.

Isaac didn't think he had any appetite, but he did now. He practically swallowed three giant pancakes with pecans in them, dousing them generously with warmed maple syrup.

"Wow, Amy. I'm impressed." Isaac eyed more pancakes, but he knew he shouldn't have any more.

"If you're still hungry, I can cook some eggs, any way you want," Cyrus said. "I know it's not restaurant grade—"

Isaac put up his palm to stop him from continuing. "Home cooked meals are the best."

Amy drank a glass of orange juice. "I was

reading my Bible this morning and praying for you."

"I could use all the prayers offered."

Cyrus's phone rang.

"Aunt Marie. I have to take this," he said. "She's still adjusting to life at SSLR."

"SSLR?" Isaac asked Amy after Cyrus left the kitchen.

"You've been away too long. It's the Savannah Senior Living Resort, the one that Roger Patel runs."

"I vaguely remember him. He was at your wedding last year."

"Yes. Several people in Mom's lunch group have considered moving there. Even she and Jerome have considered the idea."

"So it's a resort?"

"It's a mix of both a resort for seniors who don't want to cook and clean, but it's also an assisted living facility for seniors who need a bit more TLC." Amy started to get up to put away the dishes. "Cyrus's aunt and uncle are up there in age, and they decided to move in last month."

Isaac took the plates from Amy. "Please sit down. Let me clean up."

"I can help."

"You cooked breakfast. I'll clean. It's only fair."

Isaac rinsed the plates in the sink nearby. "Is the dishwasher clean?"

"It's empty, yes."

"Sit down and talk to me." Then Isaac wondered. "What exactly did you pray about for me?"

"For God's perfect will for your career and life," Amy said.

"Thank you. His perfect will is best for me." Isaac prayed silently that God's perfect will for him was still cooking and restaurant-related.

What if what I want to do is not what God has gifted me to do?

Wouldn't I be able to tell, though, what my talents and gifts are?

It would be ideal if what he wanted to do was the same thing as what God had gifted him to do.

"I know you've saved up for ten years to try to open your own restaurant, and it's slow coming," Amy said. "Have you considered the alternatives?"

One of the things that Isaac appreciated about his sister was her forthrightness. "All I want to do is cook. I love to cook. I can cook all day."

"Although you know it doesn't necessarily mean that a brick-and-mortar restaurant is in your future."

"I'm tired of cruise ships."

"I don't mean the sea. I meant that you might want to pray about where God would lead you."

Isaac nodded. "I see what you mean. I would pray for God's perfect will, and for Him to show me things that I may not have thought about, you know, like a food truck or something."

Amy laughed. "So you have thought of alternatives to owning a building with a restaurant in it."

"As long as I get to cook."

"God is super creative. He made the universe. He is the Creator of all. Culinary arts is a creative career. But there's also a business angle to it. God is the only One who can see through it all—past, present, future. From the creative to the commercial. All of it."

"That's insightful, little sister."

Amy waved her arms. "I have to surrender Christmastown to God every day. I used to think that Christmas was overly commercial, and it still is in many ways. I didn't want to have anything to do with this business. But God showed me, through Cyrus, that if Christian-owned companies like ours don't exist, we wouldn't have a chance to remind people of the true meaning of Christmas."

"How does that apply to me?"

"We are Christians first, before we are business owners. Whether you own a restaurant or whether you work as a chef for someone else, we are Christians first."

Isaac cleared more plates from the table. There was no syrup left, so he put that little jug into the dishwasher.

When he returned to the kitchen table to get their empty coffee mugs, he wondered what God was up to.

"Why do you think God allowed me to somehow end up working with and for Piper?" Isaac asked. "It's only for ten more days, but if we believe in the sovereignty of God, there must be a reason."

"Piper is a Christian now, so that goes along with what we just talked about, that we're Christians first, both at work and at home."

"Our spat with each other was from a long time ago. I remember I was a new Christian in high school, and she wasn't saved at all."

"Did something more happen between the two of you then?" Amy asked.

"What do you mean?"

"Were you two interested in each other in high school?"

Isaac had to think a bit. "Not that I know of. I considered her a friend, and still do. We were in the cooking club together before it disbanded, but in it, I was sort of her mentor."

"You never thought of dating her?"

"She was a sophomore, and I was a senior. She was an unbeliever, and I was in Bible Studies and church a few times a week. Our paths didn't cross except in the cooking club," Isaac explained. "Besides, she was ultra shy—so shy that you'd never know she was in the room if she just sat in a corner."

"Maybe it's because there were no other deaf people around her. Her mother moved here and put her in a regular school, where most of the kids were not deaf."

"Our high school allowed us to use ASL to meet the foreign language requirements for graduation. Nelson and his brother Marlon took the courses, and they practiced signing with Piper. Marlon and Piper took all the same high school classes so that he could interpret for her. In fact, those two dated."

Amy nodded. "Are they together now?"

"No. Marlon went out of state for college and never returned."

"So Piper is single."

Isaac stopped scrubbing dishes. "What are you getting at?"

"Piper is single. She is alone. Her parents are dead. She has no siblings. The restaurant is all she has. She lost her chefs. Her cousin stole all her money—"

"Mom told you." Isaac's heart sank.

Piper was such a private person. Isaac hoped that Mom didn't go around telling everyone in church about the crises at Piper's Place.

Something surged inside Isaac's heart, a strong feeling that he had to protect Piper.

Amy opened the refrigerator door. "Want some water?"

Isaac shook his head. "I hope they find her cousin and get her money back."

"If she doesn't?"

"Then she may have to sell the restaurant, or find new investors."

Investors.

Isaac remembered Amy mentioning *investing* on Friday.

Heaven forbid it's Mom, who has money to spare from the sale of her share of Christmastown.

"Why are we talking about all this?" Isaac looked for the dishwasher detergent.

Amy pointed to a box under the sink. "Because of two things. Firstly, I'm afraid Mom is going to manipulate her way into Piper's problems, as she did on Thursday when she told Nelson you needed a job on the same day she lost her chefs."

"Nelson had a hand in that. They conspired." Isaac chuckled.

Oddly enough, he couldn't be angry with either Nelson or Mom. He rather liked working alongside Piper—when she wasn't angry with him.

"Secondly, Piper is in the middle of some big problems—but she is alone, fighting off her Goliaths."

I'm here.

Isaac was glad he didn't blurt it aloud.

"She's alone and vulnerable, is what I am saying. She might be putting up a shield or shell to prevent anyone from taking advantage of her."

"I'm not, though."

"I know, but she doesn't know that. All she sees is that you asked her to forgive you for the past— like you want to be friends all over again, or go back to where you once were as cooking buddies. You stayed longer than the one night you said you'd work—now you're working the full two weeks they're hiring you to do. Then you showed up at work Friday with a paid Christmastown box she had canceled."

"I guess over time the sharp edges between us have somewhat worn off, but more so when I finally saw her after all these years." Isaac recalled that Wednesday night when he came face to face with her in the dim hallway.

That night had changed everything.

It had rolled back time for Isaac twenty years to the hour when he had found Piper sitting alone in the bushes behind the high school sports building, crying her heart out. She had no idea how loudly she had cried, because she couldn't hear her own voice.

But Isaac heard her.

This was Marlon's friend, he remembered thinking.

The fragile sophomore with her hair tied into a bun on top of her head recognized who Isaac was, though she was startled to see him sit down on the open grass in front of the bushes, pointing to his own shoulder.

"Cry here," he said.

And she did.

CHAPTER EIGHTEEN

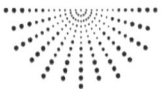

Since the Christmas decoration fiasco, Isaac had tried to clear things up with Piper, but she somehow found a way to avoid him. She had left work before Isaac arrived, even though he came in a few hours before his shift on Saturday. And she wasn't anywhere to be seen when he finished work at midnight.

Isaac and Bao closed the restaurant after the night manager shooed stragglers out of the place. Isaac went home without seeing Piper at all this evening. His second round of apologies had to wait.

After a fitful night of sleep, Isaac arose by eight to rush through a shower and quick breakfast, before carpooling to church with Mom and Jerome. He ended up visiting a mixed adult Sunday School class, in which Ming Wei taught. Apparently, he wasn't the usual teacher, but he assisted whenever the other teacher was out of town.

Unfortunately, Piper wasn't in the class.

In fact, Isaac hadn't seen any employee from Piper's Place so far. He figured most of them were either working or had the day off.

If that were his restaurant, it'd be closed on Sundays.

But it wasn't.

Many people were out of town this Thanksgiving weekend, which meant Isaac could sit anywhere he wanted in the church service during the second hour.

Isaac arrived first at their designated—by Mom—table, near a bank of windows overlooking the Savannah River. He looked around the dining room, wondering what Riverside Chapel would do if their church membership increased beyond the capacity of this riverboat. Would there be overflow rooms downstairs, or would they move back to a building on land?

He probably wouldn't be around to find out.

Not beholden to Savannah, Isaac felt that he could move anywhere. A food truck would make him mobile. A restaurant on a beach somewhere might go well with his seafood theme. Or maybe a metropolis like Atlanta, where one could find cuisines from all over the world.

For now, he had six weeks to prepare for the cooking competition in Nassau.

He had high hopes for that competition.

Cyrus came to drop off his Bible and save two seats for Amy and himself.

"Where's Amy?" Isaac asked.

"Throwing up in the ladies' room."

"Is she sick?"

"Just morning sickness."

"Ah. Okay. I hope she feels better."

"They say it goes away at the second trimester. I'm going to check on her right now." With that, Cyrus disappeared out the double doors leading to the deck outside.

Soon, a string quartet began to play a medley of hymns. He closed his eyes to enjoy the music, praying that God would help him to calm down if he saw Piper in church.

He didn't work today, so it would be noon on Monday before he went back to Piper's Place for his day shift.

As if a hint that Piper hadn't planned to keep Isaac for long, he had received a message from Nelson on the way to church that they would like his help next week in interviewing potential candidates for chef de cuisine. The interviews would be in the daytime, and it would be part of Isaac's job.

"Wake up." Mom's stern voice jabbed Isaac.

"I wasn't sleeping."

"Your eyes were closed." Mom sat down next to Isaac, and Jerome sat next to her.

"I was listening to the quartet."

"Okay. Whatever. Did you hear?"

Oh dear. "I don't gossip, Mom."

"It's not gossip." Mom chuckled. "Piper is selling her house."

I know. "How did you find out?"

Isaac hoped it wasn't from Nelson. Nelson had disclosed a lot of things to Isaac, but he wasn't sure how much Nelson talked to Mom.

On the other hand, Nelson didn't attend this church.

"You know Peggy in my Super Seniors club?" Mom asked.

"No idea who that is."

"Well, she's a real estate agent. She found the listing in her MLS database."

"So?"

"She is selling everything, including her greenhouse, in which she had been cultivating her herbs."

Whoa. Okay. Now I'm interested. "Is she selling her herb garden too?"

"Peggy said that everything in that acre lot goes, including her herb and vegetable gardens."

"She has one acre? On Tybee?" That should yield quite a profit. But first, her herbs.

Isaac couldn't remember exactly what Piper said in high school, but he recalled that her grandmother had an herb garden, which Piper was supposed to weed and water for her. They eventually moved it to a greenhouse, which her grandmother built out of a kit.

Isaac wondered if she had improved the greenhouse since then.

"Couldn't she move the herbs and vegetables before the house is shown?" Isaac asked.

"Let me ask Peggy." Mom texted her friend.

Peggy texted back and Mom read it to Isaac. "She said yes, but you have to make sure it's not part of the photo album."

"When does her house go on the market?"

"Tomorrow, as far as I know." Mom put away her phone.

"Does she have a place to move?"

"I don't know."

Isaac had an idea. "Do you still have that big old greenhouse at Amy's Christmas Tree Farm?"

"Always. We plant poinsettias and all sorts of flowers year around."

"How much does it cost to rent a corner of that greenhouse?"

"I don't rent it out."

"Just this once? Just a corner?"

Mom looked at Isaac intently. "Depends on how much space. If you rent a lot of space, I can give you a discount. We're packed full right now with poinsettias, but they are going out in the next couple of weeks."

"We need a greenhouse space today."

"We?" Mom's lips curled. "We who?"

"I mean, *she* does." Isaac glanced over to the other side of the dining room, where he had spotted a familiar face.

Piper and her friends were walking to their table, where Heidi was waiting for them. They signed to her and she signed to them, like it was the most natural language in the world.

"Mom, I need you to do me a favor," Isaac said.

"What?"

"I'm going to rent the greenhouse space, however much Piper needs, but you're going to offer the space to her for free."

Mom's eyes brightened.

"She's got a lot on her mind and a heavy load to carry, so this is my Christmas present to her."

Mom seemed to be thinking about something.

"Could you please go to her after church and offer the space? Then she could move her greenhouse herbs over this afternoon before her house goes on the market tomorrow."

Mom tapped the table. "I could send a van to help her move the herbs, but I need someone to drive it, since it's Sunday and we don't work at the tree farm on Sundays."

"Is it a commercial van?"

Mom nodded.

"I don't have the license to drive a commercial van. I think it's best if I don't participate. She and I are not exactly getting along right now."

Mom's eyebrows furrowed. "You had a fight already?"

"I tried to buy her a Christmas tree."

"Well, she has to pick it out on her own."

"Not that kind of tree. She already ordered it from Chrismastown. I just delivered it."

"And paid for it." Mom chuckled. "I bet she likes that."

"Why do you say that?"

"My dear, Piper is a very independent woman. She doesn't take gifts very well."

"Uh-oh. And here I am... Maybe I should take back my greenhouse idea."

"No, no." Mom patted Isaac's arm. "It's a great idea. It will save her herbs. You sure you don't care how much it costs?"

"Do I get a discount?"

"Twenty percent."

"Mom! Amy gave me fifty percent."

"I'm not Amy."

Before Isaac could say another word, Mom was on her feet, making a pattering beeline for Piper, who was sitting down at the table and opening her Bible.

Isaac prayed that Piper wouldn't be mad at him.

Maybe he should have prayed *before* he shared or carried out an idea.

Too late now.

CHAPTER NINETEEN

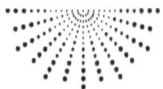

hree o'clock in the afternoon, and Piper was having a moving party with her friends in her backyard. Five of them showed up to help her move her herbs and vegetables from her small greenhouse to Mrs. Pendegrast's greenhouse at her Christmas tree farm outside Savannah. It wasn't too far away from downtown Savannah, but she would have to take the highway.

Piper's Place owned a catering van that was big enough. They'd have to make a couple of trips, even with her friends' two pickup trucks.

They had a late start because Piper returned to the restaurant to wait for Bao to pick up Forsythia, who thought she could return to work a day early due to cabin fever. Piper was happy that Forsythia had agreed to work on Sunday afternoon, since they were shorthanded with Isaac not working on Sundays.

It was a chilly Sunday afternoon, with temperature in the forties and wind chill not affected by the sunshine. Piper had bought tarps from the local hardware store to cover the back of her friends' pickup trucks. She prayed that her plants would survive the thirty-minute drive to the Christmas tree farm greenhouse outside of town.

At least it's not raining.

"I almost said no," Piper signed to her friends.

"I'm glad you said yes," Llewellyn signed back. "Otherwise you'd never see your herb garden again."

"If the house sells, though. It's so old, it might take a while to sell."

"Still, your agent told you that whatever you don't want sold, shouldn't be here for the potential buyers to see."

"I still wonder if we could have said that my herbs and vegetables are not included in the sale, the same way my furniture is not included with the house."

Nonetheless, it would be better if she moved her herbs and vegetables now.

Thus begins my emotional separation from this old house.

Piper recalled the conversation she had with

Mrs. Pendegrast at church this morning, as interpreted by Heidi. Even though Mrs. Pendegrast
would not benefit from the offer, Piper was
moved that she was willing to let her grow her
herbs and vegetables in her commercial
greenhouse.

*It's only for a short time until you get back to
normal.*

Mrs. Pendegrast seemed sincere.

But normal? What is normal anymore?

If there was any way Piper could keep the old
house that her grandmother had given to her, she
would. However, she had to choose between saving
the restaurant and saving the house. She knew she
could always buy another house and build a new
greenhouse.

But Piper's Place was historic. That was the
building Piper had to save.

Piper took Mrs. Pendegrast's offer.

She then texted Sabine to update the real estate
database to remove all photos inside her greenhouse
so that potential buyers didn't mistake what came
with the house. The greenhouse, yes. Her herbs
and vegetables, no.

So here they were.

Piper looked around the greenhouse, as if it was
the last time she would ever see it again. Maybe
some fine day, she might be able to buy back this

house. She had heard stories of people buying back their childhood homes.

Then again, this world is not my home...

Piper and Llewellyn picked up a tray of potted herbs and carried it to the van. Neither of them could sign while carrying such heavy loads, but a ray of sunshine swept across Piper's face in the November afternoon.

She looked up at the sky and smiled.

I offer up all these things to You, Jesus.

I give to You my house, my garden, my herbs, my vegetables, my kitchen, my restaurant, and yes, my life as well.

All I want to do the rest of my life is to serve You.

The weight of her own dedication to God startled Piper herself, but in her heart, she knew that the best thing she had ever done in her life was believing in Jesus. It wasn't the grandeur of going to culinary school and inheriting a restaurant.

Above all, there is God.

At the van, Piper thanked God that she had the foresight to put everything into containers inside the greenhouse, so that she could easily move her herbs outside into the sunshine during the warmer months.

Little had she expected to move her herbs clear across town to someone else's greenhouse.

"Something worries you," Llewellyn signed to her as they walked back to her backyard greenhouse, passing by her raised vegetable garden. She hadn't planted anything there this winter.

"Everything," Piper signed back.

"Name me the top three."

Piper felt touched. Only a handful of her friends were dear enough to truly care. Llewellyn was one of them.

"Is that new chef giving you trouble?" Llewellyn signed.

Piper didn't know how to explain Isaac. Maybe he could not be explained.

"He's not a new chef. He's only the temporary chef. He was supposed to work a few days over the weekend. Now he's working for two weeks."

"Was it your idea?"

"No." *Definitely not.*

It was all Nelson. Piper wouldn't put it past Nelson to talk too much with Mrs. Pendegrast.

How else did Mrs. Pendegrast know that Piper was in need of a greenhouse for her herbs and vegetables?

How else did she know that Piper's Place lost two chefs in one day?

Piper wondered if Nelson had already disclosed to her that cousin Regis had wiped out the company bank account.

"You told me a couple of years ago that you and Isaac had quarreled," Llewellyn continued.

Yes, I did tell him.

"It seems like a long time to hold a grudge."

"He held it. I just avoided him."

"He's here now. Maybe this is the time to settle it."

"Settle?" Piper wasn't sure she wanted that, although Isaac had extended an olive branch by asking her to forgive him. She told Llewellyn what happened on Thursday night.

"He chose Thanksgiving night to ask you to forgive him."

"Is that significant?"

Llewellyn shrugged. "I don't know, but I know one thing I learned in church and from the Bible. There's a big difference between forgiveness and reconciliation."

Piper nodded.

"You don't have to reconcile with him, even if you forgive him for being a sore loser," Llewellyn signed.

"I know."

But I had a crush on him, remember?

No one else knew, not even her friends.

"Maybe he felt sorry for you that you're such a workaholic. You have no life. Maybe if he cleared the air with you, he could be your friend."

"What? How did you connect the dots on that?" Piper laughed.

"We have to show him that you do have friends."

"I have friends. I don't need to prove it to him or anyone else."

"I'm going to take you out," Llewellyn said. "That'll make that chef see that you're more than just a workaholic."

"Please don't." Piper could not imagine putting on a charade.

She didn't care what Isaac thought of her.

All she wanted to do now was to straighten out the mess in her business, find a permanent place to live, and get her life back.

"Thank you for letting me stay with your family for a few weeks," Piper signed when they reached the old garden greenhouse.

"You can stay for a few months if you like. My sister and mom won't mind, considering they could use the company. My sister, especially. Being a full-time caregiver can be tiring. She gets lonely."

Lonely.

Piper wondered if she might be too, if she grew old alone.

"I'm at work all day long, and you work the night shift. So our paths are not going to cross much, and the neighbors won't talk."

"Your landlord might be upset."

"My aunt."

"I see."

"Someday I hope to save up enough to buy my own house, and then Mom and I can call it our own. We won't be renting anymore."

"Just don't hang on too much to things, friend." Piper pointed to her house across the lawn. "See, I'm losing my house. If you work towards owning your own house, don't cling to it. It's nice to have ownership, but this world is not our home, remember?"

"You're so wise."

"Painful experience, rather." Piper picked up a large container of rosemary. She had used a few sprigs of this in her cooking only yesterday.

Llewellyn followed her back on the same path across the backyard grass to the Piper's Place van. They passed by Piper's house again.

"You could stay in there until your house sells," Llewellyn signed when they stopped to rest their arms. The container was heavy, and the rosemary bushy.

"I know, but I have to detach myself from this place," Piper signed. "Also, the house is very small. Sabine said if I decluttered it or moved some furniture out, the rooms would look more spacious. I was renting pods anyway. Might as well just move out."

They passed by the other three friends on the way.

"We're faster than you two," one of them signed. "Stop talking so much and get to work. We need to get back in town for church tonight."

They're right.

Piper quickened her pace. They'd have to make two trips to Mrs. Pendegrast's greenhouse.

She didn't know how to feel—or what she already felt—yet about having to deal with the Untermeyers so much since the day before Thanksgiving.

With the exception of Saturday afternoon and evening when she had done her best to avoid Isaac, she would be seeing him at the restaurant every day for the next week and a half.

Piper wondered if she could push her memories far back enough not to think about her old teenage crush on Isaac.

We all grow up, though.

But now his mother was letting Piper put her plants in her greenhouse.

Too many reminders!

CHAPTER TWENTY

*N*elson Guilmard didn't waste any time. By Monday afternoon, he had lined up five chefs for interviews all week long. On top of that, he had somehow persuaded Piper to let Isaac sit in on the interviews.

Isaac felt that he should have a private talk with Piper about how she felt about Nelson's idea. Isaac wanted to know if Piper was really okay with it, and not just going with the flow.

However, Isaac didn't speak ASL, and must depend on texting or on Nelson to interpret. He could not ask Bao to interpret, even though that sous chef was just as proficient as Nelson in ASL. However, Bao might not be privy to all the things that were happening at the corporate level at Piper's Place.

Isaac wondered how many people knew about Piper's cousin. If the employees knew, would they quit their jobs at Piper's Place if they thought they might not get paid?

December was in four days, and surely the utility bills would be due. Where would Piper find money to pay for the utilities and all the salaries?

If Isaac were running the show, he would work on persuading Bao to move to a sous chef position to assist one of the chefs, and testing Forsythia to see if she could be a chef de cuisine. With Lillian back at work, there would be three chefs de cuisine, if Piper kept herself on the chef rotation.

And then Isaac could leave on December 6, exactly two weeks since he'd been roped in to working here.

He plated the duck dish, and let Bao take care of the rest, while Isaac went to wash his hands and eat his lunch before the first interview of the day.

He made himself a turkey sandwich, and headed for the elevator to the third floor. It was still closed until the new chef came in. At least, that was the word from Nelson.

Isaac thought it was more than that. His Christmas decorations were still up there on the third floor, but the chaser lights were turned off. Only the restaurant staff saw them, whenever they were on break or went up there to eat their meals.

Regular customers hadn't seen any of it. In fact the other two floors had no Christmas trees.

Is Piper thinking of writing off Christmas?

Walking past her office, Isaac's attention caught on a red box on her table. It was covered with hearts. The box looked like it was unopened.

Is it Valentine's Day yet?

Piper was busy doing something on her laptop, and didn't look up.

Isaac kept walking.

It was none of his business if Piper had an admirer. On the other hand, maybe she put together the box for someone else. Whatever it was, he needed to stay out of this.

His relationship with Piper was strictly professional. He had tried to put their past spat behind him, when he apologized to her.

He was still waiting for her to forgive him. He couldn't make her do it. She had to let the hurt go.

On the third floor, Isaac hesitated.

The unlit Christmas tree next to the grand piano reminded him of how angry Piper had been that he took the liberty of surprising her in her own restaurant.

Now he had ruined Christmas for her.

So make the best of it?

Isaac put his tray down on a coffee table by a

love seat facing the grand piano. He walked up to the tree and plugged it into the wall socket.

The lights sprang to life, and Isaac could almost hear Christmas carols popping out of the Christmas tree.

"Well, Christmas is about Jesus, not a pretty tree!"

Nelson's voice made Isaac turn around.

"A Christmas tree reminds us of Jesus, though," Isaac countered, returning to the small love seat.

"True." Nelson sat down in one of the two armchairs facing the love seat.

"How can I help you?" Isaac asked, putting the tray on his lap.

"I know you're eating lunch but we need to discuss a few things before the interview today." Nelson swiped his iPad.

"Okay. Let me say a blessing for my sandwich and we can talk." Isaac bowed his head, closed his eyes, and thanked God for his food.

When he opened his eyes again, Piper was sitting in the other armchair facing him.

He hadn't even heard her come in.

Her facial expression was one of concern— maybe even worry.

Isaac said a silent prayer for her that God would help her through whatever it was that concerned her.

"Chef Stephanos is coming in this afternoon, and tomorrow, we have Chef Drew Boyd," Nelson said and signed at the same time. "Both have won awards. Read: we may not be able to afford them. But they would bring attention to our restaurant, and with that, more business."

"You have a lot of business as it is," Isaac said.

Nelson signed what he said.

Isaac listened as he ate his sandwich.

"The idea is to grow the restaurant," Piper signed. "Somehow I—we all—have to make back what we lost, but if we could multiply it, maybe we have a buffer for the future."

Isaac watched her as Nelson interpreted.

Piper didn't look at him. She gave him the impression that she was holding it all in, like something was about to explode.

It couldn't be the Christmas tree this time. The tree, albeit with lights, was behind her. She couldn't see it, and wouldn't be reminded about their new spat.

"Sounds like something you two should be discussing," Isaac said. "I have no part in this business. I'm here for another week, and then I'm gone."

Isaac figured that if Piper looked straight at him, she could have read his lips and known what he said. But she had chosen to avoid him, even as she sat there, preferring to wait for Nelson to repeat his words in sign language.

Now if I knew ASL, she would have to look at me.

"Tell him that we're including him in the meeting because we want his observations and insights when we interview Chef Stephanos," Piper signed. "I want to know what his intentions are."

After Nelson explained, Isaac said nothing. He finished his sandwich, and wished he had a cup of coffee. Then Isaac asked if they knew Chef Stephanos from somewhere.

Piper must have read his lips then. She sort of moved uneasily in her armchair.

"They went to culinary school together," Nelson said.

"Oh, I see. An old friend."

"More than that," Nelson volunteered. "They almost started a restaurant together."

"Really." Somehow the word *together* bothered Isaac—when it probably shouldn't.

There was nothing going on between him and Piper, although he had always felt protective toward her. It wasn't pity, if anyone asked.

"Where's Chef Stephanos working now?" Isaac asked.

"In a restaurant in St. Augustine, Florida," Nelson said.

"Is he Greek or something?"

"No, actually," Nelson replied for Piper. "Stephanos is his name for the cooking shows he's in. His real name is Seth."

"Seth from Florida, going by the stage name of Chef Stephanos." Isaac wanted to add a snide remark, but decided not to.

Nelson looked at Piper. Signed something to her.

Piper signed something back to her restaurant manager.

"Yes, he should know," Nelson said.

"Know what?" Isaac leaned back in his loveseat. He stared at Piper now.

"Know that Chef Stephanos had proposed to Piper once. She said no."

"Why did she turn him down?" Isaac asked.

Piper must have read his lips because she was positively annoyed.

"Because her heart belongs to someone else." The words rolled out of Nelson's mouth, and he looked a bit freaked out, like someone was about to slap him.

Piper's eyes widened.

"What am I supposed to do about that information?" Isaac asked.

The relevance, though.

So Piper's ex-boyfriend had applied for the job of chef de cuisine at Piper's Place.

No one answered Isaac's question, and he decided to move on. "How did he find out about the job opening?"

"We advertised, and he saw it," Nelson explained.

"Okay. We won't leave him alone with Piper."

"Something like that." Before Nelson could say more, his phone rang. He took the call. "What? Okay. I'll be right there."

After he hung up the phone, Nelson explained to everyone. "The Super Seniors have arrived for their afternoon tea."

Isaac checked his watch. "It's not even two o'clock. When is their tea time?"

"They're always early. They stay late. Sometimes through dinner." Turning to Nelson, he signed and spoke again. "They want to know why they can't have tea on this floor."

"Tell them it's closed until our new chef comes in," Piper signed.

Isaac noticed that her fingers were shaking.

"They already know. The hostess told them. But I'll tell them again." Nelson got up. "I'll see you downstairs in your office."

He pointed to Isaac's tray. "You want me to take that? It's on the way."

"Well, sure. Thanks, Nelson." Isaac watched his friend leave.

Isaac found himself alone with Piper.

As if aware of the same, Piper got up from her armchair to leave. He saw that her eyes were glistening. Isaac reached for her hand, but only touched her fingers.

She stopped in her tracks and turned toward him.

Isaac scooted to one side of the loveseat, leaving enough room for another person to sit down. He pointed to his shoulder that was nearer to Piper.

"Cry here," he said.

And she did.

CHAPTER TWENTY-ONE

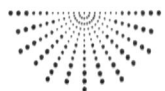

*I*f Piper had her way, she would not hire Chef Stephanos. She had only agreed to the interview—to commence in about five minutes—because he spoke ASL, and she could interview him herself.

Ironically, with Isaac invited to sit in on the meeting, Nelson had to be there to interpret for them so that Isaac could listen to the conversation and give his insight after the interview.

She only hoped that Nelson would edit his interpretation and keep to the professional. If Chef Stephanos hadn't changed a bit in the last number of years, he would find a way to talk about their personal past.

Why do I have so much past to deal with?

She did not want Isaac to know too much about her personal life.

This was Isaac. Her Isaac, the one who always seemed to offer his shoulder for her to cry on.

He was more than a friend, but some things could never be.

Unless...

The screen above her office door flashed a word.

Someone at the door.

It signaled that someone was knocking on it or just about to. The screen used to say, "Knock! Knock!"

Piper opened the door, and was surprised to see Llewellyn. She had expected someone else. She glanced outside. No sign of Nelson or Isaac.

"I'm about to go interview a chef," Piper signed.

"I was in the area, and stopped by to see if you received my gift," Llewellyn winked.

Piper laughed. Because they were signing, there was no way Isaac was going to hear their conversation.

"Did you forget?" Llewellyn signed.

"What?"

"We discussed this in your backyard on Sunday. Did you forget?"

"No, I didn't. It's not necessary. He knows I have friends."

"Is that so?" Llewellyn's shoulders sagged. "I spent a lot of money on your gift."

"What is it?"

Llewellyn frowned. He looked around the room. Walked toward Piper's desk. "You didn't open the box?"

"What did you send me?" Piper signed.

"Open the box."

"I don't have time right now."

"One minute."

Piper relented. "All right."

Now Piper was curious about what was in the box. She tore away the wrapping paper covered all over with red hearts. Inside was what looked like a velvet box.

"Please don't tell me you spend a lot of money on this." Piper opened the box slowly.

Inside was a silver necklace, at the end of which hung a plain cross.

Piper blinked.

The cross reminded her that God cared.

Piper's palm went to her chest. She signed *thank you* to Llewellyn.

He motioned for her to put it on.

Piper handed the box to him. He took out the necklace, and hung it around her neck.

Piper touched the cross.

She sniffled. "Thank you so much, Llewellyn, for reminding me about what matters."

"Jesus matters. All these will fade away," Llewellyn signed back.

Piper nodded.

She hugged Llewellyn.

Just as Isaac entered the office.

From the corner of her eye, Piper waited for his reaction as he stood there, watching her hug Llewellyn. His eyes darted to the empty box on the coffee table.

Piper stepped back.

She noticed that Isaac's eyes were now upon the new necklace she was wearing, as if he had not seen it before. Of course, he hadn't, but it also made Piper think that Isaac had been paying attention to her.

Had he?

"We're getting ready to interview some potential chefs," Piper signed to Llewellyn.

"I better go. I need to get back to work." Llewellyn waved to Isaac and walked out of the office.

"Who was that?" Isaac asked.

Even though Piper could read his lips, she chose not to reply. No, Isaac couldn't understand ASL even if she replied, but more so, she wanted him to know that it was none of his business.

Isaac tapped his wristwatch.

Piper checked her iPhone.

Chef Stephanos was late. One strike against him.

CHAPTER TWENTY-TWO

*C*hef Seth "Stephanos" Moreno brought them a tray of homemade organic chocolate cupcakes. Primarily it was for Piper, was Isaac's guess.

It was daring, to be sure. Piper's Place was known for its award-winning cuisine, including cupcakes. If Stephanos had done his research, he would have known that the last thing he'd want to feed the owner of a restaurant like this one was something resembling her own menu item.

By the time the chef explained to them where he had sourced the cacao beans and the long process by which it became cocoa powder and delivered to his kitchen in Charleston so that he could make this "beautiful cupcake" for Piper, they had not only finished eating the samples, but half their interview time was over.

Isaac felt that he needed a glass of water now to wash the bitter aftertaste from his mouth.

He could barely concentrate on what Stephanos was signing to Piper, the words of which were then interpreted by Nelson for Isaac's benefit.

For some reason, the chef didn't feel it necessary to speak in English while he was signing in ASL, as if whatever he was saying to Piper was between them only.

This wasn't a private conversation. This was a job interview.

"We don't need a business partner," Nelson interpreted to Isaac what Piper said to Stephanos. "We're looking for a chef to join the three chefs in rotation."

"Head chef?" Stephanos finally spoke as he signed.

"Main chef for one of the shifts," Piper corrected him. "I'm the executive and head chef."

"I just assumed by the title chef de cuisine..."

"My main chefs are all chefs de cuisine officially, but you should already know that, but the kitchen is mine."

As Isaac listened, he wondered whether Stephanos' assumption had been an add-on. If he knew Piper well—considering he had proposed to her—then he would have known that Piper didn't mince words.

She was in charge of the restaurant, and that was that.

"From what I understood, you might want a business partner," Stephanos signed.

Nelson seemed as though he was trying not to lose his cool, interpreting what Stephanos did not speak aloud.

Isaac felt the disrespect.

Not everyone at Piper's Place knew ASL. Piper set a rule that whenever she was involved in the conversation, everyone who could sign had to do both: speak and sign.

It was Piper's rule.

"Partner?" Piper signed back. "Nowhere did the job description say that."

"In the future," Stephanos signed.

"You're mistaken. We're looking for one chef de cuisine to work eight hours a day. It might be from 8 a.m. to 4 p.m. or from 4 p.m. to midnight."

Isaac didn't say anything. He was there to observe. He would give his thoughts later. Right now he needed some water to balanced out the tartness on his tongue. He was having second thoughts about those once-delicious cupcakes that Stephanos had brought them.

"Anyone want water? I'll go get some," Isaac offered.

Nelson said nobody else wanted any.

Isaac made a quick dash to the refrigerator down the hall, and poured himself a large glass of water from a carafe.

It was also a chance for him to step out for a minute. Two men in the room within an hour of each other was too much for him to see. First, dashing Llewellyn had brought a gift for Piper. Now, hunky Chef Stephanos was trying to charm the owner of the establishment.

Well, he hadn't received any indication from Piper that she was dating anyone or was interested in anyone.

As far as Isaac was concerned, Piper was married to her job.

She was even more of a workaholic than he was.

Isaac returned to the office, where Stephanos was still conversing to Piper in ASL. Nelson didn't have to speak anything since Isaac hadn't been in the room.

Could a guy really be that good looking? It was no wonder that Stephanos considered himself a rising celebrity chef in his resume. In fact, his resume had shown that he had been on television food and lifestyle shows. He also worked out.

The only place Isaac worked out was in the kitchen. After working there all day, he sometimes felt like a used-up dishrag, not a ripped and buff television personality.

And Chef Stephanos's credentials...

Whew. Unparalleled.

He might be too much and too expensive for Piper to afford.

"Where do you see yourself in five years?" Piper asked in ASL.

Stephanos's face brightened up. "Well, a James Beard nomination would be nice. It would put your restaurant on the map."

Isaac waited.

"And my own cooking show."

There you go. He is ambitious.

"A cooking show?" Nelson asked verbally while he signed for Piper.

"In your kitchen, of course," Stephanos said. "Wouldn't it be a sweet marriage between this historical building and my innovative career."

Isaac glanced at Piper.

"But we're not here for your personal career advancement as much as we're trying to keep the restaurant going and increasing in revenues," Piper signed.

It was a mouthful for Nelson to interpret.

"With a cooking show, Piper's Place will be on the map." Stephanos lifted his hands animatedly.

Isaac saw his perfectly manicured fingernails. Made for camera close-ups and filming.

"I'm not looking to be on TV," Piper signed. "I'm looking for a chef who can do his or her best for my customers. This is an almost thankless job, as you know, and we are open twenty-four-seven."

"I already have contracts for guest appearances on cooking shows. Surely you don't want to pass them up."

"What do you mean guest appearances?" Piper leaned forward.

"You heard me. I'm the one on TV. I'll say, 'Chef Stephanos from Piper's Place.' Product placement."

"That is to say, when you're on TV, Piper has to find a replacement to cook in your place while you're busy filming," Isaac said before he remembered he was only there to observe.

Nelson didn't interpret his words for Piper, but Isaac figured Piper had probably read his lips, although she didn't respond to his statement.

Isaac checked the digital clock on the screen above the door to see if it matched his wristwatch.

Piper must have seen his upward glance. She nodded to him.

Isaac had no idea what it meant until Nelson interpreted.

"Thank you, Stephanos, for coming in for the interview," Piper signed. "We have four other chefs coming in the next four days, and we'll make a decision at the end of the week."

"*We* who?" Stephanos asked.

Piper pointed to Nelson, Isaac, and then herself.

Isaac tried not to react, but he appreciated Piper all the more for including him in the evaluation. Granted, she had already said she would, but this was a power move on her part, to show Stephanos that he could not try to manipulate her with visions of grandeur.

"You said you need a chef ASAP." Stephanos nodded. "If I don't hear from you soon, I'll be off somewhere else."

"What about your YouTube cooking show?" Piper signed. "What happens to it if you work here?"

"That's what I meant by partnership, Piper." Stephanos leaned toward her. "We would merge our companies and go from there."

"I'm not looking to add a cooking show. My main focus is this restaurant."

"Now it can expand."

"I'm not looking to expand. I can barely handle our catering service. Did you not hear me?"

"In return I will represent this restaurant in cooking shows."

"I just told you—never mind." Piper was losing her calm. Isaac could see it.

He decided it had to end. He wasn't sure if Piper needed rescuing—she seemed to be doing well for herself—but the clock on the wall said it was almost four o'clock. The interview had gone on for an extra fifteen minutes because Stephanos was late.

"Piper's Place is looking for a chef who fits into this restaurant, not to change this successful restaurant to fit into a chef's career plans," Isaac said. "Piper is the sole proprietor and the only boss around here. Whatever you do, you need to clear it with her. You can't just walk in and change things, add this or that to what she has already established."

Stephanos gave Isaac a snarly look, and that made Isaac continue speaking.

"For example, you can't just show up one day with a Christmas tree and say you're going to decorate her restaurant for Christmas as a surprise to her." Isaac dared not look at Piper, or whether Nelson had been interpreting for him.

He kept his focus on Stephanos. "Likewise, you can't just surprise her with any of your celebrity ambitions down the road—like bringing a film crew here or something without her approval—because we are here to work and cook for our customers. It's a behind-the-scenes job one hundred percent of the time."

"Well, if we're partners..." Stephanos looked at Piper, as if looking for support.

"You're not a partner," Isaac said. "She's looking for an employee who can work for eight hours a day, five days a week. It's hard work."

"I know hard work." Stephanos smiled. "I could have taken you very far, Piper, to where you could never go on your own."

"I have no regrets being on my own," Piper signed.

"Because your heart belongs to someone else." Stephanos shook his head, speaking and signing for the benefit of both the hearing and the deaf. "You said so years ago."

Years ago? Who did Piper give her heart to years ago?

Isaac tried not to read too much into it, but he considered the implication.

Who has Piper's heart?

God, of course.

If God, then how would God lead Piper to spend the rest of her life? Alone or with someone?

Isaac was surprised by the question in his own mind.

CHAPTER TWENTY-THREE

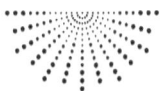

*P*iper barely had time to run outside to get some fresh air after that interview with Chef Stephanos. She had left Isaac and Nelson inside the building, telling them to take a fifteen-minute break after Stephanos was ushered out of the building.

There was no doubt Stephanos could cook. There was also no doubt that he could help publicize Piper's Place. However, at what cost? Ambitious to a fault, Stephanos had always been about Stephanos—nothing and no one else.

They had become friends quickly in culinary school—way back when—because Stephanos understood ASL. He had a deaf grandparent and had learned to sign from a very young age. As friends, Piper thought he understood her.

Until he wanted to be more than friends.

She couldn't go where he wanted to go.

Sitting alone on the loading dock, Piper felt like the whole world was pushing down on her. As though she were sandwiched inside a panini press.

Lord Jesus, why did You allow all these things to happen to me?

I thought my life would be easier if I were a Christian. In fact, it has gotten harder and harder.

In the ten years she had been saved, she had faced one challenge after another, until last year when things began to settle down. She had peace at work for about five months.

And then Chef Torkel eloped with Chef Seraphina. And cousin Regis ran away with her money. The combined fallout was more than she could bear.

It's too much.

Tears trickled into her eyes again, but she held them back this time. Piper knew if her employees saw her falling apart, they might too. She was the owner of Piper's Place. She was responsible for the restaurant, although she knew how to delegate.

And therein was her mistake.

She had delegated her money management to her cousin, who had worked for several other companies as their accountant. As far as she knew,

Regis was a Certified Public Accountant, licensed to practice in Georgia.

Why would he steal her money?

He had no reason to.

Piper knew now that it had been a mistake to trust Regis.

Lord Jesus, forgive me for my oversight. I should have hired a more trustworthy accountant.

Piper prayed that God would not only forgive her, but pull her out of this miry clay, like Psalm 40:2 said.

> *He also brought me up out of a horrible pit,*
> > *Out of the miry clay,*
> > *And set my feet upon a rock,*
> > *And established my steps.*

The verse comforted her, even as she recalled it from memory.

Forgive me, Lord, for my poor judgment.

What about the two chefs who quit on the same day. Had that been a result of her poor judgment too?

Truly, she didn't care about her employees' personal lives, as long as they did their jobs well.

And yet, Torkel and Seraphina...

Well, statistically, restaurants had high turnovers. Chefs burned out, cooks found better jobs elsewhere, and so forth. Piper knew that she could not expect everyone to work in the same place for their entire lives. If they did, those were rare gems she should pay more.

She had paid those two chefs fairly well, hadn't she?

Did I make a mistake not giving them the pay raises they asked for?

Lord, please forgive me...

Piper hung her head, even as her feet dangled off the side of the loading dock.

Behind her, the garage door was closed. There would be no deliveries until the next morning, so she did not expect to be disturbed as she sat here asking for God to forgive her—

A realization hit her heart and dragged it down all the way to the tarred driveway below. She wanted God to forgive her, but she had withheld forgiveness for a fellow human being.

Blessed are those whose lawless deeds are forgiven,
And whose sins are covered.

Paul had known exactly how wonderful it must feel to be forgiven of his sins. He had said so in that verse from Romans 4:7.

But if I myself don't forgive?

What is that verse to me?

Piper retrieved her phone from her chef jacket pocket, and searched for verses on forgiveness. She found several, including Mark 11:25-26.

And whenever you stand praying, if you have anything against anyone, forgive him, that your Father in heaven may also forgive you your trespasses. But if you do not forgive, neither will your Father in heaven forgive your trespasses."

Piper sighed.
There is someone I haven't forgiven.

CHAPTER TWENTY-FOUR

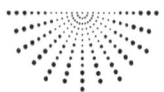

Five o'clock came and went, and Isaac was still in Piper's office, discussing Chef Stephanos Moreno with Piper and Nelson. It was time for Nelson to leave work as well, but as the interpreter, he couldn't.

Nelson didn't like Stephanos at all. "I find him bombastic and full of himself."

"He's always been like that," Piper signed.

"Doesn't mean he should work here," Nelson signed back.

Piper nodded.

Isaac purposely didn't want to volunteer his opinion about the chef, unless Piper asked. Even so, he tried to be careful in his response, in case he gave Piper any reason.

He disliked Stephanos for many reasons.

He didn't like the way the almost-celebrity chef tried to corner Piper into a two-way conversation when there were four people in the room during the interview.

He had seen people do that sort of thing before. Usually they were in cliques, and stayed within their own little elite circles, as if they were privileged or something.

Even if Stephanos had not tried to create an exclusive connection a la "I know Piper and you don't," he had given Isaac the impression that he wanted to show that he and Piper had a history.

Well, Piper and I have a history too.

"What do you think?" Nelson asked.

"What?" Isaac hoped nobody read his thoughts.

His embarrassingly ugly thoughts about someone he had just met.

Wow. That's an indictment.

I'm sorry, God. Help me to be objective.

Isaac chided himself for being quick to feel and react to something that irritated him. Even when he had been in high school, he had been ugly to Piper when she won the cooking championship.

It was as though their friendship for the entire year before had been erased by that single event.

Wasn't that childish of us? Of me?

And now Isaac was reacting again.

For all he knew, Chef Stephanos would be ideal for Piper's Place. If they could afford him.

Isaac prayed quietly that God would help him to be objective. He knew he had to put aside his personal feelings and give a professional evaluation of Stephanos, in spite of all his misgivings, having spent fifty minutes with him.

"Well..." Isaac cleared his throat.

Everyone waited.

What to say about Chef Ego?

"From what I recall, his credentials are impressive." Isaac scrolled through the email from Nelson, as he scanned for anything that jumped up. "Look at all the chefs he has worked with. So many it's blinding."

"Isn't that a negative?" Piper signed and Nelson interpreted.

"What do you mean?" Isaac asked.

"He moves from restaurant to restaurant, kitchen to kitchen, chef to chef."

Isaac nodded. "Yeah, looks like he didn't stay in one place for long."

Piper signed quickly. "He appears in this TV show, that radio program. He even tried to start his own cooking podcast to get sponsors. He is everywhere, and yet nowhere. Not one of those people seemed to have kept him for more than one or two guest appearances."

"I agree." Nelson added after he interpreted what Piper signed.

Isaac didn't feel one way or another toward Stephanos any more. Whereas he had felt a bit irritated earlier that the guy had such a big ego, right now he felt sorry for Stephanos that his so-called achievements were working against him.

He knew then that God had answered his prayer for objectivity.

"You need someone who is committed to making Piper's Place successful," Isaac said. "A team player."

Piper nodded. "Not someone focused on advancing his own career. Otherwise he will only look at Piper's Place as a stepping stone."

After Nelson explained what Piper just signed, Isaac tried to recall the interview with Stephanos. "You know, all things considered, I don't have a problem with Stephanos doing TV or radio spots if none of his extracurricular activities interfere with his job here."

"Right," Nelson said.

"After all, he speaks ASL," Isaac added.

"That's a plus," Nelson spoke and signed. "Also, he could put Piper's Place in the limelight by the fact that he works here."

Piper signed, then waited for Nelson to interpret.

"Piper said that if Stephanos gets too busy, he might not be around much," Nelson said. "She's not hiring an executive chef to oversee other chefs. That's her job."

"She established that, yes," Isaac said. "So you might want a chef who wants to stay in Savannah for the long haul."

Piper watched him. "Unlike you?"

"Me?" Isaac thought Nelson had misinterpreted.

Piper explained.

Nelson seemed to choose his words carefully so that nothing was lost in translation.

Isaac thought for a second or two. "It never crossed my mind to work at this restaurant for more than two weeks. I stayed because you needed a chef and I was available."

Was it just him, or did Piper's face look a bit disappointed?

"It has always been my dream to start my own restaurant, or at the least, operate a food truck. After ten to fifteen years of working for someone else, I think I want to be my own boss for a change."

After Nelson signed Isaac's explanation to Piper, she signed back.

"She said to tell you we appreciate the fact that you sacrificed to help us through this rough time," Nelson said.

"God takes care of all our needs." It was all Isaac could come up with.

"Thank you, Jesus," Piper signed.

At the back of Isaac's mind, it was still puzzling to him how it had all worked out. If he had arrived in town a week later, he would have missed this opportunity to clear up old wounds.

Truly, after he had apologized to Piper—even though she hadn't said she forgave him—he felt that their relationship had improved, at least in their conversations with each other.

It would improve even more if I learned ASL.

Then we would speak the same language.

"We have four more chefs to interview," Nelson said. "We'll find out who might be the best fit."

"Shall we pray for God's wisdom?" Isaac asked, surprising himself with the question.

He was even more surprised when Piper reached out to hold his hand.

His memories rewound twenty years to their Cumin Cooking Club meetings. They had always opened with prayer, because five of six members were Christians. Piper wasn't, but she had seen people pray before, particularly her grandmother, and she had joined in.

They held hands in a circle as they prayed.

The memory made Isaac feel like a hypocrite.

So pious had he been, leading their little cooking club in weekly prayers. But so pretentious was he, saying *amen* and then proceeding to hate on Piper when he lost the cooking competition to her.

What kind of a Christian was I?

Piper hadn't been a believer at that time.

So pained now, as Isaac recalled his knee-jerk reaction to the whole fiasco when he shut down their cooking club, leaving Piper in tears.

Twenty years ago.

Isaac squeezed Piper's hand, even as tears washed his eyes in shame and repentance. He drew a deep breath when he heard Nelson say, "Amen."

When he opened his eyes, Piper looked at him with alarm on her face.

"I'm sorry, Piper. I'm so sorry." It was all Isaac could say.

CHAPTER TWENTY-FIVE

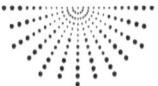

*T*he next day, Chef Drew Boyd came for his interview, made everyone laugh, and then cooked them the most delicious fried chicken Isaac had ever tasted this side of the hemisphere. He wanted them to call him only DB, but Isaac thought it had a better ring to it if they called him Chef DB.

"I taste a hint of turmeric in this." Isaac reached for another drumstick.

"It's a secret." Chef DB smiled.

"We're going to get it out of you." Chomp. Chomp. "I'm sure there's turmeric... Oh, and soy sauce. That's clever."

"Not my original idea. People in Asia fry chicken in soy sauce all the time."

"He's humble too." Isaac ate another piece of chicken. "I'm stuffed."

"Me too," Nelson said.

Isaac glanced at Piper. She seemed amused, watching Isaac and Nelson devour the entire plate of fried chicken.

Somehow, she seemed more positive today. There was a brightness in her reaction, and she also said she enjoyed Chef DB's food.

"Where have you been all my life?" Nelson ate the last piece of chicken.

"You just said that because you want Chef DB here to tell you his secret recipe." Isaac elbowed Nelson.

Nelson laughed. "I just want him to cook some more!"

"You want more?" Chef DB asked.

"He's not serious," Isaac said. "You've done enough."

He turned to Piper to see what she wanted to do next.

She was staring at her phone.

Her smile vanished.

Her laughter ceased.

And her hand began to shake.

"What's the matter?" Isaac stepped toward her.

Piper ignored him, signing to Nelson.

Nelson drew a deep breath before he spoke.

"Chef BD, Piper said thank you for coming in today. She has to leave right now for another meeting, but we can continue our interview in her office."

It was way past four o'clock. Chef Lillian had arrived, and Isaac could leave any time.

Isaac made a quick decision. "Nelson, how about if I take Piper wherever she needs to go. You can stay here to wrap up the interview."

Nelson signed. He and Piper went back and forth.

"She says they have called in their volunteer interpreter."

Although Nelson did not say where they were going, the fact that there were interpreters there gave Isaac another clue of where Piper had to go. She wasn't going to a happy place, judging from her worry-filled face.

"Let's go. We can take my truck," Isaac offered.

Piper signed.

"She said she'll see you out back after she gets her purse from her office," Nelson explained.

"I'll be waiting. Text me the address."

Nelson nodded. He seemed appreciative of Isaac's discretion in front of an interviewee, who was not privy to the disaster behind the scene at Piper's Place.

~

*S*ince Isaac didn't speak her language and vice versa, the truck ride to the Savannah Police Department Headquarters was uneventful for Piper. Even though she could read lips, it was not always an easy thing to do—especially when it came to staring at Isaac to figure out what words came out of his mouth.

Would they ever speak the same language some day?

She thanked God for the rush hour traffic, which added another three or four minutes to the seven-minute drive through old town Savannah, although the route that Isaac took avoided most of the historic squares.

Piper kept up with Isaac so that she could read his lips to see what he said to the front desk officer about their meeting with Detective Zimmerman.

Isaac turned to Piper. "He's waiting for us."

Piper nodded.

Some had said that reading lips was a skill. To Piper, it was a necessity. With many hearing employees in her restaurant, she could not expect every single server and worker to understand ASL, though their careers would be greatly enhanced if they could communicate ideas to her in her own language.

However, she was glad that at least half of the employees, if not more, had decided to learn ASL. In fact, she paid for them to take the courses. The next new round of ASL would begin in January.

But Isaac would be gone by then.

Piper didn't know yet whether she would miss him, but for now, she was enjoying his company— and feeling guilty about doing so while she harbored unforgiveness in her heart.

How on earth did it come to this?

She recalled that Thanksgiving night when Isaac had asked her to forgive him for being jealous of her winning the cooking competition.

Jealous?

He hadn't used that exact word, but his bitterness had probably been borne out of jealousy.

Piper was sure he had been unhappy that she had won what he thought was an easy competition for him. Thus, if he lost, then it must not be his food. It must have been someone else's fault.

Piper swiped her phone and scrolled through their text conversation. She reread what Isaac had said.

I am sorry I got mad for losing the cooking competition to you.

A notification popped up. It was a text from Isaac, sitting next to her in the waiting area.

Piper glanced him. He pointed to her phone.

Piper scrolled down to the last message, sent just moments ago.

I'm praying for you.

Piper looked at him and nodded. Then she tapped a reply to him, and he was quick to respond.

> **PIPER**
>
> Thank you. What a mess.

> **ISAAC**
>
> Nothing God can't fix.

> **PIPER**
>
> ASAP, please!

> **ISAAC**
>
> In God's timing.

> **PIPER**
>
> I'm about to lose everything. My house. My restaurant. My career.

> **ISAAC**
>
> You saved your herbs and vegetables.

Of course, he would know. His mom would have told him that she had offered her free space in her expensive Christmas tree farm greenhouse.

Piper thought she was done chatting. She looked around to see if Detective Zimmerman was coming down the hallway. He was nowhere to be seen.

Then Isaac texted her again.

ISAAC

Thank you.

> PIPER
>
> For what?

ISAAC

For our friendship. You could have
kicked me out to the curb.

> PIPER
>
> And break a toe?

Isaac laughed. Piper couldn't hear him, but she could see his face. Additionally, he seemed genuinely happy to be there with her—waiting at the police station. He didn't have to do this. Yet, here he was. He returned to his phone, tapping something. Piper saw her phone flash.

ISAAC

I'm sorry it took twenty years for
us to regroup.

> PIPER
>
> Regroup?

ISAAC

Please forgive me.

> PIPER
>
> I'm getting there. Give me time.

When she looked up from her phone, she found Isaac staring at her.

"I've caused us so much trouble for so long," his lips said.

Piper wondered at his choice of words.

Trouble.

Not *pain.*

To be honest, she had only thought of him on and off for twenty years. For most of the time, she had tried to put him out of her mind.

It was puppy love, as they say.

Even now that they were in their thirties—albeit still single—Piper didn't know how to begin where they had left off. She tried to feel what she had felt as a high school sophomore, but the memories were fading fast.

It was only a crush.

Teenage crushes faded with time, didn't they? In time, her own feelings for Isaac would also fade away, would they not?

However, on Monday when Isaac had offered her his shoulder to cry on and she had taken it, she thought that something was happening between them.

Her feelings for him were rekindling, not fading.

He seemed to care for her.

She couldn't describe it precisely, but he seemed to genuinely care for her more than just a friend would. Like he had to make sure she was all right.

He wanted her to have the Christmas decorations from Christmastown even though she had cancelled the order.

Oh, that.

Piper texted him.

> **PIPER**
> I'm sorry I got mad at you about the Christmas tree.

> **ISAAC**
> It was my fault. I should have asked you. Made sure you were okay with it.

> **PIPER**
> I'm fine with it now.

> **ISAAC**
> Thank you for letting it stay.

> **PIPER**
> I like the way it's decorated.

> **ISAAC**
> We basically copied the photographs that Amy took last year.

> **PIPER**
> No wonder the decor looked familiar.

ISAAC

Please don't be upset with your
employees who helped me.

PIPER

I'm not.

She really wasn't upset with him anymore.
Maybe the heaviness in her heart was starting to
lift.

But I do have to forgive him.

Or I will not be free of this burden.

The burden of a teenage crush, in which she
had imagined their lives together. And how big
their vegetable and herb garden would be in their
backyard.

How could it happen now?

Her own small garden would be sold as soon as
Sabine found people to buy her house. Her herbs
were clear across town, while she rented a room on
the other side of town.

Then again, that burden was only a dream.

Still, she had remained unmarried to this day.

All because of Isaac.

CHAPTER TWENTY-SIX

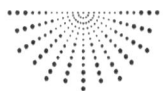

*I*saac arrived home at his mother's house to a note saying that she and Jerome had gone out to dinner, and that there was a can of spam in the pantry if he wanted to eat it before it expired.

There was a giant smiley on it, drawn out in red marker, next to an arrow pointing to the edge of the paper.

Isaac turned the paper over.

Just kidding!

It was in Mom's handwriting. She had been in a good mood, Isaac supposed.

He read the rest of the note. Mom had left him some grilled scallops she had made to prove that she could be a worthy assistant cook when she accompanied Isaac to Nassau in January.

"I don't know why you insist on going with me, Mom," Isaac said to no one.

Thing is, he couldn't find any cheap sous chef who would be willing take one week off work and help him win the cooking competition in Nassau. Everybody wanted to be paid too much.

Except Mom.

She even offered to pay her own way.

All she wanted in return was to spend time with Isaac, to make up for lost time.

Everyone is trying to make up for lost time.

Even Isaac himself. Lost time with a girl he could have been lifelong friends with, perhaps, but whom he had shunned for such reasons as could be explained only by teen angst.

And now it's too late.

Isaac left the note on the table. He found the scallops.

"Mom, you don't have to prove anything," Isaac mumbled as he heated up the scallops in the microwave. Unfortunately, the microwave probably would make the scallops go rubbery. It was a sure-fire way to refute Mom's claim that her scallops were good.

"Mmm..." It was still good. *What on earth?*

He sat down at the breakfast nook, which had been there forever. Under a too-bright light.

He was too distracted to analyze the scallops or grade the dish.

He tried to picture Piper, but all he could see was a crowd of faces.

He could barely recall what had transpired at the police station after Detective Zimmerman finally came out to the lobby to meet Piper and him, and wished that Piper didn't have to go through any of the rest of it.

Zimmerman had initially offered to meet Piper at Piper's Place to ask her some follow-up questions, but Piper had insisted on going down to the station. She did not want restaurant customers to see the detective talk to her. They might wonder if a crime had happened at their favorite eatery, especially if Piper couldn't hold it together.

Those had been her own words, via text, as they had continued to wait in the police station.

However, after almost half an hour, Zimmerman appeared with his interpreter, telling them that the entire situation had changed in Atlantic City, New Jersey.

New Jersey?

Isaac remembered the bewilderment on Piper's face. "What is Regis doing in New Jersey?"

Well, apparently that crooked cousin of hers had been making weekend trips to Atlantic City, New Jersey, to meet with his other clients.

The very place where Regis had been caught in a crossfire between criminals and the US Immigration and Customs Enforcement conducting an undercover sting operation on money laundering activities.

And now Regis was in the emergency room, fighting for his life.

Next thing Isaac knew, Piper was on the videophone with Llewellyn.

Llewellyn!

The same guy who had gifted Piper with the cross necklace on Monday.

Yep. Two plane tickets.

How does that make me feel?

Isaac let out a guttural groan.

As the scene played in his head, Isaac swiped his phone. He scrolled through the text messages to find his plea.

ISAAC

Let me go with you to New Jersey.

PIPER

No. I need you in the kitchen.

ISAAC

Bao and Forsythia can take over.

PIPER

No. I need you and Lillian to keep
your hours. I told Nelson to move
Forsythia up to night chef. She
can have any assistant she wants.

ISAAC

I don't want you to go alone.

PIPER

I'm not alone. My friend Llewellyn
is coming with me.

ISAAC

He is?

PIPER

He's bringing a change of clothes
for me. His sister is packing it for
me as we speak.

ISAAC

He knows where you live?

PIPER

I'm renting a room from him—his
family.

Stunned, Isaac remembered not being able to
speak the rest of the time, until the heroic
Llewellyn arrived at the police station, and whisked
Piper away, leaving Isaac to drive home alone.

Isaac wasn't sure how to pray about it.

Of course, he wanted Piper and Llewellyn to
arrive safely in New Jersey.

Of course, he wanted Piper to get her money back.

He wasn't so sure about whether he wanted Regis to get well soon. That was up to God, not him.

He closed his eyes and groaned.

"I should have gone with her. Why did she always have to say no?"

CHAPTER TWENTY-SEVEN

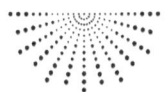

*A*fter a one-hour flight from Savannah/Hilton Head International Airport, a two-hour wait at the Hartsfield-Jackson Atlanta International, and another two-hour flight to Philadelphia, Piper and Llewellyn finally loaded their luggage into a rental car, and drove in the middle of night eastward toward Atlantic City, looking for the hospital where Regis had been admitted this afternoon.

Since Llewellyn was not profoundly deaf, and he wore a cochlear implant, he was able to sign to her and speak to hearing people at the airport and hospital, if they didn't understand ASL.

Piper was glad that Llewellyn was with her and not Isaac.

She wasn't too happy with herself for always

appearing vulnerable in front of Isaac. She hadn't been like this for years.

However, with Isaac back in town, and in her kitchen—she still blamed Nelson for that—Piper felt that many of her old suppressed memories were coming back to her, and they burst out of her tear ducts, as though the pressure was tremendous.

To be sure, it was an awful end to November for her. She had lost two chefs and all her company funds. She had lost her only cousin in town. She was about to lose her house. And if she wasn't careful, she would lose her restaurant too.

Llewellyn glanced at the navigation on his iPhone on the dashboard mount. He pointed this way and that.

Piper nodded.

Honestly, she hadn't been paying attention to the street signs. It was almost ten o'clock at night. It was dark outside. She was tired. She expected Llewellyn to know where to go since he had told her to relax and not worry.

Thank You, Lord, for bringing helpers into my life.

Nelson, back in Savannah, managed her restaurant for her, as he had done for years. On Thursday and Friday, he would interview two more chefs. Piper had asked him to let Isaac sit in, once again, to give his opinion.

Piper expected to be back in Savannah by Friday afternoon, if she didn't decide to stay through the weekend. At this point, she was using the money she extracted out of her stocks to pay for her plane ticket and the hotel room.

Thank God that Llewellyn paid his own way.

"What a friend you are," Piper signed.

He waved his usual "Don't mention it!" gestures.

Piper leaned against the passenger seat and stared outside into the highway, the lights zipping past the rental car in a neon blur. Her eyes felt sleepy.

When was the last time I slept?

When she had taken over the restaurant from Grandma, it had been a glorious time. She thought she was on top of the world, and that she had reached the pinnacle of her dream.

What she found out the next number of years was that the dream was a lot of hard work.

She prayed she was not burning out.

But working the night shift was taking a toll on her after a few months. She was glad that Lillian came back one month early from her maternity leave, but since Piper had to shuffle around the chefs, the new routine was still the old for her.

She wondered...

No. Isaac would not stay.

More importantly, he would not take orders from her as an employee.

In all honesty, Piper didn't want him to. She knew him well. Both of them were independent people, and were better off running separate businesses.

But on the personal front...

Piper sighed.

There is no personal front.

Isaac probably didn't know about her secret crush on him all those years ago in high school. In fact, Isaac had been too busy trying to get one more cooking trophy for his checklist before he went to college.

After losing to her, he rarely spoke to her again. Then he was gone, to college and beyond.

Now that he was back in town, even for a short period of time, it had affected Piper's ability to hold back her emotions, as she had been able to do for years.

She had kept herself busy as a businesswoman, a restaurant owner, and an executive chef. After her long working hours, she went home to tend her vegetable and herb garden. Every Sunday morning, she went to church with her friends.

For the most part, she had a happy life.

Her grandmother and mother would have wanted her to marry and have kids.

I'm now thirty-five.

And Isaac is thirty eight—

Wait. Why am I thinking of him?

Piper had a feeling that after next week, she would never see Isaac again. Even if he decided to open his own restaurant in Savannah, Piper knew that he wouldn't want to be in competition with her.

Isaac seemed to be meant for bigger places—maybe Atlanta, for example.

Piper recalled that Mrs. Pendegrast had an older brother in Atlanta. His children lived near him. Isaac's cousins.

Speaking of cousins...

Piper couldn't help but say a prayer for her own cousin, Regis.

Ten years older than Piper and divorced, Regis had moved to Savannah to start his own book-keeping business. Piper was one of his first clients.

In fact, Piper might have been one of his biggest clients.

She had trusted Regis.

Trusted him enough to let him log into her bank accounts.

What a grave mistake.

And now, that trust was not only broken, but the damage was probably irreversible.

CHAPTER TWENTY-EIGHT

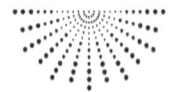

*R*egis was so badly injured in the crossfire that he had to undergo numerous surgeries while Piper and Llewellyn waited through the night at the hospital.

Sometime during the early morning hours, an Atlantic City police officer had come to talk to them and ask them some questions about Piper's relationship to Regis. However, they did not disclose to her even a little bit more than what Detective Zimmerman in Savannah had told Piper.

Sleeping in the waiting room had put a kink in Piper's neck. She opened her eyes, and found herself still lying there on a couch.

What time is it?

Piper checked her phone. Almost six in the morning.

Llewellyn made a face.

"Are you saying I smell?" Piper signed.

"Onions, primarily, like yesterday's kitchen." Llewellyn was sitting on an armchair adjacent to her.

"I went from the restaurant to the police station to three airports and then to this hospital." Piper sat up. "What do you expect?"

"You also need sleep—real sleep, preferably on a real bed."

"Give me the car keys." Piper put out her palm.

"Why?"

"I need to get some clean clothes from my bag in the trunk."

"Good idea. Me, too. I'll go with you."

"You're a good friend." Piper smiled.

"As a good friend, let me give you a piece of advice." Llewellyn walked with Piper down the hallway.

"Oh, no. Here it comes." Piper rolled her eyes.

"I'm sure many of us are praying with you," Llewellyn signed. "We don't know what is going to happen next with your cousin."

"And the money he stole from me."

"Right. I want you to be prepared for eventualities."

Piper nodded. "I may never get my money back."

At the elevator, Llewellyn pushed the Down button. "If you don't, what will you do?"

"I've put my house on the market." Piper knew that wasn't enough.

There was no offer, and no one had asked to see the house. Yes, it had only been six days, but this was a well-maintained old house on Tybee Island with a half-acre lot filled with flowers, vegetables, and herbs.

The elevator was empty, so Piper continued signing. "I cashed out some stocks. The capital gains taxes are going to be a lot. But I had to do what I had to do."

"Still not enough, is it?" Llewellyn asked.

"I think I need to downsize a bit. Maybe let some of my employees go. I may not be able to hire a new chef to replace the two I lost. Something. I'll sort it out when I get home."

"The building mortgage?" Llewellyn reminded her.

"Yes. I wish my grandmother hadn't taken out a second mortgage to help pay for my mom's cancer treatment. If I had known about it, I would have told her to sell her own house. Twelve years later, I'm still trying not to lose this building."

"I'm sorry."

"It's killing me. My restaurant is in the historic district, which is one of the most expensive places in Savannah, as you know. My building is worth quite a bit if sold today. Two doors down, they sold theirs for a million dollars, and two blocks away, for seven hundred thousand."

Piper wondered if she could have done something differently, but her grandmother had left her with the mortgage when she willed the restaurant to her. "I would like to save my restaurant, if at all possible."

"Maybe you need investors. Partners," Llewellyn signed. "You need an infusion of cash to keep the restaurant running."

"I don't know about partners." Once upon a time, the only person Piper had wanted to share a business with was...

No. Banish the thought.

CHAPTER TWENTY-NINE

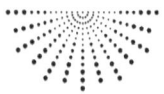

*P*iper had been gone for at least fourteen hours.

Isaac tried not to count the minutes. He tried to focus on the breakfast he was making. It was a custom order for banana pancakes with macadamia nuts and Nutella.

Piper needs to stop these custom menu items!

Isaac wondered how costly in time and money all these custom dishes were. If Piper could cut her costs, streamline her menu, put fewer items on it, she might not need so many chefs and cooks running around in the kitchen.

This wasn't even a five-star restaurant. This was a mom-and-pop family restaurant that had been around for decades and decades.

Nelson told him that, over the years, Piper's

Place had been called a café, a coffee shop, and a restaurant.

Isaac had no idea why it had so many descriptions, but now he did.

The restaurant was all things to all people.

It was a pancake place to the breakfast customers. It was an icecream shop to tourists just passing through. It was a bakery for people ordering cakes or who knew about its famed cupcakes.

It was also a lunch place for working people in town, or tourists grabbing a bite before they went on the next tour stop. It was a dinner place for big events and family gatherings.

And then it was the "best place ever" for night owls looking for small dishes and munchies as they came in at various times of the night.

It was, like he said, all things to all people.

Isaac could not even begin to tell Piper what to do, and he didn't want to. However, the thought of two truckloads of leftover food leaving the loading dock every Wednesday and Friday made him wonder if he should at least talk to Nelson about it.

Isaac plated the breakfast dish, but there was no time to look for Nelson.

It was Thursday morning—almost Friday, it felt like.

Isaac might be paid, but he was nothing more

than a guest chef in the kitchen. Five more working days, and he'd be gone.

He didn't know whether he would look forward to spending a whole month testing out various menus for the upcoming cooking competition. He was getting excited about it though, starting with his mom's scallops.

She was right.

She could cook.

Then again, she had been cooking for their family of five since the kids were little, and for their friends from school if they dropped in to do homework with the Untermeyer kids. Even though Mom hadn't gone to culinary school, she cooked by instinct.

And she was a retired photographer who had picked up a new trade: food photography. Although Isaac hadn't seen her take photographs lately, he had seen Mom's Instagram posts.

I guess I could let her come with me to Nassau. Give her something to do.

The rest of the morning went like a blur, as fast as the kitchen was busy.

"Any word from Piper?" Isaac said to Bao as the latter walked by, carrying a canister of flour.

Bao shook his head. "We all want to know what's going to happen next. Waiting for Nelson to brief us."

Isaac almost forgot that Piper had left her employees in the dark about her financial troubles. It had been one week and a day since her cousin stole from her.

When is she going to tell them?

Better not let them hear it from someone else.

They had to hear about the state of the restaurant directly from her.

Isaac felt that he had to hear from her too.

So why don't I text her?

Because he didn't want to bother her.

Truly, the best thing he could do was to pray for her.

And that was what he did.

CHAPTER THIRTY

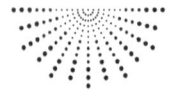

*B*arely alive, Regis Peyton finally awoke from surgery sometime late afternoon that same Thursday.

The hospital had texted Piper to let her know when he woke up. When she reached for her phone on the dresser next to her hotel room bed, Piper realized she had slept for nine hours, from seven in the morning to four in the afternoon.

Llewellyn was in another room down the hallway, and he hadn't texted her or anything. He probably knew she had to sleep.

She texted him. Woke him up right quick. Within five minutes, Llewellyn was knocking on her hotel room door, ready to drive her back to the hospital down the road.

It would take about ten minutes to get there.

Not enough time for Piper to pray long prayers for her cousin.

Does he want to see me?

Does he know I know he stole my money?

Piper prayed for wisdom and discernment to deal with the situation. However, by the time she reached Regis's hospital room that he shared with one other patient, Piper still didn't know how she was supposed to handle this.

Regis was all bandaged up. Wherever there was no bandage, there was bruising. His one non-bandaged eye registered shock when Piper walked in.

His mouth couldn't open. Both of his arms were in casts. In fact, he couldn't move much. Only his one eye moved.

"I guess we'll sit here for a while," Piper signed to Llewellyn.

"You want coffee? I'll go get coffee."

"Could you also text Nelson and Heidi back at home to keep praying?"

Llewellyn nodded.

After Llewellyn left, Piper wasn't sure what else to do but pray and try to talk to Regis. His one good eye was still following her around as she moved a chair closer to his bedside.

"I forgive you," Piper signed.

A tear fell from Regis's eye.

"When I trusted Jesus as my personal Lord and Savior some ten years ago, God forgave me of all my sins. I cannot withhold forgiveness from you."

He nodded a little bit, as if he knew where Piper was going.

For many years, Piper had tried to talk to Regis about God, Jesus, and the Bible. Each time, he not only didn't listen to anything she had to say, but he also mocked God, making some silly jokes about being his own deity.

Looks like he can't save himself now.

"Romans 4:7 says, 'Blessed are those whose lawless deeds are forgiven, and whose sins are covered.' Do you know how your sins can be forgiven?" Piper signed.

Regis shook his head slightly.

"Ephesians 1:7 tells us how. 'In Him we have redemption through His blood, the forgiveness of sins, according to the riches of His grace.' The blood of Jesus Christ at the cross covered us. In Jesus, we have redemption and forgiveness."

Regis's one eye closed. He wasn't looking at Piper any more.

He is not ready.

Piper felt sad.

We don't know if he will still die, though.

If Regis died in his sins, there would be no hope

for him, according to the Bible. Piper recalled Hebrews 9:27.

And as it is appointed for men to die once, but after this the judgment...

Piper reached for Regis's hand nearest her, but it was in a cast. He wouldn't feel her holding it.

Regis's eye opened again.

Maybe he was surprised that she was still there.

"Believe in the Lord Jesus and you will be saved," Piper signed as fast as she could, just in case her cousin closed his eye again.

He didn't move, but that one eye of his, watery just minutes ago, now steeled.

It looked pretty scary to Piper.

She decided she better stop talking about getting saved in Christ. She didn't know whether Regis understood all that she just said to him, but clearly he wanted her to stop talking.

Piper felt bad that she had taken the opportunity to preach to her cousin. She had taken advantage of his attention. At the same time, she couldn't be sure if they would have future opportunities.

The nurse had told her that it would be a while before Regis would leave the hospital.

Speaking of whom, she appeared in front of Piper now, asking her to leave so that Regis could get some rest. Or at least that was what her lips said.

Piper nodded.

She tried to meet Regis's single eye, but he refused to look at her.

Piper walked out of the hospital room, praying more for Regis's soul than for his body.

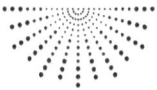

CHAPTER THIRTY-ONE

"Give me something to do," Isaac said into the camera in their private conversation. He was sitting on a rocker on Mom's back porch shortly after dinnertime, getting bitten by mosquitoes as he rocked back and forth.

Inside the house, Mom and Jerome were watching a show on television, and laughing loudly.

In retrospect, Isaac should have gone to his bedroom to check his messages, but the porch was closer to the kitchen table, where they had been having a lasagna dinner that Mom cooked.

On his phone, he could see that the app transcriber had correctly transcribed every word he said. On the screen, Piper seemed to be typing something back to him. Isaac waited until her message appeared.

PIPER

Regis is awake, but he can't speak.

ISAAC

Thank God he's not dead.

PIPER

I mentioned salvation in Christ this afternoon.

ISAAC

Praise the Lord.

PIPER

Regis looked positively angry that I did.

ISAAC

So sorry to hear that.

PIPER

He has never wanted to hear about it, but he was stuck in that bed. I took advantage of the situation. Now I feel bad.

ISAAC

You know the verse. God's Word never returns void.

Isaac looked up the verse, just to remember the exact words from Isaiah 55:11.

So shall My word be that goes forth from My mouth;

It shall not return to Me void,

But it shall accomplish what I please,
And it shall prosper in the thing for which I
sent it.

From what Piper had said, he gathered that Regis was not a Christian believer. Isaac didn't know much about Regis's background. He had been too busy cooking in Piper's kitchen to ask about crooked cousins.

Isaac wondered sometimes about his own biological family—where they lived, what kind of people they were, whether they were upright citizens or criminals.

His own biological mother had passed away before he was shuttled through the foster care system, until the Untermeyers adopted him at age four. They had doted on him like he was the best son ever, before they had two more children of their own.

The Untermeyers were his family now.

Someday, he might look into his biological family, but not at the moment.

At this very moment, he wanted to know when Piper would be back in town. He missed her somewhat.

PIPER

I don't know. I think Friday.
Llewellyn has to make up for lost
time at work.

ISAAC

What about your cousin?

PIPER

He's going to be hospitalized for a
while. More surgeries next week.

ISAAC

Okay.

PIPER

I don't know what happened to
my money. I called Detective
Zimmerman, and he said the
matter was under investigation.

ISAAC

What about the Atlantic City
police?

PIPER

They told me that as soon as
Regis is able, they will get a
statement from him. They told me
to go home and wait.

ISAAC

So come home.

Piper's face looked weary on screen. She didn't
have any makeup on to hide the puffiness under her
eyes. Isaac didn't say a word about how she looked,

but she really needed to take a few days off from work.

But she probably won't.

Isaac's last day at Piper's Place was the next Wednesday. Piper had to find another chef or reorganize her kitchen. Even if they recovered Piper's money, it sounded like it had been used for nefarious activities in Atlantic City. He wondered how long it would take for them to return the money to Piper.

He made a mental note to talk to Jerome to ask him if he knew anyone who might be able to find out what went on, and if there was any way Piper would get her money back as soon as possible.

Three hundred thousand dollars was a lot of money to lose.

Isaac could still hear the television inside the house. That meant either both Mom and Jerome were up, or it was only Jerome. He usually went to bed later than Mom.

> Isaac: I'll ask Jerome if he can help us in any way.

Piper: I can't pay him.

> Isaac: Just any information he can find, not an investigation. Maybe he could email or call someone who might have connections.

Piper: Okay. Jerome did help Iris
La Salle look for her missing sister
a few years ago.

Isaac: I heard. Mom likes to talk
about how heroic Jerome is.

Piper: My real estate agent's
husband is a PI. I know I can
ask him.

Isaac: Jerome is not a PI.

Piper: I don't know if a real PI can
help me.

Isaac: He can tell you if there's
nothing he can do. On the other
hand, he might also be able to tell
you more than Detective
Zimmerman is willing to do.

On screen, Piper's face brightened. Isaac was glad he had given her some ideas on what to do. Instead of waiting at the hospital or hotel room for Regis to get better, Piper could email or text a few people and then come home.

Piper: I can't stay here much
longer. Regis is in no position to
talk or sign. He's all wrapped up
from head to toe, pretty much.

Isaac: Sounds bad.

Piper: Yeah. They have hospital
security guards come and go. I
wonder what Regis did.

> Isaac: Better not wonder. It might
> lead to worry, you know? Best to
> get out of the way and let the
> police do their job.

Piper: Agreed.

Isaac couldn't hear the television anymore, so he said a quick goodbye to Piper, saying that he wanted to catch Jerome before he went to bed. Sure enough, when he went inside, Jerome was walking toward the stairs.

"How's your girlfriend doing?" A sly smile flashed on Jerome's face.

"She's not my girlfriend." Isaac locked the back-door behind him.

"But you know who I'm talking about." Jerome laughed.

Isaac didn't take the bait. "Do you have a minute?"

"A quick minute. It's almost past my bedtime. Got a problem?"

"Just super quick."

"Piper's cousin went to Atlantic City and got beaten up badly. He's in the hospital. We just want to know what's going on, but the police won't say," Isaac explained.

"They don't know? Or they won't say?"

Isaac shrugged. "There's more to it than that, but her cousin stole money from some people."

Jerome didn't look surprised. "Has Piper talked to Ming Wei?"

"The PI. She mentioned she would."

"He's her best bet," Jerome added. "The police usually won't talk much if an investigation is still underway."

"Understandable."

"If Piper really wants to find out what's going on, she could pay a PI to help her. If they don't find anything, at least she tried, you know?"

CHAPTER THIRTY-TWO

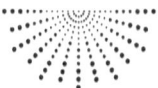

hen Piper returned to the hospital with Llewellyn the next morning to tell her cousin that she was going home to Savannah, she was surprised to find a pregnant woman standing outside the hospital room door.

"He doesn't want to see you." Her smoky eyeshadow looked smeared, like she had been crying. On her chest, just above her low-cut long-sleeved blouse, was some sort of multicolored tattoo that looked like a pendant hanging in midair.

"How did you know he doesn't want to see us?" Llewellyn asked.

"He shook his head as much as he could when I asked him if we should let you back in to see him."

"Who are you?" Piper signed.

Llewellyn interpreted when it was obvious the woman didn't understand ASL.

"The mother of Regis's child." The woman rubbed her belly. Then her eyes flared. "Like I said, he doesn't want to see you."

"He told you that?" Piper signed.

The woman waited for Llewellyn to interpret.

"I know who you are," she continued. "Regis told me he borrowed some money from you, but he said he will pay you back."

Piper tried not to react visibly. Where was Regis going to find three hundred thousand dollars to pay her back?

"Regis emptied out my bank account. I have to sell my house. My restaurant is in trouble." Piper steeled herself so that her hands didn't tremble when she signed the reply. She also slowed down a little bit for Llewellyn's sake, since he was not a professional interpreter.

The woman's shoulder sagged. "He did it for me. For us."

"You don't steal other people's money," Piper signed. "Now my restaurant might go out of business and my employees won't get their Christmas bonuses this year."

"I told you he was going to pay you back."

"How? Three hundred thousand is a lot of money that I worked very hard to earn."

The woman appeared shocked when Llewellyn explained in English what Piper just signed. "What? He told me he only borrowed a hundred thousand from you."

Oh dear. Where's the other two hundred thousand?

"Regis gave half of the hundred to someone he owes money to, and he said he could double the rest before he paid off the other half."

"Where? At the casino?" Piper felt like she had to sit down.

She hadn't expected Regis to have such pipe dreams. While she had no comments on professions related to gambling, it was a risk. She hadn't known Regis to be such a risk taker. He drove an old beat-up Oldsmobile, he rented a small apartment at the edge of town, and he managed other people's money.

Piper wondered if she hadn't paid Regis enough to be her financial manager. But how much more could she have paid him?

"We're going to have a baby." Tears flowed. "We're going to be a family. We need a house, a car, things for the baby."

Piper shook her head. "You earn your own money to support your own family. You don't take other people's money. They work hard, they get to keep their own money."

"It wasn't enough."

"Many parents earn their own incomes. They don't steal." Piper tried to steer the conversation back to Regis.

Then again, what was the point? The girlfriend didn't seem to know much. Piper had to talk to Regis again, not to her. "Regis is in very big trouble with the law."

The woman began to weep.

Piper prayed for grace to deal with the situation.

Calmly, she signed, "What is your name? I don't think you told us your name."

"Nissa." She didn't give her last name.

"How can we contact you?"

"I told you I don't know much about anything else. Regis tells me what he wants me to know and I take his word for it. I trust him."

"I trusted him too," Piper signed.

Poor Regis.

From what little she gathered from this woman, Piper deduced that Regis had used part of her money to pay off a gambling debt, and lost part of or the rest of it at the casino. Or something.

Somehow in the middle of it all, Regis ended up in a shootout between the mob and the police. What was Regis doing in the middle of a sting operation? Did Regis owe money? Or did he work for the criminals?

"Have you talked to the police?" Piper asked.

Nissa nodded. "I told them everything."

Yes, but did you tell them the truth?

People could say anything they wanted, but the truth might or might not be there. Piper didn't know this woman from Eve. Who was to say that Nissa wasn't lying?

Piper decided that she would let Detective Zimmerman know about this encounter, even though Piper was confident he already knew about her from the Atlantic City Police Department.

Piper felt sorry for her cousin and this woman and their baby.

What a mess.

CHAPTER THIRTY-THREE

*I*saac was so overjoyed to see Piper at church on Sunday morning that he decided to sit at her ASL table, regardless of what Mom or anyone else might say. As he pushed the chair closer to the table, he glanced over to his family's table, and found Mom grinning like a schoolgirl.

He didn't know what to make of that.

All he knew right now was that Piper was home again, and it made him very happy.

He even felt grateful to Llewellyn for accompanying Piper to and from New Jersey, driving her around, and interpreting for her at the hospital.

About that, Isaac had thought that Llewellyn was deaf too, since the latter hadn't talked to Isaac much. However, when Isaac picked them up from the airport on Friday evening, Isaac found out that Llewellyn was only hearing impaired.

On the other hand, Piper Peyton had been deaf since birth. Isaac wondered what it was like for her to never have heard a spoken word in her entire life.

And yet she could read lips. How hard was it for her to learn to read lips when she could not hear anything?

As Isaac sat there, he realized no one was talking to him. Piper's friends were signing to one another and to Piper and Llewellyn.

Maybe I should go back to Mom's table.

Then he heard a cello playing a hymn medley. He was watching the string quartet, when he saw Heidi walking towards their table, her Bible in hand and a surprised look on her face.

"Isaac." Heidi put down her Bible at an empty seat closer to the piano and lectern. "Learning ASL?"

Isaac nodded.

Am I learning ASL?

Should I?

He looked around the table. The five people were all signing animatedly. Every now and then a couple would glance over at Piper with some sort of mischievous grinning.

And they kept repeating the same gestures.

They'd hold up their pinkies with one hand, and tap their shoulders with the other hand.

What on earth?

Isaac glanced at the time on his phone as he sent a quick text to Piper, sitting next to him. He described what he saw them do.

She opened her purse to retrieve her phone. She seemed to hesitate. Without looking at him, she replied.

> **PIPER**
>
> I gave you an ASL name, or a name sign.

> **ISAAC**
>
> Oh. Like a nickname.

> **PIPER**
>
> Well, you can't come up with it on your own. One of us has to give it to you.

> **ISAAC**
>
> You did.

> **PIPER**
>
> Yes, I did, so that we don't have to finger spell your name every single time.

> **ISAAC**
>
> We who?

> **PIPER**
>
> My friends and I.

> **ISAAC**
>
> You talk about me to your friends?

PIPER

Don't you talk to your friends
about me?

> **ISAAC**
>
> Most of my friends are overseas.
> Different time zones.

PIPER

In other words, you don't have
many friends.

> **ISAAC**
>
> Guilty as charged. So what is my
> ASL name?

PIPER

The pinky stands for the letter i,
which is your initial. You know
what the rest is.

Piper lifted a hand and put her fingertips on her shoulder.

At first, Isaac tried to read too much into it. And then it dawned on him.

Shoulder.

"You call me Shoulder?" Isaac spoke as clearly as he could.

Piper nodded.

Isaac felt embarrassed. He had thought that was only between him and Piper.

When did Piper name him? Had it been after

that Monday evening, when he had let Piper lean on his shoulder on the third floor of her restaurant?

Or had she named him sooner?

Like sometime after high school...

"So they know about our high school spat?" Isaac said.

Piper nodded.

"Whose side did they take?"

Piper blushed.

"Tell me." Isaac waited.

Piper balled up her fists, and then crossed them gently over her chest.

Isaac didn't know what that meant.

Was that a hug or what?

Are her friends on the side of hugs? What does that mean?

But there was no time to ask. The quartet stopped playing, and the church service started.

CHAPTER THIRTY-FOUR

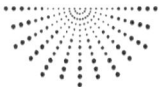

*A*fter church, Isaac did not go to lunch with Mom, Jerome, Amy, and Cyrus. Instead, he spent two hours in the grocery store, picking up an entire cart of ingredients for his test menu.

He might have overdone it, he thought, as he hauled five giant tote bags of groceries—plus a backpack filled with kitchen gear, including his favorite knives—all the way from the pickup truck, across the waterfront, up the ramp, into the riverboat, through the dining room where Riverside Chapel held services hours before, and into the empty galley.

He put his bags down on the countertop in the galley, and looked around. After church today, Heidi had shown him where the walk-in freezer was. Other than the occasional catered, custom, or wedding cruises, this particular riverboat had been for the sole use of Riverside Chapel.

But why, though?

This was a fairly large galley kitchen, with top-of-the-line stainless steel equipment everywhere, and Jerome had offered it all to the Lord, like Mary offered her jar of alabaster oil to the Lord in Luke 7:37-38.

> *And behold, a woman in the city who was a sinner, when she knew that Jesus sat at the table in the Pharisee's house, brought an alabaster flask of fragrant oil, and stood at His feet behind Him weeping; and she began to wash His feet with her tears, and wiped them with the hair of her head; and she kissed His feet and anointed them with the fragrant oil.*

Mom had said that one year after Jerome was saved, he offered up one of his two riverboats to be used by Riverside Chapel for its church services on Sunday mornings and nights, and Bible studies on Wednesday nights. At that time, Riverside only had maybe twenty to thirty members, but today, it had four hundred members, with overflow seating on two decks.

Eventually, the church would outgrow the riverboat and move back on land.

What intrigued Isaac though, was what compelled Jerome to cut his own income in half? And why was he still lacking nothing, or seemingly lacking nothing?

A few years prior, Riverside had started contributing to the utilities and upkeep of the riverboat, but other than that, the boat was no longer used in Jerome's business full time on weekends.

That was to say, Jerome footed most, if not all, of the expenses of hosting Riverside Chapel on his riverboat.

Weekends were probably his most lucrative business time of the week. Mom said that God had multiplied Jerome's business on the other riverboat, where he was still master captain.

Nonetheless, the years had worn out Jerome, and in his late seventies now, he wanted to retire with Mom and travel some. That might have been Mom bugging him to take a world cruise, tour Europe, and visit all the other places she had only heard about from both Amy and Isaac.

In the last couple of years, Jerome wanted to sell the business to his oldest daughter, who operated a tour company and travel agency in town, and Tamsyn was considering it. It would consolidate the family business under one roof, but Tamsyn wasn't sure she wanted to operate a riverboat.

In fact, Tamsyn had suggested that maybe her younger sister would rather handle the riverboat operations, since the latter had practically grown up on the river.

Isaac remembered that bit of information because Jerome's youngest daughter was adopted.

As was I.

Not only did Mom take in Isaac when he was a child as though he had always been hers, now Jerome also considered Isaac as his own son. While it was nice to have doting family, sometimes he felt that Mom and Jerome were smothering.

Or are they?

Isaac plopped his groceries on the countertop. If his fellow chef Clarence hadn't decided to take a better offer working for a restaurant in Tokyo rather than fly with him to the Bahamas to attempt to win a long-shot cooking competition, he wouldn't be alone in this endeavor.

He couldn't afford to hire anyone else, pay for their two-week stay in Nassau, and then fly them back to wherever they came from.

Piper was right. Isaac didn't have many local friends to call on when he needed help.

All he had were his Mom and sister, primarily. Amy hardly cooked.

Smothering or not, Mom had come to his rescue.

As Isaac was putting away the perishables in a nearby refrigerator, he heard steps and laughter coming down the hallway outside the galley.

"There you are." Mom entered the galley wearing clogs, but she was still dressed up in her church outfit from this morning.

Isaac hoped she wouldn't spill any oily food on that pretty wool blouse.

He had told Mom to bring a change of clothes, but it looked like she hadn't done it. Isaac himself had changed into jeans and sweatshirt after church, before he went to the grocery store.

Jerome waved to Isaac. "I would offer to help, but I'm going home to take a nap."

"I wish I could too." Isaac laughed.

Jerome kissed Mom on the cheek. "See you when you two get home."

To Isaac, Jerome had a reminder. "Don't lose my master key."

"Yes, sir." To be sure, Isaac checked his jeans pocket.

"We'll be bringing home a lot of experimental dishes," Mom said. "Don't snack too much between now and dinnertime."

Experimental dishes?

Isaac wasn't sure what to think about what Mom just said.

Still, he was glad she stepped in when he needed her most. He only prayed that she could deliver as her assistant cook in Nassau—when it mattered most.

"Thanks, Mom, for helping me out." Isaac hugged her.

"Glad to help. Where do I put my purse?" She looked around.

So did Isaac. He saw a distant unused counter by the wall. "How about there? If we can see it, we won't forget it."

"Good idea." Mom dug through her purse and found a stack of paper. She returned to Isaac, and handed him a pen. "Sign here."

Isaac's eyes widened. "What's this?"

"It's to absolve me from any blame should you lose the cooking competition," Mom said. "In life, we don't always win the contests we compete in, as you well know from high school—"

"Mom, high school was forever ago."

"I thought it was still fresh in your mind."

"It was for years, but I got over it."

Mom tilted her head. "You did? You and Piper forgave each other?"

Hmm. Isaac still hadn't heard Piper say she

forgave him, but as sure as day, he had asked for her forgiveness.

"We're working that out. Don't worry about it." Isaac thumbed through the paper. "This is three pages long. Did a lawyer write this up for you?"

"One of the Super Seniors is a retired lawyer, yes. Please sign."

Isaac paused. "I'm thinking I should read it first."

"Of course. I'm going to the ladies room while you do. Make sure to initial the part where you agree to let me see your future kids no matter what the outcome of the cooking competition."

"Mom!"

"Just to be sure."

"I'm not even married. Where am I going to find kids?"

"*Future* kids. Read it." Mom pointed as she backed away out the door. "I'll be right back."

Isaac sighed.

Did I make a big mistake letting Mom help?

CHAPTER THIRTY-FIVE

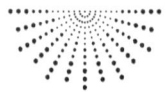

*N*o more than a minute after they discussed Isaac's menu and started the ninety-minute countdown, Mom wanted to chat. "How's Piper?"

Isaac was prepping the blender to make some of his own Southeast Asian curry paste. He should use a mortar and pestle, but he was in a hurry.

"I don't know, Mom." He dropped in some curry leaves he had plucked off the stem.

"The restaurant is hanging in there, I suppose." Mom was peeling garlic.

"I have no idea. I'm only the temporary chef."

However, in the week he had been in Piper's restaurant, he could see needed improvements already. She had too many items on the menu. Too many custom orders. The pantry and freezer were overstuffed. Piper's trips to the homeless shelter twice a week attested to the wasted food.

Wasted food?

Not wasted in ministry, of course—but if Piper were able to save more money by spending less, she could end up donating directly to charity.

But nobody asked me.

"This Wednesday is my last day at Piper's Place," Isaac added for good measure.

"She didn't ask you to stay on, at least until after Christmas?" Mom was still peeling garlic.

"Mom, I don't need the cloves whole. Just smash them like you taught me."

"Oh. I thought you wanted them whole." Mom lined up her garlic cloves on the chopping board and used the broad side of the knife to flatten them.

While the curry paste sat in a bowl, Isaac peeled the bag of shrimp and deveined them.

"You know that Piper likes shrimp?" Mom said.

"She did in high school. Maybe she still does. I don't know." Isaac checked the clock. "After you chop up the garlic, you need to be doing the next thing I put on your list, Mom. Check the clock."

At this rate, they'd never finish one dish, let alone five.

At least two of them were cold dishes that didn't need much work except plating. Even as Isaac thought about it, he had a feeling it wasn't enough. A simple salad was not going to win him fifty thousand dollars.

I don't want to settle for second place.

They had made it unpalatable with only a five-thousand-dollar prize for second place.

No, I must win first place.

"How's her cousin?" Mom asked.

"Who?" Isaac rinsed off the shrimp, double-checking to make sure they were clean.

"Piper's cousin."

"He's in bad shape, apparently, and will be in the hospital for a while." Isaac could feel sorry for Regis, all beaten up, but he felt sorrier for Piper, on the verge of losing her restaurant if her revenues didn't make up for the loss.

She's already losing her house.

Nelson hadn't said how much was at stake, but from what he gathered, it must be quite substantial.

"He'd better return the three hundred thousand dollars," Mom said.

What?

Isaac nearly dropped the colander of shrimp. "That much?"

"You didn't know?" Mom cleared the board and began to chop up some onions.

"Like I said, I only cook there. I don't manage the place."

"Right. Then how come I heard you tried to get a Christmas tree past Piper?"

"Who told you that?"

"A little bird."

"You mean a little rat?" Isaac wondered who, but he knew Mom rarely revealed her sources.

Isaac looked at the rest of the vegetables on the counter that he had assigned Mom to cut and cube and chop for him. She had just finished working on the garlic and onion.

Two down, ten more vegetables to go.

Mom was so slow that he was about to fire her, but he knew he couldn't. Who else would agree to pay their own plane ticket to Nassau with him, and even offered to pay for their villa so that she could have a "luxurious vacation," as she had put it?

We're not going on vacation, Mom!

One week later, he hired Mom and picked up the rest of the free offer.

He should've found someone else to be his sous chef.

But who?

Isaac rinsed, skinned, and deboned a red snapper next.

"So that's how you do it, huh?" Mom leaned over, watching him. "Make sure you don't leave any bones in it."

"Check the clock," Isaac said. "What are you supposed to do next?"

"Chop the rest of the herbs and vegetables." Mom waddled back to her station. "When you were young, you didn't like any vegetables. You hated kale."

"*Hate* is a strong word." Isaac put some salt and pepper on his snapper filets. *Keep it simple.*

"Well, you refused to eat them." Mom rinsed out parsley and chives. "In fact, you also hated spinach, until you sat next to the girl who loved it."

"That was in middle school. A long time ago. Why did you bring it up?" Isaac asked. "I like spinach and kale now. I like all vegetables. It's the way they're cooked that makes the difference."

"I'm glad to hear you like them, though it's funny how a girl can change things. Did that middle schooler have a crush on you?"

"I don't remember, and I don't care." *I don't want to hear any more of this.*

"Four years later, another girl also had a crush on you. This one you still know."

Who do I still know?

The realization struck Isaac like a saucepan.

No way.

"It was a secret crush, and Nelson said—oops." Mom's palms flew to her mouth.

It's Piper.

Isaac stared at Mom. "Nelson said what? Maybe he said not to tell me?"

I can't believe it.

Piper Peyton had a crush on me.

"I thought you knew." Mom backed away slowly.

"No, I didn't. I was too busy being upset about the cooking contest."

"You were like a little bulldog." Mom laughed. "Once you bit into something, you wouldn't let go."

Twenty years.

Isaac sighed. There was nothing he could do now.

Twenty years of wasted time being angry at something I should have let go.

Then again, at least we cleared it up last week so we could both move on to more important things.

At the stove, he heated a frying pan with olive oil, and sautéed the shrimp.

Mom came over with her chopped onion and garlic. The onion was supposed to be cubed, but it was in all shapes and sizes, like a crazy quilt.

There was nothing Isaac could do about it.

To be fair to Mom, she hadn't gone to culinary school. She had only cooked at home. That was not to say she wasn't a good cook. In fact, Mom could make a home-cooked meal that even the best chefs would love. However, it would take her forever to prepare it.

Forever is time we don't have.

They had ninety minutes and three dishes for the preliminary round, and if they made it past that, they would keep going all the way to first place.

Lord Jesus, I don't want to be just placed. I don't want a participation certificate. I have to show...to show...

As he stirred garlic and onion into the shrimp, he realized that he had it all wrong.

God already knew everything about him—his thoughts, feelings, concerns, desires, goals, plans, wishes.

God knew if he would make it in life, whether his career would lead him to restaurant ownership or to happy trails in a food truck or to naught.

God knew it all.

And yet I want to win that cooking competition. I need to show that I can do this.

As he stirred in his own mix of curry paste into the shrimp dish, the strong smell of curry assaulted his nose. He turned down the heat.

"That smells good," Mom said. "You should let Piper taste it."

Isaac was surprised Mom was still standing

there. "Are you watching me cook? What about the vegetables I asked you to cut up?"

"I'll get to them in a minute. Can I taste this?" Mom asked.

"We don't have a minute, Mom." Isaac counted to ten. "The cooking competition is brutal. It's not a place where we can walk around and sample food."

"What are you saying? That I need to lose weight?"

"I didn't say any of that." Isaac covered the pan of shrimp curry. "We forgot to cook the rice."

Mom chuckled. "See, even you forgot."

She walked around, looking for something. "Where are the plates?"

"Near the fridge, I think? The cabinets against the wall." Isaac was glad he had a tour of the galley today, although he could not remember where some of the things were.

Mom brought two plates. Isaac plated them with his shrimp dish as Mom took photos.

"I know we're supposed to eat this with rice, and I've got a couple of options in mind, but today's plan for the shrimp was to test my new curry paste that I mixed together using ingredients normally found in Southeast Asian dishes."

Mom held up her hand, the one with a fork in it.

"Yes, Mom?"

"Can you save the speech for later? Say a blessing so we can taste this delicious-looking shrimp."

They prayed to ask God to bless the food.

Standing there at the counter, Mom was eating and grading the food. "Is it too spicy? I can't tell."

"I don't know, either," Isaac replied.

"Slow heat. That's why. Oooh. It's hitting me." Mom fanned her mouth, but she ate more shrimp, anyway. "It's delicious."

"Thank you."

"You should put this on the menu."

"Of what?"

"Your future restaurant." Mom finished her entire plate, then eyed Isaac's shrimp.

He moved it slightly to the left, away from her. "I don't know if I will ever own a future restaurant."

"I'll invest in it. The money I have from the sale of my share of Christmastown two years ago is still sitting in the bank."

"You didn't invest it in stocks or real estate or something?"

"I was afraid to lose it, so I put it in the bank."

She buried it in the ground, like the servant did in the parable in Matthew 25.

"Mom, I appreciate it, but I want to venture out on my own. If all I can afford is a food truck, then so be it." Isaac was surer now that a food truck was on the horizon for him. If he won fifty thousand dollars in the Bahamas, he could put that toward a new custom food truck.

"A food truck?" Mom made a face. "I don't invest in food trucks."

CHAPTER THIRTY-SIX

"*R*egis was trying to pay off some illegal gambling debts." Private investigator Ming Wei—also the husband of Piper's real estate agent—explained what he had found via his contacts at the federal level, as he ate the free sandwich Piper had made him.

Piper paced the floor between the two sets of sitting areas, trying to figure out what to do.

"Working for some unsavory people was how he was trying to make up for what he couldn't pay in cash," Ming continued.

What have you gotten yourself into, Cousin?

At the table, Nelson watched Ming eat. "What exactly does *working* mean?"

"He became their courier, transferring funds

from city to city across the country, and sometimes overseas."

Piper stopped in her tracks. She didn't quite catch the last thing Ming said. Nelson signed it out for her.

"Somehow he was in Atlantic City last week, when ICE agents showed up," Piper signed.

That would tie in with what Detective Zimmerman had told her last Thursday.

"Exactly," Ming said for Nelson to translate. "As for his girlfriend, she's not charged with anything."

"My money?" Piper signed. "His girlfriend said it's gone. I don't know whether to believe her."

"ICE is sorting it all out. They'll probably let Zimmerman know how much is left, and he'll let you know."

Piper sat down. "Sounds like a long process."

Nelson spoke as he signed. "How many months is it going to take to see how much money Regis could return to Piper?"

"We have bills and salaries to pay, and it's already five days into December," Piper signed. "As you know, my house is on the market, but I don't know when it will sell, considering it's Christmastime and all."

"Regis is now a government witness. He has no other choice other than helping ICE if he wants to see his sentence reduced." Ming looked at both of them.

"Sentence? He's going to jail." Piper thanked God that both of Regis's parents were deceased. If they lived on earth and found out their only son was going to prison, it would surely break their hearts. And Grandma's, too.

"Also, the IRS might be involved due to his unpaid taxes." Ming wiped his lips. "That was a good sandwich. I must let Sabine know to ask for it when she comes here."

"Thank you," Nelson said on behalf of Piper.

"I know you insisted you didn't need to be paid to make a few phone calls, but we're not beggars," Piper signed.

After Nelson interpreted for her, Ming shook his head. "No, no. This restaurant is a favorite of many, including Riverside Chapel members. I pray you will get back on your feet ASAP."

Why couldn't Regis have been less ambitious?

Then again, people could be as ambitious as they wanted in this free country—with their own money and not with stolen cash.

I may never get my funds back, not even some of it. I'll have to prepare for that eventuality.

So help me, God.

Piper slumped in the seat.

"You might want to find other means of

funding the restaurant, at least until the investigation is completed and they return your savings—or what's left of it—to you. Do you have investors you can call?"

~

It was way past time for Piper to explain to her employees what happened to her. She would have to repeat herself three times at the three different shifts, but so be it.

At 4:15 p.m., the breakfast and lunch crew arrived on the third floor, where Piper had prayed about what she would say and prepared for possible questions.

"I want to keep this meeting short so that you can go home. I have to repeat this three times for three shifts, so bear with me," Piper signed and Nelson interpreted for those who didn't understand ASL. "I'm asking you to hold your questions until the end of my statement. Unless it's urgent and you need an answer right now, I suggest you email me your questions so that I can compile all the answers for everyone."

Many people nodded.

"By emailing me, you can be more specific about your questions. If you don't want your Q&A broadcast to everyone else, I suggest you clearly mark that your question is confidential. I will try to answer directly to only you in such cases."

Piper cleared her throat. She looked at Nelson. He nodded, signaling he was going to speak aloud what she signed as she went along, so she didn't have to wait for him to catch up. They had discussed this earlier.

Lord Jesus, please give me strength.

And grace to deal with this.

"As you might have noticed, we have temporarily closed off this entire floor since Thanksgiving day," Piper began. "Having lost a lunch chef and a dinner chef, we don't have the wherewithal to handle more than two floors of customers, until we find their replacement. We can only afford to hire one new chef at this time."

Piper looked around the room.

The elevator door opened, and more people poured in. Normally, she would have noted who came in late, but today, she gave them a reprieve.

At the back of the tardy ones, Isaac appeared. He nodded at her, as if it would make it all better. He was still late, by her watch, but Wednesday would be his last day here, so it mattered not.

"With Chef Lillian back at work but taking the dinner shift, I left myself on the night shift," Piper signed. "For the last two weeks, God sent a miracle, and Nelson found us a temporary chef who helped us keep Piper's Place going in spite of the chaos."

She hadn't begun to explain the chaos yet.

"Unfortunately for us, Chef Isaac's last day is Wednesday, and he's moving on to his other plans. He was only passing through Savannah, and I, for one, am glad he stopped by Piper's Place." Piper pointed to Isaac. "Would you give Chef Isaac a hand as we say goodbye to him in less than twenty-four hours from now?"

Isaac looked touched by the appreciation. Piper couldn't hear what the crowd was shouting, but she could see their mouths open and close as they clapped. Some whistled, and then clapped again. They seemed happy and smiling and all that.

She glanced over at Nelson, who signed that it was very noisy in the room.

Piper used the time to catch her breath, and take another sip of water from her travel mug.

Nelson raised his arms, and they all turned back to look at Piper again.

"Some of you might have noticed that we started to interview new chefs. We will be inter-viewing more chefs as the weeks go by, but only one will be hired. We want a chef who will stay in town and not run off the day before Thanksgiving, you know. Elope another time."

Many laughed.

"I have to tell you the second bad news. The first one isn't too bad anymore, since we have a solution. Thank God. However, the second bad news is going to be bad for a while."

Everyone looked at Piper.

"My cousin, whom some of you know was my financial manager, has robbed me. In fact, I found out on the same day those two chefs eloped."

Everyone was staring at her now.

Nelson signed to her that there were murmurs.

"We have reported to the police. They have assigned a detective. I couldn't say anything because they were investigating." Piper looked around the room.

"Someone asked if you don't trust them," Nelson signed.

"I trust you, but I was shocked that it happened. Stunned. Tasered. I was praying—and still praying and hoping—that maybe Regis would return my money and all would be well again. But he's caught up in some bad activities and I have little hope I will see my money again." Piper paused.

"How are you going to pay us?" Nelson pointed to the person who spoke. Then he signed the question asked.

"I've cashed out some stocks to pay you, and if I

need to take out more from my investments, I will do so." She looked around the room. "And if you know anyone who wants to buy a hundred-year-old house with a big yard on Tybee Island, please let me know. That income will go into salaries and the daily operations of our restaurant."

"Someone asked how long it will last," Nelson signed.

"I can go as far as February or March on my stocks and house. I expect to sell my house by January or February." Piper thought she might as well tell them. "If I can't find funding, I will have no choice but to sell Piper's Place, but I will try to get assurance from the new owners, whoever they are, to let you keep your positions and salaries."

Piper caught Isaac's stare. He looked sad.

Why would he look sad?

It's not his restaurant. Not his house. Not his business.

Isaac was almost like a transient migrant worker. Savannah had been just a pit stop for him. He came, he helped, and now it was time for him to leave.

Piper was grateful that they had finally met again after all these years. They had explained to each other, and come to an understanding. He had asked forgiveness...

Piper looked over to where Isaac was still standing.

I forgive you, Isaac. I forgive you.

CHAPTER THIRTY-SEVEN

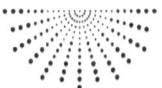

*W*hy did Jerome and Rhoda Pendegrast want to meet with her and Nelson this morning?

Piper had no idea, but with Mrs. Pendegrast, there was no telling what she was up to. They had called the meeting urgent, and asked Piper to give them half an hour, tops.

However, Piper had her third and final confessional meeting with her employees at 8:15 a.m. After having worked all night, she was loathe to have two meetings back to back—one bad and one unknown.

Yet, the Pendegrasts waited for her in the dining room, drinking their morning coffee, rich and decadent, and enjoying their eggs Benedict, cooked the way they wanted it.

It must be simply wonderful to be retired from a career-driven life, to go to bed and get up at decent hours or whenever they wanted, and to come and go during work hours as they pleased.

Piper vaguely remembered their small, intimate, private wedding the year before. It was a quick ceremony on Jerome's riverboat, officiated by an old captain friend of his, and the wedding party celebrated afterwards at Piper's Place.

She recalled that only Amy and Cyrus had been there. Mrs. Pendegrast's two sons were not at the wedding. Somehow, Mrs. Pendegrast was in such a hurry to marry that she went ahead and did it, even if her sons could not make it.

And now Mrs. Pendegrast had another idea that she didn't expect anyone to refuse.

After the employees left the 8:15 a.m. meeting on the third floor, Piper debated whether to meet the Pendegrasts there or in her office.

Well, her office was too near the kitchen, and Isaac was working today. He would most certainly see his mom and Jerome walk in or out of her office.

Did he know his mom and stepfather had asked to speak to her?

Whatever it was, let's get this over and done with.

Piper texted Nelson to take the Pendegrasts up to the third floor, and not let Isaac see them.

And then Piper spent the rest of the time praying by her favorite window, until the trio were standing by her table, waiting for instructions.

She took them to a circle of four armchairs overlooking River Street.

She didn't have to ask Nelson to sit next to Mrs. Pendegrast, both of them facing her. Nelson had worked for her for so long that he instinctively knew to face Piper so that he could interpret for her whatever Mrs. Pendegrast said.

Sadly, Piper also knew that Nelson was aware that Jerome was only there because he was with Mrs. Pendegrast. This was her show.

"I miss this view," Mrs. Pendegrast said.

Nelson interpreted, but Piper already read her lips.

"Mrs. Pendegrast and Jerome, to what do we owe the honor of your presence today?" Piper signed.

"Why are we here?" Nelson said.

Piper frowned. She read Nelson's lips, but she had expected her to interpret her exact words and meaning.

"I can understand what Piper signed—a little anyway," Mrs. Pendegrast said. "Piper, please call me Rhoda."

Rhoda?

Nobody called Mrs. Pendegrast Rhoda, not

even when she had been Mrs. Untermeyer. Everyone had called her husband Felix, but they dared not call her anything else but Mrs. Untermeyer. To this day, no one knew why they were formal with her.

She remembered Mrs. Pendegrast from high school, back when she was the scary Mrs. Untermeyer, when her first husband had been alive. She had not been the friendliest mother in school, and everyone had tried to avoid her, if at all possible.

Nobody wanted to have anything to do with her.

However, Mrs. Pendegrast had always been kind to Piper.

Always.

She had even tried to learn some ASL in order to communicate with Piper.

People might not see her kindness because Mrs. Pendegrast had a reputation for being needy and difficult—especially after Felix passed away. Piper imagined she must have been so lost without her first husband, who had been a steady anchor in their marriage and business partnership. The widow had been all alone, with her children studying in colleges as far away from Savannah as possible.

However, Mrs. Pendegrast had a soft spot for Piper. It was she who had insisted that the Super

Seniors group from church eat lunches or dinners at Piper's Place. Over the years, Piper had earned a lot of revenue from those retirees. All thanks to Mrs. Pendegrast here.

Rhoda.

That name was five letters to finger spell, fewer than Pendegrast.

Piper was sure she could never get used to calling her by her first name.

"Do you remember that I owned Christmastown with my husband?" Mrs. Pendegrast half-spoke, half-signed.

She mangled her ASL, but Piper read her lips.

Piper nodded.

"Two years ago I sold fifty-one percent of Christmastown to Cyrus, now my son-in-law," Mrs. Pendegrast continued. "Actually, he adjusted that later with Amy, so they both now own exactly fifty percent each of the business, but that's not my point."

Nelson interpreted.

Piper was grateful. Nelson knew that even though she could read lips, there were times when she missed a word here or a meaning there.

"You know that Christmastown is worth a lot," Mrs. Pendegrast said. "When I sold my shares of it, I didn't know what I was going to do with the money."

Where was she going with this?

"I was going to invest it in Jerome's riverboat business, but he's telling me he wants to sell the entire business to his daughter's tour company, and retire." Mrs. Pendegrast reached for Jerome, and they held hands.

Piper knew Tamsyn Ruttledge would take good care of her father's riverboats. In fact, she had several tour packages that included evening dinner cruises on the Savannah River. Tamsyn also brought many customers to Piper's restaurant, and in return, Piper gave them a ten percent discount if they brought their tour tickets.

Piper also gave church members the same discount if they brought their church bulletins with them to Piper's Place.

"Nelson here has been keeping me updated on what's going on with your restaurant," Mrs. Pendegrast said.

Piper glared at Nelson. "Sign for me exactly what she just said."

Nelson's fingers shook and his balding head started to sweat.

"It's not his fault," Mrs. Pendegrast said. "He had no choice."

"No choice?" Piper signed daggers.

"I made a promise to your grandmother."

"When?" Piper signed.

"Before she died. You remember I visited her almost every other day in her last days."

Piper nodded. "I thank you for that."

In spite of everybody—almost everyone—in the community trying to avoid Mrs. Pendegrast in those days, Piper knew that she had a good heart.

When Grandma had been sick, Mrs. Pendegrast baked all of her favorite cookies and brought them hot from the oven. As Grandma ate the cookies, Mrs. Pendegrast would read the Bible to her, until one day, Grandma passed away even as Mrs. Pendegrast read the Book of Revelation to her.

Piper still recalled Revelation 21:6, the last Bible verse that Grandma heard on earth.

And He said to me, "It is done! I am the Alpha and the Omega, the Beginning and the End. I will give of the fountain of the water of life freely to him who thirsts.

Two years later, Piper accepted Jesus Christ as her Lord and Savior. Perhaps it had been the effort of Riverside Chapel church members to reach out to her after her grandmother died, but Piper was quite confident that the seed had been planted when she saw Mrs. Pendegrast spend time with Grandma.

"What did you promise my grandmother?" Piper signed.

"Bless her soul. No more pain in heaven." Mrs. Pendegrast dabbed her eyes.

"What did you promise her?"

"That if you ever need something, I will be here for you," Mrs. Pendegrast said.

Jerome patted his wife's shoulder.

"What kind of *need* do you think I have?" Piper glanced at Nelson as she signed. She suspected Nelson had talked too much, as usual, but she wanted to hear it directly from Mrs. Pendegrast.

"I know about Regis," Mrs. Pendegrast said. "I know he stole your operating funds, and you might not get any of it back."

Piper leaned back against her armchair. Many people knew about Regis by now.

"Jerome and I would like to invest in Piper's Place," Mrs. Pendegrast continued.

Piper drew a deep breath. "Do you know how bad my situation is?"

Mrs. Pendegrast nodded. "If you had the three hundred thousand dollars back, your restaurant will stay open, right?"

Piper nodded. "I could hire another chef, pay my bills."

"If you sold your house on Tybee, how much will you get out of it?"

"Maybe two hundred thousand, since it has a mortgage."

Jerome shook his head. "Your grandmother left you with debts you're still dealing with twelve years later."

"It's not her fault. She did her best. My mother's cancer cost us a lot of money."

"We're here to help," Mrs. Pendegrast said. "Colette knew that I'll always be here for you as long as we are able—that is, alive. This might be the reason I felt led to sell my share of Christmastown two years ago, without knowing what would happen today. And yet, for such a time as this, here we are."

Piper wept softly.

Mrs. Pendegrast hugged her.

"You might want to wait until you find out what this restaurant is worth by the end of this year." Piper signed and waved her hand at the large space. "This floor might be permanently closed. I am not sure if I can afford new chefs, to be honest. Some employees might quit by next week. I've already pretty much lost my grandmother's house, and now I'm going to lose her restaurant. Do you still want to invest in my failures?"

"We want to invest in history," Mrs. Pendegrast said.

"We love this town, and we love to eat at your restaurant," Jerome added.

Neither of them seemed fazed by the doom and gloom.

"What do you have in mind?" Piper thought that she should at least hear it out. Mrs. Pendegrast had brought up her grandmother's memory, after all.

"Forty percent of Piper's Place with conditions," Mrs. Pendegrast said. "That should more than make up for the three hundred thousand dollars you lost."

Nelson had told her everything, hadn't he?

"Conditions?" Piper signed.

"To begin with, your menu is in small print," Mrs. Pendegrast said. She was no longer signing, as Nelson had pretty much interpreted everything as she spoke. "The Super Seniors can't read fine print. So the first thing we want you to do is provide us with a large print menu."

Wow.

It never dawned on Piper that people couldn't read her menu. If they couldn't, why hadn't anyone complained?

"Did you know that we order the same things every time because we know you have those items?" Mrs. Pendegrast said.

"Really?" Piper signed.

Everyone, except Nelson, nodded.

"Did you know we have customers who can't read the menu?" Piper asked Nelson. "That's such an easy thing to fix."

"We train our servers to talk about the dishes and specials," Nelson said.

"True."

"Well, we can fix that," Piper signed. "You don't need to invest in forty percent of Piper's Place just to get a menu in large print."

"There are other conditions," Jerome said and Nelson interpreted. "You know my wife."

Uh oh.

"Let's hear it," Piper signed.

"Your menu is the size of a magazine," Mrs. Untermeyer said. "There are too many pages, too many items. It seems to me like you kept adding to your grandma's menu, and twelve years later, you have so many items on the menu that we can't order it all. There's no way."

Piper didn't respond. How could she remove any item that Grandma had put on the menu?

"You should do what Isaac did on the cruise ship."

Isaac? How did she manage to get his name in the conversation?

"Isaac told me that they rotate menus on the cruise ships all the time. He has seasonal menus and chef's specials. And they fit it all on two sides of the menu."

"Most restaurants do that." Piper knew she should as well, but...

Maybe she had spent so much time living the same routine day in and day out, year after year, that she hadn't stepped away to assess her establishment to see how she could have streamlined her family restaurant.

Truth be told, she would love to update her menu, stop adding new items to it without taking away old items, and maybe do away with ninety percent of her custom dishes.

"Those things," Piper signed. "We could take care of without outside investors."

"Unfortunately," Mrs. Pendegrast said.

"Unfortunately," Nelson signed.

"Unfortunately," Mrs. Pendegrast repeated. "You're out of money, and you're out of time. Christmas is coming, and we haven't seen you put up any holiday decorations—except on this floor, which nobody else sees."

Piper knew she couldn't hide her troubles much longer.

"Your customers—Super Seniors, at least— already know that two of your chefs are gone. We like to send notes to the chefs, you know, and the servers told us Chef Torkel and Chef Moulton don't work here anymore."

"We've been interviewing a new chef," Piper signed.

"But can you afford him or her?"

"The sale of my house..."

"Will only take you so far." Mrs. Untermeyer leaned forward. "I've been a businesswoman most of my life. Jerome here grew up in business, too. We know what works, and what doesn't."

"A restaurant is different." Piper regretted signing it.

"Every business is different, if you want to look at it that way," Mrs. Pendegrast replied.

Nelson didn't seem to tire signing. His interpretation of what she said seemed to be increasing in accuracy. For that, Piper was thankful. She was getting tired, to be honest, due to having worked all night. It took a lot of effort for her to read lips. She was glad Nelson could interpret.

"Your offer is generous. A forty percent investment will keep the restaurant open. But."

"But," Nelson interpreted.

"But?" Mrs. Pendegrast and Jerome said simultaneously.

"I must tell you that there are two mortgages on this historic building."

The Pendegrasts appeared shocked.

"Twelve years ago, before my grandmother

handed the restaurant over to me, she took out a second mortgage to pay for my mother's cancer treatment, as a last ditch effort to save her life."

Mrs. Pendegrast swallowed. "How much was it?"

Piper told them.

Jerome didn't say a word, nor did he move even the slightest from where he was sitting. It was as though he was leaving the situation to his wife.

"Well..." Mrs. Pendegrast began. "We could pay off that two hundred thousand dollars, but it would mean our investment is now half a million. Forty percent of the company seems unjustified."

"I understand."

"However..." Mrs. Pendegrast patted Jerome's arm. "It's within the range of our investment options, right, dear?"

Jerome nodded. "That maxes it out."

"If we cut expenses, streamline the restaurant, go to a more efficient menu, we can make it work." Mrs. Pendegrast paused. "With God's help."

"You had three hundred thousand dollars in the bank," Jerome asked. "Why didn't you pay off the second mortgage?"

"I have to also take care of what's left of the first mortgage plus operating expenses," Piper explained. "Regis...Regis gave me some advice about not paying off the mortgage because I need to pay the utilities and groceries for the restaurant."

"So that he could skim off the top of it, or take the whole thing, as he has done?" Jerome asked.

Piper wasn't sure. "It took me a while to have that much savings in the bank."

"I bet. Regis patiently waited until you had enough money saved up." Jerome was upset now.

Mrs. Pendegrast looked at him. "We don't know what's in Regis's mind."

Piper wanted to cry, but she held back her tears. They were in a business meeting.

"Seems to me that you were given some poor financial counseling," Jerome said.

"All that's in the past," Mrs. Pendegrast said. "We move forward now. With God's help, as I said."

"Your generosity is from God," Piper signed. "I don't know what to say."

"You're used to being a sole proprietor," Jerome said.

Piper nodded.

"It's going to be hard for you to adjust to having two partners in your business," Jerome continued. "But you can keep in mind that we're more than happy for you to buy back our shares. We'll be reasonable."

"She likes to work alone. So much like Isaac." Mrs. Pendegrast chuckled.

"I'm not like Isaac," Piper signed.

"Oh yes, you are. You're both equally stubborn. You have to do things yourselves. You don't want any help, even if you need help. You'd be drowning in quicksand and going, 'I'm fine! I'm fine!' as you sink deeper and deeper into the hole."

"Speaking of Isaac, he's saving up for his own restaurant," Piper signed. "I'm curious as to why you're not helping him."

"He's no longer waiting for a brick-and-mortar restaurant. He's downgraded to a food truck now." Mrs. Pendegrast threw up her arms. "Food truck, can you believe it? Why would anyone invest in a food truck?"

Piper didn't respond. She looked down at the floor.

What's wrong with a food truck?

If Isaac wants to operate a food truck, why not?

I would support him.

I totally would.

CHAPTER THIRTY-EIGHT

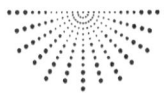

*A*s far as Isaac knew, Piper hadn't left the restaurant. She was also not in her office.

He wasn't trying to keep an eye on her, but she needed to go home and sleep some. Otherwise she was heading for a burnout.

Today was Tuesday, one day before his last day at Piper's Place. He was hoping to have a talk with Piper, to say his goodbye. He wasn't sure when he would see her again, if ever. That thought squeezed his heart in ways he hadn't felt before.

Surely I won't miss Piper.

The years had certainly taken the edge off their feud, which seemed to be one-sided, the more Isaac analyzed it. He could ask Piper if she had felt as strongly about it, but the only thing she hadn't done was to say to his face that she had forgiven him for getting mad at her over such a childish thing as jealousy.

There, I said it.

It was jealousy after all, that had caused Isaac to be a sore loser all those years ago.

Isaac glanced at Piper's office. The door was ajar. Nobody was inside.

He wondered if Nelson was out front at the moment. He had come in early for the meeting with the night shift workers, the one where Piper told all.

As soon Isaac saw that the kitchen line was sparsely filled with plates of orders, he knew there was a lull. He glanced over at the order wheel, and it too, was not full.

He put down his kitchen towel, and exited the kitchen.

Out front, he asked a host whether he had seen Nelson. He said no.

He looked around, and because he was tall, he could see across the floor, over the heads of customers and servers walking about, to the elevator that customers took to the second and third floors if they didn't want to take the stairs.

The elevator door opened.

And Isaac's jaw dropped.

Out of the elevator came Mom, Jerome, Nelson, and Piper.

Smiling away.

~

*I*saac tried not to slam the front door when he entered his mother's house. The hallway was empty, but he could hear the television coming from the living room. It was all Mom and Jerome did whenever they were home, with dinners on trays, while watching entertainment coming through the tube—well, digital streaming these days.

It was nearly seven o'clock, and he had left work almost three hours ago, but instead of going home to eat free food, Isaac drove over to Tybee Island, found a seafood joint, and ate his takeout on the beach, surrounded by sand and ocean.

He had to be alone.

Think alone.

Talk to God alone.

"Isaac." Jerome nodded as Isaac entered the family room.

"Hey, Jerome. How are you?" Isaac asked.

"Fine. You?"

"Tired. Long day."

"Sit down a bit."

Isaac didn't answer him. "Mom, we need to talk."

"Not now, dear. Episode 10 is coming up." Mom pointed to the television.

"Don't you have TIVO?"

"I want to see the commercials, too." Mom patted the empty seat next to her on the sofa. "Want to join us?"

She seemed to have no idea what was going on.

Now Isaac doubted himself. Had he been mistaken? Seeing his parents coming out of the elevator this morning with Nelson and Piper had thrown him a curveball that he couldn't catch.

And yet, he could be totally wrong about the elevator scene. Perhaps Mom and Jerome were simply coming down from the second floor, and Piper and Nelson happened to join them.

However, his instincts told him otherwise.

Mom was up to something.

"When can we talk?" Isaac asked.

"Another time." Mom's eyes were on the large-screen television. "Tomorrow, maybe?"

Jerome took the remote control from her. "Let's TIVO it. Your son is more important than a TV show."

Way to go, Stepfather!

He recorded the show live, turned it off, and motioned for Isaac to sit down.

Then everyone waited.

Mom put on her poker face.

"What's on your mind, Son?" Jerome looked concerned.

He should be.

Isaac cleared his throat. "I saw you two coming out of the elevator this morning with Piper and Nelson, and nobody told me what was going on."

Jerome looked at Mom.

"We had a meeting about how to save Piper's Place," Mom said.

"I wasn't invited," Isaac said.

"Why would you be? Your last day there is tomorrow," Mom said. "You might stay a few more weeks, but after Nassau, you won't come home—especially if you win first place and they offer you that job at Nassau Island Breeze Resort. You might then be spotted by an award-winning chef, who then might invite you to work at a five-star restaurant somewhere in Switzerland or someplace in Europe we can go visit—make sure you have a guest bedroom with a king-sized bed. You would be so far away from Savannah, that whatever happens at Piper's Place doesn't concern you."

"Come again?" Isaac's jaw dropped.

Jerome shrugged. "Sounds like we're going to Europe."

Mom wasn't done. "I'm a businesswoman. Now, I might be a so-so cook, but I've cooked most of my life. Your dad expected hot, home-cooked meals every night, as you recall—even after both of us had slaved away at Christmastown all day."

Isaac remembered. "We used to call you the Queen of Slow—for the crockpot."

"Where's my tiara?" Mom laughed.

"But you're right, Mom. You were a very savvy businesswoman."

"I still am." Mom tapped Jerome's arm. "When we saw how bad Piper's situation is, we had to step in. I promised her grandmother that I would help Piper in any way I can, as long as I live."

"How bad is her situation?" Isaac knew that he had been in the dark, but he did not expect to know anything at the corporate level at Piper's Place. His job there had been, and still was, as a temporary chef.

Mom was right. Isaac would be gone after Wednesday.

"How bad? That, I cannot tell you," Mom replied. "All I can tell you is that Nelson has kept me posted."

"Nelson? Did Piper know?" Nelson had been a spy for Mom. Isaac found that hard to believe.

"She found out this morning."

"At your meeting."

"Right. I can tell you that Jerome and I could be part owners of Piper's Place as soon as the lawyers hammer out an agreement."

"What?" Isaac held on to the armrests.

"Minority share, so we don't have too much of a say-so, and we don't want to," Jerome said.

"The goal is to help Piper ride through this low time in her life," Mom added.

Low time in her life?

"It's only for a year, until Piper gets her money back from her cousin or she earns enough to buy us out," Jerome said. "We don't want to be in the restaurant business, to tell you the truth."

"No, we don't." Mom leaned against Jerome. "We're retired, and want to stay retired. But I promised Colette so many years ago, and it will be awful if I don't help."

"If *we* don't help." Jerome put his arm around Mom's shoulders.

"You don't help me," Isaac said. "I've been saving up for years to open my own restaurant. I can't even get to that point."

Having said that, Isaac felt comfortable with the idea of owning a food truck.

In fact, the idea sounded freeing.

"You don't have a restaurant yet," Mom explained. "We're not venture capitalists. When Piper gets back on her two feet, and I expect that to be soon, she will buy back our shares, and we go our merry way."

"Merry way?"

"Tamsyn's been helping us choose a world cruise to go on." Mom clapped her hands.

She did that when she couldn't contain her excitement.

"Thing is, now we can't do it since we're investing in Piper's restaurant." Jerome winked at Isaac.

"Why not?" Mom looked stunned, like she hadn't expected it from her husband.

"Because we have to keep an eye on the money we put into Piper's Place."

Isaac didn't want to say that he had observed wasted food and cost overruns at Piper's Place.

"That's why we put all sorts of stipulations in our contract, dear," Mom reminded Jerome. "Piper will need an evaluation of spending and organization. We've already told her about her overstuffed menu."

"And custom dishes?" Isaac asked.

Mom pointed a finger at him. "Exactly. Too many custom dishes. Too many items on the menu, period. Also, the print is so small we can hardly read it."

I knew it. She would be micromanaging that restaurant.

Did Piper know what she was in for?

Isaac almost thanked God that Mom did not offer to fund his food truck.

Suddenly relieved that he wasn't involved, Isaac leaned back. Crossed his legs. "So. What else did you tell Piper she needs to fix?"

"Among other things, we want a twenty percent discount for Super Seniors," Mom said. "But Jerome said it has to be fair to all seniors. Piper said she'll consider it."

"She's already giving ten percent discounts if you bring your church bulletin," Isaac said.

Jerome nodded. "I suggested that Piper makes her restaurant a tour stop. Tamsyn said she could take small groups of people there for a Lunch Tour or Dinner Tour. They would sample the signature dishes and then tour the historical hallways and stand in front of old walls at Piper's Place."

Isaac remembered the old uneven hallways behind the kitchen. He did not recall parts of the old city on the walls, but Jerome would know more about the history of Savannah, considering his daughter ran Tamsyn Tours.

"The building might have been constructed in 1813, but it was built on top of a foundation from 1793, before the Great Fire of 1796." Jerome reached for his cup of coffee on the side table near him. "Did you know that George Washington himself walked on River Street when he visited in 1791? Legend has it that he had remarked on the architecture of the building that stood there where Piper's Place is now."

"No kidding."

"I've asked Tamsyn to see if she could find drawings or paintings of the building that was there, enough to make a tour brochure that will interest history buffs."

"A tour stop, huh?" Isaac was still digesting the idea. "That never crossed my mind."

"You are too busy working," Mom said. "We're retired. We have a lot of time on our hands to think of new ideas. In fact, the Super Seniors could volunteer as docents for the tour, thus saving Piper money to hire tour guides."

"They'd volunteer?" Isaac asked.

"For a free meal voucher, of course."

"That's a delicious compensation."

"The point is, we're doing whatever we can to prevent Piper's Place from shutting down." Mom's voice cracked a bit. "I wish I had known about Regis sooner."

"What do you mean?" Jerome asked.

"If we had known he's a crook, we could have warned Piper."

"You can't know everything. God is sovereign. He allowed what he allowed."

"We could have done a background check on him."

"You wouldn't know he needed one. We only found out when Nelson called us and asked if Isaac could help."

Isaac heard his name mentioned. "So you knew before we had dinner that Wednesday before Thanksgiving?"

Mom nodded sheepishly. "I'm sorry we could not tell you anything. Nelson took us into his confidence, and he could have been fired. In fact, I thought for sure Piper would be furious."

"Was she?"

"I think so, but she kept a lid on it."

Isaac wondered what Piper and Nelson talked about after Mom and Jerome had left the building.

"I would be mad if one of my employees went behind my back like that," Isaac said. "Nelson or anyone else."

"I'm sure Piper has forgiven him."

"So easily?" *Why hasn't she forgiven me?*

"I promised Colette at her deathbed that I'd keep an eye on her granddaughter," Mom said. "You know Piper. She's a very private person. She keeps everything to herself. Someday she might even die alone, and nobody would know."

"Mom, don't say that."

"Are you going to be there for her? I'm in my seventies now. Someone has to keep an eye on her after I die. She's going to live longer than I do, unless the stress kills her."

"Mom! Why are you talking like that?"

Jerome finished his coffee. "Let's continue another day, shall we? Your mom is tired, and she's going somewhere we don't want to go."

Isaac nodded.

He put down his coffee mug on the side table. "If we keep talking, she's going to be up all night worrying about getting a burial plot for our entire family, and I'm just not ready to go yet, you know what I mean?"

He's rambling too.

"The bottom line is that we have ready cash," Jerome said. "We have enough to bail out Piper's Place. But we're not going to invest perpetually. She'll have to try buying us back in one year, or she'll go under. She has to do whatever she needs to downsize, cut back expenses, find a way to earn more income, and so forth."

"As part of the deal, she has to hire a restaurant consultant to find a way to save money and make her operations more efficient." Mom agreed. "When we go on our world cruise for half a year, I don't want to be worried about a restaurant back home. You know how businesses are, Isaac, since you grew up practically inside Christmastown."

Isaac nodded. "It's not just increasing income, but you also have to cut expenses."

"Right."

"So we want to preserve Colette's legacy—no thanks to her other grandchild, whom she cut out of her will for her own reasons—and keep the restaurant doors open." Mom lifted a hand. "Oh, except Sundays. We would like her to keep the doors closed on Sundays to give her employees time for family or church."

"Is she okay with that?" Isaac didn't feel it had been his business to recommend that Piper closed one day a week, but he wished she had, if not for others, for herself.

"That girl never rests," Mom said.

"No, she doesn't." Isaac shook his head. "She's at work even on her days off."

"Now, she'll be forced to rest on Sundays. Speaking of rest..." Jerome helped Mom up to her feet.

I guess that means this meeting is over.

Mom pointed to Isaac. "As for you, please run your food truck the Bible way, okay? Don't borrow money. Don't go into debt. That's why we're not offering you a loan. And we're not investing a dime into your business either. You can stand on your own two feet. And I know that you're rational enough to make sure you don't hire a no-good criminal mind to manage your money."

Is she saying I'm smarter than Piper?

"I'm not saying you're smarter than Piper," Mom said.

Did Mom just read my mind?

Mom wasn't done. "I'm saying that you've got so much of your dad in you. He was very careful with our money. He thought it over in at least ten different ways before he made any business decision, and he never moved forward until he prayed over it and got clearance from God. Oh, and he would never hire a crook to run the bookkeeping."

Regardless of what Mom had implied about Piper, Isaac realized something.

Mom said I'm like Dad.

My adopted dad.

Isaac felt like crying. Somehow, God had grafted him into the Untermeyer family, given him a new name, and taught him the right way to live his life.

Mistakes are mine.

Mistakes are all mine.

Isaac felt comforted that the grace of God was deeper than his own self, his human nature, his foibles, his follies.

Someday, when he finally bought a food truck,

he would need to find a way to use it in ministry. What could he do with a food truck that would serve God and glorify Him?

CHAPTER THIRTY-NINE

*I*saac's last day at Piper's Place began like any other day he had been there the past two weeks. Put on his chef's coat, amble into the kitchen, greet everyone, and start cooking.

Today people seemed a little sad around him, more so as the hours went by, to the point that Bao hung around him and talked to him more than he had done all week.

Isaac moved back and forth between the grill and sauté stations today, passing by Bao, hoping and praying that the sous chef could someday realize he could be more.

What does this guy need? Confidence or something?

Maybe prayer. Lots of prayer.

Too many times, Isaac shot darts of stares at the

kitchen clock—ticking away the next six hours like the bells of London, tolling heavily across his chest, reminding him that the end of the day for him was coming.

He hadn't seen Piper this morning. Neither had he seen Nelson.

He assumed or guessed that perhaps they were busy discussing the terms and limitations they could put on Mom. If they had asked him, Isaac would say, "Absolutely. Mom will take over your restaurant, and she knows nothing about it."

She just thinks she knows.

And yet, Mom knew a lot.

Someone's phone chimed.

It sounded like bells.

Bells...

And backyards.

Isaac could see that day so long ago—Amy, Garrett, and Isaac on the picnic blanket with Mom. Dad had been out of town, and the kids were missing him, so Mom took them on a picnic in the backyard.

Garrett was ringing a bell he had found in their toy box.

Ring, ring, ring.

And Mom recited yet another nursery rhyme to them. Isaac could hear Mom's voice now, mixed in with Garrett's noisy bells.

When will you pay me?
Rang the bells of Old
    Bailey.
When I grow rich!
Rang the bells of
    Shoreditch.
When is that?
Rang the bells of
    Something...
When I am dead!
Rang the bells of Where's
    That...

Isaac couldn't remember the words precisely, but it didn't matter. What mattered was that he recalled those days as the happiest he had in the Untermeyer family.

Before Dad died.

After that, Mom changed.

She was cold, caustic, and calculating.

It seemed that everyone who had known her before, avoided her. She was alone, lonely, struggling to keep Christmastown going.

Every single one of her children made a decision to leave. Mom waited for years for them to come home.

Amy had been the first to come home two years prior. She said that Mom had changed.

Now Isaac had returned to Savannah. And he saw some changes himself. He was sure that God had brought Jerome into Mom's life to counterbalance her. Jerome seemed to be the steady type, reminding Isaac of Dad.

Isaac stood at the kitchen line, staring at the beautiful plates of food. Comfort food that he and Bao, and their assistants, had prepared for lunch.

Nearby, the wall clock marched on.

Isaac watched as servers came to pick up the plates. Some smiled to him, thanked him, waved to him. Out there, the customers would be happy.

Usually, so would Isaac. A sense of delight would course through him, as though he had helped someone today by feeding them. However, it would never be the same sense of delight he had as a child, in that old backyard garden, enjoying a spring day picnic between the lovely flowers Mom had planted.

Listening to bells and her voice reciting nursery rhymes.

Where is that home now?

Isaac blinked and drew a deep breath.

Maybe it's time to start a family of my own.

He wasn't sure precisely how that thought floated into his head. Maybe he was thinking too much about nostalgia while standing in a kitchen that made family meals and comfort food.

Or maybe he was starting to miss working here.

Or miss someone.

Even before he left.

Is that possible?

~

*P*iper texted Nelson to bring the cupcakes from the bakery at fifteen minutes after four, and she would do her best to keep Isaac inside the kitchen, short of throwing a party. The idea was to keep it low key, like nobody cared, and then spring the surprise on him when Isaac least expected it.

Piper went home to Llewellyn's house after she finished her night shift, and tried to get some sleep. Llewellyn's sister and mom were at the doctor's doing some tests all morning. Llewellyn himself had received an unexpected last-minute promotion at work that required him to travel fifty percent of the time, so he was gone for the next two weeks, coming home a few days before Christmas.

Piper prayed that with the infusion of ready cash from the Pendegrasts, she could move into her own apartment soon. She did not want to overstay her welcome at Llewellyn's house.

What would Isaac think if he found out that she was living here, paying no rent?

Piper rolled over in the twin bed.

Does it matter what Isaac thinks or says?

After all, they were not dating. Far from it.

In fact, today was Isaac's last day. After she took a nap, she would return to her restaurant for the surprise farewell party.

I will miss him.

But leave it to Mrs. Pendegrast to make sure this wasn't a bitter end.

Piper yawned. *We'll deal with all that later.*

Technically, Wednesday was supposed to be her day off, but due to the lack of chefs, she had worked every night since Thanksgiving. She did the same thing on Monday, her other day off.

Piper felt sleepy lying down on this bed, which wasn't even her own bed in her old house.

She set her alarm for two o'clock.

And woke up at 3:30 p.m.

Oh no! Oh no!

Piper texted Nelson to do what she had intended to do herself. She asked him to send Bao to the bakery.

Piper jumped into the shower, then jumped into her clothes, and then jumped into her car.

And somehow she made it to her restaurant with five minutes to spare before 4:15 p.m.

And her hair in a messy top bun, the ends of her hair still dripping bits of water on her wool coat.

She stepped into the ladies room, dried her hair as much as she could with a paper towel.

She looked in the mirror.

Horrors!

She had forgotten to put on any makeup.

At all.

Too late now.

She took a deep breath, and then another, as she walked out calmly and as steadily as she could, down the hallway, where Nelson and a couple of servers stood with trays of cupcakes, enough for everyone.

She nodded to them, and they made their entry into the kitchen.

"Surprise!" Everyone must be shouting—Piper read their lips.

She didn't bother to sign because Isaac couldn't understand it anyway.

Piper stood aside while the parade of cupcakes made their way toward Isaac, standing by the kitchen line. He still had his apron on.

And he was staring straight at her.

Piper felt self-conscious. She felt like hiding. But there was no place to hide.

Nelson and the cake bearers surrounded Isaac.

Piper read their lips. They were thanking Isaac for the two weeks he had been here.

Piper herself had a lot to say about it, but she

didn't want to make a speech. It was better to let Isaac go without fanfare, but this was how Piper's Place sent off chefs and kitchen staff who had been invaluable to the team.

In the middle of all the handshaking and hugging, Isaac made his way to Piper. She extended her hand for a handshake.

He took her hand, but pulled her to himself for a hug.

It surprised Piper. She didn't want to let him go.

When Isaac broke the hug, he said nothing to her, but his eyes said everything.

I wish I could stay.

Either that, or he was shocked at seeing her bare face for the first time ever.

CHAPTER FORTY

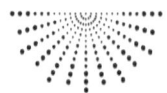

*B*efore church began on Sunday morning, Piper had a feeling that she'd forgotten something, though she knew not what. Suddenly she had nothing to do on Sunday but go to church morning and evening, and nap in between those two services.

Eat, sleep, go to church.

Is that what many Christians do every Sunday?

The instant infusion of funding from her new investors had assured that Piper's Place would be open for business for at least one year, but it had come with a price. Many prices, in fact, one of which was that the family restaurant would close on Sundays.

While waiting for their interpreter to show up, Piper watched her friends chat with one another at their ASL table. They had not left a seat for Isaac, and he had not asked to sit with them today.

Weaning us off seeing him?

Piper had no idea if Isaac was even here this morning, and she didn't want to look around—in case he saw her do so.

She sat at the table, staring straight ahead, her mind thinking back to the rest of the business meeting with the Pendegrasts, to their strange demands for the benefits of the Super Seniors and their last request that she close Piper's Place on Sundays.

Piper remembered explaining her restaurant traditions to the Pendegrasts via Nelson. "We are so used to opening every day—except Christmas. We even open on New Year's Day."

"Used to. I used to say *used to* a lot," Jerome said, as interpreted through Nelson as well. "For years after my first wife died of cancer, I lived in the past. She used to do this and that. I didn't want to do anything different. After years of grief, I walked into a random church, and the pastor there led me to the Lord. Then I learned that God made all things new."

Piper couldn't remember what she signed in response to Jerome, but she remembered the rest of what Jerome and Mrs. Pendegrast said.

"Look at your past with fond memories, yes, but you have to live in the here and now," Jerome said.

"You are a Christian now," Mrs. Pendegrast said. "We don't do things like non-believers do. We are accountable to God. When God created the universe in six days, He rested on the seventh. God set an example for us because He knows that we frail humans need a day of rest.Throughout the Bible, you see that they kept the Sabbath day holy for the Lord."

"Sabbath day? I'm not Jewish," Piper signed.

"For Christians, our day of rest is Sunday. Some think it's Saturday. Whichever day, it doesn't matter to us, although we prefer Sundays since that's the day Christians go to church. Have you thought about your testimony to your non-Christian employees when their Christian co-workers could not go to church on Sundays because you require them to work?"

"They can work around their church schedule," Piper signed. "I don't expect my employees to work more than forty hours a week, and I already give them two days off each week. If they're Christians, they can take Sundays off."

"Even if they aren't Christians and don't go to church, Piper's Place can make a statement that Sunday is employee family day." Mrs. Pendegrast was persistent. "Did you know that Chick-fil-A makes more profit than most of the other fast food places, even though they close on Sundays?"

"I know your best days are Mondays through Fridays, since you cater to the business lunch and tourist crowds," Jerome said. "Closing the restaurant on any of those days might affect your profit margin. But Sundays. Can you tell me that you earn more on Sunday than other days?"

"It's comparable."

"Regardless, think about it. You need rest," Mrs. Pendegrast said. "We've noticed that you run from the kitchen to church and back to the kitchen. Have you considered ministering on Sundays? And have you ever been to the Sunday evening service?"

"Not all churches have Sunday evening services anymore," Piper protested.

"But Riverside Chapel does."

Piper didn't realize her eyes were closed as the entire episode from four days ago played back in her mind.

I was thinking of something...

She watched a violinist step up to the microphone, nodded to the pianist, and began to play. The screen behind the violinist displayed the hymn title, "Hallelujah! What a Savior."

Jesus is my Savior, ten years and counting.

Yet, what had she done for Christ that could count for eternity?

She had been toiling in her kitchen. For what, exactly?

Did it even matter?

Standing up for something mattered. Closing her restaurant on Sundays was a way for her to show the world that she had reverence for God's holy day.

In a way, she was tithing one day of the week to Almighty God.

I wish I had done it years ago, but I was always afraid of running out of money.

Ironically, losing the funds she had held dear had turned her toward God and the things of God.

Piper's employees worked around forty hours a week, but she herself worked more than that—sometimes twice more. She felt that she had to if she wanted to have a nest egg in the future or at least be employed as long as she could.

If the Pendegrasts hadn't made her agree to closing Piper's Place on Sundays, she might not have given more thought to serving God. Wasn't it enough that she was saved?

Now that she had a forced one day off, she might consider volunteering at church. Heidi had said that sometimes the children's Sunday School was short of workers. Sometimes they need more people to help decorate the church or clean up the place after each service or activity on Sundays.

Piper had never done any ministry at Riverside Chapel because she worked day and night.

And here she was, with her friends at church, and they were all missing work today.

Now she knew what had bothered her since she came to church this morning. What she was missing was work.

Work.

Sheer back-breaking work.

Heidi arrived to interpret her husband's sermon, but the service hadn't started yet.

"How's your cousin?" Heidi asked.

"Still in the hospital," Piper signed.

Detective Zimmerman had kept up with what went on in Atlantic City, but even he said it would be a while before they extradited Regis back to Georgia to stand trial for stealing money from his clients, including his cousin. Apparently, the Department of Homeland Security, together with the Immigration and Customs Enforcement agency, wanted Regis to testify as a witness in a money-laundering trial.

Regis would be moved to a safe location soon. That could only mean one thing: Piper might never see her cousin again.

"I turned the situation over to God," Piper signed.

"Good. We'll keep praying for God to resolve the problem." Heidi smiled.

Problem?

Problems, more like it.

Piper saw flashes of light coming from inside her purse. She retrieved her phone. It was a text message from Mrs. Pendegrast, somewhere in the riverboat, asking if Piper could help her with knife skills after church.

Today?

Piper hesitated to reply. She would be free this afternoon. That, she could not lie. But to help Mrs. Pendegrast or not, it depended on many things.

Bravery, for example.

Maybe it was a mistake to accept the funds from the Pendegrasts.

Piper should have expected that Mrs. Pendegrast would be asking for favors now—above and beyond all the other requirements the investor had asked of her.

If there was anything Piper didn't like, it was unexpected things.

Last minute, unexpected things.

CHAPTER FORTY-ONE

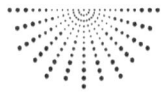

*T*wo hours after church, Isaac arrived at the riverboat in a huff, feeling warm in the cold December air. He had been unable to get the squid he had ordered. His fishmonger had messed up his orders, and Isaac ended up with octopus—which he did not want to cook at all, thanks to a memory from their high school Cumin Cooking Club, involving Piper.

Well, Piper is not here.

Still, she was on his mind this afternoon. All he wanted were happy memories of Piper, even though he no longer worked in her kitchen as of Wednesday.

But the octopus ruined it for Isaac this Sunday afternoon. It was a weird memory, but there it was. Back in high school, he had tried to teach Piper how to cook octopus, and she had not only freaked out, but cried over the death of six baby octopuses.

Isaac hated to see her cry at all.

Sure, people cry.

But not if he could help it. He wanted them to feel better. Maybe it was the result of having been in the foster care system himself, where he had experienced much unhappiness, until the Untermeyers adopted him.

Maybe it was only Piper.

Maybe Isaac had felt something for Piper so long ago, but neither had the opportunity to explore it.

Due to his own pride, he had severed a potentially long lasting friendship with Piper. Now he wondered what they had missed out in the last twenty years.

In any case, as Isaac walked down the quiet hallway toward the galley kitchen, carrying the paper sack of octopuses and some spices, he recalled vividly Piper crying over the baby octopuses he was about to teach her to clean and cook.

So many years ago, and I can still see her tears.

Isaac entered the galley—

And saw Piper, sorting out vegetables at a counter with Mom.

Isaac's eyes widened, and he tightened his grip around the grocery sack in his arms.

"What is she doing here?" Isaac was beside himself.

Mom tried to look nonchalant. "It's part of the deal."

Piper seemed to sense something was wrong—like maybe Mom hadn't told Isaac that she invited Piper to the cooking party—so she walked to the sink with some vegetables, and faced away from them.

"Part of what deal?" Isaac wondered how he was supposed to handle this.

He didn't have a lot of wonderful thoughts floating in his head right now.

He still held the sack in his arms, as if it was a buffer between him and Mom. He wanted to run and hide, to be honest, but here they were.

"I thought that since I invested in her restaurant, that she could help me out here and there." Mom stood her ground.

"Here and there? She's your business partner, not your servant at your beck and call."

Mom looked sheepish. "I don't want to embarrass myself in Nassau."

She always did that when caught, as if looking like a poor sorry girl would make up for her manipulative streak. Was this one of those times, though? Or was it an innocent mistake?

One of the big reasons that Isaac hadn't come

home was how Mom had treated her own daughter Amy and flesh-and-blood son Garrett. The irony of the whole thing was that Mom had treated Isaac the best.

And yet, every now and then, her manipulative streak showed up like an emotional cat-o'-nine-tails, lashing at the very people she tried to help.

Failing the sheepish looks, Mom usually fell back on her default: playing victim.

Not today.

Isaac prayed for wisdom and objectivity to handle Mom. God could handle anyone, but Mom was probably one of the more difficult ones— according to Isaac—because her flaws were so subtle and sly, to the point that she could pass them off as merely innocent mistakes.

This is why we don't come home much, Mom. Don't you understand?

Now Mom had brought up Nassau.

It was an oversight for Isaac to let Mom assist him in the upcoming cooking competition. His chances of winning the prize money were iffy, but without a real sous chef to help him, his chances were now at near zero.

"It's your fault you didn't want to pay your chef friend more," Mom said.

"What? It's my fault that you had to call on Piper, making demands on her?" Isaac didn't want to revisit his own failure in hiring a real sous chef. Seriously, he couldn't make his friend Clarence take a one-week vacation and spend it in the Bahamas helping him win the contest if Clarence would rather start a new career in Japan.

"I'm not making demands on her," Mom said. "I asked her at church this morning if she could help me be a better assistant to you, to show me some knife skills."

"I can show you knife skills."

"She said it was no problem. She willingly agreed."

"Willingly? Somehow I have a feeling that she felt obligated. Did you tell her I was going to be here?"

"She knew."

"Of course she knew. And?"

"And what?"

"What did she say when she knew I was going to be here?" Isaac asked.

"She asked if you'd be okay with her helping us."

"And you said?"

"I said you're totally okay with it."

"But you haven't asked me."

"I'm asking you now."

"She's already here, Mom." Isaac pointed to

Piper, still washing vegetables at the sink, still facing away from them.

Isaac wasn't sure what to do now. Should he put away the octopuses in the refrigerator so they wouldn't be problematic for Piper?

All he had left was chicken, shrimp, and cod. He had picked chicken because he thought he could pair it with the shrimp, for a modified Chinese dish he could call Phoenix Chasing Dragon on the Ocean.

With the cod in its own dish, all he would have this afternoon were two dishes.

A portion of his success in cooking today—preparing for seafood competition—was going to depend on chicken.

Yeah, chicken. The other seafood.

"I need a minute." Isaac put down the sack on the nearest counter, and walked out.

CHAPTER FORTY-TWO

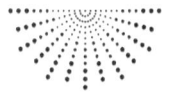

On the top deck, all the furniture had been put away, and the only place Isaac could sit was on the wooden floor. He scooted up against a low railing, a flapping banner tied to the other side providing a meager windbreaker from the chilly wind on an overcast day on the Savannah River.

He was facing the river and open skies. Hutchinson Island peeked through the side railings.

Legs stretched out, Isaac zipped up his jacket, and dug his hands into the side pockets.

He closed his eyes and shook his head.

He tried to pray, but no words formed on his lips.

Maybe it was the cold December freezing his

brain. It wasn't that cold in the south, really, and it rarely snowed here. The fjords of Norway—that was some cold place. Georgia—not even close.

He kept his eyes closed and hoped that he wouldn't fall asleep.

"I want to succeed, Lord. So badly," Isaac mumbled. "You know I've entered in numerous cooking competitions over the years. I didn't win any. I don't know why, Lord."

Maybe I should stop trying.

But Nassau.

Isaac thought that perhaps just this one time, he could get placed in a cooking competition, and feel better about himself.

Then again, what does the Bible say about tying up my personal worth to things and achievements?

"I get it, Lord, but...I want to win a cooking competition just once." Isaac wasn't sure why he felt competitive. Was it to prove to Piper that he wasn't useless?

Piper?

What about God?

"Well, Lord, You already know everything about me." The wind absorbed Isaac's voice. "I can prove nothing to You. You're not impressed with my ability to cook. I realize that my talents come from You. However, I haven't been able to win any cooking competition that I've entered over the years."

Maybe cooking competitions are not for me.

"Why do I fail so much, Lord?" Isaac mumbled again. "Here I am again, trying to win some cooking competition in which I probably have no chance against other chefs..."

Why did Mom tell me about this Nassau competition?

Once again, she was trying to help.

Maybe that was all she was trying to do. Maybe calling her manipulative was unkind.

Like I said, it's subtle.

Usually, she began with a caring heart. That would be enough for many people, but Mom would take it a step further. After she started helping, she tried to control the outcome. That was when she thought she had to do something—a lot of some-things—to reach her desired outcome.

Although the outcome might be noble, her plot to get from start to finish might not be exactly letting things take their course or letting God determine the results. It was one thing to be helpful, but it was another thing altogether to force an outcome that she wanted.

That was Mom.

What about me? Am I also not trying my best to win this competition? Don't I want to win?

Would pushing toward a winning outcome be considered manipulating the circumstances to get to what he desired? If it was fair and by the rules, there was nothing wrong with it, was there? If Isaac sought to bend the rules or overstep his boundaries, then it would be a problem.

What about this situation he was in, then?

Mom was trying to help him win the cooking competition. Knowing she had no culinary school training, she still offered to be his assistant cook at no charge because Isaac was too cheap to hire a real sous chef. To further her helpfulness, she had now asked Piper to show her some knife skills.

Isaac's head was feeling cold, but the clouds above him were parting. The wind was blowing the clouds away.

Thank You, God.

You always take care of me, even when I'm in a bad mood.

Now the sun is shining, warming up my cold head.

Somehow in the midst of the sunnier afternoon, Isaac missed Dad.

Dad had been a master at handling Mom. Isaac wondered if Jerome was able to resume that skill of knowing when to defuse Mom, when to pull her back when she went crazy trying to make things work out the way she wanted, whether her intentions were good or inadequate.

Dad had repeatedly told the family that they had nothing to prove to anyone. Rather, they would be better off trying to please God instead.

Isaac recalled the conversation with Amy in November, in which she told him about the Ephesians 4:31-32 verse that Dad had reminded her.

> Let all bitterness, wrath, anger, clamor, and evil speaking be put away from you, with all malice. And be kind to one another, tenderhearted, forgiving one another, even as God in Christ forgave you.

"Be kind to your mom because she's had a hard life," Isaac said to himself. "Or be kind to your mom. Period. It doesn't matter what the reasoning is. It's my duty to God to be kind to her."

Isaac was about to get up and go downstairs to face Mom, when his phone chirped.

CHAPTER FORTY-THREE

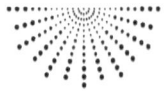

*W*hen Isaac's mom went to the ladies room, Piper wondered where Isaac was, and if he would return to the galley. She had time to help, but surely Isaac would want to give them some directions.

She found his handwritten menu and recipes inside the sack. She didn't see the rest of the sack, but the exterior felt cold, so she decided to put it in the refrigerator for Isaac to deal with later.

Based on the written recipes, Piper could show Mrs. Pendegrast how to get the vegetables ready for Isaac to cook.

Or should they wait for Isaac to return?

She texted him.

PIPER

I'm sorry.

ISAAC

Not your fault.

> PIPER
>
> I don't want to cause trouble.

ISAAC

We had trouble before you came
along.

> PIPER
>
> I'm still sorry. What should I show
> your mom?

ISAAC

Whatever. I don't care.

> PIPER
>
> I found your menu and recipes in
> the sack.

She waited for a reply. It seemed like Isaac was
taking a long time. The ellipses showed on her
phone, indicating that he was still typing something. But nothing came through. She checked the
top part of the phone. The signal was strong.

ISAAC

You don't have to stay. Mom
didn't tell me she asked you to
help.

> PIPER
>
> I don't mind. I'm happy to help.

ISAAC

I'm not happy you're helping.

345

> **PIPER**
>
> Because?

> **ISAAC**
>
> It's your day off. You need to rest.

> **PIPER**
>
> I've rested plenty.

When Isaac didn't text back immediately, Piper wondered what else was going on with that man. He didn't seem to want her around.

She prayed silently for him. Whatever he had to deal with, God was bigger than it.

At least Isaac didn't have a crooked cousin.

> **PIPER**
>
> Your mom said you had a sous chef.

> **ISAAC**
>
> He got a better offer in Tokyo.

> **PIPER**
>
> Do you want me to ask around my chef friends to see if anyone is available to go with you to Nassau?

> Isaac: I can't pay them.

Piper felt someone breathing down her neck. She was startled to find Mrs. Pendegrast over her shoulder, reading her private conversation.

"He's too cheap to pay anyone," Mrs. Pende-grast signed. "That's why I volunteered."

"You've cooked for your family for years," Piper signed. "It's not too hard to help, but he is the chef."

That is to say, next time don't override him.

"I don't know why he still hates you."

"He doesn't hate me." Not anymore.

Even as Piper signed it, she knew it to be true. In the last two weeks, Isaac had been kind to her. She smiled as she remembered their third floor meeting, when instinctively, he had known that she needed a shoulder to lean on and had offered his.

"You're smiling," Mrs. Pendegrast said.

Piper couldn't stop smiling, though. No use trying to cover it up.

"I thought of funny moments," Piper signed. It was the best she could do.

"Happy moments."

"Yes."

"So where is Isaac?" Mrs. Pendegrast said.

"I'll ask." Piper texted him.

~

*W*ith the warming sun directly on his face, and his eyes closed, Isaac thought he was slowly cruising on an afternoon nap.

Not!

Uneven footfalls against steel staircase steps reached his ears. He opened one eye. Frowning lines formed on his face.

Mom hissed as she made the last step, leaning on the railing with one hand. There was a plastic bag of some sort in her other hand. She was wearing a faux fur coat that went down to her knees.

Isaac didn't move.

Mom made the short walk across the wooden deck to where Isaac was sitting. She was limping a bit. She hadn't limped until her knees gave out a couple of years ago.

I wasn't even here for her.

Cyrus was.

Cyrus Theroux, who wasn't an Untermeyer, had taken care of Mom when her own children had shirked their responsibilities.

To be fair, Mom had not told any of them that she was heading toward knee replacement. Amy found out a year later, and Isaac found out from Amy. Garrett probably still didn't know what was going on in Savannah.

Mom dangled the gallon-sized ziplock bag in front of Isaac. It was full of cookies. "Your favorite pecan cookies."

It got him every time.

For Amy, it was shortbread cookies. For Isaac, it

was pecan cookies. Their brother Garrett could not be bought.

"Gimme." Isaac was too lazy to lift his arms.

Mom sat down next to him, and stretched out her shorter legs in the same direction as Isaac's. She handed him a cookie.

"Thank you." Isaac closed his eyes and chewed the cookie slowly. It was delicious.

This is comfort food.

"Where did you buy these?" Isaac asked, suspecting Mom had baked them.

"I know you know I baked them." Mom smiled. "But it's a compliment when you say you think they taste like I bought them from a bakery, where they have trained pastry chefs and all."

Busted.

"What time did you get up to make these?" Isaac ate a second cookie.

"Three o'clock."

Isaac tried not to look surprised, but he suspected why Mom couldn't sleep.

"Were you stressed about Nassau?" Isaac wished he hadn't agreed to let Mom become his assistant cook in the competition. He couldn't fire her now, because it would make her feel like a failure.

Be kind to your mother. She has had a hard life.

Even as Dad's words rang in Isaac's mind, he

knew that Mom's life after he had passed away was much harder than when he had been alive and had taken care of things for her.

Mom didn't reply.

"Don't be stressed about Nassau." Isaac was talking as much to himself as he was to Mom. "If we win, we win. If we lose, we still end up with a week in the Bahamas."

"It sure didn't sound like that when you were downstairs fifteen minutes ago," Mom said.

"I was upset."

"You made Piper feel bad that she came at all."

"You should have asked me *before* you asked her."

"You wouldn't have let me invite her."

"That should have told you something." Isaac reached for the ziplock bag. "How many cookies did you make?"

"Three dozen."

"That stressed, huh?"

Mom leaned against Isaac's arm. "I wish your dad were here. He'd know what to do."

"God knows better than Dad."

Mom suddenly gasped. "Don't tell Jerome I forgot about him."

Isaac laughed. "I know what you mean. Jerome is a different sort of guy. He's not like Dad. Dad was more pensive, analytical, and detail oriented.

Jerome is a nice guy and all, but to me, he is the type of person who looks at the big picture, and delegates the details to other people working for him."

"I still miss your dad."

"Me too, Mom. Me too."

There would always be a special place in Isaac's heart for his adopted father. Felix Untermeyer hadn't been a big and brawny sort of guy. He was tall and lanky, and walked with a bit of slouch because that had been his habit—leaning over paperwork and statistics, analyzing the daily and monthly sales of knick-knacks at Christmastown, months before the season began.

Until Isaac was too big to sit on laps, Dad would always let him sit with him while he calculated numbers.

However, the most pivotal moment in Isaac's life had been that day when he was four years old, finding out that his time with the Untermeyers was over. Mom had packed his lone suitcase, adding new stuffed animals for him to take.

At four years old, he hardly understood why he had to move from house to house. Where was his own mother? His father? All he knew was that he had to dress properly and wash dirt off his hands and face, or the families might not let him stay with them.

Not at the Untermeyers.

They had a big backyard, and sometimes when it rained hard—as it often did in Savannah—part of the yard would be somewhat flooded. That was where they would find Isaac, making mud pies.

When he was done playing, Mom would take him indoors, give him a good scrub in the bathtub, dress him up in comfortable cotton pajamas, and read him a storybook.

Until that day came.

Isaac had found a dark corner of the back porch, where he thought nobody would see him because the roof cast a shadow over it. It was a sunny day too, much like this one, except it was in the summer, hot and humid.

He remembered crying in that corner, the loneliest boy in the world.

Mom came to find him. Sat with him and cried with him.

"Life is hard." Mrs. U was her name at that time.

"Why?" Little Isaac asked.

"But God is good."

"How?"

More footsteps, adult shoes. It was Dad. At that time, he was only Mr. U. "There you are!"

In his hand was a popcorn bowl. He sat down

on the other side of Little Isaac. "Want some? Pecan cookies. Your favorite."

Little Isaac nodded.

All three of them ate the cookies in silence.

Then Dad spoke again. "Would you like to stay with us, Isaac?"

"Forever?"

Isaac still remembered his own words. And what did Mom say?

"Forever with God." Isaac must have said it loudly.

"Wh-what?" Mom stirred beside him on the riverboat deck. The bag of cookies had slid off her coat and was on the deck floor.

"You fell asleep." Isaac laughed.

"I did not." Mom sat up.

"You did, too."

Before Mom could reply, Isaac heard new footsteps coming up the side stairs. Pretty soon, Piper emerged, looking around. She waved to them, but she was looking out to the river. When she came over, Mom lifted the ziplock bag to her.

Piper nodded, and was about to sit down on the other side of Mom, when Isaac patted the deck floor on his side. Piper saw the gesture, hesitated, and then came over to stretch her legs alongside his.

Does that mean she is not mad at me?

They ate pecan cookies in silence, each with his or her own thoughts, Isaac supposed.

For all practical purposes, he had lost half the afternoon. But he had regained his mother's fellowship. And perhaps shown Piper that he did still love his mom.

Isaac was glad he decided not to mention the octopuses. They were still in the galley refrigerator. He would take them home after the evening church and cook them tonight.

CHAPTER FORTY-FOUR

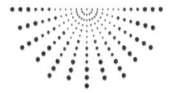

*A*s the afternoon progressed, Isaac was running out of time, and Piper knew it. If this repeated itself on Nassau, Piper was sure that Isaac would not make it to the finals.

Instead of teaching his mom to prepare this and that, Piper suggested that she and Isaac simply cooked, and his mom could watch.

That was to say, Mom sat at the counter waiting to taste samples of food, critiquing the two chicken dishes and two fish dishes, and taking photos of the "lovely couple" which she posted on her Instagram account, where she had all of one follower: her daughter Amy.

Piper herself was on social media, and so was her restaurant. Since everybody read on social media, there was no need for anyone to speak aloud. Piper could type, post videos and photographs, and nobody would even know she was deaf.

All her deaf friends were active on social media, and they did a lot of group chat and direct messages, although Piper did the least of all, since she was busy.

"Why isn't he on social media?" Piper signed to Mrs. Pendegrast.

"He doesn't know how to post." Mrs. Pendegrast finger signed her entire sentence.

"You could teach him."

"He doesn't learn well."

Piper chuckled.

"What is going on?" Isaac asked, not laughing with them. "Are we cooking or not?"

Piper appreciated the way Isaac had made an effort to speak clearly so that she could read his lips. It sometimes made her feel uncomfortable that they were facing each other frequently, but Isaac seemed to enjoy her company.

That made it worse.

This afternoon, Isaac hadn't started out in a good mood because his mom deliberately didn't tell him that she had invited Piper to assist in their practice runs.

Ninety minutes and a whole bag of pecan cookies later, the trio had returned to the kitchen, and somehow managed to salvage the afternoon. Piper went along with Isaac's menu, which he had scribbled on a piece of paper. She could handle chicken and shrimp, and cod. She almost checked what was in the unopened grocery bag in the refrigerator, but Isaac told her not to worry about it.

"Two dishes only?" Piper signed.

Mrs. Pendegrast interpreted for her.

Isaac nodded. "We don't have enough time to finish before the evening service."

Maybe Mrs. Pendegrast knew she was holding Isaac back. They were constantly having to re-chop onions, carrots, and celery for the mirepoix, for example, because Mrs. Pendegrast never cut those vegetables the same size twice. With cubes of vegetables in various sizes, they would not cook evenly.

Piper knew that. Isaac knew that.

But the assistant cook refused to respect food science.

The more Isaac tried to explain to his mom that it was important for her to cut the ingredients just right because the judges were chefs, the more rebellious Mrs. Pendegrast became.

She would have failed culinary school on day one.

Piper felt sorry for Isaac.

There was nothing she could do about it,

though. Even if Piper offered to help, there was no way she could take a week off and fly to the Bahamas to volunteer in a cooking competition in which she had no stake. Even though the prize was enticing, the money would not be Piper's. Isaac needed it to start his own restaurant or to buy a good truck.

I wish I could help him.

But I'm poor now.

Two dishes later, Mrs. Pendegrast asked what else Isaac was cooking. "Didn't you buy squid?"

Piper asked her to repeat it as she read her lips.

Did she say squid?

Was that the content of the mystery paper sack inside the grocery bag?

Isaac shook his head. "We only have time for two dishes today. We'll cook squid next week."

"Just as well," Mom said. "I can barely tolerate calamari. At least it's not as bad as frog legs. You know, people shouldn't be eating frogs."

"They choose to," Isaac said. "You don't have to eat it if you don't want to, but you can't tell others not to."

"It's gross."

Isaac glanced at Piper.

She shrugged. How was she supposed to respond? If Mrs. Pendegrast didn't like frog legs, that was her prerogative. As long as they didn't have to cook frog legs in Nassau, she should be fine.

We all have our own preferences.

Piper wondered how much Isaac remembered from their high school days, but she herself still disliked octopus meat. And no one could make her eat it.

Besides, octopuses are cute.

Not privy to her thoughts, Isaac pointed to his watch. "We'll have to finish up, clean up, change up, and go to church."

Piper kept some clean clothes in her office in the restaurant across the street, and she could very well come back in a dress or something. But Sunday evening attire at Riverside Chapel was casual, and what she had on—a long sleeved shirt and stretch pants—were enough.

Isaac was wearing a dark tee shirt under his apron and a pair of jeans.

"Do you have a change of clothes?" Piper signed. "For church tonight."

"She asked if you have a change of clothes for church," Mrs. Pendegrast interpreted.

Isaac didn't answer.

His mom called his name.

"Huh?" Isaac looked tired, like his mind was elsewhere.

Mrs. Pendegrast repeated.

"Yes, in the truck." Isaac's eyes were on his red snapper dish.

Piper knew her place and did not want to make a menu suggestion. She didn't want to be blamed. If Isaac lost the competition, whose fault would it be if she interfered with his menu? If Isaac won the competition, he might feel like he didn't do it all himself.

No chef is an island.

But Isaac would have to reach that conclusion himself.

He placed the plate of red snapper wrapped in grape leaves in front of his mother.

When he turned around, Piper handed him three small plates with three forks.

"I was going to ask you for these." He looked surprised that she had anticipated it. "Did you read my mind?"

Piper simply smiled.

She wanted to say that they worked well together, but she didn't want Isaac's mom to misinterpret her intentions with those words.

She wished that Isaac understood ASL or that she could speak. Not much she could do about her voice since she had been deaf since birth.

As Piper tasted the funny fish, Isaac watched her reaction.

Over the years, Piper had been invited to judge

a few cooking competitions here and there. If she could be honest with Isaac, something was wrong with the dish.

"This doesn't taste right." Mrs. Pendegrast made a face. "It's sour."

"Sour?" Isaac asked, facing Piper.

"Sour and bitter," Piper signed. She decided to tell Isaac later—when his mom wasn't around—that maybe he could add starch of some sort, like rice, to buffer the fish from the grape leaves.

Or invent another dish.

"She said it tastes really bad," Mrs. Pendegrast said.

"I didn't say that," Piper signed. She studied Isaac's face to see if he believed his mom.

Mrs. Pendegrast waved her off.

Piper did not like to be misinterpreted. However, she had not asked Mrs. Pendegrast to be her interpreter. In fact, she had no idea that Isaac was going to be there this afternoon.

Well, she hadn't thought of it before she showed up to help Mrs. Pendegrast with her knife skills.

Not that she hadn't thought of Isaac, but she hadn't thought through the situation.

Piper did not want to ask Mrs. Pendegrast what her motives were. Other people had said that she was sometimes manipulative, doing whatever it took to get her way.

In this case, Piper was confident Mrs. Pendegrast genuinely wanted to help Isaac, who could not afford to pay a sous chef for a week in Nassau.

Isaac wasn't in this to gain a reputation. He needed the money to open his own establishment.

"Well, we better clean up. Church is starting in forty-five minutes." Isaac tossed his fork into the sink.

Piper pointed to herself. "I'll clean up."

"She says she'll clean up," Mrs. Pendegrast interpreted.

"Let's do it together," Isaac said.

"Wonderful team work, you two," his mom said. "I'm going home. It's been a long day and I've worked hard."

"You're not going to church tonight?" Isaac asked.

"Nope. I think Jerome is coming, but I brought my own car this afternoon."

"Do you want to take some of the food home?"

"I don't want anything—particularly the fish. As for chicken, I've eaten plenty of chicken in my life."

"Could you take home some stuff for me and put it in the fridge at home?" Isaac asked.

"Like what?"

"I have some extra groceries in the fridge here." Isaac opened the refrigerator door and pointed to the grocery bag.

Piper still wondered what was in that grocery bag.

"Sure." Mrs. Pendegrast put on some lip gloss, and threw on her faux fur coat. "Thank you for cleaning up, kids. See you at home, Isaac. Drive home safely, Piper."

And she was gone, taking Isaac's grocery bag with her.

As they loaded whatever they could into the smaller of the two commercial dishwashers in the galley, Isaac spoke to Piper.

"If I give you the judge's rubric, will you fill them out for each of my dishes today?" he asked.

Piper nodded.

Isaac wiped his hands on a dish towel, and swiped his iPad that had recipes on it. He tapped a sample judge's rubric. He handed the iPad to Piper, and pointed to the barstool that Mom had vacated.

"Now?" Piper signed, but Isaac didn't understand what she was saying.

"I'll do the dishes while you evaluate my cooking." He held her hand and led her to the seat. "Please give me your real opinion, not interpreted or translated, whatever you call it."

Piper nodded. He knew his mother didn't interpret Piper's words exactly.

When Piper sat down, he still held her hand.

She looked at him, wondering what he was thinking.

Slowly, he let go of her hand.

"Thank you," Isaac said, and returned to cleaning the dirty dishes at the sink.

CHAPTER FORTY-FIVE

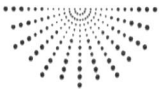

*D*etective Zimmerman chose his words so carefully that Piper began to pray for the poor man that he might have the strength of God to deal with this bear of a mess.

While it was his job to investigate crimes, his life would be easier had the criminal not escape his consequences.

Then again, one never escapes God.

Piper thanked God that she was old enough now to bear the situation, or at least know how to depend on God for help in this time of trial and testing.

If her cousin Regis had stolen money from her when she had been younger, Piper wouldn't have had the benefit of age and spiritual maturity to handle it. Even if he had robbed her after she just accepted Christ as her Lord and Savior, she would have been such a baby believer that she might have bungled her response to the mess.

I might even blame God.

Right now, sitting in her office with a nervous Nelson interpreting what Detective Zimmerman spoke, Piper felt unusually calm.

I can do all things through Christ who strengthens me.

Philippians 4:13 had been one of the first verses Heidi taught her to memorize. For ten years, that verse had returned to her mind time after time.

Now God was using it again to help her endure this problem.

Otherwise I cannot bear it.

"Between the time you visited your cousin after Thanksgiving and now, several things transpired," Zimmerman continued.

Piper had a hard time reading his lips, so she relied more on Nelson—who was sweating.

Piper now prayed for her restaurant manager, that his heart wouldn't give out. He needn't worry, truly. The Pendegrast investment in Piper's Place would continue for at least a year, giving Piper time to rebuild her funds, restructure her restaurant, cut costs, increase income, the works.

Piper patted Nelson's shoulder.

"God will take care of us," she signed.

"I know," Nelson signed back. "This is just all too much news."

"It's going to be okay."

"How can you be so calm?"

"Remember Philippians 4:13."

A light came into Nelson's eyes. He nodded.

Piper recalled the verse in her own mind for her own benefit again.

"As I was saying, something went down between the time you saw your cousin and now," Zimmerman repeated himself. "Your cousin not only stole money from you, but he also stole from some money launderers."

The detective waited for Nelson to sign.

"Since the money launderers are international, many agencies are now involved, from DHS and ICE to the Secret Service to the FBI and local police departments."

Everybody wants a piece of my cousin?

"Your cousin also has a gambling addiction, and he wasn't very good at poker. He lost most of the money he stole."

"Including mine?" Piper signed. She probably already knew the answer.

"We don't know for sure," Zimmerman said. "They're still tracking all his bank accounts, and looking everywhere for possible stashes of cash."

"How is SCMPD helping?" Piper signed.

"We're the small fish," Zimmerman said through Nelson. "We're on standby. If they need any information from us, they will call us."

"Where is Regis now? Maybe I can talk to him? We're family, so maybe he will tell me the truth." Piper paused. "Or maybe he won't tell me the truth, since I'm one of his victims."

"Still, it's worth a try," Nelson finally said.

"They already asked. Regis said he won't talk to you," Zimmerman said. "He said you're a religious fanatic."

Piper almost laughed. "I told him his soul needs to be saved. That's all."

"You probably also prayed for him," Nelson added.

"He closed his eyes, so he could not see what I prayed. I wanted him to repent." Piper's heart felt heavy.

She looked at Zimmerman. "Now you're saying Regis won't face jail time."

The SCMPD spoke aloud what Piper just signed.

"He's a federal witness," Zimmerman replied. "They need his testimony to go after the money launderers. He had worked for them for a while, it turned out, and he had information that various federal agencies want. He is out of our hands."

"Will I see him again? He's family."

"You will neither see him nor your money ever again, if he stays inside WITSEC." Zimmerman spelled it out for Piper.

She could hardly believe it. She asked Nelson to repeat.

A thief like Regis was going into the United States Federal Witness Security Program for helping to bring bigger criminals to justice, but in the process, he would continue to live freely, albeit under a different name and in a different town.

Freely?

Maybe he won't be truly free.

"Will he serve his time for stealing Piper's money before they send him to WITSEC?" Nelson asked.

"He's gone," Zimmerman said. "He gave his written testimony a few days ago. As a result, his life is in mortal danger. In return for testifying, they protect his life, and that of his family."

"I'm family too," Piper signed. "Am I in danger?"

CHAPTER FORTY-SIX

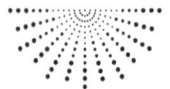

*I*saac forgot all about Mom's Super Senior Christmas luncheon after church on Sunday, one week before Christmas Eve, causing him to cancel their cooking lesson for the afternoon, but leaving him stuck with no commercial kitchen to use.

I suppose I could cook in Mom's kitchen.

When the Super Seniors did luncheons at Riverside Chapel, they went all out. Potluck or catered, they took over the entire galley kitchen, the main dining room, and then some. They recruited their grandchildren to serve tables wearing white gloves, keeping water goblets filled throughout the entire two-hour luncheon, longer if they brought in speakers who could spin long tales.

It's my fault. I should have paid more attention to the church event calendar.

When he realized what was happening to his afternoon plans, Isaac texted Piper after church to ask her not to bother showing up. Yeah, they were three weeks away from leaving for Nassau, but sometimes things happened.

Piper had already gone home. Not to her own house, but to the small room she rented from Llewellyn.

Isaac would rather she not live there, since both of them were unmarried, but no one asked for his opinion, and it was none of his business.

When Piper found out that Isaac had nowhere to go, she offered her kitchen at Piper's Place for him to use this afternoon.

After profusely thanking her for the generous offer, Isaac tried to play it cool. "I won't get there until at least 2:30 p.m."

Piper tapped her phone.

PIPER

I can wait. Sabine is doing another open house for me, but I don't have to be there. She handles everything. I just pay her when we sell the house.

ISAAC

Did anyone bite?

PIPER

Unfortunately, no. I thought the market is good. Maybe my house is too old.

ISAAC

Does it have problems—the foundation or something?

PIPER

No. It passed the house inspection.

ISAAC

We'll pray that it will sell. That's what you want, right?

PIPER

That's what I need. Cash to keep my restaurant going.

ISAAC

Even with your new investors?

PIPER

They know I'm working my way back up so I can buy their shares from them. Anyway, it's a process. So I'll see you at 2:30 p.m.

Isaac hesitated. He wanted to ask her to join him for lunch, but he wasn't sure how she was going to respond—

Oh, just go for it.

ISAAC

Where are you eating lunch?

PIPER

Haven't decided.

ISAAC

I was thinking of grabbing a bowl
at the grocery store, since we'll be
eating whatever we cook later.

PIPER

Like a progressive lunch?

ISAAC

You can look at it that way.

PIPER

Sounds fun. Let's do it.

ISAAC

Do you want me to pick you up?
Save you from driving.

PIPER

Why not!

And so that was how Isaac ended up driving over to Llewellyn's house and picking up Piper. Just as Isaac was starting the engine of his truck, he spotted a car coming up the driveway.

The driver was one tall dude with a long neck. Llewellyn. Isaac had seen him the other day at Piper's Place, when he delivered a heart-box to Piper's office. It had turned out to be a cross necklace.

Llewellyn parked his car nonchalantly.

His passenger quickly pulled her hood over her head and bent her head down.

But Isaac had seen parts of her face.

As clear as day, that was Forsythia.

Isaac reached over to tap Piper's arm. She was on her phone.

"Look who just came home with your friend." Isaac pointed.

All they could see was the bright red hood peeking up from the side window.

On his part, Llewellyn sat still in the driver's seat.

Neither one of them came out of the car.

Piper lifted her index finger.

"One minute?" Isaac asked.

Piper nodded.

See, I understand ASL now.

Isaac waited to see how Piper handled it. She went around his truck, walked up to the passenger side of Llewellyn's car, and tapped on the window.

Slowly, the red hood rose. A forehead and two eyes appeared.

Isaac had no idea what Piper signed to Forsythia. He watched Llewellyn get out of the car. He came over to the passenger side, where Piper was standing.

The trio signed without anyone speaking.

Isaac felt left out, but there was nothing he

could do except to wait for their conversation to be over. Just as he had felt in some parts of Asia, or Egypt, or other places he had cruised to where he didn't speak the language, he knew that this was harder.

There was no way Piper would be able to speak to him. Not only was she profoundly deaf since birth, she had also decided not to get a cochlear implant—unlike Llewellyn, who was only hearing impaired, and had speaking parents who helped him assimilate into the world of speaking people.

Piper did not find the need to do so, when ASL was readily available to everyone.

I need to learn ASL.

If Isaac knew ASL, then he wouldn't need Nelson—or worse, Mom—to interpret for him. He could be as precise as he wanted, convey exactly what he intended, and he and Piper could discuss many things.

Like what things?

I don't know. Many things.

When Piper returned to his truck with eyes so red and mind so far away, Isaac knew that he had to master ASL.

Not only did he think he could listen to her when she needed someone—like right now—but he could also defend her or help her in many more ways than he could at present.

And yet...

For now, they'd have to resort to texting. Just not in the car, due to Georgia laws.

Isaac drove as fast as the speed limits allowed, all the way across town to the organic grocery store where he had ordered more shrimp for his experimental dishes.

He wanted to get there quickly so that they could sit down with their lunch bowls and text each other.

Assuming Piper wanted to talk about whatever it was that had caused her to stare listlessly out of the truck window.

At the grocery store, things didn't change.

Piper didn't want to talk about it during their quick lunch. They had found a corner booth, affording them privacy, but it didn't matter. When Isaac texted Piper, she made it clear she was in no mood to rehash her problems.

PIPER

If you must know, it's about my cousin. That's all for now.

ISAAC

I'll keep praying.

PIPER

Please pray for Ming Wei, too. He's looking into the matter to find out more.

ISAAC

Will do. I've prayed for you.

Piper

Thank you. I look forward to
helping you cook this afternoon.
Cooking is therapeutic for me.

ISAAC

For me too.

When they finished their lunch bowls, Piper
turned the tables on Isaac. She texted him, asking
what was going on between him and his mom.

"That's invasive questioning," Isaac said.

Touché.

They had a good laugh about it, but Isaac knew
he had to confess his own failure even before it
begun. How could anyone fail a cooking competition weeks before it was held?

Well, here I am. Exhibit A.

"Do you have suggestions for me?" Isaac asked.

Piper seemed to be thinking for a long minute.

"Either my problem has no solution, or there
are too many solutions." Isaac laughed.

Piper pointed at him, her eyebrows raised.

"Too many solutions?" Isaac asked.

Piper nodded. She started tapping on her
phone.

Across the table, Isaac waited. He thought she

typed fairly fast, but he wished they could talk to each other verbally. It would save time.

On the other hand, Piper might be wishing that they could sign to teach other. That would save time too.

Isaac was staring at his phone when Piper's text appeared.

PIPER

Either you find a new assistant cook, or you change your menu to something she can help you with —without further training.

ISAAC

Alternatively, I could do everything myself.

PIPER

Will the other competing chefs have sous chefs?

ISAAC

I'd be surprised if they don't.

PIPER

Then you will be at a disadvantage.

ISAAC

I'm afraid of that.

PIPER

I wish I could spare a sous chef for you. But not for a whole week.

ISAAC

Don't worry about me.

PIPER

I do worry about you.

Isaac read it, looked up, and found Piper trying to delete the last thing she typed. He reached across the table and placed his hand on top of hers.

"I already read it," he said. "Can't backspace."

She looked like she had disclosed too much of her own thoughts or feelings, and was putting up a wall even as Isaac held her hand.

"Don't put up a wall," he said.

When Piper didn't answer, Isaac mustered all the bravery he had—which was very little—and tried again.

"Let me in, Piper. Let me in."

CHAPTER FORTY-SEVEN

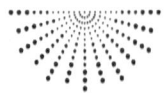

*M*ing Wei showed up at Piper's Place with a hungry stomach at two in the afternoon, almost a week later to give Piper the answer she couldn't get from Detective Zimmerman. The restaurant was crowded, so Ming agreed to eat in Piper's office so they could have some privacy while he told them what he had discovered.

This time, Piper paid him for his investigative work, although Ming gave her a discount, knowing the financial disaster that had befallen her.

"Am I in danger?" Piper signed the same question she had for SCMPD. "I'm Regis's cousin."

"No, you're not." Ming carefully cut the filet mignon.

It wasn't lunch fare, but Piper said she'd feed him anything he wanted. This was one custom meal Piper wouldn't regret. The private investigator and friend only had her best interest in mind.

So, he was saying...

"Wait. What?" Piper held on to the armrest on the sofa she was sitting on. Ming was in an armchair on the other side of the coffee table, leaning toward his dinner plate at the edge of the table.

In the other armchair, Nelson served as the interpreter, as he usually did whenever Piper had important meetings.

"Your cousin led a double life in New Jersey under various names," Ming said.

Piper's head spun. "He was in the hospital under his real name, wasn't he? I asked for Regis at the hospital desk. His girlfriend also called him Regis."

"Regis Peyton is not his real name," Ming said, more strongly this time.

Piper nearly fell out of the sofa. "But I've known him all my life."

"All *your* life. He's older than you?" Ming asked. "The police discovered that the woman who gave him a room at her apartment in Atlantic City was his birth mother."

"Wait. Wait." Piper closed her eyes and drew a deep breath. Her hands were tired of signing. "Regis's mom was Ada Peyton. She died of cancer."

"Married to Mack Peyton," Ming said. "But neither Mack nor Ada are his real parents."

"No way. Regis is a spitting image of Uncle Mack." Piper glanced at Nelson, who now looked bemused by the sudden turn of events.

"No wonder your grandmother cut him out of her will." Nelson shook his head. "No wonder."

Ming drank some water. "Ready for a campfire story?"

No, I'm not ready. Piper nodded anyhow.

"Forty years ago, Regis's mother sold him to Ada and Mack to raise as their own son. After Ada Peyton passed away, Regis went looking for his birth mother. He found her dealing cards in Atlantic City."

"Auntie Ada passed away seven years ago," Piper signed. "Regis never said a word about finding his birth mother."

"His mother was in the middle of an elaborate scheme that she was unable to pull off, and along came her own biological son, who happened to have accounting skills."

"So instead of going to the police, Regis decided to join her?" Nelson asked.

"Blood is thicker than water."

"Since the meet-up, Regis had been going back and forth to Atlantic City almost every month, and then weekly. All his travel records showed an incredible amount of money spent on plane tickets, wining, and dining—maybe even beyond his regular day job."

"He lost a couple of clients last year, so I tried to give him more work," Piper signed. "In the process, he wiped my accounts clean. If not for my new investors, Piper's Place would be no more after Christmas."

"God provided," Ming said.

"Amen." Piper signed.

No wonder Regis had no problem stealing from her.

She wasn't family.

"He was desperate, probably." Ming finished his lunch. "Thank you. Another delicious meal."

Piper nodded.

"While their planning was going on, Regis frequented the casino and became a regular," Ming explained. "And he developed a gambling problem. This was according to the people my buddies talked to. I had them cross check with more people, and they all said that Regis lost a lot of money. But he kept going back, kept trying, kept hoping."

"And kept losing." Nelson shook his head.

"He started borrowing money from loan sharks, thinking he could pay them back—with high interest rates." Ming shrugged. "He thought that if he could win big just once... The sharks sent collectors the weekend before he stole from you."

"But he didn't pay them back with my money." Piper recalled Regis's girlfriend saying that he only 'borrowed' a hundred thousand dollars from her—when in real life, he had stolen three times as much from her bank accounts.

"The girlfriend." Ming drank some water. "You told me her name. My associates looked into her. She's clueless. Regis probably didn't tell her anything."

"You keep calling him Regis, but you said earlier that it's not his real name," Piper signed.

"To you, it will always be Regis, who no longer exists," Ming explained. "I can't tell you his real name for your own protection. All I can tell you is that we haven't scratched the surface of what Regis was involved in."

"You mean the sting operation that got him injured so badly?" Piper signed. "Why he's in WITSEC now?"

Ming nodded. "While Regis and his mom were plotting their retirement funds, the feds were trying to catch the money launderers. In the middle of their deep undercover operation, they discovered those two in the thick of things. Now you know the background of what Detective Zimmerman told you last Friday."

Piper felt that she needed some fresh air.

On the one hand, she was glad that Regis didn't die in the DHS crossfire, but on the other hand, it was starting to look like other people's problems, not hers.

I can't believe Regis is not my real cousin.

Had that been the real reason her grandmother had cut him out of her will? It might also explain why Regis had taken money meant for the restaurant—which Grandma left to Piper alone. Perhaps he thought the money was rightfully his.

"The feds were investigating the money laundering. The local police departments were looking into the money that Regis stole from his clients in Georgia and New Jersey." Ming lifted one hand, then the other, like he was balancing a scale. "The feds get first dibs, you see, because their scope is wider and their fish is bigger. Unfortunately, Regis ends up being a credible witness for them to take down the money launderers, and now they've whisked him into WITSEC, so you're not going to get your money back—not soon, anyway."

"But the country is now safer from people like my non-cousin," Piper signed and sighed.

"It's a difference between half a billion dollars and your three hundred thousand dollars," Ming said matter-of-factly.

"Big fish, little fish." Piper nodded.

There was nothing she could do.

Someday, maybe it would be safe for Regis to come out of WITSEC to clear his conscience and return her money. Then again, from the sound of it —Regis's gambling addiction—her money was more than likely gone.

Suing a ghost would do no good.

"Look at it this way. You're not running for your life. So who is richer, in the end?" Ming stood up. "You know what the Bible says about it."

Piper nodded. She finger spelled Matthew 16:26, and then signed the verse in ASL.

For what profit is it to a man if he gains the whole world, and loses his own soul? Or what will a man give in exchange for his soul?

She knew the entire verse by heart because it had been her guiding verse for her business in the last ten years, although she hadn't always remembered it when she overworked or pushed too hard to earn more revenues at the expense of her own well-being.

I have no personal life.

Yes, it was way past time for her to finally accept that she needed to take at least one day off a week to rest and refresh her mind, body, and soul.

"Better choose wisely," Ming said.

Better choose wisely, indeed.

CHAPTER FORTY-EIGHT

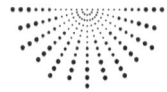

Since the invention of this particular kind of pop-up Christmas tree, courtesy of Christmastown USA, Isaac thought that the entire Untermeyer family had missed out on spending an enormous time decorating their Christmas tree every year. The pop-up trees were shorter than their usual nine-footer that Dad had loved to plant right in the middle of their old living room.

The irony in the entire situation was the existence of Amy's Christmas Tree Farm outside of town, that Mom still ran. Isaac wanted to ask her how Piper's herb garden was coming along, but he didn't have any opportunity in the flurry of activities leading up to Christmas Day.

Mom's older brother and his granddaughter

from Atlanta were coming to town "to see the ocean."

Poor, landlocked relatives.

Isaac had tried to contact Garrett, but he pretty much knew that the soldier was incommunicado. Isaac prayed that sometime in the near future, his little brother would be able to come home for holidays and birthdays, but once again, he would be missed this year.

As eccentric as Mom was, Isaac was glad that she insisted on an empty seat and table setting for Garrett.

"Just in case he walks in," she said.

"Did Mom do this last year?" Isaac pointed to Garrett's place card on the dinner table.

"Not last year." Amy waddled to her seat, drank from her water goblet, and walked away. Her tummy didn't show under her sweater, but she was acting like she was farther along than a couple of months. She even looked sick.

Her husband said it was morning sickness.

Isn't that odd? It was evening right now.

Isaac shrugged. Someday, if he ever married, he would find out all about the different types of sicknesses.

If I ever marry.

What a thought.

Isaac walked around the long dinner table that

Jerome and his daughters Tamsyn and Phoebe had set up. There was really nothing for him to do but putter around and wait. Mom had forbidden him to cook in the kitchen today.

He could hear the women in the kitchen, laughing and making a whole lot of noise with the pots and pans. He was happy that Mom got along well with her stepdaughters.

Jerome's youngest, Phoebe had flown in from Tennessee, where she and her husband lived, to be with them for Christmas. Throughout the evening, she spoke very little about what her husband did. Keenan O'Tierney was in the security business, but what kind of security? Isaac didn't ask. All Phoebe said was that Keenan was overseas at this time and could not join them.

Tamsyn's husband, Ryan, and her dad were in the backyard, playing football with her two oldest daughters in the Savannah cold. Ryan Ruttledge was an architect, and his company recently opened a branch in Savannah, putting him in charge. It also meant that the family could stay in their historic Queen Anne-style home and raise their children there.

Isaac didn't join them in the backyard because he didn't feel like it. All his life, Isaac had never been into football of any kind—whether American or Federation. Soccer hadn't been his thing since he was hit in the head by a soccer ball in fifth grade and never quite recovered from his bruised ego.

Yeah, the same ego that had caused a rift between him and Piper for twenty years.

Come to think of it, he still hadn't heard Piper literally say she forgave him for being jealous of her win.

Jealous?

Truth be told, that's what it is.

Whether Isaac considered himself competitive otherwise, he had been a sore loser because he wasn't the winner. He wasn't in the high school newspaper. He wasn't front page champion chef.

You've changed my heart, Lord. I know You have.

Whether Piper forgives me or not, I'm glad You did.

The doorbell rang, and Isaac's heart skipped a beat.

In addition to Mom's brother and grandniece, Mom had also invited Piper. It was meant to be a surprise, but Amy told Isaac because she thought he had to know.

And his sister was right.

After seeing Piper unexpectedly in the riverboat galley kitchen a few Sundays ago, and reacting badly, Isaac did not need a repeat of his own poor reaction. It wasn't like Mom had forgotten. She had deliberately not told Isaac. He had been caught off-guard, and his response had been anything but Christian.

The doorbell rang again.

"Someone get the door!" Jerome's voice came from the living room, and Isaac heard a creak from his old recliner, like he had just stretched out on it. His recliner was maybe ten feet from the front door, but Jerome must be tired.

Sure enough, when Isaac reached the living room, Jerome was exactly where Isaac thought he would be, drinking eggnog and ordering people around. On the couch next to him, Amy was stretched out, shoes off, palms on her tummy, eyes closed.

"You're not sick, are you, little sister?" Isaac asked as he walked past her.

"Just tired, is all."

Isaac looked out the side window to see who was there. Just in case.

It looked like Uncle Andros.

Isaac tried to unlock the front door, when he realized it was already unlocked. *Mom!*

It made him upset when she did this. When she expected visitors, she'd go unlock the front door. This wasn't the fifties anymore, but she did it anyway.

Anyone can walk in, Mom! You know, like criminals!

Uncle Andros surprised Isaac with his new look—well, new to him in five years. He had long hair and a beard, and wore a leather jacket and a pair of black leather pants. Under his arm was a rough-looking helmet with fire decals all over it.

Standing next to him must be his granddaughter, but Isaac had forgotten her name.

"Come in. Come in." *Whoever you are.* "We're all expecting you. Dinner will be coming soon."

Dinner was late.

If Isaac had anything to do with it, dinner would be on time.

However, Mom had banned Isaac from what she had called the Untermeyer Christmas Kitchen. Only Mom, who had called herself the Head Cook, and her two assistant cooks, Jerome's daughters, were allowed in the kitchen.

Jerome himself could come and go, for "taste testing," but the rest of them—especially Isaac—were ordered to stay away from the kitchen—until after dinner when the men would do the dishes—or they would not be allowed to eat with the family.

Mom was brutal.

What is she trying to prove? That she could cook?

Everyone in the family knew Mom could cook.

Her only problems were that she never quite cubed onions evenly, she didn't know what mirepoix was, she didn't like to try new things—like foi gras or calamari or caviar—and she made Isaac sign that paper to absolve herself from any blame if he lost the cooking competition in Nassau.

Other than that, Mom was as normal as could be.

After letting Uncle Andros and his granddaughter into the living room, Isaac was closing the front door, when out of the corner of his eye, he saw car lights coming down the road.

Maybe it's Piper.

The car drove on, down the street, and away from the house.

Isaac grabbed his jacket from the cloak closet, and stepped outside on the porch. He sat on one of the two deck chairs facing the street. Since Jerome moved in, he had slowly changed the decor of this house, to the point that it was starting to look like a houseboat. Mom didn't seem to mind.

The air at twilight was nippy by Savannah standards. It felt like all those Christmas evenings from his childhood days, after the family had eaten and played some board games.

After we have eaten.

Mom's dinner was late tonight, but Isaac couldn't complain. Mom was trying to prove something, so the family let her. It was her own idea to do all the cooking.

Really, she didn't have to prove anything.

Looking out at the street filled with cars lining it, surrounded by Christmas decorations on houses and roofs across the street, Isaac spotted someone coming up the sidewalk.

Piper.

She made it.

Isaac wanted to go to her, but he didn't want her to get the wrong idea. He waited until she came up the sidewalk before he stood up and waved.

Piper tapped the phone in her hand.

Isaac's own phone chirped.

> **PIPER**
>
> Sorry I'm late. This is the third Christmas event I'm attending today.

> **ISAAC**
>
> You're early. We haven't eaten yet.

> **PIPER**
>
> No? It's 8:35 p.m.

> **ISAAC**
>
> At the rate Mom is going, we might not eat until after nine.

Isaac extended his arm to Piper as she stepped

up to the porch. "Want to sit out here for a little bit?"

Piper nodded.

She stretched out on one of the two deck chairs, and Isaac took the other one. She texted Isaac.

Isaac read it. "Yes, I agree it's comfortable. Good idea from Jerome to put these deck chairs here."

She texted again.

Isaac chuckled. "Okay. I'll wake you up if you fall asleep."

But she didn't.

Piper looked his way, as if waiting for him to speak.

Isaac had gotten used to her facing him whenever he said something. He tried not to think about the fact that she was really looking at his moving lips.

She was reclining too far away for him to hold her hand, so he kept his hands on his side as he rolled over to look back at Piper. She looked at peace under the dim porch light, an ethereal beauty he wouldn't have missed had he not been so full of himself in years past.

He tried to find something benign to say, but nothing came to his mind.

Sometimes it wasn't necessary to say anything.

CHAPTER FORTY-NINE

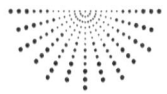

*N*ew Year's Day came and went without any fanfare as Isaac spent the two weeks following Christmas improving on his own ability to cook any dish, given the ingredients and a theme.

At the same time, he wasn't certain it was adequate preparation to win the fifty-thousand-dollar prize. This week, the organizer of the cooking competition notified everyone that, in addition to the big check, the winner would also be offered a six-figure job as chef de cuisine of a critically acclaimed restaurant in Lucaya on Grand Bahama island.

To be honest, Isaac wasn't sure if he wanted to be someone else's chef yet again. He had been there, done that. Nonetheless, he could work out an agreement where he worked for only one year.

Then again, that was one more year farther away from his dream of owning his own establishment.

But first, he had to win the cooking competition next week.

As the thoughts ran through his head, Isaac checked his suitcase one last time to make sure he had packed everything he needed. Confident he hadn't missed a thing, he zipped it up. He rolled the suitcase out of his childhood bedroom, and carried it down the old wooden stairs. He could hear Jerome and Mom laughing upstairs as he reached the living room.

At Christmas, Mom had proven to everyone that she could step up to the challenge as Isaac's assistant cook by preparing the most elaborate family dinner the Untermeyers had ever had. She had done it all with homestyle dishes that everyone remembered from their childhood.

Even Piper had been impressed.

Isaac smiled as he recalled his own delight that evening when Piper had decided to sit next to him at the Christmas dinner. Even though he could not speak ASL—not yet—they communicated using food language. Well, for the most past, they had showered compliments on the cook.

I'm going to miss her.

Loud footsteps and the sound of luggage thumping the wooden staircase interrupted Isaac's memories, as Jerome came down the stairs. Mom was right behind him.

"Are you going to be okay by yourself for two weeks?" Mom sounded worried.

"Of course. I'll eat at Amy's or Tamsyn's or Piper's." Jerome rolled Mom's suitcase to the front door. "Don't spend too much money in the Bahamas."

"I'll only buy what I need, dear." Mom pecked her husband on the cheek.

Isaac waited for Jerome to ask Mom to define *need*, but he didn't.

Should I tell him that Mom has expensive needs?

Isaac decided to mind his own business. He double-checked his backpack, which carried his favorite kitchen knives. He'd have to check those things at the airline counter, and he hoped they wouldn't be lost on the way to Nassau.

He also brought a rolling suitcase, the same one that had traveled with him across the seven seas. He'd had it for years, and it still worked. It had two compartments. He put clothes in one compartment, and spices and his favorite kitchen gadgets in the other.

Isaac figured that if he ran out of clothes, he could buy them in the Bahamas, but if he didn't have his favorite potato peeler or chopper, he could lose the cooking competition.

A man has priorities, you know.

"Ready, people? I'm going to drop you off at the airport, and then go for lunch with the Super Seniors." Jerome zipped up his coat.

Mom picked up her giant floral tote bag. She put her other hand on Jerome's sleeve. "Watch out for Eunice. She's been eyeing you up and down."

"With her glass eye?" Jerome asked, like it was serious business.

Mom slapped his arm. "No. With her good eye. She's recently widowed. Very lonely. Stay away from her. Just sit at the other table."

Jerome rubbed his scruffy chin. "Are you jealous, Mrs. Pendegrast?"

"No." Mom made a show of it. Then: "Maybe just a little."

"You don't have to worry, dear. I married you, didn't I?"

"That's what they all say." Mom started walking. "Married, but it just happened."

"I'm not like other men." Jerome went after her, kissing her noisily.

Isaac rolled his eyes.

A few minutes later, they had loaded their

luggage into the back of Jerome's SUV. Isaac was looking through his backpack to make sure he had everything he needed, including his passport and plane ticket.

Mom had her own plane ticket in her purse, which she had put inside her tote bag, next to the three hardcover novels she planned to read on the plane ride and in Nassau next week.

They would change planes in Atlanta, but the stopover would only be under an hour. Going from Savannah to Nassau by way of Atlanta would take no more than four or five hours.

Isaac expected to arrive at the Nassau Island Breeze Resort in time for sunset.

He glanced at the street in front of the house. He wasn't sure what he was expecting. Maybe Piper would come over to wish him Godspeed and more?

The street was empty this late morning, as most people were at work this Monday morning, one week after New Year's Day.

No Piper.

Just as well. After the cooking competition, Isaac's future was up in the air. In order for his food truck to succeed, he'd better go to a big city, right? A big city like Atlanta or Miami.

If he was going for money and income.

After ten years of saving and living frugally,

Isaac wondered if money was still his motivation. All along, he had wanted to run his own kitchen to show that he could do it.

Getting into the backseat of the SUV so that Mom and Jerome could hold hands one last time before she flew to Nassau for a week made Isaac think that maybe his focus had been off.

As Jerome backed the SUV out of the driveway, Mom asked him if he locked the house.

"Yes, I did." Jerome didn't sound upset that his wife had asked the question.

Sometimes you have to take things at face value and not read too much into the words or between the lines.

Wow. Where did that come from?

Isaac fastened his seat belt, alone with his own thoughts.

Had he read too much into Mom's intentions?

Over the years, she had tried to manipulate circumstances to the point of sometimes dissembling, in order to get her way, her idea of the outcome.

Isaac wished that Mom had turned more things over to God because trying to determine the outcome of any situation in such a way that would benefit everyone involved was a skill above the human pay grade.

What about me?

Have I turned everything over to God, or am I still trying to hold on to things, as if I could maneuver myself toward my desired outcomes?

"I hope you do well in Nassau." Jerome glanced into the rearview mirror. "I'll be praying for you. Me and the Super Seniors."

"Thank you. I don't know how we'll do." Isaac looked outside the window at the widening roads and increasing number of vehicles on their drive to the Savannah/Hilton Head International Airport.

The same airport that Piper flew out of in November to visit her cousin in New Jersey.

"You know the usual advice. Do your best. Maybe you'll win. Maybe you won't," Jerome said. "As long as you glorify God, you've learned one more thing in life."

Isaac nodded.

They listened to a news talk show on the radio that Jerome picked out, but after about ten minutes, he turned it off because it went to a commercial.

"May I ask you two something?" Isaac asked.

"Sure," Mom said. "Ask us anything. If we don't know the answer, we'll just make it up to look like geniuses."

Isaac laughed.

"Don't mind her," Jerome said at the red light. "She's all giddy because I said she could buy herself something nice in Nassau, and check out some places we could go back to visit next time."

"You sure you don't want to come with us?" Mom asked.

"No, dear." Jerome kept his eyes on the road. "You two will be busy cooking all the time, and I won't have anything to do by myself. While you're gone, I'm going to figure out how to sell the riverboat business to Tamsyn so that you and I can retire. Then we can go back to Nassau on a real vacation."

"After our world cruise," Mom reminded him.

"That too." Jerome laughed. "We're going to need a lot of money to do all the things we want to do now that the kids are grown."

"That's what I was going to ask you," Isaac said.

Mom gasped. "About kids?"

"No! About things y'all want to do."

"Whew." Mom made a big fuss. "For a moment there, I thought you got a girl pregnant."

"What? No." Isaac couldn't speak. "I'm a Christian man, Mom. I would never—I can't believe you even thought that. I'm not even married."

"Well, I had to make sure."

"Mom, you're impossible." Isaac laughed.

"What's your question, Son?" Jerome asked.

"You own a riverboat business. Is that what you always wanted to do?" Isaac asked.

"I grew up on the riverboat, and inherited it from my dad," Jerome said. "I guess I liked the idea at first, but when my dad died, and I had to run the business, it wasn't always easy. Most days, it was hard, especially when I had a sickly wife and two kids to feed and clothe."

"I'm sorry."

"I'm not. God used all those things in my life to bring me to Him. I wished I had been saved during all those hard years because God would have carried me through, like when my first wife died of cancer. But nothing was wasted, if you want to know."

"I'm glad you came to know the Lord when you did." Isaac knew it had been later in Jerome's life.

Saved is saved.

"So to answer your question, I didn't know any other job than to be a riverboat captain," Jerome said. "However, I found that it was useful to have a tour company as well, so I bought a fledgling business, and renamed it Tamsyn Tours after my daughter. I got her interested in it, and then sold her the company. Unfortunately, she doesn't seem too enthused about the riverboats."

"He likes it though," Mom added.

"Yes, I do," Jerome concurred. "I think that if I

had to do something else, I would always think of the river, and I would return to it."

Is that me?

I would always think of the kitchen, and return to it.

"As for Mom, I know you got into Christmastown because Dad did," Isaac said.

"We had three kids to feed and put in college," Mom said. "Your dad inherited the family business. He could sell it, but then we'd have to start over with something new. I decided to help him for the kids."

Isaac knew that it hadn't always gone well between Mom and Dad. Seeing each other too much, maybe?

"We almost killed each other at the office. Your dad and I didn't work well together. In retrospect, I wish I hadn't gotten involved in Christmastown, although after he passed away, it was all up to me."

"So you didn't want it, but you had to do it." Isaac knew that much.

"I had to keep your dad's legacy alive, long enough to pass it on to someone. None of you wanted it, except Amy, but she only wanted a minority share and even less work—at that time."

Isaac nodded.

"Now Christmastown is thriving. Amy and her husband work well together. They love going to work and running the company as partners. It's like Christmas for them every single day, all year round."

"That's nice." Isaac wondered if that would be the case had he married another chef.

"In fact, with the baby coming, I think Amy's going to close or sell off the photo studio she has downtown," Mom added.

"Oh, she still has that, doesn't she?" Isaac didn't recall Amy talking about her studio much. It must be a side thing for her these days.

"She hired a photographer to manage the studio, but business there is not as good as Christmastown."

"Makes sense. Besides, Amy prefers to be with Cyrus at the Christmastown office," Jerome added to what his wife said. "Beware, though. It's not for everyone."

"What's not for everyone?" Mom held on to Jerome's hand.

"Doing business together with your wife. Carleigh and I had opposite ideas all the time. We went as far as naming one of the riverboats after her, but then we fought over every single thing I wanted to do or that she wanted to do. It's not easy to run a river cruise company when the owners didn't agree on anything—from decorating the dining room in our time period of choice or even cruising schedules and which local businesses we should partner with."

"In the end, what did you do?" Isaac had to know.

"Carleigh and I discussed everything and came up with amicable solutions. And you know what? She was right about the period decor in the dining room. Our customers loved it. And I was right about not going into debt. When the economy was bad, our business was fine, and we rode through the storm."

"Did you both make the decisions together or did you let her get her way most of the time?" Isaac asked. He recalled that Dad often let Mom get her way, if only to keep the peace in the Untermeyer family.

"To be honest, I decided to choose my battles. As long as we didn't incur financial debts, as long as business increased, I was flexible and easy to please. If we were within budget, then we could be creative once we had those boundaries set up." Jerome thought for a minute. "I think we each got our own way. I'm the idea and concept kind of guy. She was into details, making us look good in the eyes of the customers. Value, you know. If customers see value, they'll hop on board. Both are needed for the win. And you know what? My daughter Tamsyn has both of our traits in her."

"You were quite distraught after Carleigh died," Mom said.

"Yes, I was. For years. Until I met Pastor Flores who led me to Christ. That was the best thing that happened to me." Jerome stroked Mom's neck. "The next best thing that happened to me after that was meeting you, my love."

Mom giggled. "Even so, I wouldn't want to be involved in the riverboat business. I know my own strengths and weaknesses, and running a riverboat is not my cup of tea. That tree farm is enough for me."

Isaac appreciated Mom's honesty. It also made him wonder.

What is enough for me?

CHAPTER FIFTY

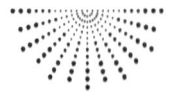

"Stop, Mom. You're stressing me out." Isaac didn't want to look in their hotel room mirror one more time. All over the vanity counter on both sides of the sink were Mom's makeup and stuff.

He didn't recall how the vanity was suddenly Mom's. Where was he going to put his one lone comb?

This was their third day in Nassau, but it felt like they just arrived. After the airport shuttle had dropped them off at the Nassau Island Breeze Resort on Saturday afternoon, Isaac and Mom crashed in their two-bed hotel room.

On Sunday morning, they took a taxi to church at Chapel by the Sea, a sister church to Riverside Chapel in Savannah. Two and a half years before,

Riverside Chapel had sent a mission team to the summer camp sponsored by Chapel by the Sea. One of the team members ended up marrying Byron Moss, the oldest son of Nancy Moss, whose namesake adorned the culinary school that now sponsored the cooking competition.

At the welcome lunch for the chefs after church, Isaac met all the other chefs—his competitors. He was also introduced to Nancy Moss. When Nancy Moss found out that he attended Riverside Chapel in Savannah, she asked him to say hello to Pastor Flores and Heidi, who were friends of the family.

Meeting the billionaire matriarch of the Moss Resorts at church had affected Mom more than Isaac—who wanted the whole week to be over and done with, once Nancy told them that they decided to livestream the entire week.

Isaac had never cooked on live camera before. How was he supposed to behave? How was he supposed to cook?

Now the dreaded Monday morning had arrived.

And Mom was fussing all over him because he refused to put on any of her foundation.

Are you kidding me? I don't care what makeup brand it is. There is just no way I'm going to paste anything on my face.

He adjourned to his queen-sized bed on his side of the room, and checked his iPhone messages. He was hoping for a note from Piper.

Piper?

Yeah, Piper.

He wanted to hear from Piper, far away in Savannah.

He wondered how she was doing. Suddenly too shy to send a text, he could only hope to hear from her.

"Smile more, dear." Mom practiced her own smile, trying to make her eyes bright. Her face was caked with foundation and powder and whatever charcoal she had rubbed on her eyelids.

She pointed to her own blouse and pants. "How do I look?"

"Mom, you'll be wearing a chef's coat, so that's the only thing showing on camera."

"Should I take off my wedding ring? I don't want to get raw meat on it." Mom touched her ring.

"We'll be wearing gloves, so I don't think it matters either way."

Isaac was more worried about kitchen safety for Mom and himself. He was unfamiliar with this special studio kitchen, and even though he had brought a few of his own things, he still had to use an oven and a stove that he had never used before.

"Remind me again why I even bother entering cooking competitions." Isaac frowned.

"You need the money, dear." Mom went back to the bathroom and powdered her face again.

How many times did she need to powder her face?

"Do I need the money?" It might be a subconscious philosophical question.

"You have money," Mom said. "You've been saving for ten years, so I would think you have enough to buy a new food truck, don't you?"

"Well, I started out wanting my own restaurant building..."

"You changed your plans. You told us so at Thanksgiving." Mom ran a comb over Isaac's hair. "I bet the other chefs have makeup artists and hairstylists helping them."

"I don't know about that. None of this was on their website." Isaac frowned.

"I think you need some makeup." Mom started digging through her cosmetics bag.

"No, Mom. I shaved."

"That's not enough."

"It has to be." It didn't seem enough if his face looked pale and sickly on camera later, but Isaac couldn't care less at this point.

Suddenly, he didn't want the fifty thousand dollars anymore.

All he wanted to do was fly home to Piper's Place, walk into her kitchen, and make himself a sandwich.

~

The Nancy Moss Culinary Institute where the cooking competition would be filmed was located one block from the Nassau Island Breeze Resort where Isaac and Mom were staying for one week.

Isaac didn't want to talk to anyone in the brief shuttle ride from the hotel to the culinary school, but Mom went from row to row, introducing herself to the chefs and their assistants. By the time she reached the bus driver at the front of the shuttle, everyone called her Chef Mom.

Chef Mom?

Mom liked it. When she returned to her seat next to Isaac, she was calling herself Chef Mom.

Ten chefs and nine sous chefs plus Chef Mom filed into the Institute through a beautiful rotunda, which Isaac noticed had a fluid design, with underwater murals on the walls.

Their adventure in the cooking competition started off with a brief tour of the building, built only a year before. It primarily served to train world class chefs and cooks. The Moss family funded the culinary school, providing scholarships and inviting award-winning chefs here for masterclasses. Interns worked in resort restaurants and cruise ships owned by the Moss family.

After the brief tour, in which Mom complained that she needed to shop for new shoes right away, they were shown the two massive kitchens in which the chefs would compete, five chefs in each kitchen, each with complete stations for the chefs.

When Isaac entered his assigned kitchen to familiarize himself with where everything was, he found Mom missing. He texted her, asking where she'd gone, reminding her that they started filming in forty-five minutes. He wanted to talk to her about a few things before they started filming.

He stayed in the kitchen, waiting.

A lady with earpieces and an iPad, who introduced herself as Esther Byrne, came to ask if he needed anything. She made sure that he knew how to operate the stove and oven, and knew where to find the pantry and refrigerator.

Isaac had brought his mom an onion chopper. It wasn't a perfect solution, but it would do. He had decided that instead of letting Mom attempt to cube onions, carrots, or whatever they might need, she'd use a chopper and be done already.

And blend everything else.

That way, it wouldn't take her forever to do anything.

He looked around.

Mom was still nowhere to be seen.

"Do you happen to know where Rhoda Pendegrast is?" Isaac asked, on the off-chance that she might know. "She's my sous—I mean, assistant cook. She was with me a minute ago."

The lady whipped out her walkie-talkie. She repeated Mom's name.

"They'll find her for you," she said. "We don't allow people to walk about all over the campus. School is still in session."

"I'm sorry. If you can page her, that would be helpful. I tried to text her, but she's not responding. Maybe her phone doesn't have enough signal."

"Sir, did you read the rules? No cell phones in the kitchen. No internet access." She opened her hand, palm up. "Cell phone, please. I will return it to you after the judges are done for the day."

Isaac handed it over.

"Once you see the main ingredient, you and your sous chef will have half an hour to decide what three dishes you will cook. And then you cook for ninety minutes."

"I know. I read that part of the contest rules."

She didn't smile. "If your sous chef doesn't

show up, you'll have to start without her, but she can't join you midway."

"No?" Isaac hadn't paid attention to that part because he had not expected Mom to go AWOL in the first round. He assumed Mom would be with him the entire time.

"No. Once you see the main ingredient, you can't leave here. We don't want people to cheat by asking someone outside or googling for recipes."

"We wouldn't do that."

"We don't know, do we?" Her walkie talkie crackled. She spoke in a British accent with a Caribbean undertone. "Yes, bring her here now."

"You found Mom." Isaac was genuinely delighted.

"Your mother?" Her eyes widened. Her eyebrows lifted.

"Yes, my assistant is my mom. In the bus ride here, everyone was calling her Chef Mom."

"Interesting." She talked into her walkie talkie again as she walked away. "Send the cameramen, too. Yes, fetch Chef Mom."

Isaac felt like a four-year-old again.

I can't find my mom.

I don't know where my mom is.

Isaac thought he should pray, but he couldn't think of anything but, "Spare me, Lord."

The good news was that he had made it to the

Nancy Moss Culinary Institute Cooking Challenge. He had waited for this event for a few months.

The bad news was that he had tossed and turned all night in the fancy resort next door. So if this day dragged on, he wasn't sure if he had enough brainpower to stay awake, let alone come up with fancy dishes on the fly in half an hour and then cook them to perfection in ninety minutes.

While waiting for his assistant chef to show up, Isaac thought of the top things he must do, and felt bad that prayer had been at the end of his long list, with the first thing being "Sharpen my knives."

Shouldn't he be sharpening his prayer life more than his knife skills?

Lord Jesus, forgive me.

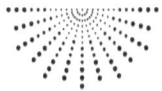

CHAPTER FIFTY-ONE

"*R*emember, Mom. Don't cut yourself. Don't fall. Don't burn anything." Isaac ran the list through his own mind as he helped Mom don the custom chef's coat that the Institute had made for the contestants.

The kitchen was clean again for Day 2, but they were not allowed to enter it yet. Some of the well-known chefs were being interviewed.

Not Isaac Untermeyer, the lesser known.

It hadn't fully dawned on him yet that the entire cooking competition had been live-streamed around the world on Day 1. Half a million views by the curious people of the planet, all watching ten chefs cook on live television.

Gone were the days of prerecorded and carefully edited cooking shows.

This was live.

On Day 1, two people had been eliminated, including the chef who burned one of his arms badly in a grease fire.

Yet that was nothing compared to what Esther Byrne had done about Isaac's missing mom.

He only found out later—after he survived the first round—that Byrne had made a huge drama about the missing Chef Mom. It became a side episode, with people on Twitter and You Tube guessing where Mom was while the cameraman made a show of going all over the building, looking for her.

Soon Chef Mom started trending everywhere, with various chefs now suing the Nancy Moss Culinary Institute Cooking Challenge organizers for using the name Chef Mom at all.

Well, Mom didn't call herself that.

"It's Mrs. Pendegrast to you," she had told the cameraman.

The rest of it, Isaac didn't want to know. He passed out as soon as they went back to the hotel room, and didn't wake up until this morning.

They had survived Day 1.

Thank God.

While Isaac had been sleeping, Mom had gone shopping with a few other sous chefs. They went to town, ate dinner, and suddenly Mom was the star of the party half her age.

Chef Mom.

"Now we're in Day 2," Isaac reminded Mom. "Old things passed away—thank God—and all things become new. Please do not disappear today, stay calm while you're on camera, and don't go viral."

Mom tried on her look of innocence.

It had worked with Dad back when he had been alive.

But it's not going to work with me.

Isaac put on his apron. He turned his back to Mom for no more than a second, when he heard a commotion. He spun around, thinking Mom had fallen, only to find her talking to Esther Byrne.

They were surrounded by a cameraman and his assistant.

"It's Day 2 of the Ninety-Minute Cooking Challenge, ladies and gentlemen," Byrne spoke into the camera. "We're live-streaming from the Nancy Moss Culinary Institute in Nassau, where we have eight chefs left. As you already know, we will be eliminating two more chefs today, and another two tomorrow. Before we find out what the main ingredient for all three dishes must be today, let's check in with Chef Mom."

Isaac backed away from the crowd.

Byrne went on to ask about Mom's evening with her friends, her night at the hotel, her morning at breakfast, and her outlook for the day.

Isaac took a deep breath and prayed that the reason he had made it wasn't due to Mom's instant popularity after her disappearance into the ladies' room to touch up on her makeup.

Don't worry about me. I'm just the chef.

He leaned against a counter, folded his arms, and watched the spectacle around Mom.

Maybe this is good. Maybe it's bad.

After what seemed to be the longest "How do you do?" interview with Mom, Byrne then announced that they were about to start Day 2 of the cooking competition, and asked if the other cameras were ready.

Eight video cameras live-streamed the event.

This would go on for six days until there were four chefs left, and they would all go to the final round. Two chefs against two. The surviving two would compete against each other for the grand prize.

Thanks to Chef Mom's help in generating attention on social media, the grand prize had increased to sixty thousand dollars. Nancy Moss herself had been watching the cooking competition, aware that whenever a part of the event trended online, it brought attention to her culinary school bearing her name.

She added ten thousand dollars to the grand prize.

Sixty thousand dollars could go a long way to buy Isaac a new and shiny food truck with brand new appliances.

Day 2 had more stakes now.

Byrne turned her attention to Isaac. "Chef, are you ready for Day 2?"

"I am." Isaac tried to be calm, but his heart was anything but.

He was on a livestream. Anything he said would be out there instantly.

"Well, good," Byrne said, quickly turning her attention back to Mom. "So Chef Mom, how do you think your son should approach today's main ingredient?"

What in the world?

Isaac scratched his head. He had said only two words, before they swung the camera back to Mom.

I'm the chef here.

He had no idea how Mom could be so calm in front of the camera.

Maybe it was good for Isaac to be reduced to a side show. He could focus on cooking instead. Let Mom have the limelight. He didn't mind. In fact, he didn't care.

As long as Mom could still assist him in cooking.

As instructed, Isaac and Mom stood in front of the stainless steel prep station, waiting for their grocery tote bag to arrive. When it did, Isaac was not allowed to look inside.

"Isn't it interesting?" Mom said. "Here we are looking at a mystery bag, wondering what's inside. You know, life is such that sometimes it's a good thing to wait."

Byrne clapped. "That is our first episode of 'Life is Such That.' We will be asking Chef Mom to give us some life tips every day of this competition."

She touched her earpiece. "I'm told that we have questions from viewers. Iceland wants to know if Chef Mom will still dispense life tips if her son fails to make it to Day 3."

Isaac's shoulders sagged.

Byrne turned to him. "Will you make it to Day 3?"

"I'll try my best," Isaac said. What else could he say?

Byrne turned back to Mom. "Can we enlist Chef Mom to dispense life tips through next week, even if she goes home to Savannah tomorrow?"

"Of course, dear. I can always tweet." Mom smiled.

"Mom, you don't even have a Twitter account," Isaac blurted too soon.

"Ooh. Drama." Byrne turned her attention back to Mom. "How will Chef Mom respond to that challenge?"

"You know, life is such that we may need to improvise sometimes." Mom didn't miss a beat. "If Isaac is eliminated tomorrow, I will get on Twitter. Meanwhile, follow me on Instagram, if you haven't already."

Mom spelled out her IG handle.

"Brilliant answer from Chef Mom." Byrne clapped. She touched her earpiece. "We're a few minutes away from finding out what our main ingredient is. The question is whether Chef Isaac will let Chef Mom look inside the grocery bag first."

Isaac sighed.

Mom isn't a real chef, but she plays one on livestream.

"You know, life is such that you shouldn't be in a hurry all the time," Mom suddenly said. "We can wait one minute or two."

"Chef Mom," Byrne said. "What do you think is in this bag?"

"Hmm. Hmm." Mom made a show of thinking aloud.

Well, at least she's enjoying herself.

"My son can cook pretty much anything, so it matters not to him what's in this bag," Mom said. "I can eat anything he cooks—except..."

Frog legs.

Isaac prayed that the organizers didn't know that. How could they know?

Oh.

Had she posted about her problems with frog legs—especially battered and deep fried—on her Instagram account?

"It's time!" Byrne declared, pushing the grocery bag in front of Mom.

Isaac assumed they were not going to ask him to look inside the bag. He would see it when Mom put the ingredient on the table.

Mom reached into the grocery bag, and lifted out a wrapped paper package. She placed it on the counter.

All eyes were on her, even Isaac's. He was trying to pray, but he realized he was holding his breath. Whatever was in the package, he had to make three dishes in ninety minutes. Could he do it?

Slowly, Mom opened the package. "Yesterday was squid, so today... I think it's chic—"

She looked down at the open package, gasped, and dropped to the floor—

Unconscious.

CHAPTER FIFTY-TWO

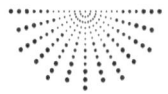

ednesday was Piper's day off, and she had chosen to spend the morning tending to her herbs and vegetables at a corner of Amy's Christmas Tree Farm greenhouse.

No one was in the greenhouse, save for one other person, who had let Piper in. Piper had her own keys, though she wondered how long Mrs. Pendegrast would let her use the greenhouse for free.

Piper's house was still on the market. Sabine had shown it twice, but neither potential buyer made an offer. Piper asked Sabine whether they should lower the price for a quicker sale, but Sabine said they should wait for at least a month.

After harvesting enough kale and lettuce for her own lunch salad, Piper washed the leaves and drove all the way to Tybee Island to sit on the sand and have lunch alone. She spread out the blanket, opened up her picnic basket, and assembled her salad bowl, topping it off with a boiled egg and slices of apple.

It was cold this January day, but it was for this very reason she was out here. The chill had kept both residents and tourists away, leaving her the entire beach and ocean to herself.

Covered from head to ankle in a hooded goose down coat that felt like a giant sleeping bag, Piper poured hot cocoa into a ceramic travel mug.

The silence all around was normal to her, but she could see the waves ebbed and flowed.

She remembered being upset when told she had to close Piper's Place on Sundays, and take another day off—like everyone else in her employment. She tried to protest, but her new investors wouldn't hear of it.

With the new funding, she was able to hire Chef Drew Boyd to handle the lunch shift. Chef Lillian remained in the dinner shift. Sous Chef Forsythia had recovered from her sprained ankle and broken heart—or at least on the mend—and seemed to be enjoying the night shift.

Reluctantly, Piper forced herself to stay away from the restaurant on Wednesdays as well. Nelson promised not to take the same day off. That made Piper feel better.

I need to turn over the restaurant into Your hands, Lord.

Her phone flashed.

Notifications.

Piper scrolled through the list, and realized that she had missed a few—especially when she had been busy in the greenhouse this morning.

Looks like the cooking competition is still going on in Nassau.

She propped her phone on top of her picnic basket, and replayed the start of the day's livestream with closed captions.

Mrs. Pendegrast appeared on the screen. "Life is such that three dozen frog legs are not going to stop you."

Her words also appeared at the bottom of the screen, scrolling left like a ticker tape.

"They tried to stop you yesterday when you fainted, Chef Mom," the interviewer said.

Mrs. Pendegrast remained calm. "I got over it, as you can see."

"Yes, after an hour in the infirmary."

"I want to thank the nurses for taking such good care of me," Mrs. Pendegrast continued. "And my son, for handling the cooking on Day 2 all by himself."

What?

Piper nearly dropped her salad bowl.

The camera panned to the station behind them, where Isaac—five o'clock shadow and all—waved at the viewers. He looked weary, like he knew he had already lost the entire contest.

"Let's talk to Chef Isaac about Chef Mom's traumatic experience yesterday with the frog legs." The interviewer and cameraman approached Isaac.

Piper felt sorry for Isaac. All his dreams seemed to be churning in an atmosphere of carnival and circus. She tapped and noticed that the video was trending worldwide, and over a million people were watching.

Poor Isaac.

"Were you surprised when you saw the frog legs in the grocery bag?" the interviewer asked.

"We were told that the main ingredient would be meat of any kind," Isaac replied. "Frog legs are meat."

"But your mother freaked out."

"She doesn't like frog legs."

"As a result, you had to cook alone. Were you stressed?"

Isaac stared at the interviewer. "You asked me the same question yesterday."

"Yes, I did." The interviewer didn't wait for Isaac to reply. She turned toward the camera. "You would never have expected three dozen frog legs to cost Chef Isaac at least a dozen marks off his score, but that's what happened. As the scores are cumulative, Chef Isaac would have to come up with something spectacular today if he wants to make it to Day 4. Three more days left before the finals. Let's get back to Chef Mom. Today's ingredient might scare her too."

Piper chewed her kale slowly.

How do I pray for Isaac, Lord?

How can I help?

Three more days, and Isaac would be home. From what Piper was seeing on the replay from this morning, Isaac had made a mistake letting his mother help him.

Piper had told him that he had to make a decision. Fire his mom or cook something she could handle.

He went for the second option.

And now this.

Piper finished her salad, and drank more hot cocoa as she looked out to sea. The Atlantic Ocean was serene and calm. A few brown pelicans glided across the surface of the seas. Above the birds, clouds drifted on another calm winter's day on the island.

She looked toward the distant horizon. Somewhere to the south of that vast expanse, the islands of the Bahamas basked in the hot Caribbean sun. Was it calm there? Or was there a storm—especially in Isaac's heart and mind?

I have to help him.

As a chef, Piper knew what to do to help him win the cooking competition.

But no. She couldn't leave Savannah. She had to work Thursday through Saturday—

Wait.

She hadn't taken any personal time off in ten years.

Maybe. Just maybe...

CHAPTER FIFTY-THREE

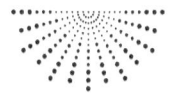

*M*om going viral on social media was the last thing Isaac had expected. But go viral she did, with "frog legs" topping Google searches and trending worldwide on Twitter.

By the end of Day 3 at the cooking competition, Isaac wanted to quit and go home.

His assistant cook was now completely distracted by her new celebrity status, with her impromptu daily doses of "Life is Such That" now becoming part and parcel of the Nancy Moss Culinary Institute Cooking Challenge weeklong contest.

Dad didn't raise a quitter, though Mom is pushing me near the edge.

Isaac decided he could not blame Mom. It

wasn't her fault the cooking competition organizer wanted drama. What else could be more exciting to a cooking show than a colorful non-chef?

Well, to be fair, Mom's newfound fame had caused the Nassau Island Breeze Resort to upgrade them from a small hotel room to a villa with its own backyard—and a personal chef on call.

Here I am, Lord, trying to make the best of the situation.

This evening, Isaac had no appetite for dinner. Mom was in the villa living room trying to start a new YouTube channel so she could do more "Life is Such That" episodes of her own outside of the cooking competition. Apparently, her new friends were online, chatting with her and walking her through the process of setting up a PayPal account so she could monetize her channel.

Whatever.

Isaac found himself walking through the grassy backyard, down meandering stone paths separating the villas from the sand and surf. He counted the number of villas he passed by, so he could back-track and return to the right one.

Above him, the sun was setting. He could hear music and laughter on one side, and the roaring ocean on the other.

Must be the life.

He sat down at the edge of the grass, facing the sea and sky.

Where am I going, Lord?

He had saved up for ten years to open his own restaurant. Somehow, he didn't think he had enough money for a place of his own bigger than a hole in the wall.

The perfect location for his restaurant in any city would cost a lot of money. The cheaper the building, the farther away it would be from the main thoroughfare, and thus, his potential customers.

A building on a popular street where locals and visitors frequent—say, River Street in Savannah— would burn a big hole through his budget.

That wasn't all.

He wanted a new and shiny kitchen, or at least a decent commercial kitchen that passed health inspection. If he had to buy new appliances, that would cost money.

He could buy an existing restaurant, together with its tables and chairs and bars, but he'd probably have to redecorate the place, retile the floors, repaint the walls, and make the place his own.

On top of that, he had to hire chefs and cooks, managers and servers.

What about utilities, taxes, permits, salaries—

Oh yes, food.

Maybe I'm not cut out for this.

He could see why many chefs worked for someone else rather than open their own restaurants.

He wondered how Piper did it. How much money did it cost her to run Piper's Place? Would her restaurant go under now that her cousin had wiped her out, even with the investments from Mom and Jerome? Would she be able to earn back in one year what she had lost in one day so that she could buy back Mom's shares?

Why am I thinking of Piper at all?

In any case, after overthinking it for years, he had settled on running a food truck instead. He hadn't intended on making that his main kitchen. He was still hoping for a brick-and-mortar kitchen, not one on wheels.

How do I pray about this?

He closed his eyes. Once again, no prayer formed in his head. Maybe he had the wrong focus, the wrong direction. How else could he explain his inability to pray about his career?

Exhaustion, perhaps?

It was by the mercy of God that he hadn't been eliminated from the cooking competition. In three days, five chefs had been sent home. Isaac dared not entertain the idea that maybe he hadn't been eliminated because of Mom, frog legs notwithstanding.

This morning's main ingredient had been better.

Mussel.

Mom could handle mussels better than frog legs, although she kept insisting that she preferred any other shellfish to mussels, no matter how Isaac prepared it.

In any case, Isaac's three mussel dishes on Day 3 had scored higher than his frog dishes from Day 2.

I think I better pack my bags. I doubt we'll last past Day 4.

If they made it to the semifinals on Day 5—

Nah.

Better pack my bags.

He dragged himself to his feet, wiped off bits of grass from his shorts, and walked back to the villa, counting again as he went.

At the fifth villa, he froze.

Someone was walking toward him.

Someone whose gait was familiar to him—but there was no bun on top of her head.

It couldn't be.

He couldn't tell in the dusk and waning light. He started walking again, assuming the stranger would walk past him.

She did not.

Instead, she smiled.

And Isaac thought he'd die right there.

"What are you doing here?" Isaac stared at Piper.

They were facing each other on the grass behind the villa, overlooking the ocean. A nearby lamppost shone on them.

"Don't look at me like that," Piper signed, then realized almost at once that he still didn't speak ASL—not yet.

Isaac reached for her hair—her wavy hair blowing slightly in the Caribbean wind. "You let your hair down."

Piper wasn't sure if she wanted him to touch her hair, since it was still damp. She had arrived an hour before, showered in her hotel, texted Mrs. Pendegrast, and here she was.

"Your hair is damp. Did you go for a swim?" He assumed incorrectly.

Piper decided she'd clear it up soon.

"I'm glad you're here. I don't know why you're here, but I'm happy to see you."

Piper reached for her iPhone in her crossbody bag.

Isaac did the same.

Standing there facing each other, they texted.

PIPER

I arrived an hour ago. I showered and then texted your mom. She said you're out walking.

ISAAC

I had a long day—three days. Walking is good for me. So is praying, although I'm having a hard time praying.

PIPER

I'll pray for you.

ISAAC

Thank you. To be honest, I just want to go home.

PIPER

I'm not here to call you home.

ISAAC

I might as well go home. I've embarrassed my profession in the contest. I need to find a rock and hide under it.

PIPER

Because of a few frog legs?

Isaac frowned and hung his head.

Piper found that amusing. She pointed to her own arm and shoulder.

"Cry on my shoulder," she signed.

He nodded, as if understanding.

He must have figured out the universal

gesture for *cry*, which looked like its emoji on social media. And he knew what the ASL sign was for *shoulder*, because his ASL name was Shoulder.

There is hope yet for this man.

Isaac blinked. In the light of the lamppost, Piper thought she saw his eyes glisten. He tried to look away.

Piper reached up to his face and wiped away a stray tear with her fingers.

Things must have been more difficult for him than Piper had seen on the livestream replays on YouTube.

I'm here, Isaac. I'm here.

Isaac held her hand against his face.

Piper stepped closer. She could feel the warmth in his chest.

Suddenly, he pulled away and started texting on his phone.

ISAAC

Have you eaten dinner?

PIPER

Not yet.

ISAAC

The restaurant at the hotel is open all night.

PIPER

Okay.

ISAAC

How long are you staying?

> PIPER
>
> I hope until Saturday or Sunday.

ISAAC

Saturday?

> PIPER
>
> You don't expect to drop out on Day 4, do you?

ISAAC

Am I missing something? What don't I know?

> PIPER
>
> You couldn't fire you mom. So I did it for you.

"You did what?" Isaac's jaw dropped, and so did his phone.

He squatted down to retrieve his phone in the grass, but he could barely get up.

Piper pulled him to his feet, laughing softly as she did.

Isaac didn't let go, interrupting her laughter with his own lips—warm and soft against hers.

The ocean serenaded them, and the evening waited on them.

His arms lingered around her shoulders for a while, as they leaned against each other, forehead to forehead.

"You keep surprising me, Piper," Isaac finally said. "You surprise me a lot."

CHAPTER FIFTY-FOUR

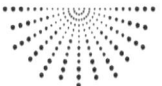

*W*ith Piper assisting him as his indispensable sous chef, Isaac made it to Day 6, the last day of the cooking competition. There were only two chefs left, and Isaac was one of them.

Two chefs.

And one dish to rule them all.

No more three dishes in ninety minutes. Today they were required to cook just one dish in sixty minutes. It was like the final examination that carried over fifty percent of the grades in college.

As they had done the rest of this week, the chefs would have thirty minutes to confer with their sous chefs about the dish. Once the time was up, they had to find the ingredients from the pantry and refrigerator, and cook like the wind.

The film crew were all over the place, and began to annoy Isaac. They were in his face, trying to record his every snarl and groan. They were repeatedly trying to capture Piper's facial expressions too.

It didn't seem to bother Piper at all.

She had said earlier that she would ignore Esther Byrne. It wasn't in the interest of time as much as the fact that the interviewer hadn't bothered to be inclusive. She had not brought with her an ASL interpreter. Instead, she was relying on Isaac—who didn't know ASL at all.

The mystery grocery bag arrived.

Byrne was doing the play-by-play for her viewers worldwide.

Mom wasn't in the kitchen studio because she was back at the villa, doing a live reaction video on the cooking competition. It was easier now with only two chefs and one set of cameras, but all through the week, viewers had to choose which chef they wanted to keep up with, since they all cooked simultaneously so that the judges could compare the dishes at the same time when everyone was done.

Isaac prayed about the mystery bag. It was the difference between sixty thousand dollars and five thousand.

The prize money was another controversy for

Isaac. When it was announced that Nancy Moss had added ten thousand dollars for first place, Isaac thought that perhaps she should have increased the second place prize instead.

But nobody asked him.

Now here he was, staring at the grocery bag.

If he could not cook what was inside, or failed one small thing—that the other chef didn't fail on—it meant he would lose fifty-five thousand dollars.

That's the cost of half of a brand new custom food truck right there.

Esther Byrne switched hats from interviewer to host. "Yesterday, the chefs were given the main ingredient—conch—and they had to cook two dishes. Today, for our final day, they have to choose one main ingredient out of two, but only cook one dish. That dish will carry half the weight of the competition, but the final points will be cumulative."

Isaac began to pray.

They had to make it today to regain the lost points that Isaac had incurred in the first three days of the competition.

Today had to be spectacular.

So help me, God.

When the time came for him to look inside the grocery bag, his heart sank.

Isaac could not believe his misfortune.

There were two choices in the bag, and both choices were bad.

If he chose octopus, he would kill the competition. He had cooked them a hundred ways on cruise ships all over the world, from Japan and Australia to Casablanca and Santiago. Anywhere, any time. He could cook any dish with octopus.

However, he couldn't possibly cook them today. He couldn't do it.

He glanced over at Piper, standing beside him, waiting.

Would she remember what had happened twenty years prior when their Cumin Cooking Club tried to cook six baby octopuses? How much she wept over the dead sea creatures? How she eventually ran out of the kitchen?

Twenty years ago.

Oblivious to his thoughts, Piper reached for the grocery bag in front of them. Before Isaac could stop her, she peeked in.

Her hands began to tremble.

She remembers.

That means I can't ask her to watch me stir-fry these little ones.

Isaac wondered if someday Piper might not become a vegetarian.

Cooking in the kitchen can be very brutal.

He reached for her trembling hand. Squeezed it.

"I choose chicken," he announced.

～

Throughout the ninety minutes allocated for the two chefs to cook spectacular dishes better than each other, Piper Peyton felt quite strongly that she might be the reason Chef Isaac was going to lose.

The other chef had picked octopus, of course.

Without a word, Piper did her best to follow the recipe that Isaac had outlined in the thirty minutes prior to cooking. It was obvious that he was better at cooking seafood than farm food.

Piper watched his worried face as he marinated the sliced chicken pieces.

Sixty thousand dollars were at stake.

She began to pray for Isaac that God would comfort him and give him direction on how to salvage this contest for both his reputation and his career.

Halfway through, she noticed that Isaac had veered off their planned recipe.

Whatever he was trying to do would make the chicken breast worse. Piper tried to tell him, but he couldn't understand what she was signing, and

Chef Mom was too busy dispensing "Life is Such That" advice to interpret for her.

The organizers had invited Chef Mom to hang around to assist Byrne on the side, but she was also supposed to be Piper's interpreter, since cell phones were not allowed in the kitchen.

"Don't worry, okay?" Isaac said to her. He even managed a slight smile.

It was enough for Piper.

It was as if the clock had turned back twenty years to that awful high school cooking contest, when Isaac was about Isaac and no one else. Back in those days when Isaac's ego was the size of a volcanic mountain.

And it was as if that clock now raced forward twenty years to this present day, when Isaac made a decision contrary to that ego, a decision that would cost him sixty thousand dollars.

Did he do it at the spur of the moment?

Did he think through before he decided?

Either way, Piper saw it now.

Isaac was not the same boy she had known in high school.

I must tell him I've forgiven him.

CHAPTER FIFTY-FIVE

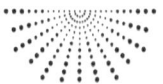

*E*ven though Mom and Isaac sat in the back pew for the Sunday morning church service at Chapel by the Sea, Nancy Moss still found them after church, and invited them to lunch with her at the Nassau Island Breeze Resort.

Mom already had lunch plans with some new retiree friends from Chapel by the Sea, so she and Isaac agreed to meet back at the villa this afternoon to pack their bags for home.

Isaac rode back to the hotel in Nancy Moss's Rolls Royce—something that Mom would have loved to be in.

Piper, not so much.

But Mom would lap all this up.

At the poolside restaurant, Nancy had a private

dining room ready for them. There was always a server in the room, so they were never alone, just the two of them.

At first, Isaac wondered why Nancy—she wanted to be called by her first name—wanted to have lunch with him, and whether she'd also had lunches with the other contestants as the contest week progressed.

Before the server even came to take their order, Nancy broached her first subject matter. "Did you fill out the suggestion box online? The one that we asked every contestant to do?"

"No. Sorry. I didn't have enough time," Isaac said.

"There's no expiration date. You could log in and fill it out, even next week."

Isaac nodded, trying not to commit to a task he might not do next week. Or any week.

"I sense that you do have suggestions for us," Nancy said.

This woman knows everything!

"Well..."

"I knew it." Nancy looked at the menu. "Would you like some appetizers?"

"No, I'm fine. Thank you. I usually eat one main course at lunch, and might even do without a salad."

"Oh, the chef's life indeed. You eat on the go a lot, don't you?"

"Sometimes just a sandwich. On the rare occasion that I get to sit down, I'll try to eat something interesting."

"You think something can be improved," Nancy said.

Still waiting for my answer, is she?

"Well, okay. Since you asked." Isaac cleared his throat. "I don't want to sound like I'm griping. I guess I am."

"Yes?"

"The original prize for first place was fifty thousand dollars," Isaac said carefully. "When the competition started trending on YouTube, and attracted much media attention, you increased the top prize to sixty thousand dollars."

"Yes."

"However, the runner-up prize didn't change. It remained at the original five thousand dollars. You did not add ten thousand dollars to it at all."

"I see what you mean."

"Don't get me wrong," Isaac continued. "Five thousand dollars is a lot of money to me. What's done is done, obviously. However, I think that for the future, fairness is helpful."

"Duly noted." Nancy reached into her purse,

found her phone, and texted someone. "There. I just asked the Institute to send you another ten thousand dollars so that your prize money as the runner-up is proportional to the first place. That way, it's fair."

Isaac nearly fell off his chair. "You did?"

"I told you I did. There is something else that bothers me more."

"What?"

"This has been on my mind since Saturday morning." Nancy looked at Isaac. "You knew that as soon as you picked chicken, you were going to lose."

Ah, that topic.

"But you did it anyhow, even though your octopus dish in the preliminary rounds in September won you a spot in the cooking competition," she said. "Why chicken?"

He didn't want to talk about it, but Nancy's question made him remember the evening before.

He recalled saying goodbye to a disappointed Piper, before she flew home to Savannah on Saturday night. She had signed up to cook at the homeless shelter after church on Sunday, so she could not stay another day in Nassau.

They had hugged before Piper took a taxi to the airport for the flight out. Llewellyn would pick her up from the airport at midnight.

A hug had been all Isaac had gotten from her. That was all. No kisses. Just a simple hug.

It had bothered him all through Saturday night, Sunday morning, and even now.

"It's complicated." Isaac adjusted the position of the knife and fork on his placemat.

"Love always is." Nancy smiled.

"What?"

"Think about it. What would compel you to give up sixty thousand dollars and a chance to be the chef de cuisine at one of my resort hotels?"

"Good question."

The server brought their main courses. Nancy had some sort of grouper.

Isaac chose grilled scallops. They were delicious. "Compliments to your chef, ma'am."

Nancy nodded. "You didn't bat an eyelid losing sixty thousand dollars in the name of love, but if I made you a job offer now that pays twice as much as that, you would also turn it down."

"I would?" Isaac was surprised at Nancy's assertiveness.

Well, maybe he shouldn't be that surprised. After all, this was the matriarch of the Moss Resorts, an empire that spread from city hotels and award-winning restaurants to custom cruise ships and island resorts. Isaac seemed to recall that she owned several yachts and one Boeing 737 that had flown the Moss family all over the world.

"I'm sure you would turn it down," Nancy repeated.

"Why would I? A hundred and twenty thousand dollars in total is a lot of money."

"Love." Nancy smiled. "You remind me of my son. He couldn't last alone in the Bahamas. He and his wife decided to move to Atlanta, where she has a pottery studio. He's attending seminary there, so it worked out."

"Makes sense."

"Does love make sense?" Nancy asked. "If I offer you a job as one of the event chefs at Moss Resort, where you have a lot of planning freedom, for a six-figure per annum salary, you'll also turn that down."

"What planning freedom?" Isaac had to ask—to prove her theory wrong.

"We have yacht parties, dinners at Moss Mansion, private island cookouts, custom cruise events, you name it."

"Wow. Sounds interesting." Isaac chewed his scallops slowly.

"The job doesn't require you to leave the Caribbean."

Ah, the catch. Then again... "Sunny days all year round."

"Absolutely. But you will turn it down."

"You got me figured out." Isaac laughed.

"It's love. Love wants to *be*, not to *do*."

"You know a lot about love," Isaac said.

"My husband and I had a very happy marriage. Unfortunately, I outlived him. That's the saddest thing of all."

"Very sad." Isaac drank some water.

"God's love is always there, even if your spouse dies. You know Romans 8:38-39? Good." Nancy checked her phone. "Here."

For I am persuaded that neither death nor life, nor angels nor principalities nor powers, nor things present nor things to come, nor height nor depth, nor any other created thing, shall be able to separate us from the love of God which is in Christ Jesus our Lord.

"Isn't that an encouraging passage of Scripture?" Nana added.

"It is. God's love is always here for us," Isaac said.

"Indeed. So when do you fly home?" Nancy asked.

"Five o'clock tonight. It'll take around four hours, and we'll be home by ten or eleven." Isaac hoped to sleep in on Monday, and then he'd spend some time praying about his career.

Now he really didn't have a job. But he had a lot of love.

Let's see if love can put food on the table.

Sigh.

Nancy drank some water. "Please send my regards to her."

And Isaac knew exactly who.

CHAPTER FIFTY-SIX

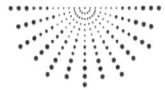

*P*iper hadn't seen Isaac since the Saturday she left Nassau. He and his mom had flown out one day after Piper. However, they stopped in Atlanta to visit Mrs. Pendegrast's brother, who lived in the outskirts of Atlanta. At the same time, Isaac was checking out some new food trucks he might be interested in purchasing, partly with the additional prize money he earned in Nassau.

Fifteen thousand dollars.

Nice.

Isaac wanted to split it with Piper, but she wouldn't hear of it. She had a feeling that as soon as he returned to Savannah, he'd bring it up again. And of course, she'd say no. Again.

Piper did not expect Isaac to be back today,

though it would be nice to see him on her day off. Even now, while planting new vegetables in the greenhouse, she couldn't stop thinking about Isaac —because this was his mother's greenhouse.

She knew that he had paid for this space. She found out when the head gardener said that Mrs. Pendegrast would never let anyone use the greenhouse for free because she paid a lot for its maintenance. Piper approached Mrs. Pendegrast and she spilled the truth. Piper took over the payment immediately.

Isaac had done much for her in such a short period of time. He had come to her rescue over Thanksgiving when she lost her two main chefs. He had stayed for a couple more weeks until she was able to hire a new chef. He had rescued her herbs when her house was put on the market.

Oh, how the tables have turned.

For twenty years, Piper had tried to forget Isaac. He was sailing the oceans, far away from home. For all practical purposes, he hadn't bothered to return to Savannah even though his mother lived here. He came home for one day for his sister's wedding, and then he left the country again.

When he showed up in her restaurant unexpectedly in November, she didn't know how to handle him. They had some rough moments, but Nelson—bless his heart—was their mediator.

Eventually, he apologized for their feud so many years ago.

And she had forgiven him, although she hadn't told him in person.

Otherwise, she wouldn't have flown to the Bahamas on her own to help him with the cooking competition. He had not asked for her to be there, but he seemed delighted to see her.

So delighted that he had kissed her.

Had she kissed him back? She couldn't remember.

All she knew was that something had happened between them. Or maybe she was dreaming. Maybe she was reliving her teenage crush.

Or maybe they had been caught up in the stir of the ocean waves and sultry Caribbean breeze.

Piper took off her gloves that were covered with dirt, and went to find water for her cups of seeds. They should sprout soon. If this were March or April, she'd want to plant them outdoors.

However, she had to find a new place to stay where there was a backyard for her to plant vegetables. The small condo she shared with Llewellyn's family had no yard.

If she found a house with a yard that she could afford, it could be way outside of Savannah. She'd be driving forty-five minutes or more each way to get to work every day. Perhaps she could find a house near this greenhouse.

Piper spotted someone walking about. He was the head gardener. Piper waved. He waved back.

She found a watering can, filled it with water, and brought it back to her seeds.

Someone tapped her on her shoulder.

She turned her head slightly.

And shrieked.

Nearly dropped the watering can too. She put it down.

"You scared me," Piper signed.

Isaac shrugged. "I don't know what you just signed, but I assumed I scared you."

Piper read his lips—the same lips that kissed her a week and a half ago.

She nodded.

"If I did, I'm sorry I gave you a fright," Isaac said. "Did you get my text?"

She checked her apron pocket. Her phone was not there. She checked her jeans pockets, then her coat hanging by the door.

I must have left my phone in the car.

She signed two words: *phone* and *car*. Isaac seemed to understand.

"I just got in from Atlanta," Isaac said. "We rented a car and drove back this morning. Jerome picked us up at the car rental place, and dropped me off at home so I could get the truck. Mom said you're usually here on Wednesdays. I called the head gardener and he confirmed that he saw you around. So I came over."

Isaac showed Piper the time on his watch. It was almost one in the afternoon. "Have you had lunch?"

No, Piper hadn't eaten.

"Good." Isaac gave her two thumbs up. "What do you want to eat?"

Piper waved her palms up. *Anything.*

"How about lunch at your place—I mean at your restaurant?"

Piper nodded.

"I'm paying," Isaac said. "I don't want you to think we're going there for free food."

Piper brushed him off.

"I'm serious. I'm paying, okay?" Isaac stared at her in some silly way, with those wiggling eyebrows.

Piper had seen it before. She laughed as she remembered.

Once upon a time, when life had been a teenage dream, Isaac used to stare at people when he wanted to show how serious he was. Unfortunately, his eyebrows would wiggle when he stared at them. Either he had done it on purpose, or he had a physiological quirk.

Probably the former.

Piper poured out the water from the watering can, returned it to its place, and then took off her work apron. She put it into a plastic bag, together with her work gloves. She tossed her small shovel and other gardening tools she had brought today—but didn't use—into her waterproof plastic tote.

She washed her hands. There were towel rolls near the wash basin.

Isaac followed her out of the greenhouse to their vehicles. As Isaac climbed into his mom's pickup truck, Piper walked to her car, and opened her trunk to put her gardening tote bag in.

She was thanking God silently for bringing Isaac home safely, when she saw him get out of his truck again and walk toward her.

Without a word, his lips brushed against hers slowly...

But she didn't let him make her wait.

CHAPTER FIFTY-SEVEN

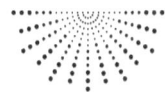

*O*n the third floor of Piper's Place, reopened since Christmas, Isaac felt weird that he and Piper were sitting at a booth, being served by the waitstaff.

"Do you feel like we're on the wrong floor here, like we should be downstairs in the kitchen, cooking?" He picked up the menu the server had brought.

Piper nodded. Her phone was on the table, as though waiting for Isaac to text her.

Isaac paged through the menu. At first, he thought it was the old one with a new background color, but then he realized it was thinner, with bigger fonts, and fewer items.

"Nice new menu," he finally said.

Piper smiled. Gave him two thumbs up.

Before Isaac could say anything, Piper's phone vibrated. She read the message. Smiled broadly.

Isaac waited for her to tap on her phone. It looked like she was replying to someone's message.

Then his own phone chirped.

PIPER

That was Sabine. Someone wants to buy my house!

ISAAC

Woo-hoo! Congrats! Do you have to negotiate pricing?

PIPER

A little bit, but I need the house sold. It's been a month and a half.

ISAAC

That's not too long, is it?

PIPER

No, but the sale will help me buy out your mom's shares of my restaurant.

ISAAC

Then we'll pray for a quick sale at the price you want.

PIPER

Thank you.

Isaac wished that he could sign so that he could pray with Piper right now.

He understood where she was coming from. They were alike in many ways. Both of them wanted to own their own businesses. Neither of them liked to share. They were happiest doing their own thing, making their own decisions.

Could two people like that be together? Isaac thought so.

Running their own companies wasn't the issue if they could talk to each other about so many other things in life...

Things like love.

Love?

Yes, love.

He couldn't put a finger on when that feeling had developed. Maybe it was November, when he worked for two seemingly long weeks in her kitchen. Maybe it was in December when she had helped train his mom to be his cooking assistant.

Regardless of November and December, Isaac knew he was in love by January when Piper literally flew to his rescue at the cooking competition.

I want to tell her precisely how I feel about her.

Yes, I wish I could sign.

How was it that he wished to learn, but hadn't done a thing about it? Determined not to let Piper down, he turned on his phone, and searched the Riverside Chapel website for an ASL class. Since

Heidi interpreted, he hoped that she would be teaching a class.

If not, he'd go to a local college to find an extension class, or take some sort of course in town at the community center.

All he wanted to do was to communicate with Piper.

He texted her.

> Isaac: Do you know anyone who teaches beginning ASL?

Piper: Are you serious?

> Isaac: Of course.

Piper: Llewellyn can teach.

> Isaac: Not him. Heidi can too, I think, but she's so busy.

Piper: She's always busy. She had an ASL class last summer. Maybe she'd do it again.

> Isaac: Summer is too late. I need to learn it now.

~

They both ordered fish. Just as well, as the last thing Piper wanted to see this week was chicken. She was sure that it had cost Isaac the cooking competition.

Why did Isaac choose chicken?

He probably hadn't known that, if forced, she would help him cook the octopus. She might throw up afterwards, but she would not let him down.

I wanted him to win. Didn't he know that?

Piper wondered when she might be able to bring it up. Maybe not for another twenty years.

She prayed that the cooking competition would not cause them a new problem on top of the old problem.

"Something on your mind?" Isaac asked.

His question was casual, his face calm.

Piper didn't want to spoil their lunch by bringing up the cooking competition in Nassau.

She wished she could say something pleasant to him in his own language. She had seen couples at her restaurant, chatting to each other, laughing, having conversations. She could never do that. She could never speak to him, hear him talk to her.

Clearly, Isaac was serious about their relationship. He wanted to learn ASL pronto.

Do you know anyone who teaches beginning ASL?

Piper didn't want to put too much hope into it, like she had done in high school. However, Isaac had been so full of himself back then, that she had given up waiting. Marlon had been a better boyfriend for her.

In high school.

They were far removed from high school now. Many years had passed by. Could things really be different now between them?

CHAPTER FIFTY-EIGHT

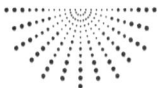

*J*erome looked surprised that Isaac led the way into Piper's Place, as though he had no problem anymore eating at the restaurant.

Well, when you've kissed the owner twice...

Isaac asked the hostess for a booth by the river, but she said they were full. The wait would be at least thirty minutes unless they'd take the first available bistro table for two.

Jerome didn't want to wait, but neither did he want a small table. He thought they should go somewhere else, but Isaac didn't want Piper to lose two paying customers.

"We'll wait for the first available," Isaac said. He picked up two menus, handed one to Jerome. "Lunch is on me."

"In that case…" Jerome followed Isaac outside where they sat on a bench facing the afternoon sun.

It was deep January, chilly in Savannah—if it could be cold by the sea in the south—but they had their jackets and boots, and Isaac really wanted to eat here.

"I guess you don't hate this place—or Piper—as much as you did." Jerome dug into his pockets.

"Hate? I didn't *hate* her—not technically." Isaac browsed through the menu, looking for something he hadn't ordered before.

He noticed that there was not a single item made with octopus or frog legs.

"I seem to recall that you had an old problem with her," Jerome said.

"In high school. We're fine now." *We're more than fine.*

Jerome closed his menu. "Glad you got over it."

"Took twenty years." If there had not been a spat between him and Piper, would Isaac still have left town? Or would he have moved to another side of town to be away from Mom, but not from Piper?

"Better late than never." Jerome put on his sunglasses. "Sorry your cooking competition didn't work out, but fifteen thou isn't bad."

Jerome must be on a roll. He was hitting every pressure point today.

"No, it wasn't bad at all. After deducting all the

money I spent on food, flight, and hotel, I still came out ahead." Isaac had forgotten his own sunglasses, so he was squinting in the sun.

"Your mom said you've wanted to own a restaurant forever. Are you certain you want a food truck instead?" Jerome asked.

"Yeah."

"What if you decide to open a restaurant in the future. What are you going to do with your food truck?"

"Good question. I'm not sure I want a restaurant anymore, to be honest. A food truck has less overhead, and I can start my business debt free." Isaac folded his arms across his chest, not because he felt the question intruded into his personal issues, but because it was plain old cold out here. "Sometimes God changes your goals."

"That's right. He can do that because He's God and He knows what's best for us. If you asked me that fifteen years ago, I couldn't tell you a thing about God's best."

"If you asked me twenty years ago, I would have said that it's either restaurant or bust."

"We change, don't we?"

"God works in our hearts." Isaac nodded. "We get older, our perspectives mature."

"We get marinated."

Marinated? Isaac burst out laughing.

"What? You think I don't know cooking terms? I tell you what else I know. I know that your mom is totally right. There is no way I'm going to eat frog legs either."

"Did you see the livestream?"

"Sure did, Son."

"Mom passed out."

"Disappeared under the table." Jerome shook his head. "I saw it on my phone. I knew it was going to happen."

"I couldn't reach her fast enough. The cameraman shoved the camera in her face. The host wanted a statement about frog legs. And there, spread out on the kitchen floor, Mom passed out a second time." Tears of laughter were running down Isaac's face.

"We have good health insurance, but it didn't cover Bahamas!" Jerome chuckled. "I was going to leave her right there. I mean, she shouldn't have gone with you."

"I know." Isaac wiped his face. "It was my fault. I apologize."

"Yep. It's your fault you were too cheap to hire a real sous chef." Jerome elbowed Isaac. And kept laughing.

Is that a joke?

Isaac felt confused. "Mom's a pretty good cook."

"She only cooks what she wants to cook." Jerome wiped his eyes.

"That's true."

"You see the irony?"

"What?"

"You switched assistant cooks halfway, right?" Jerome asked.

"The rules allow us to get new assistants for the semifinals and finals," Isaac explained.

"So Piper showed up. Top of the class in culinary school. Owner-chef of this fine establishment."

"Yes?"

"But she has a flaw." Jerome winked at him. "One word: octopus."

"Yes." And on the final day too. For the prize money.

"Your mom could have cooked it."

"She sure could."

"So you lost the prize." Jerome's voice calmed down.

"I lost."

"But you got the girl." Jerome reached over and patted him on the shoulder.

Isaac didn't know how to respond.

Did I get the girl?

CHAPTER FIFTY-NINE

*I*saac stepped into the galley kitchen on *The Rhoda*, empty and waiting to come to life again. He remembered Mom and Piper here in mid-December, when they had tried to help him practice for the cooking competition. It all ended well that Sunday afternoon, with Piper and Isaac going to evening church together.

Jerome followed Isaac around. "You like what you see?"

"Thank you for letting me rent this galley," Isaac said. "It will make a great commissary kitchen."

"It's only used whenever our church has an event. I'll be glad to see it open for business all week once again."

"Will this riverboat ever go down the river again?"

Jerome shrugged. "Not while Riverside is still using it for church services on Sunday. However, after I sell it to Tamsyn, I don't know what she'll do with it."

"Eventually Riverside will outgrow the three floors."

"Two—the top deck is only useable when it's not raining."

"Good point." Isaac stopped at the door they came in. He took another look at the galley. "When I quit my job on the cruise ship, I never expected to cook in a galley again. I thought I was going to buy a restaurant and live my dream life."

"You said at lunch that sometimes God changes your goals." Jerome leaned against a counter. "It's for the best."

"To be honest with you, owning a food truck was actually my Plan B. It didn't cross my mind that my Plan B could possibly be God's Plan A for me."

Jerome pointed a finger. "You best be sure what God wants for you before you say it's His plan for you. It might very well be that a food truck is in your future, but if you're wrong about that, then neither one might be God's plan for you."

"How do I know for sure?"

"Seek God's Word and pray." Jerome swiped his phone. "What does it say in Jeremiah 33:3?"

Before Jerome found it, Isaac already knew what that verse said.

Call to Me, and I will answer you, and show you great and mighty things, which you do not know.

Quietly, he prayed to God to show him "great and mighty things" which he didn't know, couldn't see, wouldn't be able to comprehend with his finite mind.

If a restaurant and a food truck are not for me, what is, Lord? Show me what my path should be.

"At the end of the day, whatever you do, do it as unto the Lord," Jerome added. "Colossians 3:23-24. I keep that in mind for my riverboat business."

And whatever you do, do it heartily, as to the Lord and not to men, knowing that from the Lord you will receive the reward of the inheritance; for you serve the Lord Christ.

"God knows best," Isaac added. "For some reason, I feel like a heavy burden has been lifted off my shoulders."

"Yeah?" Jerome raised an eyebrow.

"For the last twenty years, I've been doggedly

determined to own a restaurant. In my mind, if I did it, then I've succeeded."

"Now?"

"God has changed my focus and perspective. It's not the restaurant that makes me, you know?"

Jerome nodded. "I know. It's not the riverboat that makes me."

"Exactly."

"It's what I do for the Lord that matters." Isaac liked the idea of a food truck more and more.

"If you need someone to go with you to Atlanta to look at food trucks, I don't mind taking a road trip," Jerome said.

"It's a long drive. Five hours, at least."

"You're driving alone, right?"

"Yeah. I could use the company."

"I could get to know you. I know daughters. I never had a son. When I married your mother, suddenly I'm the father of two sons."

Isaac had no opinion either way. He had a brother and a sister, and parents, so he didn't feel like he was missing anything most of his life.

Sure, Mom might be difficult, but she meant well. The fact that Jerome had married her, he must have seen something in her, something to assure him that they were going to get along in their daily lives together. That accounted for something.

And now Jerome wanted to know the rest of the family.

"Thank you, Jerome. I don't mind you going with me back to Atlanta to look at some food trucks."

"I'm semi-retired, so just say when, and if I'm not needed at the riverboat, I can go."

"One thing though..."

"What?"

"You let me pay for your food and hotel," Isaac said.

"Well..."

"It's a business trip. I'm going, whether you come with me or not."

"All right." Jerome took some keys out of his pocket. "Yours. Make sure you don't lose them because I'm not driving all the way from the house to open the doors for you."

"Thank you." Isaac pocketed the keys. "You've been kind to me, Jerome."

"Don't mention it. Just pay the rent on time." He chuckled.

"I'll give you free meals from my food truck for life."

Jerome shook his head. "Bad idea."

"Why?" Isaac was surprised.

"If I like what you cook, I'd be more than happy to pay for it. If I don't, you can't pay me to eat it."

"Ah, good point." Frog legs and octopuses came to Isaac's mind.

"Now you said something about doing events in the dining room and top deck?" Jerome asked.

"Yes, sir." Isaac led the way. Having attended church here for over a month, he knew how to navigate the stairs. "The weather forecast said it might rain, so how about we start at the top?"

"Fine." Jerome pointed to the elevators instead of stairs.

The elevator they took made a funny noise.

"I better have this looked at." Jerome swiped his phone and seemed to be making a note. "If it stops working or something, you tell me right away. It's under warranty, but this riverboat is older than you are, and things can start to fall apart."

"Wow. Okay."

On the top deck, the sky was overcast. The pool was covered, and the deck chairs were still not out. Isaac wondered how many times a year this space ever got used.

"This place is huge," Isaac said. It looked bigger today than the day he, Piper, and Mom sat on the deck floor by the railing eating a whole bag of pecan cookies.

"And unused," Jerome tilted his head. "Ever considered being an event chef on top of a food truck operator?"

An event chef? "That was one of the positions that Moss Resorts offered me in the Bahamas."

"The six-figure job you turned down..." Jerome shook his head.

"I wanted to do my own thing, no matter how small," Isaac explained. "It was time for me to come home to Savannah."

"You know that at least one person is glad you're home."

Piper?

"Your mom's been crying over her children for years," Jerome continued. "Maybe now that you and Amy are home, Garrett might consider a visit. I know your mom would be beside herself if he did."

"I tried to contact him. You know how it is with the Special Forces." Isaac walked around the deck. "I can just see all sorts of events up here. Birthdays, corporate dinners, private events, rehearsal dinners, weddings..."

Weddings.

Isaac could see Piper walking down the aisle...

Banish the thought.

"If you want to add events to your food truck business—considering you're already renting the galley—I could rent you the dining rooms and this deck space as well." Jerome leaned against a railing.

Isaac tried to calculate the costs of all these things. He had put aside a hundred thousand dollars for a small food truck with all new custom appliances inside. He had also itemized the permits, licenses, and fees he'd incur to operate a food truck in the city of Savannah and on Tybee Island.

"How much is the rent?" Isaac asked.

"The riverboat is off limits on Sundays because it's a church day," Jerome said. "You'd be renting for six days a week."

Still...

"Tell you what I'll do. I'll take twenty percent off the rent."

Isaac's eyes widened. "Including the galley?"

"All your rent."

"That's generous of you," Isaac said.

"I want you to succeed so that you can have your own place."

My own place? "As in a commercial kitchen somewhere?"

"As in your own house, so you're not still living with your mom at forty."

"Be rest assured that as soon as I'm able, I'd want a house of my own."

"Kids are going to need a backyard," Jerome said.

"Kids?" Isaac was taken aback.

"When you marry and have kids, it would be nice if they have a backyard to play in."

"Oh." *Oh.*

"Meanwhile, if you have a house, you can park your food truck in your own front driveway."

How many shoes did I say have dropped? "I haven't bought my food truck yet."

"Don't you have a five-year business plan?" Jerome asked.

"Well, I can't think of even five months ahead right now," Isaac replied. "But I have thought about long-term business ideas. What I want to do with the rest of my life."

"I'll take another ten percent off your rent if you find your own driveway to park your food truck —rather than in front of the family home. I might buy a boat, and when that time comes, I will need to reclaim the parking space right quick."

Whoa. Twenty percent.

"You can use your mom's pickup for as long as you want," Jerome added. "I don't care about that."

"Why are you helping me?"

"I don't want your mom all worried about you."

"She does worry."

"Yep. So all I'm saying is if you are sure that owning a food truck business is what you want to do—and throw in being an event chef just in case your Plan B doesn't work out—you better get your five-year business plan in place. In the midst of it all, you need to find your own house to park your food truck—before you mom finds a house for you."

"She wouldn't." Isaac might or might not believe it himself. Even as he wanted Mom to stay away from his personal life, he wouldn't put it past her to try to push him along.

"You think she won't? She was driving around yesterday, and she sent me a text. A house one street down from ours is for sale, and she was all excited about it."

See? What did I say? Isaac shook his head.

"It has a fenced backyard, a swing set for the kids, and a double-wide driveway with a two-car garage." Jerome chuckled. "She said she could see you in that house."

"No."

"I'm not kidding you." Jerome laughed so hard he could barely speak. "When we go home, don't be surprised if you see a *For Sale* flyer sitting on the kitchen table. If you don't get ahead of her, she's going to take matters into her own hands, and marry you off before you realize it—you know, to Piper or somebody she knows."

Piper?

The only one for me.

CHAPTER SIXTY

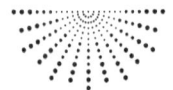

February evaporated as fast as January for Isaac, the winter months as busy as ever in a vacation city like Savannah, where tourists flocked year round—whether on their way to and from Florida, or to see the Georgian coast before the weather became humid come May through August.

While the weather on the southern state of Georgia was mild compared to snow country in the north, it was still winter, the season of wool coats and warm jackets, of hot cocoa and indoor fireplaces. Fewer people flocked the great outdoors, and thus, the food truck business suffered in these months.

That thought helped Isaac weather the wait for

his new food truck to arrive from Atlanta. There were numerous custom food truck builders across the states of Georgia and Florida, within driving distance of Savannah. However, Isaac had found one in Atlanta that met his needs.

The discount pricing via Uncle Andros's friend helped. Also, if the truck was poorly built, Isaac could also complain to Uncle Andros, who would in turn convey the message to his friend's friend via yet another friend.

In any case, the food truck wouldn't be ready until April.

Just in time for spring break, spring home tours, and one month before school was out for the summer.

Isaac had to believe that the timing was for the best.

In the meantime, Piper's Place had been streamlining its operations, handing over almost all of its catering business to Isaac's Kitchen. Piper wanted to focus on the restaurant itself and its customers.

At first, Isaac had only spoken in jest when he asked Piper to send business his way. However, when Piper actually did so, it catapulted him off into a very busy February and March. For example, he had no idea that Piper's Place catered to at least two corporate luncheons a month. Piper had said that it had been Chef Torkel's department, but since he had left the restaurant, Piper did not want to continue her catering arm.

The companies liked him, and they in turn recommended Isaac's Kitchen to their business associates, some as far south as St. Simon's Island, Darien, and St. Mary's. Another catering company in St. Simon's Island could very well be his competitor in the business, but he found a way to draw lines in the sand, so to speak, so that the two companies did not step on each other's feet.

Upon Heidi Wei-Flores's recommendations, he found ready-to-hire part-time workers from the culinary school at the University of Coastal Georgia, where Heidi taught history.

Isaac had also been in talks with the dean of the culinary school about turning his galley into a teaching kitchen. He had enough credentials to be an instructor. That would fill in the times when his food truck was not operational—like the winter months, when it rained, and during hurricane seasons.

By the end of March, Isaac had found himself a busy Event Chef. Word about Isaac's Kitchen kept spreading around Savannah, with friends of his church family calling upon him to cater birthday dinners, wedding receptions, and organizational luncheons, on top of the corporate events he was already handling.

While he had been at the university talking potential opportunities with the culinary school, Isaac asked about ASL classes. Sure enough, they had a few two-month long courses once a week for three hours on Thursday evenings. Perfect.

By the first thaw of spring, Isaac could understand elementary ASL. While he wanted to get up to speed, he didn't want to rush too much. Heidi wanted him to assist her in interpreting sermons at Riverside Chapel. He felt that it might be premature. At this time, all he wanted to do was to communicate with Piper.

Is that selfish?

"Too selfish," Piper signed to him on the last Sunday in March at their ASL table just before the service began. "You can hear and you can sign. Maybe God wants you to minister here at your own church."

Yes, Isaac had joined Riverside Chapel—which made Mom very happy, since Amy and Cyrus had also joined the church the year before.

"Pastor Flores speaks very quickly." Isaac used the ASL name Care that Piper and her friends had given the pastor.

"Learn from Heidi," Piper suggested. "She has the outline. Maybe you can practice a bit from the outline."

"Pastor Flores deviates from the outline all the time."

"Adapt."

"You really want me to do this."

"I want you to pray to God about helping in ministry," Piper signed. "Don't think of it as working for Care, but for God. It's the Bible you're focused on."

Bible.

Isaac repeated the ASL sign for it—a combination of Jesus and an open book. For Jesus, the ASL sign puts a nail on each palm.

It reminded him of the cross, where Jesus had died for his sins and the sins of the world.

Why can't I sign for Jesus?

"I'm still taking the elementary ASL course," Isaac signed. "Maybe after it's done, I'll take the intermediate course, and then get certified to interpret."

Piper stared at him.

"I'm just asking you to pray about it," she signed.

"If God wants me to do this, I will want to go all the way. I'll find out what's required." Isaac felt confident that would be the right course of action.

"Wow. I'm impressed."

The service was about to start, and Piper's friends had all arrived. They were signing to her.

All around Isaac, tables full of church members, and possibly visitors, were alive with conversations.

Isaac could hear the people at various nearby tables speak in English, Spanish, Chinese, and some Korean, as well as see his Deaf community friends chatting at his table.

In the middle of the two spheres of communication, Isaac wondered what the Lord would have him do with his free time.

Free time?

What free time?

In the front of the dining hall, where Pastor Flores would preach, a guest guitarist took his place next to the piano on the side. They started to play "As the Deer." On the screen behind them, the words to the hymn appeared.

As Isaac hummed the hymn, he saw the ASL signs in his own mind, and he knew enough to sign this hymn if he were called to do so. All he had to do was learn to sign faster to keep up with the music.

He glanced over at Piper.

Isaac blinked. Maybe it was the hymn that had touched his heart, or maybe he had been thinking about this for a while, but of all the wonderful things that God had done for him these two months of operating Isaac's Kitchen from the galley of Jerome's riverboat, he realized that none of it compared to this time that God had given him—Sunday morning at church with Piper, listening to God's Word proclaimed and explained.

Isaac reached for Piper's hand. When she turned, he signed, "I'm glad to be in church with you."

Piper smiled. Then she signed something unexpected. "Have you been spending time with God in your Bible every day?"

To his credit, Isaac was able to reply, "Yes. Every day."

And it was the truth.

Coming home to Savannah had changed his life—no, wait.

Correction: God had changed his life by bringing him home to Savannah.

He had found a job he enjoyed even though his food truck hadn't arrived. The income from catering events and teaching at the university's culinary school were enough for him to move out of Mom's house to a small house with a driveway, where he could eventually park the food truck, which he would pick up in April.

Attending church at Riverside Chapel had

helped his spiritual growth and reminded him to spend more time in God's Word. He joined a businessman's Bible Study on Monday mornings at Ming Wei's PI office in downtown Savannah. It was early enough at six o'clock so that he could go from there to his galley kitchen without any traffic snarls across River Street.

Isaac had been in prayer for two months about his life. After that conversation with Jerome about Plan C, he wanted to be sure that what he was doing in Isaac's Kitchen was of the Lord. If it wasn't, he was ready to abandon it all at once.

"Are you going to the soup kitchen with me after church?" Piper signed when the guitarist and pianist left their places, and the small choir assembled.

"Yes," Isaac signed immediately.

That too. Isaac didn't think he would enjoy helping until he followed Piper to the soup kitchen shelter in February. The kitchen was at the same homeless shelter that Piper's Place had been delivering leftover food to twice a week for years.

After two hours of serving hot lunches to homeless teens and single parents, and sharing the Word of God and the love of Christ to them, Isaac's heart broke for them. They all needed God as much as anyone else in the world.

So yes, he would be back there with Piper this

afternoon. More than with Piper, he would be with God, doing God's work.

Piper smiled. "Thank you."

"Thank you," Isaac signed back.

Can life be any better than this?

CHAPTER SIXTY-ONE

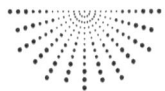

*P*iper missed Isaac all week. After church on Sunday, he had left with his parents on a five-hour drive to Atlanta to pick up his brand new custom food truck. Mrs. Pendegrast—Piper still couldn't get used to Rhoda—and Jerome were supposed to drop Isaac off at Uncle Andros's house on their way to a mountain cabin for the week.

On Monday, Isaac texted Piper, bemoaning the bad paint job on his food truck, right under the window and somewhere on the side. The food truck would represent Isaac's Kitchen everywhere it went. The idea made Isaac brave enough to negotiate a free do over. However, he had to wait a few days for all that to be taken care of.

Midtown Chapel, sister church to Riverside

Chapel in Savannah and Chapel by the Sea in Nassau, offered Wednesday night Bible studies, which Isaac attended. He took notes and emailed them to Piper, together with his copious praise for the little mission church that had grown fast in just one year.

As Piper read Isaac's email about meeting Byron Moss, Nancy Moss's oldest son, she wondered if Isaac might consider moving his business to Atlanta. After all, it was the biggest city in Georgia, a metropolis to boot, and would have more places for him to drive his food truck. Savannah was small comparatively, and the food truck business was probably not as lucrative.

Then again, who knows.

If Isaac decided to move to Atlanta, then what?

Piper remembered how Jerome's daughter, Tamsyn, had been dating a man who worked in Atlanta. Their long-distance relationship had caused them to break up, until they found a way to make it work. Now Tamsyn and her husband, Ryan, spent half a year in Atlanta and the other half in Savannah—until Ryan's company finished building their Savannah branch.

Several years prior, a former church member, Nadine, moved her virtual assistant business to Louisiana where her husband came from. They didn't return to Savannah often, but when they did, they would dine at Piper's Place and say hello to her.

Another church member and friend of Nadine's, Abilene had also moved away. After she married her British-born husband, they settled in his estate in England, where Abilene now spent her time painting the English countryside. Her goal was to paint the entire United Kingdom. Piper wondered when she would ever return to Savannah.

People come and go, and they move on.

Or they returned home, like Iris had, when her sister went missing. Or Hunter Jacobs, when he came home to write his grandfather's memoirs.

Isaac had also returned home, though his initial plan had been to stay for several weeks, try to win the cooking competition, and then go somewhere else. Instead, he had remained in town, hadn't he? He joined Riverside Chapel, started Isaac's Kitchen, and accepted a part-time culinary teaching job at the University of Coastal Georgia.

More than that, Isaac made a valiant effort to master ASL, going as far as enrolling in the next ASL course at the university to learn intermediate ASL. Isaac had learned sign language for her.

Would he also stay in town for her?

Thursday slow-crawled into another Friday. It was always busy at Piper's Place on any day of the week, but Piper didn't have to fill in for any of her chefs today.

Her new chef made the best lunches. The Super Seniors loved him. They called him Chef DB, like everyone else at Piper's Place.

For dinner, Chef Lillian also lived up to her culinary training at Le Cordon Bleu in Paris. In fact, she was the highest paid chef at Piper's Place. She received the most compliments from Piper's customers.

Chef Forsythia had adjusted to her night shift. Piper had no idea whether the promoted sous chef had gotten over Chef Torkel, but Llewellyn had treated her well. All things seemed to indicate that Forsythia had moved on from the past.

As for Piper...

She was still sitting at her desk in her office. Before her mind wandered off, she had been crunching numbers to see what other budget items she could cut. If she managed her money carefully, she could still give her employees a Christmas bonus this year.

She knew she would never see her stolen three hundred thousand dollars again. Her adopted cousin Regis—whatever his real name was—had disappeared into WITSEC with whatever information he had about her money.

If, at some point in the future, Detective

Zimmerman could recover the money, Piper would consider it an unexpected bonus.

In the meantime, the Pendegrast investment had paid off. Streamlining the budget at the restaurant upon their wise counsel, Piper had been able to cut expenses and eliminate excess food. While it meant less leftovers to take to the homeless shelter every week, Piper more than made up for that by serving in the soup kitchen after church one Sunday a month.

The only gray area that Piper had battled over was whether to keep on catering. Chef Torkel had pushed for that expansion some years before. It had not been something that Piper wanted to do. Handing catering over to Isaac had helped her to focus on the restaurant itself, and it had also helped Isaac jump start on establishing himself as the new event chef in town.

The small screen above the door flashed.

It's probably Nelson.

Piper had told him to leave early, to go home and see to his wife's needs. She was in her eighth month of pregnancy, and on bedrest. Although Nelson's mom had been staying with them to care for the kids for a few weeks, Piper felt that she could be flexible with Nelson's schedule. She would fill in for him if she had to.

After all, it was Nelson who had brought her

and Isaac back together again after twenty long years.

Well, God had done it, to be sure, but He had worked through her old friend.

Piper left her desk and went to the door.

When she opened it, she shrieked.

It wasn't Nelson.

Isaac laughed as he signed, "I scared you back in November too."

November? Why did he bring up November?

Has he been thinking of us?

Yes, November had been the first time they had met again after twenty long years. It was April now, and this time, Isaac had only been gone for five days.

She hadn't missed him that much.

Well, not too much.

Isaac didn't as much as hug her or say hello. He went straight to the point. "Want to see my new food truck?"

CHAPTER SIXTY-TWO

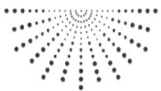

Steady rain continued to fall across the nearby cobblestone street as Isaac and Piper walked across the back parking lot to his small food truck away from the loading bay.

As Isaac held the umbrella over Piper, his other hand was around her waist so they could both fit under Piper's umbrella. The clear dome-shaped umbrella was similar to those Isaac had seen at a wedding he had catered a few weeks prior.

There might be a reason many people did not choose to get married in rainy April in the south, but the lovely couple, faculty members at the college he would be teaching in, wanted to be married among the azaleas in someone's private garden. And azaleas bloomed in April in Savannah.

Isaac looked up through the umbrella, watching

the rain fall from above. The rain cooled down the humidity, although the temperature this afternoon barely pushed through the seventies, with the cloud cover.

It was a perfect snuggling weather.

He held Piper closer, and felt like kissing her, but he didn't.

At the door of his food truck, Isaac let Piper hold the umbrella while he unlocked it. She was looking up at the sign and the front of the truck, painted in ocean colors.

"Back in November, I had wanted to call it Seven Seas," Isaac signed. "I still like the colors, even though now my food truck is called Isaac's Kitchen, which is the name of my event catering business."

Piper gave him the thumb's up sign with her free hand.

Inside the food truck, Isaac folded the umbrella and found a place to stash it.

"Well, what do you think?" He led Piper down the narrow stainless steel floor, flanked by the grill station and oven to one side and the refrigerator and work table on the other, surrounded by other equally shiny equipment he had installed.

Piper walked the length of it and turned around. "It's very small."

"It has everything I need." Isaac pointed to the

basket fryer here and the hand sink there. "It's a food truck."

"Exactly." Piper walked back to him, a worried look on her face.

"Are you upset?" Isaac spoke and signed at the same time.

"I want you to know that I have forgiven you a while back for what happened to us twenty years ago," Piper signed. "Don't let that get between us."

"I know you've forgiven me."

"I didn't say it to you like this."

"I had a feeling."

"Feeling?"

"You let me kiss you twice."

"That kind of feeling." Piper cleared her throat. "I was trying to tell you that I forgave you. Neither of us won that day. We both lost. We lost our friendship, we lost twenty years of time, and we might have lost opportunities."

"Opportunities?" Isaac was puzzled.

"For you to open your own restaurant here in town. There's room for both of us in Savannah, in spite of the fact that it's not as big as Atlanta."

Isaac reached for her, then realized that he needed both hands to talk to her in ASL. "You think I'm leaving."

Piper blinked.

"What made you think I'm leaving?" He stepped closer.

"You saved up for so many years to open your own restaurant, but you're not." Piper seemed to be studying his facial expression. "You bought a food truck instead."

"With wheels... That can take me anywhere—away from Savannah. Is that what you're thinking?"

"You might go to food festivals or travel the state."

"I can just see all the permits and licenses I would spend more months waiting for in every state I need to get to." Isaac chuckled.

"Did I kill your dream of owning a brick-and-mortar restaurant or something?"

So that's what this is about. "Let me explain. Once upon a time, I dreamed of owning a restaurant somewhere. I was determined to get there. I thought it would be the end of my career if I didn't."

"You helped me so much at Piper's Place. You could run your own restaurant easily. We don't have to compete with each other."

"I agree. We definitely don't have to compete with each other." Isaac smiled. "However, God used the cooking competition in Nassau to teach me a lesson about living with less money and learning to focus on the riches in Christ."

Piper was on the verge of tears. "That was my fault."

"Not at all. The fault was mine. The *pride* was mine."

"You didn't win first place because of me. Again!" Piper buried her face in her hands.

Isaac gently pulled her hands away from her face so that she could see him sign.

"No, it's not your fault at all—not back then, not now." Isaac fingered a stray strand of hair at the base of Piper's hairline He was trying to push the strand behind her ear, when he decided to reach for her topknot bun.

When Piper didn't stop him, he tugged at the hairband around it. The wavy hair fell all around Piper's face and bounced on her shoulders.

"In fact, you were amazingly helpful. I wouldn't have made it to the final day without you." Isaac ran his hand through her hair, like he had done at the vacation villa in the Bahamas. "Remember our time on the island? I'm glad you went to Nassau for me."

She closed her eyes, as though she was feeling and enjoying his touch—and perhaps having the same memories she had of their short time in the Bahamas.

"Tell me something," Isaac signed when Piper

opened her eyes. "I heard you had a crush on me in high school."

She blushed. "Who told you?"

"So it's true?"

"I never told anyone..." Her facial expression changed. "Except Nelson."

"Don't blame him. He's a good friend." Isaac tried to remember the ASL signs for what he wanted to say. "Do you... Is it still there?"

Piper's lips quivered.

"We know that compared to eternity, life on earth is only for a moment. We can go through life waiting for our ideas of moments that may never come, or we can thank God for the daily moments He has given us and is giving us now." Isaac continued. "We make choices and decisions, and we think we have time to recover later, but we can't when time runs out—speaking for myself."

"Is time running out for us?" Piper's lips quivered.

"God gives everyone an allocated time to live. Someday, when this life is over, we will be in heaven with our God for the rest of eternity."

"I will see my mom and grandma there. You will see your dad again."

Isaac nodded.

"I will be able to hear in heaven," Piper signed.

"You can speak to me and I will hear you with my own ears."

"There are many people with ears who don't hear God, like the Bible said in Zechariah 7:11."

> *But they refused to heed, shrugged their shoulders,*
> *and stopped their ears so that they could not hear.*

"See, they refused to *heed* and *hear*," Isaac added.

"Where did you get that verse?"

"When I was at Midtown Chapel on Wednesday, I had a good talk with Byron Moss—you know, Nancy's son. I had no idea he's a counseling pastor now."

"Really. A counselor?"

Isaac nodded. "I talked to him about becoming an ASL interpreter and whether that's something God might want me to do as a ministry—as opposed to doing it to impress you."

"Impress me?"

"Uh-huh. I realized that being deaf is not a deficit." Isaac gently kissed Piper's ear. Her earlobe was soft and bare, without any earring in the way. "If you can't hear with your ears, listen with your heart."

Piper's lips quivered.

"You and I are chefs, and we're very conscious

of time." Isaac watched to see if Piper saw where he was going with this.

She simply waited for him to finish.

"There is a time to cook... And there is a time to love." Isaac was on his knees.

Piper gasped.

Isaac reached into his pocket. The ring was still there. Whew!

He lifted it toward Piper.

Tears ran down her face.

Isaac didn't want to see her cry, but he knew those were tears of joy.

"I have prayed about this for weeks." He finger spelled Piper's entire name. "I want to spend the rest of my life with you, to love you every day for as long God gives me days to live. Is that possible for us?"

"With God, all things are possible."

"Thank you, Love." Isaac smiled. "Your name sign is Love."

Piper chuckled through her tears.

"Will you put up with me, care for me, and lend me your shoulders to cry on? Will you marry me, Love?"

Piper nodded. "Yes."

Slowly, Piper extended her left hand toward Isaac.

This ring better fit.

The week before, he had texted Llewellyn— who then asked his sister to find a ring in Piper's room that she had worn recently, draw the outline of the ring on paper, and bring it to church on Sunday.

Isaac hadn't been sure when he was going to buy a ring, since he was still praying about how to approach Piper about it. However, the delay in his food truck delivery made him stay in Atlanta for several extra days. The next thing he knew, he was attending Bible study at Midtown Chapel, and asking his new friend Byron Moss if he knew of a reasonably priced and trustworthy jeweler. Byron told him about a jeweler that his wife liked.

Isaac had bought the ring on Thursday, and here he was on Friday.

The diamond sparkled on Piper's ring finger.

Isaac kissed her hand.

She pulled him to his feet. She looked happy, contented, and at peace.

Isaac drew her to himself, and brushed strands of hair from her face. His thumb gently wiped another tear trickling down her cheek, and he kissed the rest of the salty tears away.

CHAPTER SIXTY-THREE

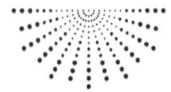

*D*ue to a regularly busy summer season in Savannah and Tybee Island for both Piper's Place and Isaac's Kitchen, the Peyton-Untermeyer wedding had to wait until the school year started again.

For the next five months, their own businesses kept Piper and Isaac busy. Piper offered Isaac a place to park his food truck in her restaurant's back lot, as long as the food truck didn't get in the way of the delivery vans and her employees arriving and leaving. The parking location was closer to Isaac's commissary than his mother's house.

Piper was glad that their agreement worked out because the landlord of the small house that Isaac rented decided at the last minute not to let him park his food truck in the driveway. Soon after, the landlord suddenly wanted the house back for his newlywed daughter to stay.

After searching all over town, Piper and Isaac decided to rent a loft apartment within walking distance of the restaurant and the riverboat. They could use Piper's car to go places, and Isaac could return the truck to his mother.

While they were engaged, Piper thought she could continue to stay a while longer with Llewellyn's family and let Isaac have the loft apartment, but Isaac didn't like the idea—even though Llewellyn was now happily dating Forsythia, with talks of possible nuptials themselves. In the end, Isaac returned to his mother's house for a few months, while Piper moved into the loft apartment with whatever furniture she could fit into the small space.

The rest of her furniture was still in storage, and they decided to rotate or take out only what they needed for day-to-day-living. Isaac had been on cruise ships overseas for years, living in a small cabin with no place to accumulate his own furniture. All he had to call his own were his Bible, his suitcase, and his backpack of kitchen knives.

By July, all of Isaac's permits arrived, in time to catch the last groups of summer vacationers in Savannah and on Tybee Island. The rest of the time, Isaac busied himself preparing a curriculum to teach at the University of Coastal Georgia culinary school, and catering to events at Jerome's riverboats and at other venues in the area.

Piper was surprised when Isaac offered to buy up some of his parents' shares of Piper's Place. She had not expected him to be interested in her restaurant, but he knew that she would prefer to have full control over her business. In spite of that, she had decided to keep the place closed on Sundays, regardless of ownership.

On a bright Saturday morning in late September, family, friends, and Riverside Chapel church members congregated on the top deck of the riverboat *Rhoda* to celebrate Piper and Isaac.

Piper had not thought that her own turn at marriage would come. Having loved only one person since high school, and having been unable to love anyone else, she was sure that she would have remained unmarried the rest of her life—had Isaac not returned to Savannah.

To everyone who would ask, she'd have told them that she was too busy with the restaurant for relationships.

The truth of the matter was that she had been using her restaurant as an escape from her broken heart. The more she worked, the less she thought of Isaac.

Until he had shown up in her restaurant nearly a year ago now.

Bringing back memories.

But God!

Yes, God had used that to set in motion the beginning of their healing.

Thanks to Nelson, who had earned the privilege of being Isaac's best man. It had been Nelson who had hired Isaac to rescue Piper's Place almost a year ago.

Piper glanced at the clock on the wall in the women's parlor—or whatever stateroom this was. Piper didn't mind and didn't care, as long as she had a place to change into her wedding gown.

And go get married!

Heidi interpreted for her, so that the makeup artists and hairstylists knew what she wanted.

Heidi, lovely Heidi, the pastor's wife and her Sunday School teacher, would be doing double duty today. She was both her matron of honor and the interpreter for the entire wedding ceremony.

All of Piper's friends were probably already waiting upstairs on the top deck.

They had helped her pray for clear skies for this riverboat wedding.

And God had answered their prayers. The weather this afternoon was perfect. Low seventies and pretty clouds everywhere.

In a few hours, Piper and Isaac would fly out to the Bahamas. This time they would fly together, unlike back in January. This time, it would be for the pleasure of a honeymoon, and not for the pain of competition.

But first, the wedding ceremony and reception must happen.

Piper prayed for Isaac. He had been anything but relaxed today. He had been all over the galley kitchen, micromanaging Bao and Forsythia.

Piper supposed that he had to one-up her catering at his sister's wedding two years ago. But she didn't mention her thoughts to Isaac. She let him do what he wanted with the reception.

She had to choose her battles.

And she liked his menu, anyway—all of it.

Piper practiced her smile in the mirror. In order to fit the headdress and veil over her head, she had to forego her topknot bun and let her hair down. It was what Isaac had requested, but to be honest, Piper would rather tie her hair up in a bun, thank you very much.

Before she knew it, it was time to climb the deck stairs in her wedding gown, all the way to the top deck, without falling down the stairs, swirled in yards and yards of pleated chiffon and lace—and train.

Who's bright idea was it to wear such a voluminous gown?

Well, it had been a beautiful idea—until the elevator to the top broke an hour before the wedding ceremony was to commence. Maybe from carrying too many passengers?

There's always something old, isn't there?

Heidi helped her up the steel staircase, reminding her to tread lightly. Piper often forgot that because she could not hear herself. She had no idea how loud her wedding shoes were against the steel treads of the staircase.

"The processional has started to play," Heidi signed.

Piper nodded, trying to hold back tears.

She had opted to use a hymn rather than a classical song. She had chosen a hymn with words that meant something to her grandmother and mother, who could not be here on her wedding day.

An old hymn, it had to be.

Something old.

"Amazing Grace," of course.

Reaching the top deck safely was a feat. Piper thanked God for it. Heidi looked relieved. Everyone stood up as Heidi walked to her position near Pastor Flores.

Piper walked alone down the aisle. She had never met her earthly father. Her maternal grandfather had died in the Korean War a long time ago. Jerome had offered to walk her down the aisle, but she hardly knew her future father-in-law. Several Super Seniors had also offered, but if she picked any of them, the others would feel slighted.

In the end, she walked alone.

And there, ahead of her, waiting for her at the end of the aisle, was the bridegroom, wearing a silly grin on his face. She almost signed to him about it—except everyone who knew ASL would know what she was signing.

She chose to smile instead.

And Isaac winked.

That was unexpected.

As unexpected as the entire last year had been. From seeing Isaac after twenty years of losing him, to their unexpected chemistry working together in the kitchen and their special time in the Bahamas, to his brand new food truck, and now, this wedding.

She felt like she needed to pinch herself, but everyone was watching.

Piper walked closer and closer to her almost-husband. She looked past him so that she wouldn't feel too nervous. Beyond the floral wedding arch, Savannah River flowed, as it had done for thousands of years.

Above the river was God's glorious sky.

Something blue.

A beautiful blue sky that could also sometimes turn to gray.

Yes, gray.

It might rain from time to time. Such is life. However, whether rain or sun, Piper knew that God Himself would be with her and Isaac.

God, the healer of broken hearts.

God, the Lord of true love.

May God alone be honored in their sacred marriage, their holy matrimony, their family together.

Piper was impressed that Isaac repeated his vows after Pastor Flores without missing a beat signing ASL. He had memorized it, but still, he had texted her that he was nervous.

I'm nervous too.

"...for as long as we both shall live on earth," Piper signed.

The vow over, Pastor Flores announced that they could kiss, as interpreted by Heidi.

Isaac grinned broadly—like a school boy all over again.

In spite of the lines on his face, the slight graying of some of his hair, Isaac still had the charm that had first caught Piper's eye way back in high school.

He had started out as a shoulder for her to cry on, but he was more than that now. Now he was her strong defender, confidant, someone she could pal around with and yet still rely on, someone she could trust with her deepest thoughts and feelings. Her life partner, her best friend—and soon, her husband and father of her children.

She had waited twenty-one years for this very moment—a moment she hadn't expected would come at all.

And yet here she was, anticipating her wedding kiss.

Isaac leaned toward her.

She closed her eyes, and slowly tasted his lips...

Apple flavor with a touch of honey?

And Piper was almost distracted by an immediate thought of a new recipe for her kitchen.

Later. Later!

She opened her eyes. Gazed directly into his.

He seemed to know what she was thinking. He'd put on that new fruity lip balm on purpose.

Something new.

Yes, something new.

In the sunlight, Isaac's big brown eyes spoke to her of things to come, of their future together as husband and wife, of walking with each other in step with their Lord Jesus Christ through the rest of their lives.

What will come? Only God knows.

No matter what, she and Isaac would be each

other's shoulders to lean on, to cry on if they have to, comforting each other in tough times and cheering on each other to greater heights.

Above them, the southern sun rose higher into the late morning sky, warmer and brighter than ever.

It marked a new beginning for Piper and the only man she ever loved.

God had indeed brought them full circle back to each other. And He had made all things new.

Thank You, Jesus!

DEAR READER:

Thank you for reading *Call You Home* (Savannah Sweethearts Book 10). I hope you enjoyed the story of Piper and Isaac. In *Call You Home*, we meet other chefs in Piper's kitchen, including sous chef Lennon Bao. The final novel in the Savannah Sweethearts series is Lennon Bao's story. To be notified when *Let You Go* is published, sign up for my book news mailing list:

JanThompson.com/newsletter

While each book can stand alone, the entire

Savannah Sweethearts series is interconnected in a chronological fashion. In *Call You Home*, you might have noticed named friends and family of the bride and bridegroom. Many of them have made past appearances in the same series. Here are some of the main characters and their own books.

Sophie and Leon Watts first meet in *Ask You Later* (Savannah Sweethearts Prequel), when Leon tries to display his mixed-media sculpture in Sophie's dad's art gallery on River Street.

Needless to say, Sophie is totally not impressed with his messy folk art. After ten years of traveling the country, Sophie and Leon return to Savannah to buy back Sophie's dad's art gallery.

Ask You Later (Savannah Sweethearts Book 1)
JanThompson.com/ask

Pastor Diego Flores is in all the **Savannah Sweethearts** stories (in fact, he also makes cameo appearances in many of the **Vacation Sweethearts** novels).

Diego kicks off our series when he is still a single pastor in *Know You More* (Savannah Sweethearts Book 1), alongside Heidi Wei, an active church member and old college friend. Heidi is a deaf interpreter, and it is due to her ministry in Christ that led Piper Peyton to the Lord.

Know You More (Savannah Sweethearts Book 2)
JanThompson.com/know

Heidi's brother, Private Investigator Aidan Ming Wei, tries to keep his career together in *Tell You Soon* (Savannah Sweethearts Book 2), where his financial situation is so dire that he has to sell his oceanfront cottage. Real estate agent Sabine Hu is here to help, but Ming's job puts her in danger.

We see Sabine again in *Call You Home* (Savannah Sweethearts Book 11), when she helps Piper sell her beloved house to keep her restaurant afloat.

Tell You Soon (Savannah Sweethearts Book 3)
JanThompson.com/tell

Then we swing back to Simon's Gallery in *Draw You Near* (Savannah Sweethearts Book 3), where Riverside Chapel church member Abilene Dupree works as an art teacher. She doesn't need the money, but she loves to paint and draw and teach. Along comes a visitor from overseas who has fallen in love with a painting of hers.

Abilene and Lars Cargill are only mentioned

briefly in *Call You Home* (Savannah Sweethearts Book 10) because they live in England now, where Abilene is busy painting the English countryside.

Draw You Near (Savannah Sweethearts Book 4)
JanThompson.com/draw

Abilene's brother, Dante Dupree, is also mentioned in passing in *Call You Home* (Savannah Sweethearts Book 10) because he still lives in New Orleans. However, when he is trying to date Nadine Saylor in *Cherish You So* (Savannah Sweethearts Book 4), Dante finds every excuse to go back and forth to Savannah frequently.

Cherish You So (Savannah Sweethearts Book 5)
JanThompson.com/cherish

Another character who appears in *Call You Home* (Savannah Sweethearts Book 5) is travel agent Tamsyn Pendegrast. She first appears in *Walk You There* (Savannah Sweethearts Book 6), in which I introduce to you the Pendegrast family. We will see them again in *Reach for Me* (Vacation Sweethearts Book 2), but Tamsyn's father, Jerome Pendegrast, is already in multiple books in the Savannah Sweethearts series. In *Walk You There*,

Tamsyn is in a battle to save old Savannah, her beloved city of great cultural inheritance.

Walk You There (Savannah Sweethearts Book 6)
JanThompson.com/walk

Jerome Pendegrast is also in a vital supporting role in the next book, *Love You Always* (Savannah Sweethearts Book 6). This novel is a romance with suspense. Camden La Salle, who first appears in *Tell You Soon*, with his friend Ming, now returns for his own story. His college sweetheart is in town with a whole truckload of problems...

Love You Always (Savannah Sweethearts Book 7)
JanThompson.com/love

In *Call You Home*, we find Isaac's brother-in-law's aunt and uncle moving to the Savannah Senior Living Resort. Mentioned in several books in the the Savannah Sweethearts series, that retirement community is the setting of *Kiss You Now* (Savannah Sweethearts Book 7).

One of Piper's regular customers at her restaurant is Roger Patel, the director of the resort, where a number of the older members of Riverside Chapel have planned to retire. *Kiss You Now* is about Roger's cousin, Priyanka, at the crossroads of her life.

Kiss You Now (Savannah Sweethearts Book 8)
JanThompson.com/kiss

The next novel, *Find You Again* (Savannah Sweethearts Book 8) is Roger Patel's story. Finally. He has been a faithful member of Riverside Chapel for many years, but he came to Savannah after Isaac has left town. That's why Isaac doesn't know Roger very well. As I mentioned, Roger has been a regular customer at Piper's Place, and in *Find You Again*, he finally has a promising girlfriend.

Find You Again (Savannah Sweethearts Book 9)
JanThompson.com/find

One year before *Call You Home*, Isaac's sister, Amy Untermeyer, returns home to deal with a business decision their mom has made that affects her. She meets her new business partner and majority shareholder, Cyrus Theroux, who seems to be more interested in preserving the Untermeyer family business than people give him credit for. If you have read *Wish You Joy* (Savannah Sweethearts Book 9), you might recall that Amy and Isaac keep in touch even though the siblings work in different parts of the world.

Wish You Joy (Savannah Sweethearts Book 10)
JanThompson.com/wish

And then we are back to the top of this page, when I started talking about *Call You Home* (Savannah Sweethearts Book 10), the book you just read. A reader asked me about Deaf culture, and here is my response: "I am not Deaf myself but I did a lot of research into the Deaf culture and hope that I have respected it in *Call You Home*. For example, Piper doesn't try to be hearing. She is profoundly Deaf and remains so. Isaac enters her world and adapts to her world. Everyone in her kitchen knows ASL, and e.g. they have flashing lights in addition to fire alarms. However, my readers are mostly hearing, so when Isaac and Piper text each other, I use the English grammar to communicate and not the ASL grammar because this book is in the Savannah Sweethearts series so I have to maintain the same linguistic style throughout."

Call You Home (Savannah Sweethearts Book 11)
JanThompson.com/call

I hope the **Savannah Sweethearts** series have been encouraging to you. Ultimately, I wrote all these books to remind Christians to remember God in our daily lives. He alone is worthy of our praise. He alone is worthy of all honor. To God alone be the glory.

Savannah Sweethearts
JanThompson.com/savannah

Savannah Sweethearts has two spin-off series: **Vacation Sweethearts** and **Protector Sweethearts**. While the latter is a Christian romantic suspense series, **Vacation Sweethearts** is Christian travel romance, with five novels in all, featuring people from Savannah on vacation.

In *Call You Home*, Isaac and Piper flew to the Bahamas for his cooking competition. A year before that, Riverside Chapel church members were in Nassau to minister at a summer camp there. Donovan's brother, Byron Moss, runs into her nemesis, Tina MacFarland, in *Smile for Me* (Vacation Sweethearts Book 1). This novel is the next book after Savannah Sweethearts wraps up.

Smile for Me (Vacation Sweethearts Book 1)
JanThompson.com/smile

Continue reading for an introduction to the next series, **Vacation Sweethearts**, and a sneak peek of the first novel in that series, *Smile for Me*...

THE NEXT SERIES IS VACATION SWEETHEARTS

From *USA Today* bestselling author Jan Thompson come these clean and wholesome, sweet and inspirational Christian vacation romance novels set in some of her favorite vacation places.

Travel with these Savannah residents to the coast and to the mountains, and cheer them on as they celebrate the immeasurable grace and undeserved mercy of God through Jesus Christ.

Vacation Sweethearts begins with *Smile for Me*, the story of Byron Moss and Tina MacFarland, spending their summer on the Caribbean islands of the Bahamas where the water is blue and hearts are warm...

- Book 0 (Prequel): *Time for Me*
- Book 1: *Smile for Me* (Beach Romance in the Bahamas)
- Book 2: *Reach for Me* (Romance with Suspense in the Smoky Mountains)
- Book 3: *Wait for Me* (Romance with Suspense on a Cruise Ship)
- Book 4: *Look for Me* (Romance with Suspense in a Florida Beach Town)
- Book 5: *Pray for Me* (International Romance in the City of Atlanta)
- Book 6: *Care for Me* (Small Mountain Town Romance)
- Book 7: *Cheer for Me* (International Romance)

The **Vacation Sweethearts** novels are a spin-off of Jan's **Savannah Sweethearts** series, and fans will recognize familiar faces from Riverside Chapel, a church in the coastal city of Savannah, Georgia. In fact, we do visit Savannah and the beach town of Tybee Island from time to time to see old friends and beloved families.

Vacation Sweethearts:
JanThompson.com/vacation

To receive Vacation Sweethearts book news:
JanThompson.com/newsletter

THE NEXT BOOK IS SMILE FOR ME

VACATION SWEETHEARTS BOOK 1

She is laid-back.
He is uptight.
Never the twain shall...kiss?

A deadline-driven workaholic assistant school principal who meticulously plans his schedule months in advance meets an easygoing art teacher and studio potter with no sense of time, living her life as the seasons come and go. When they cross paths again at the Summer by the Sea Day Camp sponsored by his church in Nassau, Bahamas, how can they get along if they cannot see eye to eye?

From *USA Today* bestselling author Jan Thompson comes *Smile for Me*, book 1 in the **Vacation Sweethearts** collection of wholesome, sweet and inspirational Christian romance novels set in some of Jan's favorite vacation places around the world.

 Vacation Sweethearts is a spin-off of Jan's **Savannah Sweethearts** Christian beach romance series, and we might travel back to Savannah and Tybee Island to meet friends, old and new.

 To start off the **Vacation Sweethearts** series, we travel to the Bahamas in the Caribbean, where the waters are clear, skies are blue, hammocks sway under coconut trees, and hearts are in love...

TINA MACFARLAND IS LAID-BACK...

When invited back to the Bahamas for a second time two years after a disastrous mission trip there, potter and art teacher Tina MacFarland isn't sure she wants to face the obnoxious assistant principal of the Chapel by the Sea Christian School again. The last time she encountered

Byron Moss, he found fault in everything she did. It seems that nothing she ever does is good enough for Mr. Uptight, as attractive as he may be to her.

Regardless of her personal concerns, they need art teachers at the Summer by the Sea Day Camp, and Tina answers the call to go. Surely God will help her last for four short weeks. What can possibly happen in a month? Nothing she can think of.

BYRON MOSS IS UPTIGHT...

Assistant Headmaster Byron Moss is at a crossroad in his career. On the one hand, he has worked very hard to get to this position at the Chapel by the Sea Christian School. One more step up from this assistant principal position, and he'd be in charge of the entire school.

On the other hand, when Tina returns to Nassau, Byron suddenly feels hemmed in by his career choice. He is restricted from showing his transforming feelings for Tina. He fears he has taken a wrong turn in his career, and that if he keeps going on that route, he may lose his chances with Tina. More importantly, what is God's will for his life? Somehow, he knows that Tina is part of all that. But she's so...chaotic! And it drives him nuts.

For the first time in his life, Byron is confused about what he needs to do.

NEVER THE TWAIN SHALL...KISS?

Ah, Byron and Tina... How will they navigate the super-conservative work environment where office romance is frowned upon? Can they change the old rules? Or will the old rules change them?

Smile for Me (Vacation Sweethearts Book 1):
JanThompson.com/smile

Vacation Sweethearts:
JanThompson.com/vacation

Subscribe to Jan's book news mailing list:
JanThompson.com/newsletter

Continue reading for a sneak peek of *Smile for Me.*

SMILE FOR ME CHAPTER 1 SNEAK PEEK

VACATION SWEETHEARTS BOOK 1

Byron Moss had called that woman *Veronique* in a singsong fashion, and that had rubbed Tina MacFarland the wrong way.

She would have to admit that Veronique was a pretty French name—too French for this ex-British colony, but then again, nobody had asked her.

She watched both of them whisper to each other at the front of the long school bus, identical iPads hanging off their necks like some sort of Horn books from the nineteenth century.

At first Tina had thought that Veronique was taller than Byron, but that idea went away when Tina saw the day camp assistant director's five-inch stiletto.

Try walking on Bahamian sands with those—

Lord, forgive me.

Thank You, Jesus.

Tina didn't know what had overcome her, but every time she had been with Byron, she only thought of the worst of him.

Meticulously overbearing was the last double adjective she had used for him.

Uptight.

A pain in the neck.

The moment the volunteers from Riverside Chapel, Savannah, and a couple of other churches had disembarked from the airplane, Byron was at baggage claim waiting for them.

The way he had checked off their names as if they were school children had bothered Tina.

Then he had herded them into this non-air-conditioned school bus. Everyone just cracked jokes and laughed with him as he checked off their names one more time.

However, when Tina passed by him, he didn't say anything except to call her name.

The way Byron had said her name was very unlike how he had called Veronique's name. Veronique's name rolled off Byron's tongue in a smoother way than when he had snapped out Tina's name.

"Ti-nah!"

It was curtly British, clipped at the end of the second syllable, as if his disgust of her had taken its toll and he couldn't bear to say her name at all this time around.

Two years ago they had butted heads like two rams or goats. Horns locked as Byron had hissed out her name and stretched it in the air as though he was mentally wringing her neck every single time.

"Tee-yee-yee-nah! Teeenaaah!" Byron would yell at her in disgust because she hadn't done things the way he had wanted.

Well, sure, there was the bell before and after class, but she hadn't finished teaching, and besides, the kindergarteners were having fun, weren't they?

After all, it was Vacation Bible School, not a bar exam.

Come on!

In any case, her name sounded awful when Byron had said it aloud.

Well, it wasn't her fault she was named after a citrus fruit. A tangerine, to be exact.

Clementine Gracielle MacFarland.

No one ever called her Clementine, not since birth, according to everyone. It had always been Tina, as if Clementine was a shame of a first name.

Her brother had the better name, Martinelli, though everyone called him Martin.

But Tina.

"Tee-yee-yee-nah! Nah! Nah! Nah!"

"Stop," Tina muttered. "Stop it..."

A nudge and a couple of hard jabs on her shoulder made her jerk straight up and open her eyes.

"Oww... Who did that?"

Two brown eyes, eyebrows raised, edged by a smile, were in her face.

Tina recoiled, but there was nowhere to go. The seat back was stiff. She bumped her head on the metal bar that went all the way across the top of the seat.

"Ouch." She rubbed the back of her head.

Byron Moss straightened up, looming over her. Byron with the lovely brown eyes that kept her out of focus whenever she remembered them—

She cleared her throat.

"You fell asleep. Had a tiring flight?"

His voice was somewhat gentle and quiet, and

Tina was beginning to think she had been dreaming that his tone had a sharp edge to it.

Yeah, must be having a nightmare.

She yawned and rubbed her eyes.

"We got off the plane?" As soon as she had said it, Tina felt dumb, like she had just given Byron one more "scatterbrained" remark for him to pick on later.

"You got off the plane. We loaded your luggage —all five pieces—onto this bus. We drove all the way from the Lynden Pindling International Airport to Montagu Bay, taking thirty-one minutes due to traffic. And we are now parked outside the Nassau Island Breeze Resort."

Byron waved toward the window. "We unloaded your luggage—three heavy, hard case luggage, two soft sides, but equally heavy—what in the world did you bring?"

Tina didn't feel obligated to answer him.

"Everyone is checking in at the front desk."

"Now?" Tina tried to get up, but her head spun.

"Yes, dear. Did you take Dramamine or some air-sickness meds, perchance?"

Dear?

Perchance?

Yep. That was Byron for her. He'd say strange literary things like that.

Byron stretched out his hand to help Tina to her feet.

She felt groggy. "Sorry. I stayed up all night to pack my art supplies. Then I couldn't sleep on the flight. Turbulence or something."

"We can get art supplies in Nassau, you know." Byron smiled with his eyes.

He was the only man Tina knew who could smile with his eyes.

"Well, I thought that—I mean, the last time I was here..." Tina wasn't sure how much she should remind Byron of what had happened two years ago when she had come to the Bahamas on her first mission trip outside the United States.

"Yes. Two years ago." Byron stepped back between two seats to let Tina go first toward the exit at the front of the bus. "You forgot all your brushes and canvases."

"You don't miss a thing, do you?"

"I missed you last summer," Byron said. "Why didn't you come?"

Missed?

Did he just say he missed me?

Tina tried not to read too much into it.

Byron was the last person on earth who would miss Tina.

"The kids at day camp asked for you by name.

Where's Miss Tina? Why isn't she here? Doesn't she love us anymore?"

Love?

Tina stumbled out of the bus into eighty-something-degree heat. The June sunshine was bright, bright, bright. The sky was clear and blue, and Tina wanted to go for a swim.

Behind her, Byron was on his iPhone.

Tina shed her cardigan she had worn since she sat down in the cold cabin on the tarmac at the Savannah Hilton Head International Airport. She was always cold in an airplane cabin, even when the flight was full and the passengers were packed in like paint tubes.

But now she was hot.

"What time is it?" Tina rolled up her cardigan and stuffed it into her worn, oversized zippered tote bag she had been using as her purse for over a year now.

"Two o'clock. Actually, six minutes after two."

"Are you sure it's not six minutes and fourteen seconds after two?"

Byron frowned at his watch. "Well, I don't know..."

Tina gently punched his arm. "Lighten up."

"Did they give you lunch on board?" Byron stood there a minute.

"I guess. I slept through."

"Why didn't they wake you up? You paid for the meal."

"Why are you asking me all these questions, Byron?"

"Because I don't want you to be hungry. Everyone else said they've eaten." Byron stepped toward her. "If you haven't, I'll take you to lunch."

"You'll take me out to lunch?"

Byron nodded. "Yes. Is that a problem?"

"No." Tina wondered why they were standing on the sidewalk. Shouldn't she be checking in?

Then she saw her.

Veronique and her five-inch stilettos, walking briskly toward them as if she were strutting on a catwalk.

She was amazingly graceful.

Clumsy me, I can't compare.

Tina watched as Byron dangled the bus keys in front of Veronique. "Thank you for taking the bus back to the school."

Tina wondered how Veronique was going to drive this mammoth of a bus in those heels. Then again, it wasn't her problem, was it?

"How are you going to get home?" Tina asked Byron.

"I left my car in the hotel car park."

Car park? His way of saying parking lot.

"You thought of everything." Tina started walking.

"Not everything. You still haven't eaten lunch."

"Don't worry about me. I'll just eat in the hotel restaurant. Surely they have a café of some sort."

Byron stopped at the lobby, and so did Tina. She turned to see what the matter was.

"We need to learn to get along, Tina. Otherwise the Lord's work is not going to happen the next few weeks you're here, or two months, if you decide to stay for the entire camp."

"What does that have to do with where I eat lunch?"

"I get along with everyone else."

"So do I."

"But you and I don't get along with each other."

"Maybe it's best if we stay out of each other's hair," Tina said.

"Or we can have lunch and do things together to break down this wall of ice between us."

"Do things?" Tina widened her eyes. "Like what kind of things?"

"Like maybe we could work in the same classroom and be on the same field trips this summer."

"No. We'd drive each other insane."

Tina went to the end of the shortest line. There were gobs of people in the lobby, checking in. Summer vacationers, possibly. She waved to her teammates and the other fellow volunteers, some of whom were in the front of their lines while others were done and wheeling their bags to the elevator.

"Not if you try to be on time—for once," Byron said.

"Whoa. You just insulted me, and I haven't even checked in."

Byron stared at her.

"Go away, Byron."

"Can't. I'm in charge of the Summer by the Sea Day Camp, remember?"

"Well, bummer. I'm not going to congratulate you for being promoted to assistant headmaster." Even though he probably deserved it. Byron Moss, in spite of his many flaws, was one of the most hard-working men Tina had ever known.

"Can we still do lunch?" Byron's voice was almost pleading. "We have to make the day camp succeed."

Tina's tummy growled.

"Your stomach is begging you on my behalf," Byron said.

Tina burst out laughing. "All right. I'll have to give it to you. You're not only stubborn, but you're also persistent."

"I think those two words mean about the same thing."

"Just say thank you, Byron."

"Thank you, ma'am." Byron glanced at his watch. "I'll help you take your bags to your room after you check in, and we should be on our way by three o'clock."

"You'll help me with my luggage because you don't want me to be late coming back down here to meet you for our already late lunch?"

"No, because your bags are heavy."

"Oh." *How considerate.*

"While you check in, I'll get you a Fanta Grape."

Tina froze. It had been two years since she last had that soda. "You remember."

"I remember everything about you, Clementine Gracielle MacFarland." And off he went.

Smile for Me (Vacation Sweethearts Book 1)
JanThompson.com/smile

More Information about Vacation Sweethearts:
JanThompson.com/vacation

Subscribe to Jan's book news mailing list:
JanThompson.com/newsletter

ACKNOWLEDGMENTS

As per usual, not all of my extensive research makes it into my books, but I feel that it is necessary to thank everyone for their time and kindness.

For American Sign Language fact checking, I thank Paula Mowery, ASL Interpreter for the Deaf and Hard of Hearing, for answering my questions about communication.

For Deaf Community information fact checking, I thank Madelon Stone and Lenda Selph. Thank you, ladies, for your time and patience.

For law enforcement and operational fact checking, I thank private investigator and former FBI agent Steven Kerry Brown, and Detective Dony Jay, both of whom have been generous with their time and knowledge.

Many thanks to my Georgia Press publishing team for keeping up with my writing schedule.

With God-given eyes for copyediting details, Lenda Selph is my patient proofreader extraordinaire. I appreciate her and thank God for her invaluable hard work.

For additional proofreading, I thank fellow author Valerie Comer, who took time out of her busy schedule to read this book.

I appreciate my early readers who kindly read this novel ahead of the world: Debbie Jamieson, Paula Marie, and Julia Wilson.

I am grateful to God for my husband and son for their support and encouragement.

And I'll always remember my dearly loved widowed mother and my late father for having instilled in me the love of reading and writing from a very early age. I miss my father here on earth, but I will see him in heaven some bright day.

Most of all, I am eternally thankful to my Lord and Savior, Jesus Christ, who died on the cross to save me from my sins and rose again from the grave to give me eternal life. Without Him, I can write and do nothing.

Jan Thompson
John 3:16

BOOKS BY JAN THOMPSON

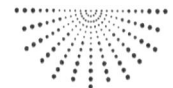

CONTEMPORARY CHRISTIAN CITY, COASTAL, AND BEACH ROMANCE

Seaside Chapel (7 Books)
JanThompson.com/seaside
Savannah Sweethearts (12 Books)
JanThompson.com/savannah
Vacation Sweethearts (8 Books)
JanThompson.com/vacation
Midtown Christmas (4 Books)
JanThompson.com/christmas

SEASIDE CHAPEL

Welcome to *USA Today* bestselling author Jan Thompson's Seaside Chapel Christian beach romance series. These novels are set on real-life St. Simon's Island, Georgia—a beach town where history is all around and the future is a moment away—and the neighboring fictitious Seaside Island, where the rich and famous live.

Savor the small-town atmosphere and the warm southern beaches of St. Simon's Island and the idyllic Golden Isles along the Atlantic Ocean. Enjoy the music of the orchestra and hymns of the church, and hang out with our Christian friends who attend Seaside Chapel, a little church by the sea known for its beach weddings and fair share of love and life.

As these Christians grow in their knowledge

and understanding of God, they are tested in their spiritual maturity, their love lives, and their relationships with others. Share their heartaches and healing, and cheer them on as they celebrate faith, family, and friends.

JanThompson.com/seaside

- Book 0 (Prequel): *His Surprise Proposal*
- Book 1: *His Longing Heart*
- Book 2: *His Wake-Up Call*
- Book 3: *His Morning Kiss*
- Book 4: *His Quiet Serenade*
- Book 5: *His Waiting Love*
- Book 6: *His Beach Retreat*

SAVANNAH SWEETHEARTS

Welcome to the new south! From *USA Today* bestselling author Jan Thompson come these clean and wholesome, sweet and inspirational Christian romances set on the romantic beaches of Tybee Island and in the coastal town of Savannah, Georgia. Meet a group of multiracial and multiethnic churchgoing Christians who love the Lord, work hard in their careers, and seek God's will for their love lives. Against a backdrop of ocean, sand, and sun, these inspirational romances showcase aspects of the human need for God and for one another. Have some tea, settle in a comfortable reading chair, and enjoy these sweet celebrations of faith, hope, and love in Jesus Christ.

JanThompson.com/savannah

- Book 1: *Ask You Later* (Artist Romance)
- Book 2: *Know You More* (Multiracial Romance)
- Book 3: *Tell You Soon* (Asian-American Romance with Suspense)
- Book 4: *Draw You Near* (International Romance)
- Book 5: *Cherish You So* (Wheelchair Billionaire Romance)
- Book 6: *Walk You There* (Old-Meets-New Tour Guide Romance)
- Book 7: *Love You Always* (Romance with Suspense)
- Book 8: *Kiss You Now* (Multiracial Romance)
- Book 9: *Find You Again* (Multiracial Romance)
- Book 10: *Wish You Joy* (Christmas-Themed Romance)
- Book 11: *Call You Home* (Deaf Chef Romance)
- Book 12: *Let You Go* (Asian-American Romance with Suspense)

VACATION SWEETHEARTS

Travel with our friends from Savannah, Georgia, to the coast and to the mountains. Cheer them on as they celebrate the immeasurable grace and undeserved mercy of God through Jesus Christ.

The Vacation Sweethearts novels are a spin-off of Jan's Savannah Sweethearts series, and fans will recognize familiar faces from Riverside Chapel, a church in the coastal city of Savannah, Georgia. In fact, we might even visit the beach town of Tybee Island from time to time to visit old friends and beloved families...

JanThompson.com/vacation

- Book 0 (Prequel): *Time for Me*
- Book 1: *Smile for Me* (Beach Romance in the Bahamas)
- Book 2: *Reach for Me* (Romance with Suspense in the Smoky Mountains)
- Book 3: *Wait for Me* (Romance with Suspense on a Cruise Ship)
- Book 4: *Look for Me* (Romance with Suspense in a Florida Beach Town)
- Book 5: *Pray for Me* (International Romance in the City of Atlanta)
- Book 6: *Care for Me* (Small Mountain Town Romance)
- Book 7: *Cheer for Me* (International Romance)

Read *Time for Me* (Prequel) for free: JanThompson.com/time-free

MIDTOWN CHRISTMAS

Big city romance, small town feel. Four Christian couples minister at Midtown Chapel in metro Atlanta, and Midtown Village, the community of tiny homes for needy families. From November to January every year, this place turns into a Christmas Village for a small-town feel right there in the metropolis of Atlanta, Georgia.

- Book 1: *Let Me Hold You* (Levi Theroux and Maggie Jacobs from *Pray for Me*)
- Book 2: *Let Me Want You* (Erika Song from *Look for Me* and Hiroki Yamada from *Walk You There*)
- Book 3: *Let Me Need You* (Forsythia

McDevitt from *Call You Home* and
Owen Grayson from *Find You Again*)
- Book 4: *Let Me Love You* (Leila Patel
  from *Find You Again*)

PROTECTOR SWEETHEARTS

Private investigator Helen Hu and her associates specialize in searching for missing persons and hunting for lost treasures. Join them in their adventure suspense around the world in *USA Today* best-selling author Jan Thompson's Protector Sweethearts, a series of Christian Romantic Suspense with a side of mystery.

Protector Sweethearts is a spin-off of Savannah Sweethearts and Vacation Sweethearts.

JanThompson.com/protector

- Book 1: *Once a Thief*

- Book 2: *Once a Hero*
- Book 3: *Once a Spy*
- Book 4: *Twice a Fighter*
- Book 5: *Twice a Convict*
- Book 6: *Twice a Soldier*

DEFENDER SWEETHEARTS

Defender Sweethearts is a sister series to the Protector Sweethearts Christian romantic suspense collection. While the heroes in Protector Sweethearts search for lost treasures and lost people, the Defender Sweethearts novels focus on protecting the helpless and hopeless. The main characters in Defender Sweethearts come from the supporting cast in Protector Sweethearts.

JanThompson.com/defender

- Book 1: *Never a Traitor*
- Book 2: *Never a Hostage*

DEFENDER SWEETHEARTS

- Book 3: *Never a Fugitive*
- Book 4: *Always a Maverick*
- Book 5: *Always a Champion*
- Book 6: *Always a Guardian*

GUARDIAN SWEETHEARTS

Guardian Sweethearts is a collection of Christian suspense novels in between other books in Jan Thompson's story world. These sandwiched stories feature married couples who met in the books before the present ones. Therefore, the books in this series are both prequels and sequels or preludes and postludes.

JanThompson.com/guardian

- Book 1: Once Bitten, Twice Shy: A Christian suspense novel in between Tell You Soon (Savannah Sweethearts

Book 3) and Once a Thief (Protector Sweethearts Book 1)

- Book 2: Check Once, Check Twice: A Christian suspense novel in between Love You Always (Savannah Sweethearts Book 7) and Never a Traitor (Defender Sweethearts Book 1)
- Book 3: Going Once, Going Twice: A Christian suspense novel in between Reach for Me (Vacation Sweethearts Book 2) and His Mercenary Sentinel (Watchfire Widows Book 1)
- Book 4: Fool Me Once, Fool Me Twice: A Christian suspense novel in between Wait for Me (Vacation Sweethearts Book 3) and Her Billionaire Warrior (Watchfire Security Book 1)

BINARY HACKERS

Like more suspense with your Christian romance? Like to read suspense thrillers? If you're looking for clean near-future romantic suspense without compromising the Christian faith, these books are for you.

From *USA Today* bestselling author Jan Thompson come these inspirational near-future cyberthrillers combining technothriller and romance, starting with Binary Hackers that feature computer specialists living at the edge of cyber-space, where they have to juggle being law-abiding truth-telling Christians while carrying out their assignments by any and all means possible.

The Binary Hackers series is set in the same story world as Jan's other books, and characters from the other series may make cameo appearances in this series and vice versa.

JanThompson.com/binary

- Book 1: *Zero Sum*
- Book 2: *Zero Day*
- Book 3: *Zero Base*
- Book 4: *Zero Trust*

ABOUT JAN THOMPSON

USA Today bestselling author Jan Thompson writes clean and wholesome contemporary Christian romance with elements of women's fiction, Christian romantic suspense with an air of mystery, and inspirational international thrillers with threads of sweet Christian romance. Jan's books are for readers who love inspiring stories of faith, family, and friends.

Raised on a tropical island in the eastern hemisphere, Jan now lives and writes in the western hemisphere. Her international background gives her a unique multicultural and multiracial perspective to her novels and books. The island has never left her, and she reminisces about beach life in her beach romance novels.

When Jan is not busy writing small-town stories, she writes big-city romantic suspense and international technothrillers, a nod to her previous career in computer science. She weaves technology with human interests, reflecting the current and future digital world. And romance. There's always romance.

Beyond the printed page, Jan is a wife, a mother, an avid reader, an occasional artist and potter, an erstwhile piano player and quilter, and the chief of staff to the family cat. Jan's life verse is John 3:16.

Find out more about Jan Thompson:
JanThompson.com

Subscribe to Jan's book news mailing list:
JanThompson.com/newsletter

For God so loved the world
that He gave His only begotten Son,
that whoever believes in Him
should not perish but have everlasting life.
—John 3:16

www.ingramcontent.com/pod-product-compliance
Lightning Source LLC
Chambersburg PA
CBHW030741030726
47497CB00001B/79